The Shadow of Her Smile

Highlander Heroes, Volume 3

Rebecca Ruger

Published by Rebecca Ruger, 2019.

This is a work of fiction. Names, character, places, and incidents are either a product of the author's imagination or are used fictitiously, and any resemblance to actual persons, living or dead, events, or locales is entirely coincidental. Some creative license may have been taken with exact dates and locations to better serve the plot and pacing of the novel.

ASIN: B07XPBSNFX

The Shadow of Her Smile

Written by Rebecca Ruger

Disclaimer: The material in this book is for mature audiences only and may graphic content. It is intended only for those aged 18 and older.

Rebecca Ruger

www.rebeccaruger.com[1]

1. http://www.rebeccaruger.com

Chapter One

February 1304
Near Happrew, Scotland

ADA MONCRIEFE STOOD atop the battlements at Dornoch Castle as her betrothed and his army returned. There was much to appreciate about her soon-to-be husband; he was tall and striking upon his large destrier, his chain mail shiny, his tabard bright, always untarnished it seemed by this war. John Craig somehow kept his person fastidious, even as all those who followed showed the effects of what Ada must assume was a terrific battle: swords and hands were caked in blood, dried and darkened to suggest the battle was hours old; faces and brows, under narrow brimmed helms, were swathed in sweat and grime; horses showed still a glossy sheen of lather from their labors this day.

Ada watched John dismount and shout orders to his officers. She'd been a guest of Dornoch for almost a month, when her father had sent her along—despite her earnest protests—to her future husband. Ada imagined that John Craig, with his shiny dark hair and pleasing blue eyes, might have thrilled any young girl at first glance. Ada, herself, admitted to a modicum of relief that he was so pleasing to look upon. It had only been a few days before her good opinion had been corrected.

Her betrothed, a Scottish baron with an allegiance to Edward I and England, was a monster.

Initially, Ada had only been unnerved by his discourtesy to inferiors, soldier or servant and his own sister, but soon this was amplified into dread as she'd witnessed greater atrocities, attesting to his true character. She supposed she should be thankful she'd been shown his rightful personality from the start; it would have been worse to have been deceived, to have gone into the marriage completely blinded, believing him to be noble and kind. She now had no false illusions about what her marriage, and thus her life, might be.

She watched as a line of prisoners was herded inside the gate. A sickening fright knotted in her belly, knowing these men would suffer the same fate as the previous lot of hostages. They would die, slowly and without mercy.

With a sharp cry, which she interrupted with a hand over her mouth, Ada saw that one of the prisoners was no more than a boy. His eyes darted to and fro, taking in everything inside the yard of the castle, while his freckled cheeks showed a bright red flush of distress. He couldn't be more than a dozen years of age, Ada decided, or only a very small framed older boy, but a child, nonetheless.

There were six prisoners, she counted. Each one wore a tartan of red and blue and gold, though Ada did not recognize either the tartan or any man bearing it. The prisoners were not as the last group that John had brought to Dornoch. Only the boy showed any fear, his shoulders tense, as if only waiting and dreading some violence against his person. The others held their heads high, their broad shoulders neither cowed nor bent. Ada wondered if what some might perceive as bravado—their eyes were not lowered in subjugation but took in everything and everyone around them—was truly only prudence and strategy; they noted every detail of their surroundings, mayhap already plotting a confrontation and escape.

As they came fully into the bailey, Ada stepped back, ducking under the eaves of the overhang along this part of the keep, pulling her gray cloak more tightly about her dark hair. She had no fear of being discovered—her betrothed loved an audience, she'd learned—but thought to separate herself from any coming violence. She had no desire to witness again exactly how brutal John Craig could be.

The prisoners were instructed to dismount. One sizable soldier was dragged off his mount, already wounded, the blood-soaked tartan said. The boy fell to his knees as he landed on the ground and was quickly rewarded with a hard kick to his side. One of his comrades jumped in front of him, taking the next blow and throwing back a ferocious growl as the boy managed to gain his feet behind him. John Craig approached the man who'd come to the boy's defense, standing eye to eye with the large warrior, who was cowed not at all by either John's intentional menace or his own lack of weapons.

From this distance, the words exchanged between John and his captive were lost to Ada. She caught only hints of the sounds. The man's voice was deep, his diction heavily accented, so unlike John's practiced and precious English. John threw his head back and laughed at something the man said. Ada cringed at the sound, so false and terrifying.

Ada studied the brave man, who did not flinch before her betrothed. Mayhap he knew not how precarious his own position was just now. Perhaps all that bravado came with some erroneous belief that he might still be alive come this time tomorrow. When one of John's soldiers reached again for the youth, the man threw himself in front of the lad. His hands were untied, and he pulled the boy behind him. John liked to prove his own courageousness, his own superiority, by leaving hands unbound; easy to do when surrounded by your own loyal men-at-arms. For his efforts to defend the lad, the man received a gauntlet-ed fist to the face, and blood dripped immediately from his lip. He stumbled but did not fall. And he did not release the arm of the boy.

Ada considered him more closely as he straightened and stood eye to eye with her betrothed once more. She had an impression of height and breadth; he stood as tall as John but was broader across the shoulders. He wore no helmet—none of his comrades did—and showed a mane of very dark blond, long and tousled with sweat and dirt and blood. An angry frown furrowed his brows and she thought his teeth might be clenched, but that was all Ada could distinguish across the distance of the yard.

Her betrothed was saying something to him and his lip seemed to curl at the words and then the boy was yanked from his grasp by another Craig minion. He reacted instantly, trying to regain hold of the boy's arm while the boy cried out, giving up what had remained of his own courage. One of John's soldiers dragged the lad away while the big man was beaten to the ground by three more Craig men for his attempts to stop it.

Ada had seen enough. She swallowed her revulsion and slipped away, back inside the keep.

SOMEHOW, ADA MANAGED to dine with her betrothed, as expected, without giving any hint that she had witnessed his return, or the happenings in the yard, only hours before.

"And what have you been about these three days while I was gone, my dear?" John asked.

Reveling in your absence, was her first thought. She felt Margaret, John's sister, nearly jump out of her skin at her side at the sound of her brother's voice.

"We've been very busy with the mending," Ada answered vaguely and thought to add, "and yesterday we helped out with the candle-making."

He chewed upon the dried-out meat and her words. Ada cast a glance at Margaret, but the girl would not lift her eyes from her plate, though she ate not at all. Poor Margaret, who seemed only a shadow of a true person, submissive and subjugated. Margaret was only a year younger than Ada's twenty-one years but behaved as might a child of many fewer years. Whether her cowed and simple manner was due, in fact, to her brother's temperament and his violent tendencies, Ada could not be sure. She guessed the girl's only hope was to be married and removed from her brother's volatile presence.

If Ada herself could not somehow achieve her own freedom, she imagined that as John's wife, she could push him to arrange a marriage for his sister to see her removed from the hell she lived.

Seeing her own self freed was Ada's priority. If she had to simply walk away from Dornoch, she would, though the remoteness of the castle and the desolate nature of the surrounding countryside offered not much more hope than her circumstance here. She'd thought, when John had left on this last short campaign, that the opportunity might present itself to escape. This had not been the case. She was under constant and watchful eyes, all the people of Dornoch seeming so attuned to her every movement, whether by instruction or not, that she was never alone but when in her chambers at night.

John eyed her critically, though not with any outright displeasure. "You have made yourself very useful, Ada. That is a very admirable quality." He cast a hard glare at his sister, who had yet to lift her head. "Would that all the ladies of Dornoch were so constructive."

"Margaret and I appreciated how well received our presence was. I think the women were very happy for our assistance." She did not know if that were true, as so many souls of Dornoch seemed only spiteful and nasty people, their dark moods and fretful scurrying no doubt dictated by the baron. But Ada added a pretty smile, and this seemed to pacify John. She watched his dark brown eyes settle, not for the first time, upon her bosom. As before, he appeared wholly entranced by her chest, and she wondered if she bounced them up and down, if he might lick his lips.

Ada Moncriefe had been raised in a fairly pleasant household, when her own father was not blustering—this often controlled and contained by her dear mother—where she had never known fear and had been often allowed to speak her mind. She had to assume that her father did not know of John Craig's violent bent when he'd contracted the marriage agreement with him. Likely, he'd been won over, as had Ada in the first few days, by his coolly pleasing manner, his pretty speech, and his finely tailored garments. She'd swiftly learned how to be afraid, to fear what the future might hold. When she thought of what she'd witnessed of his vicious nature and coupled that with his leering at her breasts, she became truly fearful of what marriage to this man might entail.

"Did you find success in your endeavors, sir?" She thought to ask. It was always safer to have the discussion be about him.

He turned to her, his face softening just enough to suggest he was pleased with her query. "Great success, dear Ada." The smile that followed was oily and sickening. "Greater than I had hoped, even. We've captured some infidels—done in by their own weakness—and we shall show them exactly how we deal with dissenters of our liege lord, King Edward."

Ada gave a brief thought to the man who'd stood against John and his men in defense of the youth. "I wonder they find themselves upon a field of battle, if they are besieged by weakness."

Her betrothed shrugged, spearing a scrap of meat onto his knife. "Actually, they put up a good fight, 'twas only their softness in returning for a lad we'd captured that had so many of them also trapped." He plopped the morsel into his mouth and chewed a bit before adding, "Weakness."

She would not have characterized that as weakness, but she would never say this to him.

Later that night, plagued by frightful thoughts of what that sorrowful imprisoned lad must be thinking and feeling right now, Ada dozed and dreamed that John had the youth executed in the same manner he had another man slain just two weeks ago. That man had been suspected of poaching sheep from the vast Dornoch land. He'd denied the charge, and though there had been no witness or evidence to prove him guilty, he'd been pronounced so and had been sentenced to die. Ada could still see the man's face, when he'd been told of his fate. His lips had quivered and parted. All color had drained from his flaccid face. He'd wrung his wool hat in his hands and had looked around, mystified, surely thinking he lived his own nightmare, waiting only to be wakened. He had not been, and because John had insisted that both she and Margaret be present while his punishment was meted out, Ada could still hear his cries, could still see his body, stripped and flogged, before he'd been hung. There had been no mercy in the hanging, as he'd not been dropped from tall gallows, his neck broken and death instant. He'd been hauled up slowly by a rope around his neck so that he was aware of his entrails being spilled onto the yard until, thankfully, death had claimed him. And still, his limbs had been secured to four horses, whose rumps had been struck with the flats of swords, scattering them off in many directions to tear his body into four pieces.

Ada jerked up on her bed, wakened by these horrific recollections. And she knew she must act, must do something.

She would leave tonight. She must save that poor boy.

Again, she considered the bravery of the prisoner who today had stood against John Craig, the man with the tawny hair and arms the size of tree limbs. If she were to put her own life into his hands, she'd bet he could see her safely removed from Dornoch and her fate.

Previously, she'd invited Margaret to give her a tour of Dornoch while her brother had been gone. She'd pretended an interest in the keep and the Craig family history but truthfully, had only wanted to know any and everything she could that might one day help her escape. It was a small vat of knowledge, but she would employ it tonight.

Rising, she considered her chambers and its contents, and her personal belongings she'd been allowed to bring with her from home. She would not be sad to leave them behind; they were only things. A quick glance out the lone window of her chambers showed her it was indeed full dark, though she had no idea of the time, as she might have dozed for twenty minutes or two hours.

From the cupboard where hung all her gowns that she would leave behind, Ada pulled out a small leather pouch and attached it to her belt. She debated donning her cloak; it would make her figure dark and surely conceal her identity, but it would also give rise to questions should she happen upon any persons outside her chamber. Leaving the cloak behind, Ada blew out a terrified breath and snuck out of her chamber before her fear insisted she stay.

Chapter Two

Bare streaks of light shone into the cells of the dungeons, landing upon the cold and wet stone floor. Mildew lived here, the stench hanging heavy in the air. Jamie MacKenna wasn't often afraid—truth be told he couldn't recall a time when he'd ever been afraid—but today, tonight, he was fearful. While he and four others had been tossed into the dungeon, young Henry had been taken elsewhere and they had been neither informed of his whereabouts nor why the boy had been separated from the rest. Jamie and his lieutenant, Callum, had agreed the reason no doubt had to do with leverage over them, and not some dastardly plan to harm or brutalize the boy.

Jamie prayed they were right, hoped it wasn't just wishful thinking.

He swiped his hand over his jaw and chin and leaned his head against the bars of the cage, watching and listening.

They ought not to have been caught, he mused with frustration. But then, the entire day had been one mishap after another. The English had come, under Segrave and de Latimer, and—to the chagrin of loyal Scots—Robert Bruce, intent only upon capturing William Wallace and Simon Fraser. Smaller houses, Craig's included, had supported the English campaign. Jamie's MacKenna army had joined the fray, along with Conall Macgregor's forces. It should have been a rout, the English hadn't more than a thousand men all told. Jamie had an idea that Robert Bruce might have been behind the divide-and-conquer strategy, as their forces had wreaked havoc all around Stobo and Peebles and Happrew, burning fields and farms, coming and going in small groups, confusing the Scots with this practice, so different than their normal siege tactics.

Jamie's forces had been divided by a surprise attack. The lad, Henry, who was no soldier proper but the son of one of Jamie's officers had quickly been trapped. They'd had to at least try and save him. Jamie might have considered it fortunate that only six men had been captured, save that so many others now lay dead upon the Cademuir Hills.

Behind him, further back in the cell, Donald groaned. Will sat next to him, applying pressure to his wound. He wouldn't last long and there wasn't anything Jamie could do for him. Donald would be the lucky one, would escape the suffering come the morrow, Jamie guessed.

"A man dinna bring prisoners to his own keep," Callum had said earlier, "but to trade for his own prisoners, or to make an example of them."

Jamie couldn't imagine that his army or the forces of the MacGregor had been able to secure any prisoners. They'd barely managed to stay alive, intent on getting Wallace and Fraser out of harm's way.

He felt a hand on his shoulder, pulling his face away from the cage door. 'Twas all it was, really, a cage. Short and squat the cell, he and his soldiers had been forced to stoop to enter, and were obliged to remain upon their haunches or sit or kneel as the metal rails that were the ceiling of the cage were no more than four feet off the ground.

His captain pointed to Donald, who now lie still and silent. Jamie said a prayer for his soul, realizing his friend's body would not be afforded a proper burial.

Callum held his forefinger to his lips, his eyes like black glass, and then pointed to the steps at the far end of the dungeon, the ones they'd been forced down earlier today.

Jamie listened but heard nothing. There was no guard down here, in the dungeon, in the space outside the cages. Undoubtedly, there were several Craig soldiers in the yard, above the dungeon and very near to the heavy but well-greased door.

He threw a frown at Callum, for the silence, and then heard the noise just as Callum raised his thick brow. The door above was being pulled open. There wasn't any reason for the door to be opened at this hour of night, unless pain was on the agenda.

Jamie gritted his teeth and met the eyes of Will, while Callum kicked the feet of Ned and Malys, both of whom had fallen asleep, but came quickly awake. All five sat or hunched, ready and alert, with an effort to seem uncoiled. Jamie's frown deepened as some sound revealed that a person walked down the winding steps though no flickering light guided their way. Who came without a torch?

The sun had set many hours ago and the men were accustomed to the dimness of the dungeon, but this did not help them to recognize the figure that emerged into the space before their cage. Several sets of brows raised as they comprehended the bare swish of sound and the unmistakable silhouette of a woman's skirts.

"Please do not speak," said a low voice. The dreary darkness and the distance showed no face yet. "We haven't much time. I aim to set you free, but only on the condition that you take me with you." Though her voice was silky and soft, Jamie could well distinguish the tremor in her words.

No one answered, shocked as they were by this turn of events. Many a dungeon they'd collectively seen in their lifetimes, but no woman had ever either effected their freedom or insisted they remove her with them.

"Aye," Jamie said finally, as she'd gone still at their silence. He saw only a shadowed figure, no face showed itself even as she stepped nearer. He had the impression of a rather tall but young woman, with a pretty voice and long hair that fell over her shoulders when she bent to apply the key to the lock.

Before she turned it, and awarded them freedom, she insisted again, "You must take me with you."

"On my honor," Jamie said, so bemused by this circumstance that he didn't give thought that she might well have no idea who he was and thus, his honor might be a disputable thing. But she turned the key, and the hand he'd fisted upon the bar pushed the gate toward her.

Jamie stepped outside the cell, rose and stood very close to her, but saw only large and frightened eyes, the only shining thing in this hole in the ground. "We need the lad."

This seemed to startle her. Her eyes moved over all his men. They stopped briefly on Donald's body. She recovered quickly, however. "He would be in the tower, then."

"I saw four towers."

"The northeast one. The armory is on the first floor, prisoners above. There will be soldiers."

With little hope, he asked, his lips curving, "You wouldn't have dared to have brought along any weapons now, would you, lass?"

Another guilty, flustered look. "I-I did not. But the guards atop—they're sleeping. They are, or were, armed."

"Sleeping?" Callum asked with some suspicion.

"With help," she told them, patting a leather pouch at her hip.

"Malys, Ned, and Will, get the lass outside the wall. Wait for us on the road to Stobo," Jamie instructed. "Callum and I will find the boy. We'll be right behind you."

Will stepped forward and took the lass's elbow and Jamie led the way out of the dungeon, up the stairs. The torch light of the bailey showed three guards slumped on the ground, just outside the door, a dull leather flask near one man's hand.

Callum and Jamie and Malys each claimed a sword from the Craig men.

"Sleeping or dead?' Callum asked, shoving his boot into one man's thigh.

"Sleeping," the lass said, and then with less certainty, "I think."

Jamie turned to look at her, while Will's hand was still attached to her elbow. Her eyes were indeed large, round with fright, inside a face that would make for pleasant dreams, he imagined, and surrounded by a wealth of dark hair, glossy and curled down to her hip. "Thank you, lass."

She nodded. Her fear was palpable, and Jamie inclined his head to Will to get her away. He spared only a second to watch the three men and the lass scurry across the yard; he hadn't time now to inquire of her circumstance that had her jeopardizing her own life to see them released. He turned then to follow Callum to the north tower, using the inside wall as cover, not daring to cross the middle of the yard.

They met with little resistance inside the tower, their stealth well practiced that the few soldiers within heard them only when it was too late. They were swiftly overtaken and incapacitated, and Jamie and Callum raced up the circular steps to reach the top floor.

Thankfully Henry was unharmed, and Jamie quickly surmised his quarantine had only been a mental tactic used to cause fear and panic. Jamie could well see that Henry's first instinct upon seeing who opened the door was to run to him. But the lad caught himself, stopped within a few feet of Jamie and only nodded, no questions asked for his laird's appearance. Jamie grinned and tousled the lad's hair.

"C'mon, then." Callum tried to hurry them along. But he was too late. Loud noises broke the stillness of the night, shouts and calls heard all across the keep and yard. Jamie pivoted just as Callum slammed the thick wooden door shut. His captain threw up his hands, helpless, seeing that there was no brace on this side of the door. As one, they turned toward the windows. They hadn't the weapons or the numbers to face the coming horde, even now loud upon the first floor.

Jamie led the way, using the butt of his pilfered sword to knock out the solid wooden shutters. It was many seconds before they heard the pieces crash to the ground.

Callum looked at Jamie, who said with a shrug of his shoulders that they hadn't any choice.

"Get on with it," Callum said. "Might be, we can scale down the wall." His tone offered little hope that this might actually be the case.

Jamie lifted Henry into the window opening, and gave him an encouraging nod with the advice, "Like going down the side of a mountain, lad. Just hang on and dinna look down."

The laird and his captain exchanged a glance before Jamie tipped his head toward the window. "You first," Callum said. Jamie didn't waste the seconds arguing. His captain would never leave him behind, he knew. The door still hadn't burst open. He sheathed the sword in his own belt and climbed out the window, turning his back and clinging to the stone. He moved immediately to the left and called for Callum to come.

This side of the tower did not overlook the bailey, or likely they'd have been put upon instantly with missiles of some kind to thwart their escape. Jamie only managed to descend about half a floor before he lost his grip and fell the rest of the way, another fifteen feet perhaps. He landed hard on his back and grunted with the impact but quickly saw Henry's hand, outstretched to pull him up. Jamie came to his feet just as Callum's large body thumped next to him with an equally pained grunt.

In the next moment, the three skirted around the keep, further away from the yard, deeper into the darkness. They found the postern gate with only seconds to spare, as torch light now flickered along the wall, heading toward them. Jamie had to put his shoulder twice into the door to free it and soon they were sprinting away from Dornoch Keep.

They waited for more than an hour, tucked within the trees that framed the Stobo road. Callum and Henry had already walked quite a distance east and west inside these trees, but there was never any sign of Will or Ned or Malys, or the lass who'd freed them.

Twice now, Callum had stopped him from returning to Dornoch.

When he could stand it no more, when he knew they weren't coming, he resolved that they must scour the vicinity of Happrew, find the MacGregor army if it remained, or any left of his own, and come back.

Jamie cursed volubly, anger warring with helplessness.

He'd never left a living person behind.

"It's all we've got," Callum said.

They'll be dead by morning, Jamie knew, if they weren't dead already. Looking into the eyes of both Callum and Henry, he could see they knew this as well.

Jamie shook his head. He needed another plan, or an additional plan. There was too much going against them. "Callum, take Henry to Inesfree. Wait there, for MacGregor or for me." His captain wanted to argue again. Jamie pinned him with an intractable glare. "If there's none still near to Happrew, Inesfree is our best hope."

ADA HAD ONLY THOUGHT she'd known fear earlier today, or any time in the last many weeks under the same roof as John Craig. That had not been fear, she learned now. Maybe it had been dread, maybe it was anxiety, but it had certainly not been fear.

She knew this for sure, because she now felt true terror.

They'd been stopped near the gates, they're attempt to flee discovered by a soldier unexpectedly emerging from the gatehouse. No sentry atop the wall had noticed them. But this man, brought up short, just as surprised as they had been, raised a hue and cry and immediately struck out, engaging the sword wielder. The Craig soldier had been quickly joined by his comrades and one man from the dungeon, the only one with a weapon, had been swiftly overpowered and killed.

Another had been cut done only moments later by John Craig's very angry captain. Having been detained yet unharmed by soldiers near the gates, Ada and the remaining two had stood surrounded, weighing their options with grim countenances. Sir Rodric had walked right into the group, drawing his dagger as he marched toward them. He hadn't stopped, just kept coming until he was close enough to swipe the blade across the throat of the man, who sputtered and gurgled while blood spurted from his neck. Ada supposed she had been too shocked to react, having gone completely still. She hadn't even gasped at this gruesomeness.

Her hand had been released, belatedly, by the one who'd tugged her along since she'd freed them from the dungeon. But Sir Rodric had seen this, had put together the entire scenario right quick, and had turned a snarl upon Ada.

"He's not going to like this at all." Somehow, she hadn't flinched, even as he added, "And he'd had such high hopes for you." He'd left then to meet her betrothed, who'd come from the keep, his head bent as Sir Rodric spoke to him in a low voice as they strode across the yard. Ada saw, even from the distance, the thick but neatly trimmed brow of her betrothed rise just as he lifted his gaze to her.

And then he was standing before her, looking not at all as if he'd been jostled from his bed at such a late hour, but dressed finely in his bright red tabard and buff breeches. His boots, though he'd returned only earlier today from battle, showed not one speck of dirt. He'd bothered to collect his gloves, slapped them against his thigh as he looked at her now.

With a bravery that she absolutely did not feel, she met his gaze. It seemed all but her mind was numb.

The remaining prisoner, who Ada feared would breathe for not much longer, spoke up as John Craig regarded her with some foreboding calmness.

"Aye, but your lasses should no be wandering the yard at night, Craig. Almost had us our own prisoner."

He was cuffed upside the head by Rodric for his efforts. While Ada appreciated his attempt to remove blame from her, she could see that John did not believe him. He did not even deign to glance at the man, just continued to pin Ada with a hard stare.

"I'm waiting, dear Ada," John finally said, and shrugged, "for some explanation for your unruly behavior." There was nothing about his handsome features that spoke of the grim fate that awaited her. No lines marred his forehead, no darkness shrouded his eyes, no curl turned his lip.

She would die, she knew, or she would wish she were dead. He was that manner of man.

"I wished only to be away from you," she answered. "You are cruel and inhuman, without a shred of decency."

"So your politeness over this past month was all a lie?" He asked, seeming unperturbed by her response.

"Very much so." She was numb no more, could feel her legs about to give way.

"I am cruel and inhuman," he repeated, and turned his head to incite a reaction from the surrounding soldiers. They laughed, barely and uncomfortably. John Craig faced Ada again. He leaned close and whispered at her temple, "My dear, you have no idea."

She heard a small panicked cry and realized it had come from her.

Ada consoled herself with only this: from start to finish, it had taken the alleged sheep thief about thirty minutes to die; thirty minutes was naught when compared to the lifetime she'd surely suffer at the hands of John Craig if she'd only married him.

John Craig stepped back and Ada breathed again.

He struck out so quickly then, so unexpectedly, that she didn't see the hand coming until it was too late. He backhanded her, his knuckles glancing off her cheek and mouth, jerking her head to the side with the force of the blow.

Ada tasted blood and swallowed as his shape blurred before her eyes. So caught off guard was she, so stunned by the strike, Ada stumbled as her legs finally gave out. She collapsed at his feet, her skirts billowing briefly before they settled around her. John Craig grabbed her hand, away from her cheek, and bent over her. He held her hand in front of her face as at last he demonstrated his true self, spitting in her face as he ground out, "You will learn just how cruel and inhuman I can be. When the sun comes up, sweet Ada, I will make you beg for death."

That had been a couple hours ago. And because John Craig was a master of horror, it was too simple, too easy, to have her locked in some room while she waited the morning and the torture to come. No, Ada and the man who'd been caught with her had ropes slung around their necks and had been stood upon wooden crates, which seemed not sturdy enough to handle even Ada's slight weight. Their hands had been tied behind their backs. John Craig, himself, had adjusted the ropes around her neck and that of the man, so that they needed to keep on their toes to maintain the slack. Standing flatfooted pulled the rope too tight around her neck.

Several soldiers had, at first, stood close to them, taunting them. The man next to her had his face sliced up, though he couldn't move away from the knife that sliced him, lest he stumble off the crate and hang himself. Ada had only turned her head minimally to see what they did to him, afraid of losing her balance. John Craig had left them to find his bed, content to wait for the morrow to begin his entertainment. But his soldiers, those on the overnight detail, had sought to alleviate their own boredom with the man hanging next to her, one man being so dastardly as to force his dagger, inch by inch, into his side. She thought the man might have passed out, or pretended to, so that they bored with him and moved on to Ada. They had come to her then and she had received similar treatment, a shallow slice from each side of her nose to almost her ear. When this was done, one Craig soldier used his dagger to carve a line across her chest, just above the neckline of her kirtle.

Neither Ada nor the man had cried out or truth be known, made much fuss, as their precarious footing required they remain so still. The soldiers tired of their play soon and thankfully, they'd been left alone after that.

The man next to her was Will, she'd since learned. They'd talked almost constantly to each other, as it was imperative that they remain wakeful lest they stumble off the crates.

He was of the MacKenna clan. The large man who'd promised to take her with them, who'd yesterday stood up to her betrothed in defense of the boy, was Jamie MacKenna. Will insisted that he would come for them.

"He'll no let us die," Will had promised.

"It's been hours," Ada had countered. There was no point in having hope, if there was to be none. "Mayhap they are dead."

Out of the corner of her eye, she saw him shake his head very slowly. "The MacKenna'll no be killed by an insufferable Craig man." There was so much conviction in his fierce words, Ada was compelled to believe him.

Her toes and the balls of her feet were cramped and sore. She could not maintain this position much longer. She felt drained, bloodless, and about to collapse.

Will suddenly slumped and scrambled, his toes dancing about the crate to find purchase. After a moment, he righted himself.

Ada talked, told him of her life back in Newburgh, with her dear mother, and her favorite sister, Muriel. Told him how she'd arrived here only a month ago, that she was to wed John Craig. Was. She spoke of riding across the heath of Lomond Hills on a sunny day and the last festival she'd attended down near Glasgow. She whispered a raunchy ditty she'd learned here at Dornoch, anything to keep them both awake.

Will tried to do the same, told her he was the fourth son of a fine merchant, that he'd been in the MacKenna army for seven years, that he was in love with a girl named Beth, but he'd never told her. He said he hoped her blue eyes were the last thing he saw.

"Aye, but she hasn't your heart, Ada Moncriefe," Will struggled to say. Blood now dribbled from his lip, coming from deep within. "When Jamie comes, lass—and he will—you tell him I'm sorry."

Ada sobbed woefully.

When it was near to dawn, they'd exhausted their efforts to remain on their toes, to remain awake. Will slept first, not even waking as he slumped, as the rope was tightened around his throat. Tears fell as Ada hissed his name to rouse him, to no avail, even as she refused to believe that he was likely dead now. Her own weariness finally overtook her, and she slumped just as Will had and the rope constricted.

MARGARET CRAIG SAT pensively at the ornate writing table in her chambers, tapping the quill upon the ink stained surface. Her brother, Andrew, presently near Perth, would not come, summoned only by his little sister. She knew this because she'd many times written to him, begging him to take her away from John. He'd ignored every plea. His history with their eldest sibling was rife with its own abuses and malignancies. But if John were gone, Andrew would then be baron Craig.

She was a coward, she knew, unable to bring herself to confront John on her own, even as he continued to torture and abuse dear Ada. Tears slipped from her eyes, for what John was doing to Ada, what he had done over the last three days since she'd tried to leave Dornoch with the prisoners, all of whom were now dead or gone. John would not be swayed by the pleas of the sister he despised. John had always only and ever been swayed by violence. So be it.

Her hand shook as she finally put pen to paper.

"John is dead. Come home," was all she wrote.

Aye, it was a lie at this moment, but it would bring Andrew home, she knew. And before he arrived, Margaret was determined either to make it truth, or to have somehow managed to have freed Ada.

Chapter 3

May 1305

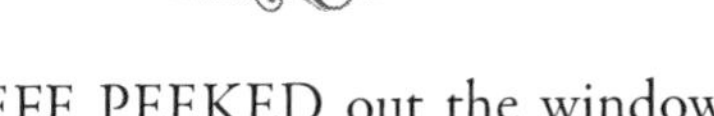

ADA MONCRIEFE PEEKED out the window and scanned the yard, her eyes moving left and then right. She thought she'd heard an unnatural sound. Her heartbeat quickened even as she could distinguish nothing out of place. But she stayed like that, watching, for several minutes.

When she was satisfied the noise and it's source were not a threat, she moved away from the window. The dagger in her hand was lowered and she again sat near the cold hearth.

Today might be the day she struck out again.

Or, like all the days over the last many months, today she might only tell herself that she would move on and find her landing place, but then find one project after another to occupy her time until she reasoned it was too late now to start such a journey. Not that she had any idea what said journey might entail, having no clear idea where she was, or exactly where she might be going.

Will hadn't moved, even when Ada had jumped up several minutes ago. She clicked her tongue, and while the noise lifted Will's ears, he did not rise from the floor at her feet. He'd returned last night, having been gone for three days. While Ada did not begrudge him his freedom, and his need to roam, she never felt quite as safe when the wolf pup wasn't around. Not so much a pup anymore, as he'd grown considerably since she'd stumbled upon him many months before. She'd been searching the forest for stray nuts or seeds over the long winter and had come upon the shaggy and scraggly pup not far from the cottage. She'd had no intention of stealing a wolf's pup and had felt the entire area near him was a dangerous place to be. She'd skirted around him and left the yipping pup to his own devices, or the return of his mother. But he'd been in the same area the next day, and the day after that, his yipping having grown plaintive and desperate that Ada had finally taken him home.

Home. No, it wasn't that, these four walls and that lone window were only a resting place. She'd only stumbled upon the cottage herself by chance, hadn't yet found the courage to go further. She seemed only to be in some state of not really living and too afraid to die.

Ada blamed three people for her present circumstance: John Craig, for the scars she carried; Jamie MacKenna, for her inability to trust any human being; and herself, for being too cowardly to accept her fate and move on.

John Craig.

Not a day went by that thoughts of him did not come to mind. Curiously, she could scarce recall the first many weeks at his keep, only those last four days. He'd heaped on the abuses, day after day, until she feared her mind would be hacked away as were other little bits of her. And all the while, as daily tortures were inflicted, he kept reminding her, the worst was yet to come. He had no intention of killing her, he'd told her with some twisted glee. But a rape was coming, he kept promising. It would be the decisive finishing stroke, he'd said, "Though still I fear I cannot find it in my heart to kill you, sweet Ada." And then dear Margaret had found her, broken and bleeding in the tower on the fourth night. Ada would never know how the timid girl had arranged it, but she had helped Ada out of the tower and away from Dornoch via the postern gate. Half mad with pain and grief, Ada had stumbled away on foot, had asked no questions, hadn't even thanked Margaret, she recalled too often these days.

It had taken her weeks to return to her family in Newburgh, and she had arrived nearly incoherent. Her recovery had taken many more weeks and had been only a slightly lesser hell. She'd not lasted long there, her father had been unable to lay eyes on her, her scars a revulsion to him. Her mother had done naught but cry, her sisters were aghast and, sadly, unsympathetic; Sarah had asked her if she would please not attend her wedding, as she didn't want her day to be ruined by the sight of Ada. Only Muriel had been able to look at Ada, only she had been a comfort to her. Nevertheless, Ada had left the Newburgh house, had slipped out during the night, had taken naught but the clothes on her back. She'd find a nunnery, she'd thought, 'twas all she was good for now.

Peace, she'd mused. Maybe she'd find some peace.

She'd walked for weeks, slowly, aimlessly, thinking only about some direction of south, before she'd stumbled onto the cottage in the forest. She'd planned to spend only a few days, had discovered Will within the first few weeks, and had yet to find a reason to leave.

"Aye, Will, let's get outside," she said now, rising from the stool. It was her movement, less so her words, that roused Will.

He followed Ada to the door and outside, both of them squinting a bit to adjust their eyes to the sunshine. Will stayed near as she walked the now well-known path toward the creek. The little stream was close and provided Ada all the water she needed for washing and drinking, and as the base of all her very bland soups and stews.

Just before the small ridge that crested above the stream, Will's ear's pricked up. He listened intently, his head cocked to one side. Humming a low growl, he stepped a few feet away from Ada, watching one particular spot in the trees. A stripe of hair rose along the center of his back. Ada withdrew her knife and scanned the forest. A flash of movement caught her eye. Her stomach constricted and dropped, a feeling that was all too familiar to her.

And then so many faces and forms came into the clearing, soldiers bearing an unfamiliar green and blue and gold tartan. To a man, their eyes were trained on Will and not on Ada. Will, God love him, did not leave her. He was angry at the intrusion, at the threat, but stayed in front of Ada, between her and the soldiers. His eyes moved from one to the next until both his and Ada's gaze settled on the mountain of a man who walked through the horde and stood at the front. He was big and dark, with black hair and beard and black eyes. The eyes he kept trained on Will even as he stood casually with his thumbs looped through his belt.

"That's quite a hound you've got there, lass," he said, his voice deep, the sounds thick.

Ada said nothing, didn't move her blade, even as the black eyes considered it.

"We mean no harm, lass," he went on, "but you're on Kincaid land and we need to know what you're about. That you taken up at old Mungo's place?"

Of course, she wasn't sure to whom the borrowed home had once belonged. But they seemed to be aware of her presence there, and it would explain the recent feeling she'd had of being watched. Ada nodded.

"Now if you be needing a place to stay, we'll take you on down to Stonehaven. The Lady Anice will no stand for a nice lass being on her own in the forest."

"I am only passing through," she said, eyeing all the soldiers in this man's company. "And apologies to you, and your Lady Anice for having encroached." She hoped her scratchy and pale voice reached them.

"Where you headed, lass?"

She hesitated. *I was hoping to find a cloister that might take me in*, sounded absurdly pitiful. Ada pulled the hood closer around her face. "Again, I am sorry to have caused alarm. I'll be on my way."

"Stonehaven's no a bad place to take some refuge, lass."

He didn't seem unkind. He seemed...fatherly.

And John Craig, at first glance, had seemed a young girl's dream of a bridegroom.

"We'll move on today, sir," she insisted.

The big man regarded her thoughtfully for a few minutes, taking one step closer, shortening the distance to less than twenty feet as his big booted feet crunched upon the hardened earth and crispy leaves. Will lunged, but only a few feet, giving several deep warning barks.

"He looks like a wolf, but that yapping is hound, aye?"

Ada didn't know anything about her pup's lineage. "Will is asking you to stay back, sir."

The big man grinned, as if Will's name amused him.

"I'll no come closer, lass. I am Torren, captain of the Kincaid army. I really think you'll want to come meet our Lady Anice."

"You are very kind, sir. As I've said, we are only passing by—"

"Aye, but here's my dilemma, lass. I dinna ken you. And you're no giving me anything to make me think you dinna mean any harm to mine down at Stonehaven. I dinna think you want your wolf sprinkled with missiles," he said, and threw his thumb over his shoulder to point out the several soldiers with arrows nocked and aimed at Will, "so I'll ask you again to kindly come down to Stonehaven and meet Lady Anice."

Ada could not be sure they wouldn't kill her wolf-pup, but somehow thought this man wouldn't allow it unless it was justified.

"Will you come closer, sir? Will is a good judge of truth."

The big man grinned again within his dark beard. "Aye, I bet he is." He walked slowly toward her.

Ada was aware of his bowmen repositioning themselves, to keep a clean line on Will. She breathed slowly, purposefully, trying to relax herself. She did not want her own heightened emotions to instigate any defense in Will. She stepped forward and placed her hand on the scruff at his neck and caressed the fur there, to let him know she wasn't afraid. He would let her know if she should be, she hoped.

The man, Torren, continued to come, his gaze on Will, his hand on the hilt of his dagger.

When he stood only a few feet before her, Ada said, "I cannot leave him behind."

"Aye, if he dinna eat my hand, he can come. But if he even looks sideways at one person, he'll be locked up."

It was a good response. A person with nefarious intentions wouldn't have threatened even that much. They'd have assured her of anything.

Ada lifted her hand from Will's neck. He moved, with halting steps, towards the big man, sniffing his way along. When he was close enough, he sniffed at the man's hand, his head moving close and then not, until finally he began licking the man's fingers.

Ada's bottom lip fell.

The man raised his thick slanted brows at her and gave a wink. "Aye, 'twas bacon at our first meal."

She laughed. She couldn't help it, surprised herself even. Ada clamped a hand over her mouth to stifle her mirth. She certainly hadn't expected this. She reined it in quickly, unsettled by what she was feeling. She hadn't felt...*anything* in so long, certainly not joy, even one as simple as this.

And then, as if her laughter had been an invitation, the soldiers began to crowd around Will, whose tail wagged at the friendliness and attention.

"He's a big one, aye?' said one, scratching behind Will's ear.

"Look at his paws," said another, on his haunches, setting his own hand on the ground to compare the size.

"Aye, but you've got your mam's wee hands, Kinnon," someone teased.

The pale-faced young man was unperturbed by the ribbing. He stood and faced Ada. "Why'd you name him Will? He needs a better name to suit him."

"Like Zeus," someone suggested.

"Warwolf!" Came another idea.

"She'll no be naming her hound after an English war machine, Tamsin!"

"Wallace!" Cheers followed this suggestion.

But Ada barely heard. The distance had kept her face in the shadows of her hood, but this close, the shadows offered no protection. She felt her cheeks redden instantly and saw that both the lad, Kinnon, and the big man's eyes were fixed on her face. They'd gone completely still, the youth gaping at her with some mix of horror and shock.

Best to get it over with, she told herself. While they suddenly seemed like good people, she had an idea that showing her face to them might actually be a means to escape. They'd take one look and likely send her on her way, politely and firmly.

Ada lowered the hood, curling her fingers around the edges, letting it fall down her back.

Someone gasped.

"*Jesu*," another muttered.

She clenched her teeth. She met the pale blue eyes of the boy, Kinnon, not brave enough to look beyond him, to see all their expressions.

"That why you keep to the forest, lass?" His initial shock having worn, his tone was now level, giving no hint of either repugnance or sympathy.

Ada nodded. Will growled low, sensing a change in the atmosphere. The big man, Torren, absently offered his hand again for Will to sniff, his eyes upon her face.

The silence then stretched on, until Ada gave a nervous laugh, and said, "I haven't actually seen it myself yet, but I guess your reaction tells me...that I probably do not want to."

Many spoke out then, filling the air with lies.

"It's no so bad, lass."

"I almost did no see it."

"You can hardly notice...."

And Ada knew then they were good people, indeed.

"Aye, c'mon, lass," said Torren. "We'll get you down to Stonehaven."

She nodded, just as someone said, "Sister'll take good care of you."

ADA RODE BEFORE THE big man, Torren, and let her jaw gape for the second time that day, seeing the magnificent castle that was Stonehaven. It sat atop a flat-brimmed hill, with only the sea behind it. Carved of pale, sand colored stone, it boasted a tower in each corner and a massive wooden door, which stood as high as the third story. They rode through an arched tunnel to gain the bailey, where Torren immediately shouted out, almost into Ada's ear, "You'll no be running, lass! No running!"

Ada looked around to find the recipient of his chastisement, expecting to see a small child in harm's way, for the vehemence behind his dictate. She saw only a blonde woman with curious short hair and a very large belly. The woman stopped and threw her hand onto her forehead to block the sun, to see who came.

"Torren, I've told you, I'm not breakable."

He reined in and swung himself onto the ground and pointed a finger at the woman. "I see you running again, I'll lock you in the keep. And the Kincaid'll support me in this!"

When he turned to assist Ada in her dismount, she saw the woman stick her tongue out at him. Ada was set onto the ground and saw Kinnon rush over to the woman's side.

"Sister, look what we found in the forest!"

Torren brought Ada around to face the woman, and chided Kinnon, "She's no a *what*, boy."

"Sister can see that, Torren," was Kinnon's response. He stood beside the woman, smiling as if he'd brought her some rare present.

"This is Ada, lass," Torren said.

Ada met the woman's gaze. She had never met a more beautiful person. While her hair was unusual, being cropped so close to her head, her eyes were an amazing shade of blue and her skin was perfectly creamy, and completely unblemished. Ada could read the shock in those very pretty eyes, but to her credit, the woman tamped it down quickly and offered her the kindest smile Ada was sure she had ever received.

"I am Anice."

Ada nodded and bit her lip, not knowing what she might say.

Torren said, "She's only passing through, lass, but we agreed she'd fare better in the keep than out in the forest."

The woman did not hesitate. "Of course."

Will burst onto the scene then, having sniffed most the ground inside the walls.

Torren was quick to shield the woman named Anice, stepping somewhat in front of her, his hand once again poised on his dagger. Ada guessed it was instinctive. But Will only tore through the group, headed for other things to sniff out.

"That's Will," Torren said, relaxing his stance.

"Is he yours?" Anice asked Ada, with some excitement.

Ada nodded again. "I found him."

"He'll probably no be kept away from her, lass," Torren said. "Maybe the north tower would suit her, to keep the wolf away from the hall."

Ada stiffened, which did not go unnoticed by the pretty blond. Anice was quick to explain, "It sounds awful, I know. But the tower room is one of my favorites. It's very pretty. And it has its own entrance." She pointed to a door at the base of one of the rear towers.

"And why were you running anyway, lass?" Torren asked of Anice.

Ada watched as the woman gave a sheepish glance to the big man. "I was hoping to catch Nellie before she was gone for the day."

Torren rolled his eyes. "How much bread can you eat in one day?"

Anice shrugged and grinned at him. "Apparently, quite a bit." And while Torren rolled his eyes at this, Anice said to Ada, "Have you eaten, Ada? Very good. Then come along, we'll get you settled in."

The woman, Anice, led Ada inside the keep and through the hall. At the far corner of the large hall, they entered a long corridor with light stone columns and an arched ceiling. It turned left and then right and finally showed a door at the end. The corridor was dark but not unnaturally damp, despite their proximity to the sea.

"If you decide to use this entrance, I can see to it that the lamps are lit daily," Anice offered.

"You said there was an exterior entrance?"

"Yes, and you are more than welcome to use that," said the lady. They reached what Ada assumed was the area directly beneath the tower, entering the room through an arched doorway. Anice pointed to a door across the room. "We might need to have Torren open it the first time. It's rarely used and likely stiff." She picked up her skirts and mounted the stairs, which were narrow and attached to the outer wall. A second floor showed only the storage of some things and Anice kept walking up. Upon the third floor, there was a landing and another arched wooden door. This one opened easily at Anice's insistence and revealed to Ada, as she'd been told, a very pretty room with a timber ceiling and two glass-less windows. Anice took a moment to lift the furs away from the openings, bringing light into the space. The room itself, while the floor and walls were only more of the same stone, was made cozy with a beautiful carved wooden bed, topped with a delicate embroidered cover with flowers of green and blue and gold. A small table and chair and chest were the only other furniture, but the walls were covered in tapestries of burgundy and gold and there were three rugs of fur upon the floor.

"This is lovely, and I thank you for your kindness," Ada said. "But this feels—am I putting someone out of their chamber?"

"Not at all," she was quickly assured. "It belonged to my husband's mother and she has left us." Anice turned from the window then and rubbed her hands idly over her belly.

"Is Torren your husband?"

Anice shook her head, her coming smile wry but lovely. "Torren is my keeper."

Ada did not know what that meant.

Anice waved off her own silliness. "Pardon me. No, the Kincaid is my husband. Torren is the captain of the Kincaid army, though in truth he seems to think he's in charge of only me. May I ask where you come from? Or what you were doing in the forest?"

While she did seem very nice, Ada wasn't sure how much she wanted to divulge about her own circumstances. "My family is in Newburgh. It became...impossible for me to stay there." She chewed the inside of her cheek for a second before adding, "I had hoped to find refuge in a cloister, but only made it as far as the cottage when the winter came. Haven't been able to get myself back on the road again, I guess."

Anice nodded. Ada was sure she'd have liked to ask more questions but kindly refrained from doing so.

"I won't stay long," she promised. "I won't intrude any more than I—"

Anice rushed forward. "You intrude not at all. *We* have, or Torren did, and I apologize. He is overprotective of Stonehaven."

"Of you," Ada guessed.

This was acknowledged with a small grin.

Ada wondered briefly how that felt, to be so well protected, to be so valued and loved. She guessed it felt as this woman looked, happy and healthy and whole. She sighed.

"Now, what do you need?" Her host asked. "A lie-down before supper? A bath in the garder robe? Have you possessions that should be fetched from the cottage?"

Ada shook her head. "I-I haven't anything I need, that is, I haven't any possessions, really. But might what little I've collected remain at the cottage for when I depart?"

"Of course," Anice assured her. "Mayhap you and I will walk back there one day and look things over, pack them up, just so that no other stumbles upon the cottage and decides to make use of your things."

Ada had a thought. "Would that man, Torren, allow you to walk that far?"

She giggled wonderfully. "Possibly, no. Certainly not without him, or a very large armed retinue, but it can be done. All right, so we need then to outfit you. The laird's mother left some things when she departed. I fear my own gowns would be too short for you. You are wonderfully tall."

"Why are you being so kind to me?"

Anice frowned, though managed to look still angelic and sweet. "Why would I not?" She stepped closer still, took Ada's hands in hers. Ada flinched, hoped it went unnoticed by this woman. "You've been through something, Ada. I won't insult you by pretending I don't see the evidence of it. You should never suffer so again. You are welcome here for as long as you need or like."

Something warm and unfamiliar churned inside her. She didn't dare name it; to do so was to give it hope. But she smiled back at the woman, who squeezed her hands before releasing them to thread her arm through Ada's. "However, you will have to suffer my attendance at your bath. Stonehaven is wonderful, but it is a decidedly male domain, with so few females in attendance."

Chapter Four

Over the next few weeks, Ada began to think less and less about leaving, about striking out on her own again. Stonehaven was wonderful, as was every person who resided within. She'd met Lady Anice's husband, Gregor Kincaid, that very first evening, at dinner. He was incredibly handsome and doted on his wife. And Anice left no doubt in any onlooker's mind that she adored him in return. Her eyes fairly lit up when he entered the room or came anywhere near her.

Anice had kindly shared many pieces of wardrobe with her, so Ada felt a little more human, more so than she had since leaving Newburgh. By the end of the first week at Stonehaven, she felt confident enough to leave off trying so hard to conceal her face. Most all had seen it by now, and their initial shock had worn a bit. They stared less and less, and Ada appreciated this. She had mentioned to Anice on the first day that maybe she should wear a wimple, it would at least cover her neck, leaving only the scars upon her face visible.

"Ada, whatever your tale, your scars are like Gregor's I presume—bravely fought and honorably achieved. You should not be ashamed of them. They mark you not as a victim, but as a survivor. Embrace them. You are stronger, more remarkable for them."

Ada accepted this and did learn, slowly and around certain people, to at least be somewhat less self-conscious about her disfigurement.

Very quickly, she discovered that the beach behind Stonehaven was absolutely her favorite spot in all the world. There were stone steps, along the steep cliff behind the castle that would take a person from the rear yard directly down onto the beach, but Ada did not care for those; they were too narrow and too high, and she feared the wind of the North Sea would blow her right off them. And, thankfully, Torren, would absolutely not allow Anice to navigate those treacherous steps, or even look at them. Anice instead led her out through the arched tunnel and down the slope at the front of the castle. At the bottom of the hill, they turned sharply right and took the foot path until the packed earth turned to bone-white sand and the trees opened up to reveal a wide but shallow expanse of beach. Ada stared with awe at the dark blue water slapping against the shore, breathed deeply of the salty air, and watched with some delight as Will bounded ahead of them, charging directly into the surf.

Facing the beach from the back of the castle, Ada saw that further to the right, the cliff on which the house sat jutted out into the water, so that the sandy beach ended at that point. To the left, a cairn of rocks stood as tall as Torren and reached almost to the water. Anice explained that around that pile of rocks, there was another beach, wider but more shallow; at night, Anice had said, when the tide rolled in, it was not possible to get around the ancient cairn, so she usually only visited it during the day. "But not today, when Torren is here," Anice had whispered to her.

"What *are* you allowed to do?" Ada teased her, but again was imbued with a sense of envy for Anice Kincaid being so well loved and cared for.

"Not much," Anice said and made a face, "and likely even less as my time draws nearer."

"Mayhap he'll transfer his overprotective bent onto your child and you'll be allowed more freedom."

Anice's charming dimples appeared as she smiled at this. "That, dear Ada, is my hope."

Kinnon was with them today, as they were once again at the beach. Ada liked the lad very much. He was kindly and unaffected, curious about so many things, and always so good natured. And Will had really taken to him. They cavorted now, Kinnon splashing the wolf pup every time Will darted by him in the surf. Ada laughed as Will chomped at the low waves with his teeth. She was again becoming accustomed to the sound of her own laughter, though she knew it was huskier, as was her voice, since Dornoch.

"I want to put my feet in the water," she said suddenly, Will's enthusiasm raising her own interest.

Anice turned from watching the wolf and Kinnon. "It'll be cold, but oh so refreshing. Leave your shoes here."

Ada sat in the sand, and lifted the bottom of her borrowed blue gown, taking only a moment to unlace her soft leather shoes. "Oh, but my hose..."

Anice waved off this concern with a crafty little smile. "I went barefoot here for almost the entire summer last year," she admitted, a wistful note in her voice. "You can absolutely remove your hose and garters without lifting your skirts and no one will be the wiser." She glanced up and around. "Torren and Kinnon cannot see—I'd join you myself if I could reach around this belly to untie my own shoes."

Ada needed no more enticement. She had never walked in the sea. She doffed her hose and garters and rolled them up and tucked them into her discarded shoes. "Anice, come here," she said and came onto her knees. "I'll untie your shoes."

Her friend's eyes lit up and she obeyed, standing before Ada, her hand on her shoulder while Ada removed her shoes and then her hose and garters as well, hiding them just as she had her own. Ada stood and Anice took her hand and they dashed down to where the waves lightly crashed in, lifting their skirts as the water rolled over their bare feet.

Ada dug her feet into the sand, squishing it between her toes, letting the receding wave pull it all away. The water was indeed very cold, but it was a remarkable feeling. Anice cried out with joy, and swung Ada's hand high as they darted away from a larger incoming wave. This alerted Torren of their nearness, of their presence in the water. He turned and his frown was immediate. He started shouting something straight away, though the words were lost for the noise at the surf. He walked towards them, frowning and hollering.

Ada and Anice laughed and giggled.

"I'm not sure what poor Torren is going to do when I actually have to birth the babe," Anice called as Will skimmed by them, still biting at the waves.

"He'll be standing just outside the door, scolding you to not push too hard, nor feel any pain."

"Now that's enough of that!" He ordered now.

They could hear him but only laughed more. Anice kicked up her foot, splashing water at the big man as he closed in on them. He rolled his eyes but refrained from returning the gesture. Ada could see that he very much wanted his dear Anice to have fun, but that he just worried too much. He hovered close then and allowed them to play yet more in the ankle high surf.

Ada lifted her arms and spun around, tipping her head back to let the sun warm her face. Oh, but this was exhilarating. And it was joyful.

She was truly happy here at Stonehaven.

JAMIE MACKENNA FOLLOWED Gregor Kincaid down to the beach behind the majestic Stonehaven keep. He'd been here last fall, when they'd hidden William Wallace down here, after they'd accidentally recovered Anice from kidnappers. He'd returned several times since. He liked being at Stonehaven, liked the Kincaid's lass and the people of Stoney. He considered it so much less lonely than his own Aviemore, in which he'd barely resided in years. For so long, he'd been a faithful companion to William Wallace, but unlike Gregor and even their friend, Conall MacGregor, Jamie hadn't anything—anyone—to draw him back home. He liked the sea, liked the air down at the beach here, which smelled of salt and sand and never of blood and sweat.

"She's already here," Gregor said beside him. They'd come looking for Anice, as Jamie could not pass through without giving a proper greeting to the lass. "Ada's with her."

"Who is Ada?" There were so few women at Stonehaven, Jamie thought he knew all of them.

"We are no exactly sure. Torren found her making use of a shack in the forest," Gregor answered cryptically. "Be warned, Jamie: Ada's face is scarred, rather gruesomely. Dinna stare, lest you suffer Anice's wrath."

"Where did she get the scars?" Only scars he'd ever seen had come from battle.

"She's no said. Anice said were no to pry."

Jamie nodded, looking out toward the water. He saw the Kincaid's woman standing with a few other people. With her short blonde hair and growing belly, she was easy to distinguish. He recognized the Kincaid captain, Torren, and another Kincaid tartan-ed soldier. Jamie knew that if Gregor himself was not with the lass, Torren would be. He wondered if Anice ever just wanted to be alone, as he knew full well the lass was rarely, if ever, left unattended.

The little group stood within the water, Torren giving no mind to his boots in the surf, keeping close to the Kincaid lady.

The woman named Ada stood with her back to them as they neared. She was taller than Anice by several inches and slim, with long and shiny dark hair, was all Jamie could see. Anice was speaking but broke off as she said something to Ada, seeing her husband and Jamie.

She smiled beautifully.

Jamie heard Torren admonish, "No running, lass."

There was no need for her to run. Gregor jogged toward her the last dozen feet, scooping her up in his arms just at the water's edge. Jamie frowned, watching their happy reunion. They'd been separated for three days, by his reckoning, not three months.

When Gregor released his wife, she turned to Jamie. "You, sir, have been too long gone from Stonehaven."

"What I'd tell you about the *sir*, lass?" He accepted her hug, even patted her back lightly, having never touched an expectant woman before. In his peripheral, he was aware that the woman, Ada, kept her face averted—because of her scars, he guessed, but had no sure knowledge of this.

Gregor pulled Anice away from the water and the entire small party followed suit, standing just out of reach of the highest climbing wave.

"Will!" Kincaid's soldier called suddenly, moving away from the group, walking toward the keep. Jamie turned to see the pasty-faced lad chasing down a huge beast. His eyes widened, realizing the animal was possibly part wolf, and widened more when he realized the wolf was named Will. The lad—Kinnon, if Jamie recalled correctly—gave a whistle and the wolf lifted his head and charged at him, tail wagging.

Anice laughed behind him and Jamie turned to her. There'd been no wolf when last he'd visited Stonehaven. The woman named Ada was watching Kinnon and the wolf as well, showing her profile to him.

Jamie forgot to breathe for a moment.

"Ada, call him off," Kinnon hollered with a loud chuckle, while the pup had his huge paws on the lad's shoulders and was licking his face.

"Will! Come, you big oaf!" She called. Several of those watching laughed at Kinnon's predicament and the wolf's playfulness. But her voice held no lightness, was scratchy.

An elbow dug into Jamie's rib. Gregor was next to him, frowning at Jamie for his rude gawking.

He couldn't *not* stare. He couldn't believe his eyes. It couldn't be....

Yet, he knew that face. A shadow of this face had haunted his dreams for more than a year.

"Ada, you must meet Jamie," Anice said, when the wolf had left Kinnon alone and the circle turned away from watching.

He was still staring at her, despite Gregor's hard elbow.

Soft hazel eyes turned to him just for a second. Her very small and thin smile vanished. She didn't recognize him. She was only now shy, afraid to be the object of any attention, he imagined. She stared only at his chest. He could not look away.

"Jamie MacKenna, this is Ada Moncriefe."

She knew his name. He wasn't sure how, but she now knew who he was. Her eyes jerked back to his. Her lips parted.

Their gaping at each other could not have gone unnoticed—did not, as told by the keen silence around them.

Jamie opened his mouth to speak, but no words came forth.

She clenched her teeth, as announced by the tremor in her lips and the tightening of her neck, the skin of which showed a distinct and puckered red and white line from left to right, disappearing into her hair.

"The wolf's name is Will?" He didn't know why those were the first words he said to her.

She said nothing, did not answer. Finally, with a shake of her head and quick grimace to Anice, she skirted around the group and darted away, stumbling until she yanked up her skirts and bolted from the beach. Jamie was shown a glimpse of bare feet and slim ankles as she ran away.

Those that remained turned stupefied gazes onto Jamie.

He took in Anice's confusion and the heavy frowns of Gregor and Torren.

"You and Ada have met," Anice said unnecessarily.

How did he explain it, though? He kept his gaze on Anice, would not look away from the censure in her eyes. How could he tell her that all those scars were because of him?

It was the lass to whom he owed the explanation. Ada. With a foul obscenity, he pivoted and chased after her.

ADA CURSED THE TEARS that fell. She could not comprehend that these people, who had been so kind to her for so many weeks, were friendly with that devil! It was beyond her understanding. My God, how could Anice embrace him? And smile at him!

She heard her name called. *Please, no!* She ran faster, out of the sand, onto the flattened grass of the worn path around the side of the keep.

"Wait!" He called again.

He was closer. Why did Anice let him follow her?

Ada kept going, heartened when she heard Will barking. He was not far away. Ada chanced a glance behind. The man had stopped, unable to get around Will, who'd come between him and Ada. His snarl was mean now, as Ada had never heard it.

She stopped, breathless, and stared at him, while more than twenty feet separated them. On one side, trees flanked the narrow path to and from the beach; the other side was only a tall jagged cliff of rock, on which Stonehaven sat at the top.

"Lass, how came you to be here at Stonehaven? I thought you dead."

She saw it now, that the face was the same as the one she'd barely seen that night down in the dungeon and then in the sparse light of the yard at Dornoch. The piercing eyes, whose color she had not known, and the squareness of the jaw were all that were familiar to her. His hair, which she recalled being rather long, was tied at his nape, while the sun glinted like gold in the blond strands.

Jamie MacKenna. She had not forgotten his name.

"You thought me dead?"

"Aye."

"But I am not." She straightened her back.

"But how?"

"Aye," she said bitterly across the space between them, "you'd not know, because you left me there. And Will. You said you'd take me. Will swore you'd come back for us."

The look of horror that washed over him was well done, she decided. Indeed, all color seemed to drain from his face.

"Will died believing that. He said you'd never leave us behind."

"Lass, I...."

Ada lifted a brow, gave him a derisive glare. "What? You forgot? You're sorry?"

Anice came rushing around him then, ignoring Will, who still held Jamie MacKenna at bay, and lumbered toward Ada.

Ada softened her tone as much as she could, but her words were still laced with fury. "Do not come near me," she advised.

Anice was brought up short by such vehemence.

The Kincaid and Torren and Kinnon were close now as well.

Ada drew a ragged breath, holding her hands out, palms forward. "You have been very kind to me...and I do not want to seem ungrateful...." She was crying now, couldn't make the tears stop, or her voice not quaver. "I thank you for...everything."

And she turned and walked away again, knowing Will would give her a good head start.

ANICE TURNED TO JAMIE, her mouth open, waiting for some explanation, but he said nothing, looking as if he'd seen a ghost as he watched Ada disappear around the front of Stonehaven.

"Kinnon," Anice said, "take Will up to the stables. Lock him up." Her gaze remained fixed on Jamie as she explained to those around her, "She won't leave without Will."

Kinnon nodded and patted his leg as he walked past Jamie and then Will, who gave one last snarl at MacKenna before trotting after the lad.

Jamie ran his hand over his forehead and eyes and let it rest on his jaw for a minute, before finding Anice's gaze again.

"Jamie?"

Dropping his hand, he found Gregor's eye. "Remember that action down at Happrew last year?"

Gregor nodded. "Aye. You and Conall getting Wallace away from Segrave's forces."

Torren recalled this as well. "You were caught up by some English."

Jamie nodded. Blowing out a heavy sigh, he shook his head and filled in the details he'd not shared with any but Wallace himself, and that had been only this year.

"Six of us were taken by this devil, Craig. Mean son of a bitch. Locked in the dungeon, save for Andrew's lad, Henry—they take him up to the tower." He put his hand to the back of his neck, squeezing, let his hand hold there. "This lass comes down near to midnight, says she'll set us free if we take her with us." This was the hard part. "I swore, on my honor, I'd take her with us. We separate, the lass and a few head straight for the gate. Callum and I fetch the boy." His eyes met the troubled gaze of Anice. "We get out—Callum and Henry and me—and we wait on the Stobo road as planned. They dinna come. We can no go back, we've only got two stolen swords." Another deep breath. "I send Callum and Henry to Conall at Inesfree, said I'd get back to Happrew, see if any MacGregors or MacKennas remained, would charge back at Craig." Jamie shifted his feet, planted a hand on his hip. "Happrew was wasted, no one 'round. Conall hadn't gone straight home. He'd heard de Latimer had us prisoners, went after him. I had to get to Aviemore and back." A long pause, and then, "Took me five days to return."

Jamie only stared at the ground, somehow peripherally aware of Anice covering her mouth with her hand, her sorrow no more than a silent cry.

"I found Malys and Ned, or parts of them, scattered about," he continued. "Will was hanging still, had been dead for days." In his mind, he saw still the ashen bloated face of his friend, crisscrossed with so many slices and cuts. The rope had been nearly embedded into the skin of his neck. "A lass hung near Will, barely alive, but it was no...her. Found out later, after we strung John Craig up exactly where Will had hung, that the lass there was Craig's own sister. She'd helped—I dinna ken her name was

Ada—helped her escape. We chewed up and spit out every inch of ground around Dornoch for weeks. Never found her."

"*Jesu*," Torren breathed, swiping his hand over his chin and beard. "So her face—that's what they did to her?"

Jamie nodded. "I saw her for not more than five minutes total, and in bare light; spoke no more than ten words, maybe. But she was...her face was uncut, her voice was sweet and soft." There was a huskiness to it now. "Aye, Will's face had been carved up as well."

"There's...there is more than just her face and neck," said Anice with a catch in her small voice. "Her chest, her back...." This brought three sets of dark and perturbed eyes to Anice, who nodded sadly. "It's inhuman, what they did to her."

That took the last of the wind out of Jamie's sail. He sank to the ground, onto his knees, let out a strangled noise.

"Tell me you made John Craig pay for all that, for everything," Gregor demanded.

"He did no go kindly. Or quickly." But it hadn't helped then, didn't help now.

"But poor, dear Ada," Anice lamented. "I must go to her." She picked up her skirts and turned away from them.

"Nae, lass," Jamie said. When Anice faced him again, he said, "It'll no make it better for her. You'll want to explain that I tried, and she will no want to lose her hate. Might be all she has, or all she thinks she has. Dinna take it away." He stood again, leaned his hand on the hilt of his sword.

"Jamie, she needs to know you returned to Dornoch—"

"It'll be no but excuses to her ears, lass. Better she hate me than herself."

Anice nodded, tears sliding down her cheeks. "But I will check on her." Anice left the path, followed the route Ada and Kinnon had taken. Torren shook Jamie's hand with a sorrowful grimace and went off after Anice.

Jamie said to Gregor, "I will no stay. Only make it worse. Wallace should return within the week. I can head out with him then."

Gregor nodded and changed the subject. "He is expecting to be well situated by the end of summer."

Jamie tipped his head at Gregor. "You going to be able to leave Anice?"

His initial expression said that he would not, but he told Jamie, "The babe will be here by then. Wallace will have thousands again if you and I and Conall meet up with him—and, if he can talk Bruce into joining. We need to finish this."

Jamie considered this. "That's a lot of people then knowing his whereabouts. Who's to say not one of them claims the 300 marks Edward put on his head?"

With a shrug and a grim look, Gregor said, "Canna hide forever, worrying about it. The nobles are lost, Edward made sure of that. We need Wallace and Bruce together to get this started again."

"When's he to meet with Bruce?"

Gregor shrugged, then grinned a bit. "Wallace sent a letter to Bruce, told him to come quietly and claim his throne."

They walked back to the keep. Gregor continued talking but Jamie only half listened.

He interrupted whatever Gregor was saying. "You'll keep her here? Keep her safe?"

Gregor nodded immediately. "Anice will insist. She's safe, Jamie."

This put him somewhat at ease, to know she would be cared for. However she came to be here, Jamie knew Anice was the perfect person for Ada to have found.

Her face swam before his eyes, crowded his mind. He hadn't noticed it that night so long ago, how beautiful she was.

Or, had been.

The scar on her right cheek was larger, more grotesque, being curved and jagged, as if the original cut had been made with slow, taunting incisions. It was raised and pink, only the thinnest parts white, but significant enough to be visible from a good distance. On her left cheek, in the same manner, stretching from her ear to the side of her mouth, it seemed to have been made with a quick, solid slice, being smoother and flatter against her cheek. The bastard. And of course, the rope mark around her neck would be with her for a very long time, if not forever.

"How long has she been here?" He asked Gregor.

They stopped, at the bottom of the sloped hill that led to the castle gate. Jamie kicked some small rocks off the pathway.

Gregor grimaced. "I dinna think you were heeding anything I said."

Jamie stared at his friend.

"Few weeks," Gregor told him. "Torren and the lads found her up in the forest. There's a rundown cabin up there. She'd been there for some time, Torren reckoned. Anice said she does no give up too much, so we hadn't any idea about her history."

"She named the wolf Will." Why? To remember him? To torture herself further?

"Aye."

"Jesu."

Chapter Five

"Anice is looking for you, lass."

Ada shifted to find the big man, Torren, walking along the battlements. She said nothing to him, returned her eyes to the sky above, and remained slouched against the wall.

He sat next to her, stretched his long legs out before him, and let out a long sigh.

"Where is Will?" She'd come to the rooftop to scan the yard and grounds for her wolf, that she might stealthily claim him and be off. But she'd not found him, and then had ducked when the Kincaid and the demon Jamie MacKenna had walked through the tunnel.

"Kinnon has him below...somewhere."

Ada lowered her gaze from the sky to Torren. He did not turn toward her, seemed content to stare at the half wall across from them. "He is mine."

"Aye, he is." And now he turned, gave her a steady black eyed stare. He and Anice were among the few who could look into her eyes, not at her scars. "You dinna want to be running off, lass. Take some time and think about things."

"I do not want to be here if... he is."

"He dinna ever stay long. And where would you go?"

Ada felt tears threaten again. "Very discourteous of you to remind me of my pitiful choices."

"Now, lass, you ken you're the only one who believes you haven't any choices."

"What choices do I—"

"You have the same choices and opportunities as anyone else," Torren insisted with a fair amount of gruffness. "You ain't a leper, lass. You ain't mad or lame or even English. You've been here now a few weeks. You see they treat you same as everyone else, no better, no worse, no different."

"They stare and—"

"Shite, lass. They stare at me and I've lived here for years. They stare at Kinnon's dough face. They stare at Anice's hair. They stare at the hole in Gavin's head that used to be an eye. Listen, I'm sorry for what happened to you. It's awful, no matter how you look at it. You going to hide away all the rest of your life?"

"I was going to try," this, in a small voice, very close to tears again.

His voice was softer when he responded, "That ain't living, lass. You dinna want to do that."

"But at the very least, it raises the question: what will I do? What should I do?"

"Go back to find that answer," he said. "Before this happened to you, what did you want?"

Ada shrugged. "Torren, you may not realize this, but for a female, that is rarely a question asked. I didn't *want*. I simply did as I was told."

"And did that satisfy you?"

Ada harrumphed, which made Torren chuckle.

"Of course not."

"Well, then there's the good then, see? Aye, you suffered, but now it's done. Been done now for a while. So you get on, and now you get to do as you please. No one to answer to."

"You make it sound easy, Torren. What—do I just say I want to be this? Or do that? And it becomes so?"

"Depends on what the *this* or *that* is, I ken."

They were quiet for a moment, until Ada said, "I'm sounding ungrateful, Torren, and I apologize for that. I'm glad you found me in the forest. At the very least, I've learned that my fear of people's reaction is often greater than people's actual reactions."

"That's something, then. The thing is, lass, your life will be whatever you decide to make of it. You want to be angry and lonely, that's what you'll get. You want friends and company, you can have that, too."

Ada nodded, leaned her head back against the stone wall again. "I'll make my apologies to Anice. I had no cause to be rude to her."

ADA FOUND ANICE LATER in the day, when she'd been assured by a passing Kinnon that the Kincaid and MacKenna were outside the keep. Anice was in the solar next to her private chambers, weaving the reeds she regularly collected from the beaches into mats and baskets and sometimes, completely useless items.

Ada paused just at the threshold, warmed by Anice's gentle smile. "I sit here for a few hours every day," she told Ada, "to give

Torren a break." The rolling of her eyes, which accompanied this confession, brought a grin to Ada's face.

"I apologize for my earlier behavior, Anice," Ada said. "I should not have taken out my...dismay on you."

Her hands stopped moving, the reeds forgotten in her shortened lap. Anice looked up at Ada and insisted, "There is no cause for any apology. None at all, I assure you. I hadn't bothered you at all for any details of what happened to you—truly, I thought it would come out when you were ready. But your upset earlier made me force it out of Jamie, I want you to know." She let this settle before she continued, with a most sympathetic expression, "Ada, what you did was so damnably remarkable and selfless, it makes me feel so wholly unexceptional in comparison."

With Torren's recent lecture still fresh in her mind, Ada did not demur outright, only tucked her head, away from the startling admiration in Anice's gaze.

"Jamie has asked that I not speak on his behalf and so I will not," Anice said. "But, Ada, I think you might want to hear what he has to say."

Ada was shaking her head even before Anice had finished her sentence. She disliked immensely disappointing Anice, but could only offer, "It just doesn't matter."

Almost to herself, having resumed her weaving, Anice said, "I do wonder, though, if this is the basis for Jamie's ever-present sorrow."

Still, Ada said nothing. She wouldn't have suspected Anice of resorting to manipulation, yet these words came across as such, transferring sympathy onto that man. Ada would have none of it.

Anice bit her lip, clearly wanting to say more on this subject. Mayhap her vow to Jamie MacKenna kept her quiet on this score. Finally, she asked, "Ada, promise me you will not run away. Jamie will only stay for a few days. Everything will be as it was when he goes."

Ada inclined her head in agreement to this. Silently, she acknowledged to herself that her acquiescence came with some relief; she hadn't wanted to leave Stonehaven.

"Will you at least give him an opportunity to explain?" Anice wondered.

Ada tightened her lips. It was unfair of Anice to ask this.

"Very well," Anice said, reading Ada's stillness. "But I insist you also promise that you will not disappear while Jamie is here. Knowing the truth—even if you do not want to hear it—means that I cannot have Jamie, as our guest, made to feel uncomfortable."

Ada then reluctantly arrived in the hall for supper in the early evening. She took her usual place at the trestle table near the head table, in her usual spot of the past few weeks between Kinnon and the very large soldier, Arik. Across from her sat Tamsin, a friendly soldier of about her age, who suffered much ribbing from his comrades as he thought and spoke slower than most. Next to him was Sim, who was smaller than Ada, with a heavy lidded gaze and serious nature.

Ada resolutely ignored Jamie MacKenna when he entered the hall and took a seat at the family's table on the dais, seated with Gregor and Anice Kincaid, and Torren and another lieutenant, Fibh Kincaid, a distant cousin of Gregor's. Seated as she was, it was almost effortless to pretend he was not there, her back the only thing she presented to him, should he spare her a glance.

Other tables soon filled with persons who lived within the castle; the stablemaster, Gavin, and the lads under his supervision shared another table with Robert, the smithy, and his wife; across the aisle sat another group of soldiers, those to whom Ada was polite, but not as friendly as those who surrounded her; and yet another table was occupied by the baker and his wife, Wilbur and Nellie, whose work in the bakehouse across the yard usually started before the sun rose and was finished by noon each day; Alastair, the castle's steward, shared a table with his family and that of the bailiff.

Several times now, Ada compared the carefree and animated atmosphere of Stonehaven's suppers to those somber and dreadful meals at Dornoch, happy once again that fate had landed her here. Daily, she found great amusement in the bantering of the men around her. Truly, some of them seemed no more than boys, but when she considered the horrors they must have seen, having engaged in numerous battles she knew, she attributed manhood to them, despite their youthful veneers.

"But where does she put it all?" Tamsin was asking just now, drawing Ada's attention.

"Where does who put what?" Ada asked, wondering what she had missed.

"The Lady Anice," Kinnon said around the food in his mouth. "She eats more than Torren, or even Arik here."

"She is eating for two," Ada reminded them.

"Two what?" Arik asked, his eyes crinkled with laughter. "Horses? Oxen?"

Ada grinned. Anice did consume a lot of food throughout the day. Still, she meant to chide the big man for his playful disrespect but heard Anice behind them before she could speak.

"I heard that, Arik."

As one, all heads on Ada's side of the table, her own included, turned to find Anice staring at them, even as her loaded knife was held before her face. Because her own eyes were lit with mischief as she shoved the food into her mouth with a saucy look, everyone laughed.

Except for Ada. Her eyes had lit on Jamie MacKenna. He'd been watching her. It was the heat of that gaze that had drawn her eyes from Anice. A small gasp welled within as a result of his stony, unfathomable eyes on her. Ada faced forward again, settling both hands upon the table to steady herself. A man's scrutiny, no matter how sharp or compelling, should not perturb her so.

Just as she believed herself composed again, she found Sim's eyes resting with great sympathy upon her shaking hands. Ada met Sim's gaze only briefly before lowering her eyes and her hands into her lap, under the table.

Drat him! Jamie MacKenna could not leave soon enough. He'd been here only several hours and already he'd disrupted the serenity she'd found at Stonehaven. If not for Anice's begging her not to disappear while he visited—which indeed had been Ada's first instinct—she'd have kept to herself for the next few days.

She tried, with a fair amount of concentration, to ignore his presence, or the very ridiculous idea that he stared often at the back of her head throughout the meal. Yet, there was no other reason the hairs at the nape of her neck had repeatedly risen with a prickling awareness.

Most at the table had only barely finished their meals when Ada begged of Arik to allow her to exit the bench. Unless she wished to climb off the bench in some unladylike fashion, she needed the big man to slide off the end. Arik did not question her early departure but stood up and Ada scooched along the wooden bench seat to the end.

She said good night to the men, thankful none questioned her early leave-taking, and stood. She sensed a presence very close to her. She knew it was him, didn't need to turn to confirm this. In a split second, she elected —for Anice's sake, for surely she watched—to not pretend she had no notion of his presence and run from the hall. Drawing a deep breath and straightening her shoulders, she half turned to face him, curling her fingers into her skirts.

"Might I have some of your time, lass?"

Now, she knew the color of his eyes. They were blue, cold as the waves of the sea, fringed with tawny lashes. Surely, he was out of doors more often than not, his skin darkened by the sun, the planes and hollows of his very pronounced cheeks shadowed by a few days' growth of stubble.

She would have said no. There was nothing she wanted to hear, nothing she wanted to say to this man. But for Anice, who had been so unbelievably generous since the very first moment they had met. A chance glance confirmed Anice watched them intently.

Ada swallowed and nodded tightly.

Jamie MacKenna lifted his hand, as if to take her elbow. Ada squeezed her arms against her sides and swept past him, thinking the always busy bailey a fine place to give him no more than two minutes to say what he felt he needed to.

To her dismay, the bailey was unusually empty, owing to the dinner hour, she belatedly realized. She turned, just outside the door to the hall, crossing her arms over her chest, against him and the cold.

"Let us find some warmth," he said, and he did now take up her elbow and turn her toward the tunnel. His hand was firm but gentle upon her arm, or she was sure she would have protested his manhandling. Two things prevented her from making a fuss over this: first, she thought she would be at a disadvantage, if she stood before him, body shivering and teeth chattering, the early summer air was that cool; and, perhaps more importantly, she could not deny that she had been intrigued by Anice's claim that she would want to hear what he had to say. She'd spent the better part of the afternoon rejecting any interest, and then wondering what Anice might know, what he had told her.

He did not direct her into the tunnel, but opened the door next to it, the very one she used often to find peace and sometimes just a spectacular view, atop the battlements. Gently, he steered Ada ahead of him, up the dark stairs and onto the walkway above the yard and the space outside of Stonehaven. A few sentries milled about, gathered near the metal-barreled fires that were lighted every evening, while several others patrolled the walls, ever watchful. Jamie MacKenna directed her to a fire barrel where no other persons gathered.

Ada lifted her hands to open them over the flames, to avail herself of its warmth, but stopped herself, her fingernails still pressed tightly into her palms. As smoothly as possibly, she lowered her arms, held them at her sides. She would show him no weakness.

"Step closer to the heat, at least," he said, letting her know—intentionally or not, she would not know—that he was aware of her intent to put on a brave face. In her mind, she chanted, *I do not care what he thinks of me.*

Ada did not move. "What did you want to say?" She tried to hurry along this discussion, hoping that aside from simmering glares and false promises, he also practiced brevity.

Fairly surprised to see him all but shuffle his feet in indecision, Ada waited until he finally met her gaze again, across the barrel, the flame shadows licking at his face, lending a golden hue to his eyes.

"Ada," he said, making loose with her name, "I need to know what happened. When I could no return...I—I'm asking you to tell me how—" he stopped, ran a hand over his stubbly jaw while a muscle ticked in his cheek. "I have only bits and pieces."

Ada could only stare at him, rather taken aback.

She'd expected that he wished to defend his actions—or lack thereof. She'd thought he'd requested an audience to relieve his mind of whatever culpability might live with him, if any at all. She had not—not at all—imagined he would ask this of her.

"You'd make me relive it? To...what? To give you peace? To make *you* feel better?"

Straight brows slanted over stormy eyes. "You think me hearing how awful it was for you, and what they actually did to Will before they killed him will be easy for me?"

"I do not know what kind of person you are, so I cannot answer that."

"The fact that you entertain the possibility that it might be easy for me to hear this tells me what kind of person you believe me to be."

She only shrugged, not of a mind to allow for any benevolence toward him.

One day she would talk about it. Both Ada and Torren had hinted, over the last few weeks, that it was necessary, if she desired to move on from it. Perhaps one day, she would even think Jamie MacKenna needed to suffer through an accounting of it. But it wasn't now. She barely knew him, and she wasn't ready herself. True, it would lie between them until it was said, until he knew, but this was no hardship to Ada. He would be gone from Stonehaven soon. Maybe one day soon, she would be as well.

They stared, eyes locked over the barrel of fire. "I owe you nothing." Ada clamped her lips, felt her breaths now rush out through her nose.

His own nostrils flared, but his tone was level. "Aye, you do no. And aye, if you dinna want to share the tale with me, I canna force you. I can only say I am sorry." When Ada said nothing, remained motionless even, he added, "I owe you that. More, if you feel the need to claim it."

She would never know what prevented her from accepting this, his apology. He seemed genuine enough, she supposed. Perhaps Anice had the right of it, there was much sorrow in the man.

But she could not absolve him, couldn't give him any trite words she did not mean.

For so long, she'd lived with her hatred of him, and of John Craig, and for her father, and everyone else whom she'd known before, who had sent her to Dornoch or left her at Dornoch. She was unwilling to give up something to which she'd become so attached, the very thing that now defined her. Maybe if Will had lived, maybe...something would be different, maybe she'd be able to forgive.

"Three people live because of you," he said, she did not know why.

"Three people died because of you," came quickly to mind, and out of her mouth.

His entire face seemed to harden, became like stone, until he said to her, "I dinna need reminding of that, lass. Everyday, it is with me."

She'd had enough. Giving him one last look, pooling all her hatred into her stare, she turned and walked away.

Chapter Six

"Favorite color?"

"Blue, as the sky," Ada answered, tilting her head back. Today's sky was wonderfully cloudless and bright. She disliked immensely gray and rainy days.

She and Kinnon walked toward the little town of Stoney—Stonehyve, properly—the lad excited to show Ada the stained glass window in the church. She'd never seen one before, had only been given descriptions, which Kinnon promised would pale in comparison to the real thing.

This morning, with a hope to avoid Jamie MacKenna while seeming to Anice to not be doing so, Ada had begged prettily of Kinnon his company into Stoney.

"Favorite food?" Kinnon asked, swatting at some flying thing that buzzed near his face.

"Sweet cakes, of course."

"Favorite...person?"

"Presently? Or ever?"

Kinnon shrugged. "Presently."

"Lady Anice."

"I knew you'd pick her."

"Wouldn't you?"

Kinnon stretched his lips, so that what little color they did possess, faded. "Aye, or the laird."

Ada allowed, "He seems nice. Fair. You don't mention Torren, though he's your captain?"

The lad tossed his head and groaned comically. "If you spent one day training with us, lass, you'd no be throwing his name into that lot."

Ada grinned at this while the basket that Anice had made for her swung over her arm. She twirled around, gave some appreciation to how beautiful Stonehaven looked from here, halfway to the village, in the glen between rolling hills. The castle appeared as if it floated above the spare line of trees at the bottom of the knoll upon which it sat. They were far enough away that she could only make out movement of the sentries on the wall, but not really their faces or forms.

"My turn, Kinnon," Ada said, ducking off the dry, packed earth of the road, into the spring grass, likely not as tall as it would be when summer was fully upon them, and brown yet, showing only hints of green. Occasionally, the brown and sparse green were broken by bursts of color, summer flowers blooming. Ada plucked at more than a few pink and round-headed thrift flowers, laying these into her basket, alongside the frothy spears of meadowsweet. "Favorite food that you haven't had in a long while?"

He didn't answer, and Ada looked up from picking her way through the grasses, thinking he hadn't heard her. Kinnon had stopped in front of her, standing in the middle of the empty road. One hand gripped the sheath at his hip and the other reached across his front to wrap around the hilt of his sword.

He was completely still, watching the road where it entered the deeper span of trees that separated Stonehaven from the town.

"Kinnon?"

"Stay close to me, Ada," he said, without turning toward her. Ada did as he instructed, coerced by his voice, suddenly less youthful, sounding very manly and stern. When she stood on the road, a few feet behind Kinnon, while he stared still at the trees, Ada felt it. The earth beneath her rumbled. She looked down, at pebbles bouncing on the ground.

A horn sounded behind her. Ada guessed it was Stonehaven's alarm. No sooner had she acknowledged the noise, plaintive and low and drawn out, than the trees before them erupted with so many horses and riders, Ada squeaked out a cry at the sight. The horde charged at them, the hooves of a hundred horses pounding against the dirt and grass.

"Turn and run, Ada! Run and don't look back!" Kinnon called loudly, drawing his sword and planting his feet apart.

Ada whimpered, whipping around just as the gates of Stonehaven opened. She would never make it. She might be halfway between the coming army and the gates, but she would be quickly run down while on foot.

"Give me your dagger," she pleaded with Kinnon, coming to his side.

"Nae!" He shouted loudly, angrily. He shoved Ada away. "Go on, lass! Git!"

She would have never imagined such ferocity from the always pale and affable Kinnon. Seeming to have no other choice, Ada picked up her skirts and ran toward Stonehaven. It was impossibly far, and truth be told, the speed at which she ran reflected her belief that she would be cut down before she was even halfway there. She chanced a glance back at Kinnon, still holding his position. It was an eerie picture, the silhouette of a lone boy standing so straight and still against the coming mass, awash in dust and grime and shiny steel.

Tears stung her eyes. Facing the castle again, she cried with relief when she saw Kincaids charging out through the tunnel, dozens of riders intent on meeting the enemy. She ran toward them, aware that more Kincaids came from the north side of the castle, from the training field. Leading these was Gregor Kincaid himself, his sizeable outline easily identified.

Those coming from the castle were closer and Ada focused on them, beginning to believe she now stood a chance, that she might reach them before it was too late. Tears fell as she ran, thinking of Kinnon, afraid to turn and know or see his fate, even as the sound of those in pursuit closed in on her, meaning they had already met or passed the boy. She was belatedly aware that missiles flew overhead; the Kincaids on the wall sent arrows out to assist.

Ahead of her, the riding soldier closest to her stretched out his hand as he neared. Panicked, Ada realized he meant to grab her up while the huge destrier still moved. She slowed, stumbled really, seeing that it was Jamie MacKenna who reached for her. He leaned forward in the saddle, his feet kicking furiously at the steed's flanks, his eyes the most savage thing Ada was sure she had ever seen. She lifted her hand, and squeezed her eyes shut, sure she was about to be trampled by his horse. In the next instant, his hand met hers, his grip strong and sure, and Ada was lifted off the ground and swung up behind him. She yelped and was barely able to swing her leg around the back of the huge beast. But his hold was firm, and he did not let go of her hand until she was safely perched behind him. MacKenna had slowed the racing horse after all, but only minimally. Her instinct toward self-preservation bade her to wrap her arms around his middle while he charged forward. Without thinking, Ada held him tightly and pressed her head against his broad back just as the sounds of steel meeting steel found its way to her.

"Kinnon?" She cried out, too afraid to lift her head.

"On his feet still," Jamie MacKenna advised her, his voice as harsh as his entire battle mien.

With her left cheek pressed against the MacKenna's broad back, Ada saw only what was presented to her from the right side. As they seemed to be just in the thick of the fighting, she had to assume Jamie MacKenna had reached her just in time. She felt every part of him move with each lunge and swipe of his sword. He jerked the horse to a quick stop and Ada saw the reason, another steed on the ground in their path, missing two legs, a man trapped and howling beneath him. MacKenna directed them quickly left just as Ada caught sight of close movement out of the corner of her eye. She screamed, digging her fingers into the leather of his breastplate at his front, wincing with the expectation of a coming blow or sword thrust. But MacKenna's war horse was amazing, stopping dead as the MacKenna tugged the reins hard, as told by his leaning so far back into Ada. The assailant then overshot his plunging sword, which glanced off the MacKenna's, raised in time to deflect the blow. Two more parries and he sliced the brigand's arm off just as it lifted to come at them from a different angle.

He urged them forward, directing the huge beast to jump over bodies on the ground. A lane must have cleared, and he dug in his heels, spurring the horse faster. And then Ada saw Kinnon, amazingly still standing. She pulled her head away from MacKenna's back, about to alert him of Kinnon's position, when he turned right, toward the lad. Kinnon's back faced them, shoulders sagged, the point of his blade dug into the ground. He seemed to be leaning on the sword, having no more strength to lift his weapon even as he stood in one man's charging path. She didn't fear for him; they were already closer, and she'd just been witness to what the MacKenna and his mount could achieve in battle. It seemed only a jousting move, the MacKenna charging into the pathway of the coming warrior, both men raising their swords. The infidel hadn't the strength or speed of the MacKenna and he was quickly dispatched, and they pivoted again, coming to a full stop just near Kinnon.

"Let go," the MacKenna ordered, even as he began to slide out of the saddle. Ada released him and he bounded off, yanking Kinnon by the collar, steering him toward Ada.

"Get up there," Jamie MacKenna directed the lad, "and get her back."

Kinnon did not argue, his battle-weary gaze meeting Ada's terrified one for just a second before he took Jamie's place on the horse. Ada clung to him just as she had the MacKenna, turning her head as Kinnon steered them out of the battle, to watch the MacKenna. He met another of the enemy, using only one hand to raise his sword and deliver the killing blow, his arm and his blade being so much longer than most men.

When they reached the outskirts of the skirmish, Ada breathed easier, as Kinnon navigated the destrier through the same grass and flowers through which Ada had traipsed only a short time ago. With one arm still around Kinnon's much narrower frame, she turned fully in the saddle to witness the atrocity that had sprung out of nowhere. Considering the whole of the wide open field between Stonehaven and Stoney, the fight consumed only a tight and small circle of space, though there must be hundreds of men, alive or not, in that diameter. She tried to find the MacKenna's brawny figure in the crush, but could not, the air all around steeped in dust and clouds of dirt.

As the enormous wooden gates were once again opened, to admit Kinnon and Ada, she ducked her forehead against Kinnon's sweaty back and wept.

THEY PASSED THROUGH the tunnel and were greeted by several soldiers inside the yard, Torren included. Ada had regained enough coherence to wonder that he was not at his laird's side. The big man scooped her off the steed and set her on the ground, onto her wobbly legs. Ada then had to squint against the sunshine as she looked up at him. Somehow, that beautiful sun was now especially offensive, daring to shine while such tragedy took place just outside these gates.

"Anice?" She thought to ask.

Torren was quick to assure her. "Tucked away, safe."

Kinnon had dismounted. He stood beside Ada, a glazed look about him, his hands and sword smeared in blood, a smattering of it splashed across his forehead.

Ada threw herself into his slim embrace. He pressed his chin onto her shoulder, squeezing her tight, sharing all that relieved fright. "You are amazing, the bravest man I have ever known," Ada spoke into his collar. She pushed back, kept her hands on his shoulders. "But how did you manage it? You are only one man. There were so many of them—"

"'Twas the archers, lass," he said, his face for once flushed to near red. "They kept up a steady stream. I had only to handle one at a time." His youth showed then, his mouth trembling with what could have been. Ada hugged him again.

"Get inside now, lass," Torren instructed. "Kinnon, up on the wall."

"Aye," said Kinnon and he scampered away.

Ada obeyed as well, her eyes scanning the yard briefly, which showed only grave-faced soldiers moving about. Likely, the initial fretting and scurrying of people within, triggered by the warring army, had been done while Ada was still outside. Torren followed her inside the hall, which also was eerily quiet for this time of day. That cheerful sunshine slanted in through the thin and glass-less windows high on the walls, creating lines of brightness across the rush-strewn floor and the tables.

"Lass, can you stomach giving aid to any wounded when they come?" Torren asked. "I'm bound to keep Lady Anice locked away and safe for as long as I can."

Ada's dullness of mind was lightened for a moment, at Torren's overprotective bent toward Anice. This, then, explained why he'd remained inside the castle; Gregor Kincaid must lead his own army, and Torren was the only one he'd entrust with his wife's safekeeping. "I can be helpful, though I haven't much experience." Save for the tending of her own trauma when Margaret had helped her flee Dornoch, and she'd been lost somewhere near Stobo for weeks, bleeding and shattered. "Where?"

"Right here," answered Torren, even as the steward, Alastair, came into the hall, followed by two kitchen girls, their arms laden with stacks of linens while the steward hauled in a steamy cauldron of what Ada guessed was heated water.

Torren moved the trestle tables and benches to the perimeter of the room, six against each wall, leaving the center of the hall clear. The girls draped each table with the full linens. Ada helped with this while Alastair announced he would fetch the medicinals.

Torren left them, too, intent on returning to the wall, just as a loud cheer swept throughout the castle and yard. The two serving girls exchanged relieved smiles. "We have triumphed," said the blonde one. And then their pace quickened, expecting now to be met very soon with many in need of their attentions.

The blonde lass, Lucy, ran back to the linen storeroom and found an apron for Ada. She tied this around her waist, over her borrowed gray kirtle and then Lucy shoved another item at her "Put this on, too," she said quickly. Ada opened the folded fabric to reveal a kerchief, which she tied round her neck and swept up over her forehead, pushing all of her hair down her back.

All three girls jumped then as the door was thrust open with such force it slammed against the wall behind it. They moved quickly, realizing it was the Kincaids, bringing in the wounded. It was Arik who had crashed open the door, having the arm of another man wrapped around his neck. Sadly, they must be accustomed to this, for without hesitation, Arik half-dragged the man to the nearest table and lifted him up on to the linen covered top. The man groaned and removed his hand from his middle. Blood oozed immediately. Ada gasped, and while Lucy and the other lass seemed only rooted to the floor with dismay, Ada stepped forward, grabbing up some of the strips of linens. She rushed to the man's side, and slapped the linen over his stomach, pressing firmly upon the gaping wound. She met Arik's gaze across the table. His brown eyes displayed adequately his assessment of the wounded man's fate.

Perhaps she had misspoke about having experience. She knew nothing, knew not what to do other than to staunch the flow of blood.

"Just stay with him," Arik said, possibly having read her horrified expression. He moved around the table to whisper to Ada, "No one wants to die alone, lass," before he left the hall.

More wounded came, either on their own, or carried or hauled in by those not injured. Ada saw the two girls had since moved, each busy with other wounded at different places in the hall.

Ada returned her gaze to the dying man on the table before her, who still writhed in pain and despair. Carefully, with little hope and an unavoidable grimace, she lifted the linen away from his tunic. Blood still seeped, if only with slightly less force. She knew him only by sight, had seen him in the hall. She did not know his name. His face was absolutely colorless, as his blood continued to escape.

"Shh," was all she could think to say. She cried yet again today. She only realized this as a teardrop splashed onto the back of her hand pressed still on the man's stomach. "You're going to be fine," she promised him, even as he stopped moving. Ada's lip fell open, staring at the lifeless man on the table. Her eyes scanned the room for assistance, saw Alastair at the table with Lucy, struggling to wrest some object out from a screaming man's leg while two soldiers held him down and Lucy stood ready with hot and wet linens. "Help," Ada whispered, her voice cracking. The other girl, Fiona, was at another table, chasing down the swinging arm of another lad while the lieutenant, Fibh, hollered at him to stop wrestling.

The hall was filled with people now, at least several dozen, wounded or not, moving or milling about the room.

"Help," Ada croaked, her hands still pushing the linen firmly into the dead man's belly.

Fingers touched her arm. Ada faced forward again, saw a large hand covering her wrist. Her eyes followed the fingers and the hand, up the strong arm and wide shoulders to find Jamie MacKenna standing next to her. "He's gone, lass," he said, his tone mild. He flexed his fingers, pulling her hands away.

She nodded, seeming to recall none of her hatred of him at the moment. She continued to nod and pulled her hands back, leaving the gauzy fabrics in the man's body. She hated war and blood and death and all the evil and greed that made it part of her world.

"Ada," he said fiercely, his hand moving up her arm to give her a little shake. "Harden yourself," he ordered, lacking any hint of sympathy. "There's more who need your help."

She met his gaze, perhaps only the second time she'd ever done so without rancor or loathing. "But I cannot—"

"Aye, you can," he cut her off, his frown deepening. "You, more than most, are equipped to handle this."

She gave her own frown. Yes, she was. "I meant I haven't any idea how to be helpful. I know nothing of medicine or tending wounds like these."

"Then do as you have. Hold their hand, stop the flow of blood, until Alastair comes 'round."

Jerkily, she nodded again, and glanced around the room, to see who might need attention.

JAMIE WATCHED HER WALK away, speechless and overcome by what he felt just now. There was something about her that drew him, his gaze, his attention, a desire to shield her from atrocities as she'd seen today, and at other places. He'd not felt like this, not ever, about any other human, not even his own wife while she'd lived. Having no other explanation, he supposed his own guilt was the basis for such leanings.

When the alarm had been sounded today, he'd left the hall and had sprinted across the yard and up the stairs to see what danger came. He hadn't thought of anything or anyone, 'twas only the soldier in him that needed information before decisions could be made, knowing Gregor was out in the field. Observing then the army stampeding out of the trees, directly toward Stonehaven, had straightaway set him into warrior mode. He needed no further explanation—a party came to make war, he would stop them. He'd turned away from the sight, intent on finding his destrier and making quick time before they came too close to the keep. A shouted call of, "Kinnon and the lass are outside!" stopped him, and Jamie had jerked back to the wall. He'd not noticed them before, his gaze having been so intent on the coming militia. He'd not seen the two small figures in the forefront. He'd squinted, just as Kinnon had pushed Ada away from him. She'd run toward the keep, her pace sluggish. Quickly, he'd judged the distance, between her and the keep, and between her and the enemy. She had no chance.

"Archers! Keep that lad alive!" Was all he called as he left the wall and took the stairs three and four at a time. He grabbed the reins of the closest horse, as Gavin and the stable hands were already saddling several and swatting their rumps to send them out of the stables and into the yard for whoever came.

Gregor's army was well trained and well disciplined. The gate had begun to open before he'd needed to give that order, as others raced around the bailey, gaining the seats of their mounts.

He would never forget the sight of her, as he'd neared, of that unmitigated horror in her gaze, her face a frozen mask of terror even as she stumbled along the lane. He'd had some angry thought, wondering, *My God, what will You throw at her next?* But he'd reached her in time.

This time.

The relief he felt as his hand met hers, mere seconds before she would have been carved up on that road, had not gone unnoticed. Only when she wrapped her arms around him, when he knew she was safe, did he release his breath and switch his intention to getting to the lad.

Jamie closed his eyes briefly now. It made no sense, served no purpose to entertain the what-ifs and could-haves. Opening his eyes, he saw her now at another table in the hall, holding the bloodied hand of another wounded. She spoke softly to him, her head bent near his, her hair falling around her shoulders, out from the kerchief, and onto the man's tunic.

Spotting Gregor finally coming into the keep—Jamie knew the man would not leave the battlefield until all his men were accounted for—Jamie crossed the hall and sought answers.

"It was de Musselburgh," Gregor said, before Jamie had put the question out. He was looking around the hall. "Where is Anice?"

Jamie shrugged, but pointed out Torren. Gregor approached his captain, who had his thick hands upon the shoulders of a lad, pushing him firmly onto the table while Alastair wielded needle and thread to close the hole in his side. Gregor grabbed Torren's arm.

"Anice?"

Jamie could well discern the panic in his friends voice.

Torren quickly put him at ease. "Locked in the chapel."

"Walk with me," Gregor said to Jamie and strode quickly from the hall. Jamie followed as directed, and Gregor repeated, "It was de Musselburgh."

"That bastard who caused me grief last year?"

"Aye. We've been through three sheriffs in the territory in the past six months—de Musselburgh is the current pet of Longshanks, installed just last month. I'd wondered how long it would take him to stir up trouble, because I'd no sworn fealty," said Gregor, as they wended their way through dark corridors to the north side of the castle.

"That's some bollocks to come crashing in with only a hundred men," Jamie murmured.

"And so I'm wondering: did he mean only to warn me that he's got his eye on me? Or is that only the forward army, promising more to come if I dinna make a vow to England?"

"He's no but a sheriff," Jamie said, with a thoughtful frown, "how much more of an army does he command?"

"Good question. Wallace had shared some rumors he'd come upon, said England was sending some of the Welsh mercenaries to get a better grip up here in the north," Gregor said, as they reached the arched door to the chapel. "God damn it, Torren must have the key,"

"Gregor?" Came Anice's voice from within.

"Back away from the door, Anice."

"All right," she called, and then added, mere seconds later. "I'm away."

Gregor shoved his shoulder into the door, which splintered away from its lock, while Jamie gave some thought to Gregor being unable to wait to see Anice only the few more minutes it would have taken to procure the key. Gregor rushed in and took Anice into his arms, while Jamie remained in the corridor, leaning his shoulder against the cracked wood of the doorjamb and watching the couple express their relief and gladness to each other.

Anice eventually pulled away from Gregor's embrace and ran her hands over Gregor's face, assuring herself of his well-being. "I would have waited for you to fetch the key, love."

"Would you have?"

"Not happily, but aye, I would have."

"I couldn't." He kissed her brow again and set her away from him. "It was de Musselburgh," he said to Anice, who gasped before Gregor continued, to Jamie, "which makes it even more imperative that Wallace and Bruce join forces and expel England and all its henchmen, and with all due haste."

Jamie nodded. They all knew what had to be done. It was a matter, after so many years of fighting, so many years under the thumb of the English, to convince the nobles that they would prevail, but only if they all came together.

"Where is Ada?" Was the first thing Anice thought to ask.

"In the hall, helping with the wounded," Jamie supplied.

Anice made to leave the chapel, but Gregor's hand did not allow her to go. She turned back to her husband and before Gregor could even refuse her, she said, "I know. I know. I'll stay in the hall. I'll not touch an open wound. I'll not do anything strenuous. I will remain within Torren's sight at all times."

"Jesus, am I that bad?" Gregor asked with a frown.

"Yes, and I love you." She kissed him briefly again and was off, Gregor and Jamie following slowly behind her, Gregor much more relaxed now that he knew that Anice was safe.

"Now what?" Jamie wondered, about de Musselburgh.

Gregor shook his head as they turned a corner in the long and dimly lit hallway. "I need more information before I decide. I dinna want to get caught up with this now, as Wallace needs us focused and ready for him. But we just decimated them out there—half his army dead, at least. A dozen prisoners, maybe."

"Aye, and I'd wager they have intelligence they'll be pleased to share," Jamie said with a predatorial glint in his eye.

"My thinking as well," Gregor acknowledged.

They'd reached the hall again. Jamie's eyes searched immediately for Ada. She was still with the same wounded warrior, but now Alastair was at her side, inspecting the man's trauma.

Torren and Fibh joined them, giving Gregor a report on the Kincaid injured and dead, thankfully so much less than the number of de Musselburghs. Jamie continued to watch Ada, over Torren's large shoulder. The man whose hand she held was no more than a boy actually, showing barely enough stubble to have need of shaving. He cried and she lowered her head to his, being almost eye to eye, soothing him with soft words. Her free hand skimmed the hair off his forehead, resting on the top of his head as he lie on the table. Observing her compassionate attendance of the boy made Jamie think he was glad she was with Will when he died—he had to assume she had been, that she'd been right there beside him. He could now imagine, or pretend, that Will had known some comfort, just hearing her voice, knowing he wasn't alone.

An hour later, Jamie entered the hall once again, he and Gregor having made a tour of the village, which mercifully, had suffered no visitation from the de Musselburghs. The initial chaos of the surprise attack and aftermath was well settled by now, so much so that they returned to find Anice facing Torren, arms akimbo, berating him for daring to actually lock her in the chapel. Her tone was filled not so much with anger but composed of a long-standing frustration as she insisted she was not an idiot to be treated so, but actually quite capable of taking care of herself.

Torren was cowed not at all by her chastisement, and dared to insist, "Squawk all you want, lass. You'll be locked away for safekeeping every time danger comes near."

Ada stood nearby, her hands washed of all the blood they'd been soaked in today, holding a stack of clean linens, these pressed against her chest. She stared between the two and seemed to smile at Torren's last words. When Anice threw up her hands, portraying her continued vexation over this oft-repeated discussion, Ada said, "Would that every one of us were as fortunate to be so well safeguarded."

Though she hadn't meant it as a rebuke—Jamie could well read the wistfulness in Ada's stance and gaze—Anice seemed to take it as such and lowered her arms to consider Ada. After a moment, Anice said to Torren begrudgingly, "I appreciate your concern always, Torren. And I love you dearly." Torren beamed, but too soon, for Anice added, "But if you ever lock me in a room by myself again, I will poison your ale with buckthorn and rhubarb."

Gales of laughter sounded all around when it was realized that Anice had just threatened him with a purgative. Jamie himself grinned, more so at Torren's puckered brow and lips, but his eyes stayed on Ada. She smiled as well, as those around her did, but it did not reach her eyes. She just stood there, hugging that pile of fabric to her breast, pretending a levity to match the company she kept, but her mind was elsewhere, Jamie was sure.

Would that every one of us were as fortunate to be so well safeguarded.

She has no one, he guessed. Whatever her complete circumstance, whatever her familial situation, she had no one to look after her. How many times had she been let down in this regard? How many persons—aside from him—had forsaken her?

He would say it seemed a pitiful situation, but there was something about her—her poise, the tilt of her head, her oft-angry eyes—that near screamed to any and all that there was nothing pathetic about this fierce lass. She was a survivor. She would carry on, trudge through. Giving up, giving in—these were not choices she would ever make, he somehow knew.

Jamie sighed and looked around the hall. The wounded were well situated. All evidence of the medicinal maneuvers over the past hour had been tidied up: the blood soaked rags were nowhere to be seen, the bodies of the dead had been taken away, the treated injured men had been moved to the barracks. Even now, two soldiers moved the trestle tables back into their usual places toward the middle of the room. Alastair and those serving girls were nowhere to be seen, and Anice and Ada themselves disappeared down a corridor now, possibly heading to the kitchens.

Jamie left the hall and found the stables once again. He needed a long and hard ride, to rid himself of the unrest that coursed within him still. He should have calmed down himself by now, should feel drained at this point, many hours after the fight. He refused to acknowledge, or believe, that thoughts of Ada Moncriefe were what kept him yet so riled up.

Chapter Seven

Ada lie awake late into the night, her mind tortured by all that had happened today. Closing her eyes brought not darkness and rest, but visions of that army charging upon the figure of Kinnon, or a picture of that soldier crying in despair, his eyes glassy with fear, because he knew he was bound to die. She kicked at the suffocating blankets and shifted upon the mattress and pillow more than once.

A long and mellow howling, climbing in through the window of her tower room, brought her upright in the bed. Dear Lord, she'd forgotten all about Will. Earlier, she'd considered it unwise to allow Will to bound along side her when she'd planned to walk to Stoney, but with everything that had happened, had given him no thought the rest of the day.

Jumping from the bed, Ada wrapped herself in the cloak that had once belonged to the Kincaid's mother and shoved her feet quickly into her leather shoes. She was afforded just enough light to find the door to the tower, though the narrow stairs down were shrouded in complete darkness and she checked her want of haste to navigate these carefully. Luckily, Torren had since pounded his thick shoulder against the door on the first floor, so Ada pushed it open now with ease and scampered across the bailey, into the stables just as Will let out another plaintive howl.

She found his kennel by the light of the bare moon and lifted the latch without hesitation, whispering sincere apologies for having ignored him all day.

"Oh, you poor thing," she said to him, scratching at his ears and kissing his nose. "Come along, darling." She left the stables with Will still pushing at her hand for more love. "Let's get you down to the beach for a good run."

But the gate, of course, was locked, at this time of night. Ada had to call, in a whispered hiss, up to the guard on the wall. Luckily it was Arik who smiled and waved down to her.

"I forgot about Will," Ada said to him. "Can I take him down to the beach?"

Arik nodded and held up one finger, asking her to wait.

Ada did so, while Will reacquainted himself with every nook and cranny of the bailey.

In another minute Arik appeared at the door to the right of the tunnel and two more sentries peered down from the battlements now. Arik pulled a torch down from the wall and handed it to Ada. "I canna go with you, lass. I've got duty for several more hours." He directed her through the tunnel and surprised her by unlocking and opening a man-sized door that she'd never noticed actually within the tall wooden and metal gates.

Arik smirked at her surprise. "Only go to the beach, lass. We'll keep an eye on you from up here. Lady Anice does this all the time—well not any more, since she's with child. But she did, at one time."

"Thank you so much, Arik."

He nodded. "Keep the torch lit. If it goes out, you come up. When the light's gone, we'll know to open the door."

"Perfect, thank you." Ada smiled, and called to Will, who bounded through the doorway ahead of her. She passed through and descended the slope while Arik locked the small door behind her. Will dashed this way and that, marking territory and scaring up some nesting critter from the brush. But mostly, he followed Ada around the side of the castle and along the path that opened up to the beach.

Ada stopped, just as the entire beach came into view and stared with no small amount of wonder. She didn't need the torch, the moon shining so bright, its reflection upon the smooth sea doubling the light upon the beach, bathing everything in navy and gold. The tide was higher but not dangerously so and Ada jabbed the torch into the sand about halfway between the water and castle's cliff. Will raced past her, ran straight at the water, splashing through the surf and chomping at the waves again.

Pulling the cloak more snugly about her, wishing she'd taken the time to don more layers, Ada plopped down in the cool sand and waited for Will to expend much of his energy. She breathed deeply of the salty air and concluded that the beach at night must rival the lure and beauty of the daytime beach, for all its peaceful, if eerie, solitude.

No more than a few minutes had passed when Will went dashing by her, heading to the left side and the cairn rock formation. He began to bark, which had Ada clambering to her feet and peering into the blackness of the rocky cairn. Will only ever barked at people. No sooner had she thought this, than a shape appeared over the top of the cairn.

Franticly, Ada sent a nervous glance up to the wall and relaxed only minimally, seeing that two guards seemed to be watching her, as Arik had promised. The shape moved over the rocks, coming enough into the moonlight that Ada could distinguish it as a man.

She wasn't sure how, when the man remained in shadowed blackness for several more steps, that she knew it was Jamie MacKenna. But she did, and it was.

Will had quit his harsh bark, having replaced it with a rumbling growl that caused Jamie MacKenna no hesitation at all. He leapt down from the last knee high rock and landed on the sand very near to Will.

Ada heard a brief, not unkind, "Hush, Will."

Nervously, Ada turned and went to pick up the torch. She would leave. Her nighttime foray into blissful seclusion was no more.

"Wait." He called, neither too loudly nor too sharply.

Will no longer growled, but he did prance over to stand in front of the man.

Ada faced him but said nothing. Jamie MacKenna stopped so that only Will and a few feet separated them. His hair, his eyes, everything about him that was light and fierce in sunlight, was dark and unfathomable in moonlight.

"What are you about, lass?"

Ada blinked. "I—I'd forgotten about Will today, with...everything. Arik said it was all right for me to be here." Why did she feel the need to defend rather than simply explain?

He nodded. "He seems right at home in the water."

Ada blinked at him. They were going to make conversation? As if no great calamity hung between them? She squinted through the darkness. Over his shoulder, she would swear there flickered the light of another torch, on the other side of the cairn. Did the MacKenna, too, find solitude near the water?

Ada had spent some of the last few hours, lying sleepless in her bed, with some irksome bit of guilt that she had not spoken even one word of appreciation to Jamie MacKenna for what he had done for her today. Admittedly, she balked at the idea even as it plagued her, thinking he deserved no such thing. If it had not been him, likely another soldier, a Kincaid, would have lent his hand or his aid in that circumstance.

But she hadn't cause to be so callous. She could quite easily give him her thanks and not regret later that she had not.

Swallowing the lump in her throat, she said, "I have neglected more than Will today. I failed to properly thank you for what you did—for me... earlier." Honestly, she thought it sounded as about sincere as a verbal appreciation from Edward Longshanks to any Scot.

It was a long time before he responded. Or it only seemed so while she mulled over the insincerity of her words.

"I dinna ken that puts us on similar footing, though."

Ada gave him a quizzical look.

"Lass, I can yank you out of a hundred battles looming, and I'd still no have repaid you for what you did for me and mine. And for Will.' He shuffled his feet a bit, which Ada had to believe was something Jamie MacKenna rarely did. That man who'd charged headlong into battle today was not the man who stood before her now. "I watched you with those lads today and I hope to God you were with him. In the end."

She hadn't expected this, either a reference to Will or what seemed an honest desire of his. Her lips trembled, those last moments with Will brought to mind. She surprised herself, being able to meet and hold his gaze, being able to tell him, "I was. We—we talked all night, to keep each other awake...so that our feet wouldn't slip off the crates." The words came haltingly, in a low voice, filled with unpleasant memories. "But he—he couldn't stay awake, or...or the blood loss was enough that he passed out. He slipped off.... He didn't even wake, didn't try to regain his footing." The words, once began, seemed then to come easily. Ada began to cry in earnest. "I called his name. I kept calling, but he wouldn't wake up. And I—I—"

He lifted his hand, as if he would touch her, but he did not. "You did all you could, lass."

"I didn't!" This, as a painful keening. "I was so angry at him, so angry that—that he died. That he left me. I was so afraid to be alone."

"'Tis only natural—"

"It is not natural! It was wrong of me to wish him alive for so selfish a reason!" She sobbed and whispered, "Why didn't you come back! Why?" She raised her head, glared at him through watery eyes. "Why, damn you?" and she slapped him across the face as hard as she could.

It wasn't fair, that she had to live with it, but he did not.

Ada slapped him again. His head turned sideways with the force of the blow. Breathing heavily, Ada locked her gaze with his as he faced her again. She hit him once more. He grimaced, but she had the fleeting and pathetic notion that the face was made as some sort of apology that her small hand could not inflict more harm. She struck out again and again, smacked his face and his shoulders, and beat her fists against his chest and he just stood there. She knew she cried but heard no sound, only the thud of her fists on his leather breastplate. She pounded and pounded until she could only breathe raggedly, and her legs wanted to buckle. However, she kept at it, and somehow in the fringes of her mind understood that his hands hovered, touched lightly near or around her waist, to keep her steady and standing so she could continue to rail at him with her fists.

Some sound splintered her ears, her own voice calling him *bastard* and *unworthy* and wishing him to hell, telling him he didn't deserve a friend like Will. The noise was scratchy and airy and the words doubtless incoherent.

She didn't care. She hadn't cried like this...in forever. It wasn't long before she was drained and stopped moving and she slumped, might have fallen but his hands held her, lowered her softly to the ground.

He stayed on his haunches before her, held her steady. Her shoulders shook with her now quiet weeping, but no other part of her moved.

Ada looked at her fingers, gripping Jamie MacKenna's biceps while his strong hands held at her elbows. She lifted her eyes and found his, lightened only barely by the lone torch, to dark pools of simmering blue. Some belated awareness made her glance around, wondering why Will had not intervened. The wolf sat nearby, on his belly in the sand, his face so close to the ground while he regarded Ada with a blazing uneasiness. He whimpered when their eyes met.

"I'm sorry," she said with another sob, the ghastliness of her outburst just now fully realized. She pulled her hands away from Jamie MacKenna's hard arms and covered her face, her shoulders dropping while she continued to cry.

"You'll no apologize," Jamie MacKenna said, his tone rather fierce. "No to me."

Lowering her hands, she lifted her gaze again and stared at him, befuddled.

And then she laughed. It surprised her but she could not stop it, only supposed her heightened and precarious emotions just now were to blame. She clamped a hand over her mouth, her eyes meeting Jamie MacKenna's with a great guilty expression, even as she failed to rein in her mirth. It just wouldn't stop; indeed, it seemed the harder she tried, the more she giggled. It was so ridiculous.

He stared at her now as if only concerned for her state of mind, his brow creased.

When she still could not regain her composure, Ada flopped down onto her back in the sand, and managed to explain, after several attempts interrupted by her laughter, "I was apologizing to Will, for having frightened him."

She wasn't looking at him now but had some sense of the tension draining from him. Out of the corner of her eye, she saw him sit next to her and shake his head, but not, she thought, in crossness. Ada laid her forearm over her forehead and considered the inky moonlit sky. She wasn't exactly sure why Torren's words came to mind. *Lass, your life now can and will be whatever you decide to make of it.*

Sighing, she decided she liked the feel of laughter, no matter how untimely. It was so much better than anger and sorrow, so lovely.

"The thing is," she said after several long and quiet minutes, sure she was surprising the MacKenna with her casual tone, "when I'm not upbraiding myself for being angry at Will for abandoning me, I'm still angry. Holding on to the rage seems to nullify the guilt a wee bit. So...I court it daily, the anger. I purposefully think on you and John Craig. I plot out revenge. I dream of exacting vengeance. I've wished truly horrible things on you and yours. So often, I hate you more than him; he only did as I'd expected him to, but you gave me hope when there was none. A greater crime, to my mind."

He turned his head, rested his chin on his shoulder, to look at her. He did not speak immediately, and then not until he faced the sea again. "If I could...do it again, take it all back, make different choices...."

She nodded against the sand. She would say no more about his role. She'd said and done enough. It served no further purpose.

"Will mentioned someone named Beth," she said after a while.

This time, he turned rather sharply to gaze upon her. "My sister?"

Ada shrugged, then realized he might not have seen it. "He only said Beth, said he was in love with her, but had never told her." She recalled how his voice had softened when he'd spoken of her. "He said he hoped her eyes were the last thing he saw."

Some sound came from his throat, loud enough that Ada discerned it over the hum and smooth crashing of the surf. He turned away again.

"How long did he...?"

"He was gone before the sun rose. They'd been...crueler to him in those first hours. Shall you tell Beth that he loved her?"

He nodded, so Ada was surprised when he said, his voice lower, "Beth is dead."

All that lightness she'd known since laughing, since opening up, evaporated. "Oh," she breathed on a fresh wave of tears. More heartache. Why was life so mean, so awful? "I'm sorry."

Jamie MacKenna nodded again and did as Ada had done, slumped backward onto the sand. He lifted both arms and folded them under his head.

Silence for several minutes while they stared at the moon and sky.

Jamie broke the not uncomfortable silence first. "Where did you go after Dornoch?"

"In due course, back home, to Newburgh." She imagined he would ask the natural follow-up question and saved him the trouble. "It didn't work out—mayhap it would be better now, since the...scars are older, faded maybe. They could barely look at me. Seemed I had brought so much grief—tension, actually—to that house." She didn't want to speak about her family. "What would you say if I asked you to take me to Dornoch?" If anyone could help her make John Craig pay for what he'd done, she was sure it would be this ferocious and fearless man. "He should not be allowed to have committed such atrocities and live."

Without turning, he said, "John Craig is dead."

Ada turned her head upon the sand, to face him. She saw only his profile, and a muscle ticking in his cheek. "How can you know that?"

"I killed him."

Ada froze. Anice had told her she might want to hear what Jamie MacKenna had to say. But that would mean that....

"I strung him up where Will had hung," he said, seeming to speak through gritted teeth.

She digested this, sniffled and swallowed, and choked out, "When?"

"Five days later."

It was many long minutes before Ada said only, "Oh."

And then a more prolonged silence, while Ada understood that the quiet waited for her to apologize now for her judgment of him and her ill treatment of him. Her lips trembled with so many new and conflicting emotions, but she could manage no words.

THE DAY AFTER THE ATTACK on Stonehaven, there was still so much to be done. The entire morning was set aside for the funerals of those killed, casting a mournful quietude over the entire day. Ada felt as if ever person of Stonehaven, and maybe even some surrounding villages, attended. At one point, the entire funeral cortege was near brought to its knees with awe over the magnitude of the grief of one lost soldier's mother. She'd flung herself onto her son's cold, shrouded body and had sobbed so outrageously, Ada wondered that no one felt as ill at ease as she, witnessing so fierce a sorrow, a most painful thing to behold.

Later, Ada had accompanied Alastair as he made his way through the army's barracks, checking on the those wounded, who must remain abed for several days or longer. Those wounded who could found some relief, and a brighter clime, lounging around the smith's shed in the bailey. There had been only need for Ada to change two bandages, with Alastair giving her instruction, telling her it was a useful, practical skill for her to learn.

She'd spent some time with Anice in the chapel, offering what surely must be inept or unheard prayers. While she and Anice sat silently with their devotions, Torren and Fibh, with the help of Stonehaven's carpenter, worked to repair the door to the chapel, which had somehow been busted away from the metal hinges. Anice had looked pointedly at Torren when Ada had asked how the door had been broken, but only answered, "Do not ask."

Ada had debated telling Anice about her late night conversation with Jamie MacKenna, but she did not. Stonehaven had just seen its own misfortune so that her trials seemed to pale presently.

By late afternoon, Ada was tired. She'd not been able to sleep after meeting the MacKenna on the beach. This had come as no surprise; seemed to be, she thought, that her lot in life would frequently see her wrestling with some manner of guilt.

She'd treated the MacKenna unfairly. While she didn't know the entire circumstance, he had obviously and indeed returned to Dornoch as promised.

Five days later.

She'd left—escaped with Margaret's help—on the morning of the fifth day.

What she had done to him last night, the fury she'd unleashed on him, now sat within her in the form of overwhelming embarrassment and remorse. The words she'd not been able to force out last night needed to be said today.

When supper came, Ada straightened her shoulders and entered the hall, knowing she must seek some of his time, as he had hers—and hope he allowed this, even if begrudgingly—and she must make this right. She thought it odd to find Anice at the lower table, with Kinnon and Fibh and only a few others.

She smiled at Anice, even as a question lit her eyes. Just as Ada sat down on the end of the bench, Anice explained, "Gregor and Torren and a few others are seeing off Jamie and...others. They're down at the beach."

"He's leaving? Now?"

Anice's brows lowered at the disappointment she heard in Ada's voice.

"Yes."

Ada stood. "I have to tell him—on the beach, you say?" She did not wait for a confirmation but lifted the skirts of her warm woolen gown and dashed from the hall, sorry that she could not take the time to explain to Anice, who was calling after her.

She must tell him she was sorry.

The gate was closed today, even though it normally was not while the sun shone. But Arik had just showed Ada the door within, and without bothering any of the sentries on the wall, Ada let herself out of the castle yard and raced down the hill and around to the right.

She reached the woefully vacant beach and felt her shoulders slump. He was gone. Oh, this was awful. She'd been an absolute wretch to him—and the man had stood there and allowed her to beat and berate him, knowing full well that she had no cause at all to do so. And now she couldn't even tell him she was sorry.

She was so damn sorry.

Tears blinded her as a constricting heat narrowed her throat. Thumping her hands onto her hips, she tilted back her head, trying to calm herself. A noise drew her attention to Left Beach, over the large boulders of the ancient cairn. Ada realized it was voices and wondered if she hadn't missed him at all.

Relief surged through her and she scrambled up and over the rocks, having to use her hands to steady herself as she climbed. At the top of the cairn, she saw that at least a dozen people were on this beach. She spied Jamie MacKenna straightaway, even as he had his back to her, and now descended. Gregor Kincaid, speaking to the MacKenna, inclined his head when he noticed her.

She couldn't see his expression when he turned to find her, as she'd stumbled and needed to put her eyes back on the rocks. She gained the beach, planting her feet in the sand as Jamie MacKenna strode toward her. She met him, halfway between the cairn and the men who seemed to have stopped what they were doing. Ada ignored them and drew a fortifying breath. The wind was harsh and blew so much of her hair across her face. She gathered a thick tail of it in her hand, holding it near her shoulder.

"I'm sorry," she said. She thought his blue eyes rather dazzling in the light of day, now that she truly looked at them, didn't go out of her way to avoid them. But she realized he was frowning at her now. She had to raise her voice, almost holler, to be heard over the wind and the waves. "I am sorry for having misjudged you, and for the way I lashed out at you."

She didn't know why she cried now. Her emotions, since Jamie MacKenna had come to Stonehaven, seem to overwhelm and astonish her quite often. She bit her lip and stared at him.

"Like as no, I deserved it." There was no need for him to raise his voice, it being naturally deep and projected from his diaphragm. "If no for what I failed to do for you, then surely for some other misstep."

"You didn't fail!" She cried with larger misery, for what she'd assumed of him, for the names she'd called him. "I behaved shamefully. I cannot take it all back—I'm sorry for that. But could you just imagine I'm only a wretched person and not give it any thought? I—I don't know how to...not be angry."

He shook his head, breathing, it seemed, through his nostrils, waging some inner battle.

"Oh, please," she begged, while tears dribbled down her scarred cheeks. "I'm sorry I couldn't save him. Or Malys or Ned. Why do I get to be here, and they do not?"

They'd stood this close yesterday, while she'd attacked him. She'd had no true idea what his expression had been last night, but right now, she was all but bitten by the harshness about him. He struggled mightily with some emotion and she wondered if he only tried to talk himself out of striking her, as retribution.

Ada closed her eyes. 'Twas no more than she deserved. Dear God, the things she said to him!

He did not strike her. She felt his arms wrap around her and press her head against his chest. And now she really sobbed, for this forgiveness, and from this man, her only link to Will.

He was so large and warm, she nearly melted at the instant peacefulness that settled over her. She did not open her eyes, but inhaled deeply the scent of this man, leather and cloves, and discovered that her fingers clung to his breastplate. Suddenly, she felt an acute sense of loss that Jamie MacKenna was leaving, that her tenuous connection to Will would leave as well. She gave no thought to why she so desperately wanted to hold on to Will's memory.

Just as it registered with her that his hand rubbed lightly in circles on her back, sounds that originated not from her or Jamie

MacKenna penetrated her dismay. Reining in her tears, sniffling loudly, she lifted her head and heard Anice calling her name.

"God damn it, Anice!" This, roared from the Kincaid, effectively broke through Ada's numbness. "I'm going to lock you up myself, I swear to God." The Kincaid rushed over to the cairn, where came Anice, lumbering over the tall rocks with Kinnon chasing after her, exasperation plainly written on his face.

Jamie MacKenna's arms fell away from Ada as she turned to face her friend.

"Ada!" Anice called, her hand now in Gregor's, her husband's face stiff with displeasure at what he deemed his wife's recklessness. She stood before Ada, her confusion clearly visible as she stared between Ada and the MacKenna behind her now.

Ada sighed, completely drained of tears. "I was saying farewell."

Anice's gaze took in all the other people down here at the beach, behind them, the ones Ada had not considered since she'd approached Jamie. "Yes, well, let us get you back to the keep."

She reached for Ada's hand, but Ada turned away, facing Jamie MacKenna one more time. She looked directly into his blue-as-the-sea eyes and tried so hard to give him a smile, one of apology and regret and indeed, farewell. She had a sense that a headache she'd struggled with for years was now gone, as if that constant tightness in her chest was loosened. She took in a deep and long breath of salty air and said to him on a slow exhale, "Farewell, sir. I wish you Godspeed."

He said nothing and Ada was infused again with the notion that he wrestled still with something inside. His gaze burned into her, his strong features seeming to be made of stone just now.

"Come along, Ada," Anice prodded still, her hand at Ada's elbow.

"She comes with me," Jamie MacKenna said, his tone firm, while his gaze remained inscrutable and fixed on Ada.

Ada blinked. The words did not immediately have meaning to her.

"Jamie—" Anice's voice hinted at a protest.

"She goes where I go," Jamie MacKenna said.

This, now, registered. Ada frowned and looked up at him. His eyes were neither kind nor soft. A muscle ticked in his cheek. In the name of all that was holy, what had possessed him to make such a statement?

And then she saw it—or supposed she did. Beneath the tightened jaw and behind the impenetrable gaze, Ada was very sure there lived much sorrow. Just as she struggled to comprehend this complexity, he blinked, seeming to shutter all emotions, his gaze now flat.

She goes where I go.

"Why?" She asked of him.

It was a long time before he responded. "I've a debt to repay."

Duty. Or, pity. Sadly, she shook her head. He owed her nothing.

Chapter Eight

Jamie stared down at her. Something screamed inside him, *what have you done?* but he could not retract the words. He had a responsibility to her.

This was the right thing to do.

She met his gaze steadily, every scarred and tightened feature of her face screaming with resolve. "You have no debt to me. I—I do not need your charity."

"'Tis no charity," he claimed. "I failed you once. I should no do so again."

Brilliant hazel eyes regarded him with profound wariness. "Where do you go?"

He was fairly surprised she entertained the idea even so much to ask this. He was more amazed that something inside him was adamant now that he not go without her.

"About, for now, on some business," he answered vaguely. "Eventually, to Aviemore, my home."

"Jamie," Anice spoke up again. She'd moved, stood now beside him and Ada. "She cannot go where you are going."

He felt his jaw tighten at Anice's interference, well-intentioned though he supposed it was. Ada's lips parted. Anice took her hand, intent on leading her away.

But Ada nodded, even while her expression showed a mix of wonder and uncertainty. He could well see that she tried very hard to maintain a silent courage, even as her fidgeting hands, clenching and unclenching in the folds of her skirt, belied her steady gaze.

"She'll be in good hands, Lady Anice," said a deep voice behind them.

Bluidy Christ. Aside from Anice and Gregor, before him, Jamie had all but forgotten about the undoubtedly captivated audience behind him. He blew out a frustrated breath and turned to face the other men who'd come for him, those with whom he was meant to leave.

He met the untroubled blue eyes of William Wallace, hoping the grimace he gave correctly conveyed his apology. William only nodded, his gaze seeming to show approval for the odd encounter and consequence as he stepped forward to tower over Ada.

"I have met some remarkable lasses in these highlands," he said, resting his gaze momentarily on Anice, "and yet I find I am still somehow astonished that there seems to be rather a surfeit of courageous ladies in Scotland." He lifted her hand and introduced himself. "I am William Wallace, lass, and I am pleased to assure you that your presence would be most welcome."

Jamie himself might have laughed at her expression just then, save that this circumstance was still fairly grave, to his own thinking. Ada's jaw gaped but a moment before she collected herself and dropped into a deep curtsy. Her tongue-tied reverence did afford a spark of pride to swell within Jamie and he introduced her to William when she rose before him.

"Ada Moncriefe," Wallace repeated. He gave her a thoughtful perusal, which included briefly eyeing the hand he held and staring at length at her neck and cheeks while his jaw worked side to side. "I am always disturbed to disagreeableness by the mishandling of the bold and true daughters of Scotland. As ever, I am proud to call Jamie MacKenna a true and noble companion, and then more so when he seeks to right these wrongs."

Jamie was quickly getting used to the fact that Ada wore every emotion on her face, at all times. However, he could not at present discern if her beguiled expression also showed a satisfaction. Whatever the case, she said nothing, seemed only to consider the words, biting her lip as her gaze slid away from Wallace and found his.

"Come along then, Ada Moncriefe," William Wallace said, making the decision for her, moving away as if the matter were settled. "You will be in good hands with the MacKenna, I vow."

"I need to collect Will."

"Her hound," Jamie explained to Wallace. And to Ada, "You have bits and pieces to collect as well?"

She turned those hazel eyes onto him, showing something of an awkwardness. "I-I haven't any possessions."

"But the gowns—you're welcome to take them," Anice insisted. "And you'll need your cloak." Anice said to Jamie, "We won't be long."

She pulled Ada away, toward the cairn, their heads pressed together. Jamie could not hear their words to know if Anice spoke for or against his plan and Ada's seeming agreement.

Jamie shook Gregor's hand. "See you again in a few months' time."

"Aye," said Gregor. He inclined his head toward Wallace. "You ken to bring him back by sea if needs be." With Jamie's nod, Gregor pivoted and caught up with his wife.

Wallace said, in his low and deep voice, "She's the lass from Dornoch, I presume."

"Aye."

"Then it is as it should be, I imagine." And he stepped away, taking the reins of the horse Gregor's man held ready for him. "The war grows old, my friend, and I weary of it," he said as he gained the saddle. "Let us end it, and soon, and rid ourselves of all these shameful byproducts."

Jamie attended the loading of his saddlebags onto his steed, which Ada had interrupted with her coming. He made a point to breathe evenly, wondering that what he felt right now seemed to be relief and not unease.

Not more than ten minutes had passed when the sound of Will's barking preceded his bounding over the rocks. The huge beast crested the rocks, standing still but a moment, spying the party below, before he nimbly made his descent, racing toward Kinnon and begging his attention.

"'Tis no hound, but a wolf," said Wallace. And then he mused, "A wolf named Will."

Ada appeared then, carrying only a small rope-tied bundle. Jamie jogged over to the cairn and offered his hand. She spared him only a glance, her expression now fairly reserved, as she put her hand in his.

She bade fare thee well to Torren with a long embrace, and to Kinnon with a bittersweet smile and hug. Jamie watched the lad scrunch up his face, as if he battled greater emotion than shown.

When she faced him again, and while the party waited still, she looked only at Jamie, displaying her first trace of true doubt. He allowed no time for this to expand but lifted her into the saddle and swung up behind her. With a nod to Torren and Kinnon, Jamie turned the horse to follow Wallace and the others and breathed in the scent of lavender and honey that surrounded her.

ADA BENT TO ARRANGE the skirts of her gown to cover her exposed ankles, but the horse moving rather jerked her back against him. She let out a little 'oomph' just as his arm slid around her middle. His touch surprised her, but she found herself clinging to the arm, having not expected to be moving so fast so quickly.

With a knot in her belly, she contemplated all that had happened this afternoon, and in such a small amount of time. From the second she had come to find Jamie MacKenna, only to ask for forgiveness, until this moment now, riding away from Stonehaven with him, she believed not more than thirty minutes had elapsed.

What have I done? Came to mind, and more than once.

"It will be all right," Anice had said to her when they'd walked back to the keep. Those hadn't been her friend's first words, though. While Gregor Kincaid strode beside them holding Anice's hand, his countenance giving no sense of disapproval or alarm, it was almost comical the way dear Anice had fumbled and stumbled over words, until finally she'd blurted, "Ada, what just happened?" And then, before Ada could respond that she herself wasn't exactly sure, Anice had asked, "Are you really leaving with Jamie?"

Her reply had come quickly, hinting at a bit of defensiveness. "Unless you tell me he is evil, or bad, then yes, I am."

"I would—could!—tell you no such thing. Jamie is..." she'd waved a hand, searching for words or thoughts, "he's quiet and moody and frankly, I think he carries much sorrow."

"But your husband would not be friendly with a depraved person?"

Gregor had furrowed his thick brows over his dark eyes. But it was Anice who had answered, "He would not."

"Then I will go with him. I cannot stay here forever, living off your generosity—" Ada quickened her words to prevent the argument she saw rising in Anice "—and the idea of living out my days at a cloister never did sit well with me. This is...something, at least."

Anice had made no further attempt to deter her, yet her expression showed still some hesitancy. "But if you should ever need anything—anything at all—you are always welcome here."

Ada had embraced the very dear woman and told her, "You've given me more than you know, and I will forever be grateful."

But now, as the very kind Anice and Stonehaven grew smaller and smaller behind her, Ada bit her lip, and could only hope she'd not made another mistake where Jamie MacKenna was concerned.

His voice came at her ear, his breath warm. "We've a long road ahead, lass. You'll no want to be so stiff. Ride the rhythm, dinna fight against it."

"I feel as if I'm about to fall," she confided, not without a bit of worry in her voice.

"I'll no let you fall, lass." His arm tightened around her. "But swing your leg around astride, you'll feel more solid on him."

He slowed, only briefly, while Ada did as he'd suggested. It took two tries while her own fingers clung to his arm, but she managed it, despairing of the greater amount of skin now exposed as she sat astride. However, she did immediately know more security in this position.

For the first time, Ada considered the other people of this riding party. Four soldiers rode in front, followed by William Wallace and another man, with Jamie MacKenna and Ada bringing up the rear. She knew also that two more men on horseback had ridden out fast and far when they'd first taken off. Ada gave a brief thought to the fact that when she had first seen Jamie MacKenna at Dornoch, he'd been surrounded by soldiers all bearing the red and blue and gold MacKenna colors. No one in their present party sported these or any colors but for Jamie's tartan, draped around his wide shoulders.

"Who are these men?" She asked the MacKenna, turning her head to the side. "They wear no colors."

"They are loyal to Wallace, and to Scotland's freedom, but have no familial connections —or any that remain. When all the supporters finally gather, there will be dozens and dozens of different plaids and banners, as all come together to end this war."

"When will that be?"

"When Wallace feels he has recruited the numbers to win our freedom," Jamie answered, his voice low against her ear. "He hopes to make a final and decisive stand within a few months."

"And you will be at his side?"

"God willing."

"Where do we go now?"

"Ultimately, to Aviemore, as I've said. But first, we will continue to recruit loyalists along the way. You should ken that we might be several weeks on the road."

"Oh," was all she said.

Ada was thankful that the horses were never given their legs, even as they eventually left the thin trail through the trees and came upon a wide open, heather strewn meadow. Through tall or short grass, over rocky ground and across meandering streams, they kept the same pace always, rather a slow trot, which never made Ada too terribly uncomfortable.

When the sun set low to their left and darkness came, the weight of the day's events began to consume her. Ada shivered as the cooler air began to seep into her skin and felt her eyes begin to flutter as exhaustion overtook her.

Ada awoke sometime later, surprised she slept at all. She roused, finding herself slumped against Jamie MacKenna, his arm still secure around her waist. But her own arm no longer draped and clenched over his, but was covered by his hand, his fingers wound around her wrist, holding her close. She straightened, and glanced left and right, around Jamie MacKenna's broad frame. She couldn't see or hear Will anywhere.

"He's around, lass," she heard at her ear. "Keeps up for a while, then trots off into the thicker trees. He's no ever too far from you."

"Might this be too much for him? He's not accustomed to running for such a long time."

"He's holding his own," he assured her. "We'll be stopping soon."

Almost an hour later, William Wallace called for a halt. Will had indeed shown himself several times. They turned off the narrow road upon which they presently travelled, ducking into the trees.

They dismounted only when they were deep within the forest. Jamie eased smoothly from the saddle and reached for Ada. She did not often have to tilt her head back at people but did so now as her feet touched the ground, as they stood so close. She might have only spared him a glance and moved away but his hands held yet at her waist.

"Stand for a moment," he advised. "Your legs will want to crumble."

Ada was surprised to realize he was right. She lifted one leg under her skirts and gave it a shake and remained for only a moment more before nodding and moving away from him.

Ada found relief much deeper in the trees and brush. When she returned to their little camp, she saw that this was not to be a brief stop. A fire pit was being dug out by one man. Another dumped kindling and larger branches into the hole in the ground. Jamie MacKenna was nowhere around. William Wallace walked back into the clearing, coming between the gathered and hitched horses, with Will trotting beside him. He stretched out his long arm and offered a leather flask to Ada while Will dashed off again into the trees.

She accepted this with a small smile and took a long drag of the warm ale. She returned his flask just as he sat upon the cold hard ground, lifting one leg to drape his arm over it, the flask then dangling from the hand over his knee. Having no other idea what she might be doing, she sat as well, on her knees, tucking her legs and skirts beneath her.

"From where do you hail, lass?" Wallace asked her.

"Newburgh. My father is a merchant."

William Wallace was exactly as the tales of him advised, larger than any man she'd had ever seen, with long legs and arms. His shoulders were broad and his chest thick. Ada had imagined, from the stories that had been told, that the man must be at least fifty years of age, but she saw now, that while his face showed a weariness and an aged wisdom, he was not that old. His deep set blue eyes showed much of the fatigue, and, too, the wisdom.

While Jamie MacKenna had yet to return, and the other soldiers were still about their own business, or camp readiness things, Wallace said to her. "It is a fine happening, lass, that you find yourself now entrenched with Jamie. A fine son of Scotland, braver than most," he said, and then bent his head, giving her a slow blink, "excepting a lass such as yourself."

"It is not a brave thing, good sir," she defused, "to have been caught and punished."

"Nae, it is no, lass," he agreed readily. "Any man can do that. That's no where your valor shines. But you saw a need, and saved lives. And you are here now. 'Tis the surviving it, lass, the living with it that shout your courage."

Ada gave this some consideration, tried to find some validation in this reasoning.

William Wallace continued, "Two dark souls though, lass." He shook his head with a new sadness. 'Tis no good. One must shine, teach the other to do so as well."

While she understood that he referred to her and Jamie MacKenna, of course, she wondered if the MacKenna could credibly be labeled a *dark soul.* This, then, had her questioning the sorrow she'd recognized in him, which Anice had seen as well, and she questioned its origins.

Jamie returned then and sat upon a flat rock next to Ada. Will had come with him and, after many hours of running along with them, collapsed next to William Wallace, who spent a moment scratching behind the hound's ears. Jamie carried a small loaf of bread in his hands, tore it into two pieces and handed one to Ada. "The lads'll hopefully scare up some rabbit or pheasant, but this for now."

"Thank you."

It occurred to Ada then that she was now dependent upon Jamie MacKenna for...well, everything. It seemed strange, as she had at one time seen to every one of her own needs, few though they were. She would make an effort, she decided, to not rely too heavily upon him. At one time, she'd scrounged up her own food, had snared rabbits and squirrels herself, had slept on the forest floor, had travelled hundreds of miles on foot, she was sure; there was no need to be reduced to such reliance upon another now.

One by one, the numbers around the warm fire grew, the other men having completed all necessary tasks. They formed a circle now. Ada stayed seated between Jamie and William Wallace, more than once catching the eye of different persons upon her. One in particular, whom Wallace had addressed as George, gnawed at one of his fingernails and sent glances every other second to Ada, until she found herself ducking her head away from his discourteous perusal.

Jamie MacKenna must have noticed this as well. Shifted so that she rather faced only him, she saw him level a threatening glower at the man.

These men, or most of them, must have been keeping company for a while now, she guessed, listening to their conversation, talking about people they knew and places they'd been. They kept their voices low, and the fire was never allowed to become too large or bright, even as the air grew chillier and Ada rearranged her cloak to cover her head.

They slept where they'd sat around the fire, Ada one of the first to succumb to her sleepiness, curling onto her side on the cold ground, using her arm as a pillow. She did not sleep immediately and knew when Jamie MacKenna laid down next to her, facing her. At the same time, she felt Will settle down against her back, between her and William Wallace.

"You dinna seem put out, sleeping on the ground, lass," Jamie commented, just above a whisper.

She hesitated a moment, then informed him, "There were many nights, over the past year, that found me in a similar situation." The fire crackled and hissed and provided enough of a glow that she could see his eyes, which seemed to regard her with their usual intensity.

"Still, I should have thought to beg a fur from Anice."

"It's not so bad," she lied, not bothering to wonder why she did.

But he knew she lied as well. "Aye, it is. Are you even now regretting your decision?"

"To come with you?" Ada hoped only Wallace might be able to hear them, if even that, as she kept her voice as low as Jamie's. "No regret," she said honestly. "But I've been wondering *why* I said yes. I liked Stonehaven very much. And Anice. Everyone, really. I'll miss the beach."

"You'll let me ken when you figure out the why?" He asked.

She grinned at this even as she accepted that she might never know.

"There's a loch at Aviemore," he told her. "No so grand as the beach at Stonehaven, but it might prove a good substitute. And we'll see Aberdeen tomorrow, and the North Sea once more before we go inland."

Someone, on the other side of the fire, began to snore loudly, snorting on the inhale.

"Do you think I'll ever see Stonehaven again? As I think on it, I might only regret that I made a decision not considering that I might never see Anice again."

"We'll get back there," he assured her.

His use of the word *we* struck Ada. As if they were a pair. As if she were now forever entwined with him. Maybe she was, or was destined to be, because of Dornoch, because of Will.

Chapter Nine

Ada woke before the sun did and felt a weightiness around her middle. It was only a second before she recalled her circumstance and knew that Jamie MacKenna had, sometime during the cold night, sidled up against her and wrapped his arm around her. She stiffened, disconcerted by her position, which had her face buried in his chest and his other arm, inexplicably, under her head. But for the satisfying warmth, Ada felt a tremendous awkwardness and made to separate herself from his hard body.

His voice vibrated against her hair, even as his arms proved immovable. "You'll set your teeth to chattering again."

She did not relax, but neither did she attempt again to disengage herself. Wakeful now, she was very aware of all the parts of him that pressed against her. While the warmth was indeed welcome, Ada was glad for the pre-dawn grayness that allowed only her to know of her blush. She stayed very still, only relaxing when she believed he slept again. While one hand was curled against her own chest, the other was splayed out against his. Ada stared at her light skin, so stark against his dark plaid. Experimentally, she moved the fingers. She felt only hardness and heat. The bare morning light showed where his tunic, under his plaid, ended at his collarbone. Rather without conscious thought, but imbued with a curiosity, Ada moved her fingers up over the middle of his chest until they touched his bare skin. Whisper soft, she skimmed the tip of her index finger over the depressed space between his clavicles. It then seemed natural to trace along the jutting bone, intrigued by the spark ignited by her skin touching his. Ada moved her finger along his collarbone and back to the middle before it dawned on her what she had actually just done. Her eyes widened at this lapse of good sense, at her daring impropriety, just as Jamie MacKenna's hand covered hers, holding it still.

Hugely ashamed, Ada lifted her eyes to his, but saw only his jaw as he did not look down at her. He squeezed her hand and murmured, "No more, lass. I canna pretend to sleep while you go about exploring."

Ada gasped, again at her recklessness and too, at his candid description of what she had just done.

"Aye, dinna fret. Close your eyes now and let us sleep yet."

Ada did not close her eyes and there was no way she would be able to sleep now.

IT DID NOT GO UNNOTICED by Jamie, when they eventually rose and breakfasted around the stoked fire, that Ada Moncriefe absolutely would not, or could not, meet his gaze. She bustled about, without a chore to attend, seeming more flustered than usual.

And he understood completely her nerves being on edge. Her brief and innocent endeavor this morning had woken every sense he had, some he hadn't used in years. He wasn't quite sure how he'd managed to remain still, or how she could possibly have been unaware of his thudding heartbeat or accelerated breathing.

Lord love a sinner, he mused, but that should have seen him packing her and her pitiful belongings up onto his horse and riding her straight back to Stonehaven. *Jesu*, the last thing he needed was the distraction of so alluring a person as she.

As if no more than an inexperienced lad, he stole glances at her all morning, appreciative of the grace with which she moved and the lustrous shine to her dark hair. When she smiled at Will, begging bread from Wallace at her side—which Wallace seemed quite happy to share—Jamie drew in his breath at beauty of it, wishing he'd been the recipient of so glorious a thing.

And when the camp site had been abandoned and they'd ridden away, further north, and she was seated again before him, Jamie had to call upon every ounce of discipline to not return the favor of so enticing an exploration. His arm was once again folded around her slim waist. Every so often the ride required a bounce in the saddle, which tightened his arm around her, rather reflexively. Twice now, when he'd done so, his arm had ridden up against the plump firmness of her breasts. Jamie was no eunuch that he then did not imagine exploring this further. But imagine was all he allowed, and that only fleetingly.

Around noon time, they stopped just outside the sometimes bustling town of Aberdeen, hanging back across the river that ran through it. It was planned that Jamie and George Goody and Roger of Balweny would ride into Aberdeen and find Simon Annand, who was expecting them. Wallace would remain secreted across the river until they delivered Annand to him.

Jamie was sorry that he had to leave Ada behind, but knew her to be very safe in Wallace's care. But Wallace himself wondered if it might be of benefit to take Ada into town.

Jamie's frown was instant, over Ada's head, and across to Wallace.

"No," he said, promptly.

Wallace raised a brow at Jamie. "'Tis not held by the English, nor inhabited as such. The lass's presence would dampen any interest in three soldiers. And you need only to meet with Annand, determine his suitability and allegiance, and return him to me," Wallace argued. "There is no danger to her."

Jamie opened his mouth to refuse this still, but Ada spoke up before him.

"I will go." She turned, only her head, so that he was presented with the cheek with the lesser scars. "Sir William has assured us of the safety. And should he have erred, I have faith that you can see me removed without harm."

Clenching his jaw, Jamie met William's eye, the big man's brow raised as if he thought similarly to Jamie, that she practiced sweet manipulation well.

So it was that not more than thirty minutes later found Jamie and Ada seated next to each other and across a table from Roger and George inside a traveler's inn. They'd requested ale and food to give a pretense of only seeking sustenance for a journey and this was delivered posthaste, steaming platters of fish and wild fowl and a plate of cheese and bread. George shimmied off the bench and walked away, intent on inquiring of Simon Annand.

Jamie watched him leave, pursing his lip as he considered the man. George Goody was as loyal as they came, but Jamie had always considered him a bit of a weasel. The man could not make conversation that wasn't either salacious or outright incendiary and Jamie was regularly put off by his disappointing hygiene practices, so that the man always seemed greasy and grimy. William Wallace had been living in forests and safehouses for years, with few amenities, and seemed never to appear so bedraggled as Goody.

Roger of Balweny, on the other hand, dressed not expensively but neatly, and carried himself with the bearing of a titled and learned man; he could speak well on many subjects, crops or religion, babies or the system of roads in the Highlands, that Jamie valued his opinions and fellowship more than most. Presently, he appreciated that Roger was tactful enough that even as he spoke with Ada, he appeared—or pretended—that he saw her scars not at all. Unlike that fool Goody, who continually gawked and puckered his brow at Ada so that Jamie knew he was going to have words with the man.

Ada wrapped up several pieces of cheese and a long strip of fish in a square of linen provided with the meal. Jamie was surprised to see her tuck this into the pocket of her cloak.

He and Roger exchanged curious glances over this, while Ada apparently did not know or did not care that they had witnessed her secreting away food.

With a small chuckle, Jamie asked, "Is that for Will?"

Ada turned her face up to him, unembarrassed. "It's for Sir William, though like as not, he will share with Will."

"Aye," said Roger with an agreeable grin.

Jamie turned and watched as Goody sidled up to the innkeep and leaned close, speaking softly to him. The bald little man, who ran a crowded and lively establishment, inclined his head toward a table at the rear of the room. Only minutes later, Goody returned with Simon Annand in tow.

Annand gave the impression that he was a man who preferred to escape notice. While his eyes showed an intensity and, Jamie judged, an intelligence, he dressed with a mind toward blending in, rather than being noticed. Goody returned to his seat on the bench and Annand followed, only showing a minimal faltering, from which he recovered swiftly enough, as he spied Ada's face.

Roger handled much of the conversation with Annand, to gauge his willingness to abet the cause while Jamie observed, trying to ferret out the person he was. William Wallace just could not be too careful.

While Ada had conversed rather easily with Roger, she was quiet now, her hands in her lap, the plentiful fare forgotten. It occurred to Jamie, surely as it had to her, which had her suddenly stiff and downcast, that she was drawing attention. The inn teemed with scores of people and pulling his gaze from Annand showed many of these casting what they supposed were hidden peeks at her. It was not to be avoided; from afar, one would be rather entranced by her shining hair and beguiling lips, perhaps the shape of her eyes as well. It was those who drew near, or sat close, that noticed the detail of her face. One woman, sitting across the aisle from them, had grimaced crossly at Ada before requesting that her traveling companion trade seats with her, undoubtedly so she wasn't faced with Ada's visage. Jamie gnashed his teeth together and wanted to get Ada out of there, though knew that he could not, yet. Completely ignoring their guest and this mission, Jamie reached his hand under the table and wrapped it around Ada's in her lap. Uncaring who watched, he leaned over and put his lips directly at her ear, felt her stiffen more, until he whispered, "Dinna you lower your head, Ada Moncriefe. You are the most beautiful woman here."

With these words, Ada gave a nervous smile of appreciation, though she did not turn toward him. While he kept his hand clutched around hers, she straightened her shoulders and lifted her head, attending again the conversation.

His hand remained covering hers and he allowed his own shoulders to relax, but this was short-lived. George Goody was speaking to Annand, his head tipped to the side, his words muted. But Jamie heard them, saw him lift his hand and point to Ada.

"Ye want that for all your womenfolk? That's what the supporters of Longshanks do to 'em. Likely more, that we canna see."

Roger, appearing nearly as furious as Jamie, his eyes stricken with some horrified expression, swiveled his head swiftly to Goody, while Jamie's hand upon Ada's tightened with his rage.

"They hanged her, least some of the time," Goody said, his eating knife suspended over one of the platters. He pointed again at Ada. "Show 'im yer neck."

"That will not be necessary," Roger of Balweny intoned, his voice chilly. "At any rate, we must wrap this up. MacKenna, would you mind collecting our mounts?"

Unable to control the curl of his lip, knowing if he remained he would likely kill Goody, Jamie nodded tightly and rose, pulling Ada along with him. He made a curt farewell to Annand, supposing they would meet again, and steered Ada ahead of him with his hand at the small of her back. Bless the lass, but she held her head high as she navigated the many tables and benches and chairs. She even stopped at the door, so that Jamie moved forward and swung it open for her, as if only her minion. *Good for her*, he thought, even as he seethed still over the dastardly and unscrupulous tactic Goody had employed.

Outside, she did not stop but walked across the well worn road, to where they'd left the horses with a lad.

"Is that why you didn't want me to accompany you to the inn?" She asked, even as she continued walking, her gait so stiff as to have Jamie supposing she might snap in two if he but touched her again. "Did you know he was going to use me like that?"

"I did no," he ground out. "Under no circumstance is that acceptable. I will address this with Goody."

Jamie flipped a coin to the barefooted and unclean lad as they neared him. Ada stopped just next to Jamie's destrier. He was aware that she drew a deep breath before turning around to face him.

"I'm not sure why it didn't occur to me, when Sir William proposed that I accompany you, that I hadn't truly been in a public place since... Dornoch."

Jamie shook his head. "Lass, you ken, it's only the people who matter who should be given any of your thoughts. You do no need to concern yourself with strangers and what they see or think or even say."

She surprised him by waving a hand at this, appearing more resolute than troubled. "I agree. Yet it was still awkward. I'd like not to repeat it, I think."

"Aye."

Roger and Goody exited the inn then and while Ada's lack of proper distress had calmed him, Jamie still snarled at Goody as he neared.

Roger pursed his lips as he strode past, toward his horse. "Imbecile," he muttered, shaking his head, glaring at Goody even after he'd found his seat in the saddle.

They rode almost a mile to where Wallace and the others waited. Roger dismounted quickly and strode to Wallace, to give him the details of their meeting with Annand. The man had an army of almost five hundred, and he was monied, to afford more if Wallace delighted. Thus, the meeting had proved fruitful. Jamie just wished it hadn't come with such disrespect to Ada.

Leaving Ada on the horse, Jamie swung down and approached Goody, who'd dismounted as well. Towering over the much shorter man, Jamie thumped his finger into Goody's shoulder.

"Never—never!—use Ada thusly again." He hadn't shouted, but his tone was chilling and his stance intimidating, that Goody rather recoiled, his face pinched with dread. "She is no a propaganda tool, to be treated so," Jamie growled. "I'll slit your throat if you ever dare mistreat her again. And keep your fucking eyes off her, do you understand me?"

Goody's mouth gaped, showing what lack of hygiene had done to his teeth, and he nodded with some fright, even as he dared to say, "But it's so perfect, her face all messed up like that—"

Jamie saw red and slugged him, threw his fist right across his face, and now roared, "I just fucking said you will no mistreat her!"

The man hit the ground, scrambling away, one hand held up defensively. Jamie loomed over the little man until he nodded again, this time knowing better than to open his mouth.

Still scowling, Jamie pivoted, brushing past Wallace, who'd likely come to intervene.

He didn't lift his gaze to Ada until he was almost upon her. Abruptly, he pulled her off the horse, ignoring her aghast expression, and took her hand to lead her away from the attentive onlookers. Jamie led Ada over a small knoll and down to the river, only releasing her hand when they stood just at the water's edge.

He pressed his hands onto his hips and said while he stared out over the muddy river, "I apologize for that—" just as Ada murmured, with the hint of a question in her voice, "Thank you." This made him bark out a short laugh, though he found nothing funny, was still antagonized by his fury.

He squatted and scooped up water in his hands, throwing it onto his face and swishing it around his mouth. He stood and flicked his hands and spit out the water, back into the river.

With about as much levity as he supposed he'd ever noticed in Ada Moncriefe, he heard her say behind him, "Your knuckles will be scraped raw if you attack every person who stares at my face."

Jamie turned. The barest hint of a smile hovered about her, curving her very tempting lips. "'Twas no so much for the staring but for his performance at the inn."

She knew this, and nodded, leaving her serene expression to offer still her appreciation. She stood with one hand folded over the other at her front, her eyes riveting while they regarded him so thoughtfully. The scars did nothing, truly, to take away from the fact that she was exquisite, her skin otherwise creamy, her lips pink and full and inviting. She'd tied her hair up at her nape, showing her long and slender neck, where her cloak now fell away.

Her lips drew his attention again and he strode with purpose toward her. She neither backed away nor showed any sense of retreating, even as he did not stop until his boots met the hem of her skirt, even as his gaze surely alerted her of his intent. Without preamble, he placed a hand on each side of her face and drew his thumbs along the line of her scars, and he made no effort to diminish the smoldering desire of his gaze while she kept hers locked on his.

And then he kissed her.

ADA SUPPOSED SHE SHOULD have expected the kiss. Why else would he have put his hands on her as he had? And what else might she have read in that blazing look he'd given her? But no, she was still very shocked when his firm and warm lips touched hers.

She gasped silently. He stopped but did not retreat. Waited. Ada swallowed and breathed again. His lips touched hers once more. It wasn't intentional that her eyes fluttered closed; they seemed only to sigh and drift downward. He moved his mouth back and forth. She felt his breath against her face, was aware of a great turbulence inside her belly.

She kissed him back and clung to his forearms.

"Open for me," he said against her lips, using his thumb to draw down her jaw while his tongue licked her mouth. She did open, not sure why, and then his tongue was inside her mouth, engaged with hers, and Ada felt her knees weaken. She'd had no idea that the tongue was involved with kissing and felt instantly that this was both carnal and exciting. He moved his mouth over hers, sending delicious sensations swirling about her.

She liked it very much but was still fairly shocked at her own eager response, and then was quite sad when he stopped, when his mouth left hers, so that only their ragged breaths touched now.

"I've never been kissed before," she breathed.

He set her away from him, letting his hands fall away from her, but with a look about him that said he didn't want to let her go, perhaps only believed it was something he should do.

"You can no say those words ever again."

It took Ada a moment, and a poor reading of his very handsome face, for her to realize he meant that now she had been kissed and the words were no longer necessary, or truth.

"Yes," was her very un-clever response to that. To her own ears, her voice, even raspy still, held a dreamy and delicate quality.

This produced a smile in him, which shocked her nearly as much as his kiss had. Jamie MacKenna was indeed a very handsome man, but now, with his smile, he was absolutely beautiful. Ada had never seen him smile and was made almost breathless again at this sight. It transformed him, showed him as extremely approachable—almost boyish—removing all traces of hardness and sorrow.

"You should do that more often," she murmured, captivated by the change his smile had wrought.

His lips curved more, looked downright devilish. "Kiss you?"

She was innocent yet to understand the nuance of flirting, and answered honestly, "Smile. You should smile more."

He appeared unperturbed that she seemingly preferred his smile to his kiss and pressed, "Mayhap more kissing will instigate more smiling."

This, being so blatantly manipulative, made Ada blurt out a giggle. She covered her mouth with her hand and stared at him, realizing she liked everything about this circumstance very much. His kiss was splendid, and she hoped there might be more, indeed. She enjoyed as well how she felt right now, light and bubbly and rather carefree.

Maybe it was the matching ease written so plainly on their faces, or the lack of the anger that had driven them away from the group, that lifted William Wallace's brow upon their return. Or mayhap, it was only Ada shyly stealing glances at Jamie MacKenna that twitched the great warriors mouth with some pleased expression.

Belatedly, Ada remembered the scraps she'd tucked away for the giant man, and presented these to him quite happily, having no idea that her lips, indeed her entire face showed very clearly that she'd been kissed quite spectacularly. She smiled at Wallace and accepted his thanks, assuming the smile he returned was borne only of appreciation and not also of awareness.

Chapter Ten

Because of his own lighter mood, and because the impression of Ada's lips against his own was still unmistakably discerned, Jamie left off growling again at George Goody when they joined the group again. They would remain here, near Aberdeen, until Annand showed himself to meet personally with Wallace. Roger had assured Wallace of the man's cleverness and fervor, which served as a suitable endorsement to Wallace.

Ada excused herself to duck off into the brush quite a distance away from the lounging circle of men after she'd shared her bounty with Wallace. Jamie watched her leave, wondering at his complete lack of remorse for having kissed her—and then wondered at his questioning this lack. Why should he feel remorse? Remorse for what? The kiss had been brilliant, had stirred in him something he'd assumed long dead, something he'd thought he'd buried with his wife many years ago, mayhap even before that. He examined how long he might have been thinking of kissing her. It seemed not something that had crashed into him suddenly today, only something that had been building up, whether he'd recognized it or not.

"Roger enlightened me about your cause with Goody," William Wallace said.

Jamie startled, caught unawares by Wallace, who stood just beside him. He'd not heard him approach. Jamie sighed. It had not been his intention to cause any dissention and he said as much to Wallace, but justified, "It was wrong, what he did."

"I agree, lad," said Wallace, though he wasn't more than a decade older than Jamie. 'I'd not have insisted the lass go into Aberdeen had I'd known he would have used methods so disheartening."

Jamie waved off his concern. He would never suspect Wallace of being behind that sort of behavior. "'Tis done, and I'm sure he'll no repeat it—I'll no allow it."

Wallace shifted just slightly, to put his gaze onto the spot where Ada had disappeared. "Amazing—a woman scarred like that, all that violence so visible upon her person, and all a man can see is her beauty. Remarkable, isn't it?"

"Aye, she is," Jamie responded automatically and glanced sharply at Wallace to see that he'd been caught in one of his little games, making a statement as such, to elicit the response he sought, which answered any questions he might have had. Jamie could not help but smirk at Wallace, who clapped a big hand on his shoulder and chuckled as he so rarely had cause to do.

"Aye, Jamie MacKenna, if the lass's eye strayed at all from you, I trow I'd give it my best."

Wallace was still chuckling as Ada returned, and even as Simon Annand showed himself in their provisional camp.

First thing Jamie noted upon her return was that her gaze was shy now. She rolled her lips inward, and he was struck by the idea that she did so to keep from smiling. Holding back his own grin, in pleased reaction to this, he advised her that he needed to be at Wallace's side now. At her nod, he followed Wallace away toward Annand.

ADA UNDERSTOOD AT ONCE, as they mounted to ride again almost an hour later, that since Jamie MacKenna had kissed her, everything was changed. Simply riding with him, seated before him, was beheld in a completely different context now. Yesterday, she'd sat before him, happy for the security of his arm around her, and the warmth of his chest against her. She'd kept her hand atop his while they were on horseback, to steady herself. Today, the heat she felt at her back was more charged as Ada was aware of each part of her that was pressed against him. The hand around her middle was now familiar and intimate, it seemed; her hand settled atop his stirred with a fantastic awareness of his skin beneath her.

That evening, when they camped again, Wallace outlined for everyone Annand's commitment to their cause. "He will meet us in three months' time," said Wallace, pulling meat from the bones of a rabbit as they gathered around the fire, "with numbers in the hundreds."

"Where next?" Asked a man simply called Crumb. Within this group, Crumb talked the most. He was wiry, both in personality and appearance, his voice scratchy and his face and body bristly and muscular. Ada had never encountered a more chatty man, who never had so much to say, only liked to hear words, or his own voice, Ada reckoned. But she liked him, as he seemed always to be of good cheer.

"North still," Wallace answered.

Roger expounded, "The MacBriar has agreed to meet with us."

Ada supposed this was how it was done, how Wallace had amassed supporters over the years, meeting face to face to rally patronage, using only his persuasive voice and his personal dogma that Scotland should only and ever be free, no matter the cost.

When the bones of a half dozen hares had been tossed into the low burning fire, Ada excused herself and found her way to the river's edge. She rinsed her hands in the water and then chose to sit a while, intent on watching the sun set across the river, over the gray and green capped hills in the distance. It did not compare to the beach at Stonehaven, but it was peaceful, the only sounds being the honks and hinks of some pink-footed geese floating upon the water.

To her mind, it seemed it had been longer than only a couple of days since she'd left Stonehaven. She hoped that Jamie had spoken truth when he'd said they'd get back there one day. As if conjured by her very thought, Jamie came to the river then. As Ada had done, he washed his hands in the water and then sat beside her on the brownish-green grass, his palms on the ground behind him.

"The MacBriars who were mentioned are within a day's ride to Aviemore," he told her. "I said to Wallace we'd part ways there. I need to call in my own army, to be ready for Wallace's summons."

"Is the MacKenna army very large?"

"Decent enough," he allowed. "Half what it used to be, before Falkirk and all these years of warring."

"When was the last time you were home?"

"Been almost a year, I guess."

"Do you miss being home?"

He shook his head. "There is little to draw or keep me there."

"Is Aviemore very large? Don't the people need their laird?"

"My uncle Malcolm and Aviemore's steward, they look after things. Agnes Nairn runs the household for me—she's Malcom's mistress."

Mistress raised Ada's brow, but her question did not pertain to that. "Do you never get tired of sleeping on the ground, scrounging for food? Do you dream of a true bed?"

His shoulders lifted and fell with a noncommittal shrug. Tipping his head toward her, he countered, "How long were you at Mungo's place, up in the forest at Stonehaven?"

"A long time," she said after a moment. She hadn't thought in a while about that cottage. She'd woken every morning, not really thinking of a future, not dreaming of what comforts she missed or amenities she wished she'd had. She'd just lived, one day at a time, with a schedule of things to do—feed herself, warm herself, busy herself. Maybe that's how he approached so much time away from his own home, one day at a time, with no thought to the future. This, then, begged the question, "Do you think you'll die fighting for Scotland's freedom?" She stared at him, caught his quick frown of surprise.

His gaze left hers soon enough. He picked up a large stone next to his leg and tossed it into the water. Then he lifted his knees and rested his arms across them, his hands joined.

"I dinna rightly think about dying, it seems," he finally answered. "Aye, but neither do I give much attention to the *after*, when the war is done. So aye, maybe I expect I'll die."

"Doesn't that scare you?"

He shrugged again. "I imagine you need something worth living for, to make you afraid of dying."

These words struck Ada as sorrowful, though he'd uttered them in a level and practical tone. She almost asked why he felt he hadn't anything to live for but stopped herself. Ada imagined that was indeed a very personal question, or at least, would require divulging things of a personal nature, should he have chosen to answer.

Ada sighed, weary enough that she was only slightly disappointed that it seemed there would be no more kissing. Still, the awareness of him was new and different. She knew every move he made, sitting next to her, even something so small as scratching his arm or shooing away a fly. Every time his hand moved, something inside her tingled, and she knew it was in happy expectation of him touching her. But he did not, and when complete darkness shrouded the lake and Will howled close by, they returned to the camp site to settle down for the night.

She was sure she would never get used to, or have a liking for the cold, hard ground. She sat, debating if her bundled belongings might make a good pillow, when Jamie said, in his now familiar nighttime voice, "Might be easier to sleep if you lie down, lass."

Turning, she found him already reclined, one arm under his head and his feet crossed at the ankles. Honestly, she thought it looked terribly uncomfortable, spreading himself out so that the cold could seep into every part of him. Ada opted to lie on her side, rather curled up, hopefully giving the crisp air access to only her back. She pulled the long close-fitting sleeves of her kirtle down over her hands and tucked them under her head. It wasn't long before she slept.

She dreamed she was at Dornoch again, with the rope around her neck. Curiously, it was not John Craig who tortured her, but Will. He stood before her with a feral gleam in his eyes and applied the knife just as John Craig had, even as his own face and torso showed so much of the cruelty inflicted on him.

"Oh, Will," she moaned, her heartbeat racing while fear twisted her belly. Will cackled with glee at the sight of her fear, waving the knife before her eyes. Ada began to shake, having learned that her fear—the expectation of pain—was actually greater than the pain itself. "Will, no," she pleaded with him.

"Ada."

Will shook her and she cried out, having lost the very fragile hold over her control.

"Ada!" This, given sharply, and not being Will's voice, woke Ada.

Jamie MacKenna hovered over her.

"Aye, wake up, lass," he said, his tone was harsh, putting her to rights so that she understood it had only been a dream.

"I'm sorry," she murmured, hoping she hadn't woken anyone else. She shivered, even as she realized she was flush with perspiration. Swiping at tears on her cheeks, she closed her eyes, shutting out the frowning scrutiny of Jamie MacKenna. But closing her eyes brought the picture of Will again to her. Ada whimpered and covered her mouth with her hand.

Opening her eyes showed Jamie still risen on his elbow above her. He appeared harsh still but there was some agony in him, and she wondered if she'd called Will's name out loud and he knew then of what she'd dreamed. In an effort to deflect the pity, or assuage his anguish, she told him, "Will was incredibly brave. He—he tried to assume all the blame, pretended he'd only stumbled upon me, that I'd had no part in it...."

It was a moment before she heard his whispered reply.

"Aye, he was one of the finest."

Ada could see the outline of him, saw his shoulders relax. And then he stretched out again. Turning her head, to consider the sky, and so she wasn't staring directly at him, she listened to Crumb's and another's snoring and a few embers crackling and wondered how long she'd slept.

His low voice reached her again. "Beth never had any time for him, thought him only some annoyance. But she was all he saw, he worshipped her. I was always amazed that she chose to ignore it. She was spoiled though, truth be told," he said. "Always hoped she'd marry some rich baron and be a grand lady of great lands and many people. Will would've been happy in a hovel with her."

When it seemed he would say no more, Ada asked, "How did she die?"

"Hmph," he snorted quietly. "She married a rich baron and went with the birthing, the babe, too." And then, "She cried when I told her about Will, was distraught, really."

"She did love him," Ada guessed.

"Aye, in her way, I suppose she did."

"Do you have other family? Brothers and sisters?"

"All gone, another sister to a fever as a child and a brother lost at Stirling Bridge years ago. But lass, what were you doing at Dornoch? Why were you there?"

The question surprised her, both for its timing and for the sound of it, rushed out, as if he'd been thinking on it, or had held it back for a while.

"I was betrothed to John Craig." She guessed there was really no way for him to have known. She let that sink in and only thought to add, "I'd been there a month. I'd seen enough."

"'Twas beyond brave, what you did."

She didn't acknowledge this; it had never been that to her. "I watched as you and the others were brought in. It was the sight of the boy, that lad with you that twisted my heart with fear."

"Henry," he supplied.

"Henry. He is...well?"

"Aye, you'll see him at Aviemore."

There was boundless satisfaction in that.

"I often think...if that hadn't happened that night, I'd likely now be married to John Craig and I sometimes wonder which is, or would have been, worse—what has been, or what might have been."

Jamie MacKenna rolled toward her, his eyes bright in the darkness. "Ada Moncriefe, you are...exactly where you are meant to be."

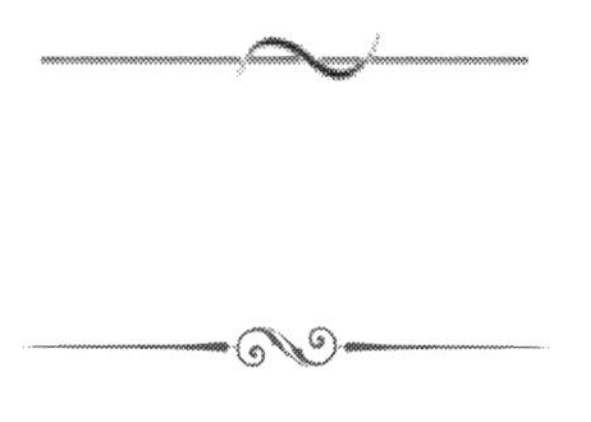

THEY DID NOT BREAK camp the next day until late in the morning, Ada continually surprised that this group, with so noble a purpose, never seemed to be in so great a hurry.

Once again, Ada rode with Jamie, who'd advised her they would have a long day in the saddle. She dozed for a while against him and was restless when she woke. To pass the time, and while Crumb hummed loudly and sometimes put bawdy words to his own melody, Ada recalled the game she and Kinnon had played on their way to Stoney. With some thought to preserving her own sanity, she resolved not to think of the atrocity that had interrupted their game. As any and all of her conversation with Jamie while they rode usually found her turning her head to the side so that her voice would carry back to him, Ada twisted, turning her cheek toward his chest.

"What's your favorite food?"

If he were surprised by her out-of-the-blue query, she could not know.

But he answered rather promptly, "They've a fair orchard down at Inesfree. The cook bakes up apples with cinnamon in the bread."

"What is cinnamon?" She'd never heard of this, but decided she liked the word.

"It's a spice. Leans more toward sweet, as opposed to savory."

"Apples in bread?"

"Strange, I ken," he admitted. "But it's right tasty."

"What's your favorite color?"

"Favorite color? Why would I have a favorite?" While Ada waited, he wondered, "How would I know which was my favorite?"

"Which one makes you happy? Blue is mine, like a cloudless sky on a sunny day."

"Green, then," he answered easily then.

"Do you have a favorite song?"

"I dinna ken any songs."

"Crumb seems to know quite a few," she said with a grin and felt Jamie harrumph against her. Crumb had trotted his horse up ahead, sidling alongside Roger and patting him on the back. He lifted his voice, trying to encourage the Balweny man to join him in song. Roger only chuckled at the silly man and shook his head.

"Why do you want to ken these things?"

Ada shrugged, leaning her back against him, her cheek resting against his breastplate. "Passes the time." Feeling more relaxed than she could recall in recent memory, she twirled her hair in one hand while holding Jamie's hand at her waist with her other. "Where's the farthest you've ever traveled?"

"I went to France once," he answered, "when I was very young, with my father."

"What did you do there?"

"I dinna recall, save that I was mostly bored. Much more color there, in the streets and the buildings, and the peoples' costumes."

"Would you like to go back there, to see it not as a child?"

"Nae, Wallace says it's filthy, said he'd feared the smell of sewage and body odor would kill him even as the war had not."

"What's your favorite—" Ada's words died as something sliced through the air and barely missed crashing into George Goody as he rode a little ahead and beside Jamie and Ada.

Ada bolted upright, just as the entire party danced their horses around, trying to find the source of the arrow that had been shot into their midst.

"It came from above," Ada announced, having been witness to its trajectory. This had all eyes scanning the hills behind them.

"Get into the trees," Jamie shouted, and kicked their horse to race toward the promised cover of a grove of pine and birch trees, quite a distance away to the west.

Sitting straight again, Ada clung to Jamie's arm, which had tightened around her when he'd spurred the animal into a hard gallop. Only Roger and another soldier ran ahead of them, the rest of the group being in their wake. A strangled scream told Ada that someone had been hit. Panicked, she glanced behind them, around Jamie's arm, just in time to see George Goody fall from his horse, the arrow that jutted from his back snapping in two as he bounced on the ground. His steed did not stop, but continued his gallop, keeping pace with the other animals. Another yelp sounded, this one lower, almost guttural. Another arrow, lodged into Crumb's thigh, contorted his face into a mean grimace. He kept stride, did not lose his seat, and reached the canopy of trees only seconds after Jamie and Ada did. The amount of pines, and the closeness of all the trees necessitated that they slow measurably.

At the same time, Jamie and Ada straightened from their low and hunched positions, which the greater speed had dictated. Her thighs and shins bounced against his as the horse clopped through the scrub and underbrush within the woods. Ada faced forward again but could hear the sounds of the dozen horses of their party crunching and crashing along behind them.

It wasn't until they were nearly half mile into these trees that Jamie halted, and the entire party gathered round.

Ada watched the men and saw that every one of them looked not at each other but at their surroundings.

"Bit of a trail," one man commented, looking down at the clear but thin path.

"Aye. Settle all about the path and wait?" asked another.

"Aye," said Wallace. "Spread out, twenty to thirty feet, three units on each side."

"Call the goshawk when they come," another instructed.

"Jamie, you and the lass take the furthest point," Wallace said.

And without additional instruction, or any other division of the men, they all trotted off, disappearing at varying spots along that narrow trail. Jamie and Ada moved ahead, and Ada did not need any clarification to know that Wallace had put her farthest away from any potential coming danger.

A good twenty feet or more off the trail, Jamie directed Ada to wait near a fallen tree. She sat on the stump, from where the rest of the trunk had broken away and watched Jamie lead the horse even further away and hitch up the reins to a small and spindly tree.

He returned and pulled his sword from its sheath, pointing to the ground. "We'll stay low."

They sat side by side, their backs against the stump, the remaining fallen trunk giving them fair cover from the trail. The ground was damp and cold, and the sun had yet to show itself today from behind heavy gray clouds, but Ada left off asking any questions about how long they would wait, or why they hadn't just kept riding away. After a while, she leaned her head back against the smooth bark and closed her eyes but could not maintain this position for long, for the kink it formed in her neck.

When the question did begin to hound her, she finally asked of Jamie, "We weren't followed, after all, so why don't we just get back on the horses and get away?"

"We need to ken if Annand had any part in this."

"But I thought it was decided he could be trusted."

Jamie spared her a glance, his eyes shining at her. "Trust is only assumed, until it is earned, lass."

"But you had a good feeling about him?"

"Aye, I did, but some are more clever than most, can hide their truths."

After a while, as night came and darkness thickened, Ada felt her head bobbing as she drifted off. But each bob would rouse her, until she dared to lay her head upon Jamie's shoulder.

"ARE YOU GOING TO SLEEP?" She whispered through a yawn.

"I canna sleep, lass. We all must be wakeful." He shifted against the stubby trunk and patted his lap. "But here, you put your head down now."

She scooched closer and did so without argument.

With her head in his lap, she asked, "Do you think Crumb is all right?"

"I dinna ken." His voice was low, barely more than a whisper. "There's a spot in the leg, about the same on each man, where blood seems to just rip right out of you. I've seen it, blood spraying five feet into the air from that spot. I dinna think it had struck him there."

He sacrificed a moment of watchfulness to glance down at her head, nestled on his left thigh. Her hair had long since lost whatever contraption she'd set it into, and now fanned around her face and his legs and over her cloak onto the ground. Jamie used his free hand to sweep the long tresses off her cheek, which revealed that her eyes were closed. He moved another strand off her face and repeated the gesture again and again. His steady gaze returned to watchfulness, near and around the trail, even as his hand continued to caress her hair and scalp in soft strokes.

They hadn't any need of the call of a goshawk as an alert, as the enemy, when they came nearly another hour later, held torches aloft as they slowly picked their way through the trees. Jamie pressed his hand over Ada's mouth, startling her to wakefulness, for which he was sorry. But he could not have her cry out if she were woken by the light and noise that came now. Her eyes opened wide, but she acclimated quickly and moved her head against his palm so that he removed his hand. Ada sat up slowly, without a sound, and Jamie took her hand and tugged until she understood he wanted her on the other side of him. Keeping his hand low, she was forced to crawl over him, and Jamie stopped her when she had one leg over his thighs and her face was very close to his.

He put his lips to her ear and whispered, "When I go, you stay here. Dinna move at all. Dinna make a sound."

"I understand."

"Even if I fall, lass, you canna make a sound."

Now, she hesitated, but did soon nod and settled herself next to him.

The lights came closer. Jamie knew that Wallace, or whoever might be in the lead position, would wait until they had passed by, so that they could surround whoever came.

When they drew nearer to Jamie's position, and because they were thick-headed enough to employ torches, Jamie was able to crane his neck and surmise some numbers. The trees were thick yet, but he could make out about eight or ten for sure, guessing there might be more straggling behind as they seemed to be almost single file on the trail.

Jamie had just risen to his haunches, to be available to spring into action, when he heard the long squawk and three short jips of the goshawk call. At this point, the call was an order to move and Jamie leapt out from behind the tree trunk and chased down the first horseback rider, who had only seconds ago walked his steed past Jamie's position.

Chapter Eleven

Ada in no way wanted to witness this skirmish, having seen such viciousness and death at Stonehaven only days ago. But she couldn't *not* watch. She had to know that Jamie prevailed.

Pulling herself onto her knees, she hunched still behind the stump and bemoaned the very cover of trees that had secreted them but that now prevented her from knowing what happened. She saw only golden light and lines of shiny steel in motion, heard the grunts and groans of a battle met, and knew that several horses already were racing away from the skirmish.

At one point, Jamie entered her line of vision, just a foot of space between two trees. She could not help the stricken cry that burst forth when she realized he had no sword but was using one of the torches as a weapon. She watched, horror choking her, and proved what a coward she was, for ducking low when the huge man, circling Jamie, seemed to face her directly.

She supposed they must be greatly outnumbered, as none of their party came to Jamie's aid, though his disadvantage was clear.

To their left, Ada saw the body of another man, quite a distance from where Jamie dodged and parried this man's attack. The man was quite obviously dead, his horse gone and his bow useless at this side. Ada crept through the brush and pounced on the dead man, just at the edge of the bare trail. As she hovered just near a thick tree, she could see little of the battle that raged. She yanked at the man's bow, around which his fingers still curled. She tugged harder and gained possession of the large thing and searched around for arrows but saw none. Falling to her knees, she pushed the dead man onto his side and found the projectiles, in the quiver at his back. She wrapped her hand around what few remained and pulled them free before the body fell back.

Ada ducked back into the cover of the trees, hopefully before she was noticed. Near to the stump, she found a spot with a clear but narrow view of Jamie's bout. With more determination than know-how, certainly wishing she'd paid more attention when she'd watched the training with Kinnon at Stonehaven, she whipped her cloak back off her shoulders, and nocked an arrow onto the bow. A cry burst forth, for the sight of her trembling hands, as she tried to aim. Adjusting her focus brought the fight into view beyond the tip of the arrow. Jamie was still standing, ducking, and deflecting each thrust of the man's long blade with the torch. The flame was beginning to dwindle. They were standing and circling fairly close, the two men, and her hands were shaking yet too much for her to chance a shot now. She waited, drawing deep and even breaths, for an opening. She needed Jamie well clear of the man, suspecting it not so easy as it looked to fire a missile through the air, and have it land where you intended. The blue tartan-ed man lunged again, catching the sleeve of Jamie's arm with the tip of his blade. Jumping away from the swiping sword, Jamie created quite a bit of space between him and his assailant.

Ada let the arrow fly. And hit nothing. But the arrow sailed directly between the two men, surprising them, that they both turned, to locate the new adversary. Jamie recovered first, and swung his torch as a club, catching the man on the side of the head. The man fell and Jamie kicked him hard in his gut, divesting the man of his weapon and using it to end his life.

Rather than come to her, Jamie squinted into the trees with a surprisingly ferocious scowl before he sprinted away from her, along the trail, toward the rest of the fighting.

Briefly, she wondered if she might be helpful to any other, with her newly acquired bow and arrow, but thought then she'd only been lucky with her solo shot. And her hands were still shaking, now with even greater force. She was about to find cover again behind the fallen tree when she heard the unmistakable sound of Will's growl. Whatever he was about, and Ada could not see from this vantage point, he was clearly and directly involved in this battle. She could well discern the growl as being similar to the one he used when he playfully tugged at some item he wanted from Ada. But this growl was vicious, and she could well imagine his head moving side to side, his teeth clamped down on some unfortunate thing or person.

Ada heard a shout of, "Go on, Will!" and thought it might have been Wallace who'd hollered. Will did not obey, Ada guessed, now frantic as she heard a renewed growl and more steel clanging. Frightfully upset, she stood frozen, forgetting even to hide herself.

And then, rather all at once, the noise stopped.

"Catch him!" She heard Roger call, followed quickly by another's exclamation of "God damn it!"

The night darkened as torches were either stomped out or faded on their own. Several low moans reached her ears, but Ada remained where she was, unable to move.

Another of Wallace's comrades interrogated a wounded man, asking who'd sent them, what they were after. The man groaned and cried but gave no answers. Then his cries stopped.

Someone walked through the trees and came toward her. Ada's relief was palpable as she recognized Jamie's silhouette and his purposeful pace as he neared.

He strode right up to her, put his face in hers and snarled, "Which part dinna you hear? The *stay put* part? The *dinna make a sound* part?"

"I—I—"

"God damn it, Ada! That's how people get killed—they dinna listen!"

Truthfully, even as she knew he was right, and that his anger was possibly justified, she believed his fury overdone. She was unharmed, after all. And she had helped him!

He ground out, "I specifically recall you saying that you understood my order."

With her own burst of annoyance, she revealed, "When I said that, it didn't mean that I agreed. It didn't even mean I understood." And then, lamely, and with a bit of remorse, "Unfortunately, it didn't even mean that I was listening."

He threw up his hands, his frustration evident. "Then why did you say it?"

He was shouting still, which then had Ada yelling back at him, "It seemed to be what you wanted to hear." She was quite distressed to notice that tears seemed imminent. Damn that man. It was all his fault anyway!

He collected their mount and marched toward the others. Ada followed, and saw that the thin trail was laden now with dead bodies, including two of their own.

She was then distracted by others riding away. She stared, counting only she and Jamie and William Wallace and Roger that remained.

Of course, George Goody was dead, left somewhere in a field of heather. When she asked about the leave-taking of the others, Wallace answered, "Mr. Crumb had need of medical assistance, so the lads bore him straightaway to Aberdeen, where their role was twofold, in that they were consigned to ferret out from whence came this cowardly attack."

They rode yet again, but only for an hour or so, to put the battle, and the evidence of it, far behind them. When they settled down to sleep, and without the benefit of even a small fire, Ada curled up with her back to Jamie, her jaw clenched in resentment and cold, childishly wishing she could take back the aid she'd given him, such as it was.

She stiffened when she realized movement behind her, knowing he was lying down as well, and then was quite surprised when, despite their harsh words and residual frustration, he hauled her up against him. "Aye now, dinna fuss," he said when she stiffened. His voice demonstrated still a particular ire, even as he pressed himself against the length of her and wedged his arm under her head. "Dinna disobey again, lass. I need to be clear headed, and no be worrying about you."

And that changed everything. He had been worried about her?

Ada chewed her lip for a moment. She turned in his arms, so that she faced him. She opted to tell him the truth but wanted to be sure that no one overheard her. The stubborn man wouldn't lower his head. Ada waited. When he still didn't and being rather embarrassed by the confession she was about to make, Ada whispered, "I didn't *mean* to not listen to whatever you had said to me." And then haltingly, "It's just that I could not truly listen, or at least not make sense of it—you were so close and your...your lips were nearly touching me, and I was thinking about...I was wondering if you were going to kiss me again."

He hadn't been moving, of course, was just lying there, but Ada felt every part of him become rigid. She was convinced she could actually hear his teeth clenching. So much for her apology by way of explanation begetting any peace between them.

"I'm sorry." She couldn't help but bristle. "Mayhap any future directives should be given with a minimal distance between us," she said, uncaring that it sounded so ridiculous.

He lowered his head now, and Ada waited for more harsh words from him. But he only kissed her forehead and drew her even closer to him. Ada sighed with the release of anxiety, aware of the tension leaving his body as well.

Several minutes passed, before he murmured into her hair. "Minimal distance of three feet? That sound about right for any future directives?"

Ada smiled into his chest. "I should think five or more."

WHEN NEXT SHE WOKE, the sun was not yet risen, but hovering just over the hills to the east. Ada turned her head and saw William Wallace walking back toward their little circle, sans his chain mail and surcote, rubbing a length of fabric over his naked chest. His hair and skin glistened as if wet, and Ada assumed he'd only taken himself off for a bath and wondered how she might manage that.

She sighed and closed her eyes, groggy still and now dreaming of heated water and the stout wooden tub she'd used at Stonehaven.

"That's a wistful sigh, lass," came Jamie's voice very close to her.

"What I wouldn't give for a bath," she said. She was quite comfortable, and kept her eyes closed, hoping Jamie MacKenna was in no hurry to move. Will was on her left and Jamie on her right, that she rather enjoyed the warmth, being squeezed in between them.

Jamie's arm flexed underneath her, where it rested beneath her neck and head, as if he wished to rise. Ada ignored it, receiving a chuckle for her stubbornness.

"Was thinking much the same," he said. "Aye, now, let me up, and we'll see about making your dreams come true today."

This opened Ada's eyes. She sat up, as did Jamie. Will lifted his head, but not for long, only stretching out his front paws before applying his chin to them.

Jamie disappeared into the brush while Ada sat idly, rubbing the fur behind Will's ears. William Wallace had donned a fresh tunic and returned all his accoutrements to his person, sitting now with his psalter, as he did often throughout the day. Will had risen and sat now quietly at his side.

The bath did not come until they'd ridden all day, their pace unhurried so that Ada thought they hadn't traveled more than ten or so miles. When they finally stopped, late in the afternoon, the four each contributed to setting up a transient campsite. The ground here was rocky and Jamie left off digging, using several large stones to make a circle for their fire while Ada gathered kindling and a few heavier pieces of wood. Wallace and Roger each removed their bow and quivers from their mounts and announced they'd see about hunting their dinner.

When Ada had supplied what she thought was a fair amount of tinder and Jamie had arranged the pieces and started the fire, he turned to her and suggested, "You'll want your bath now while the sun still shines."

Ada nodded. To find this secluded campsite, they'd walked their horses around a small loch. The sun had shimmered over the water, and though she knew it would be cold, it certainly looked inviting. She fetched her bundled belongings from Jamie's horse and walked down to the water. To her surprise, Jamie followed her, and she hoped she didn't have to insist on privacy or hoped that he didn't need to be told that she expected it. But Jamie only scouted the area at the water's edge, pointing toward the right, where a section of tall brush and trees extended almost into the water.

"Should have some privacy down there, lass," he said, and Ada breathed a sigh of relief.

She ambled in the suggested direction, glancing back to see Jamie turning away and walking back to camp. When she was completely out of sight, Ada divested herself of her cloak, hanging it over a red flowering bush. Her gown and chemise, and shoes and hose followed, all but her shoes being rolled into one bundle that would need laundering eventually.

She recalled well enough from so long in the forest outside Stonehaven that it was best to submerge herself quickly and completely, as the longer it took her to force herself into the cold water, the more dreadful the bath seemed. With this in mind, she walked rather purposefully into the water, surprised to find that it dropped fairly quickly to be above her shoulders. Truthfully, it wasn't as cold as she'd feared, but it wasn't warm either. She held her breath and dunked her head, spending a few minutes scrubbing at her scalp with her fingernails, dunking again and again to clean her hair.

She emerged at one point and heard a splash, clearing water from her eyes just in time to see Jamie MacKenna's head surface, from deep in the water, and far from Ada, closer to their camp. He went about the same business as her, ridding himself of a traveler's grime.

While Ada was not disturbed by his presence, being as she was covered up to her chest in the water and he was quite a distance away, she hoped he was quick with his bath as she wished neither to have to walk naked from the loch in full view of him nor to remain in the chilly water any longer than necessary.

He was considerate enough that he did not dawdle but after only a few minutes began to climb from the water. Ada held her breath, realizing Jamie MacKenna had no similar qualms about striding naked, it seemed. Without purposeful intent, she lowered herself so that her chin hovered just at the water line as she watched him exit the loch. The space between them now posed a hindrance and Ada was presented with only a hazy image of pale skin and hard muscles and a catlike grace as he moved. When he reached the bank of the loch, he bent and retrieved his plaid, applying it to his chest and back and arms to dry himself. And then, seemingly indifferent to the surely cool air, he gathered up his boots and other items, and walked, still naked, back to their camp.

Ada shook herself and returned her attention to her bath, chastising herself for having ogled the MacKenna so eagerly. When she could stand the cold water no more and when she was satisfied that she was so much cleaner, she started toward the bank herself, only to be stopped by the sight of a large snake, sunning itself at the base of the bush where she'd hung her cloak. She stood now, covered only to her waist, frozen in place by the reptile's poor timing. She debated what to do, knowing she wasn't brave enough to walk even just close enough to grab the cloak and run, with only the unsupported hope that the snake wouldn't move. The cool air hit her, chilling her so much more than being submerged in the water had. Ada reached into the water, found one of the bothersome rocks at her feet and hurled it at the snake. She screamed then, as the rock landed very close to the snake, which sent it scrambling to safety, into the water. With another shriek, Ada dashed from the water as fast as she could, yanking at her cloak and managing only to clutch it to her chest just as Jamie MacKenna burst onto the scene, sword in hand, his other hand holding the ties of his obviously hastily donned breeches.

He raced over to her, his chest and feet bare, eyes ablaze.

Horrified, Ada looked down to make sure her cloak covered all of her, which it barely did. With limited success, she tried to pull the cloak wider, around at least one hip, and said with some panic, some apology, "'Twas only a snake." She was very sure that her cheeks were bright red with both her fright and her embarrassment.

He stopped, within ten feet of her, the tensed muscles of his arms softening as he lowered his sword. Ada bit her lip and stared at him, at his chest. She couldn't not stare, even as she knew he stared at her as well.

She didn't know what the word was to describe her reaction to him, to the sight of his very bare, very solid, very...manly chest. But she supposed her response, being abruptly breathless and filled with some novel sense of wonder, at the very least, hinted at some appreciation for his appearance. Forgetting that she stood naked, with only the cloak that no doubt showed just as much as it concealed, Ada stared at his rock hard stomach and the sculpted muscles of his massive shoulders and strong arms. His chest was only sparsely covered with hair, which intriguingly tapered to one thin line as it disappeared into his breeches. True, she could determine no term for what it was that swirled inside her at the sight of him, but she knew the word for what she gazed upon. Beautiful. Jamie MacKenna was beautiful.

"Aye, now, dinna be staring like that," Jamie said.

His voice, low and husky, startled Ada's gaze away from his chest and onto his face. She was mortified at her overlong—indeed, wanton—perusal of him. But for the life of her, she couldn't manage any statement of apology for her gawking. And then, as if they'd a will of their own, her eyes strayed again to the perfectly symmetrical pectoral muscles and the flat brown nipples.

A flick of his wrist sent the sword, blade first, into the ground, which pulled Ada's gaze, but only for the space of a second, to see the hilt sway back and forth. Jamie covered the distance between them in a few quick strides and wrapped his fingers around her upper arms.

"I warned you, lass."

Chapter Twelve

He kissed her. He shouldn't, some part of him cautioned, but how could he not? The gaze she'd put to him, all that awe and wonder she could not contain amounted to a silent siren's call, no matter how artlessly given.

Ada stood motionless, but Jamie was aware of her shoulders going limp, while her hands clutched the cloak tightly still, crushed between them. Every fiber of his being was aware of how perfectly naked she was beyond that cloak.

Softly, slowly, as not to startle her, he let his kiss inform her of his intent, and indeed, his extreme reverence for how very fine she was. He was besieged with a brilliant desire—not to possess her, but just to hold her, to feel her in his arms. Something in her, that strange combination of hard-bitten innocence intrigued him as nothing else ever had.

He cupped her face, pressed his lips to hers, and gave up his own sigh at the feel of her. Then Jamie pulled away to meet her fascinated and beguiling eyes. With great tenderness, he kissed each cheek, paying homage to those scars. Ada whimpered at his ear.

"I—I have no clothes..." she said, breathless.

Against her lips, he murmured, a smile in his words as there hadn't been in so long, "Aye, and dinna I ken it."

He continued to kiss her, pushing his tongue into her mouth, reveling in the feel and taste of her. Slowly, he lowered his hands and circled her waist. Sweeping his hands around her slim hips, his breath caught at the sensation of the cool nakedness of her buttocks. Her skin was unbearably soft and smooth, and he was not oblivious to the gooseflesh that rose with his touch.

She clung to him, returning his kiss as she'd learned from their previous encounter, arms stealing around his neck while the cloak remained crushed between them, her mouth opening to give him full access. Jamie pushed a hand between them and yanked the cloak away so that it fell to their feet. He cupped one breast, widened his fingers to circle it, her nipple pressed against his palm. Sliding his hand downward, his fingers grazed her nipple, teasing the bud into a peak. He lifted his head, watching her sigh a shaky little breath of air, enjoying the sight of her face alight with stirrings of passion, her lids closed, eyebrows arched expectantly, her features completely without tension. Jamie glanced down at her breasts; they were perfect, as perfect as he imagined all of Ada would soon prove to be. Full and milky white, her rosy nipples pointed around two circles of pink.

But Jamie's heart nearly broke at the sight of the thin white marks that crisscrossed so much of the skin of her beautiful breasts. And above them, a foot long scar ran from right to left, just above the top of the globes. His nostrils flared, while he fought back a rage so brutal it curled his fingers into her flesh.

Ada gasped and opened her eyes, saw what held his attention. Every inch of her stiffened, and then all at once went completely limp. "I'm sorry," she whispered. "I—I should have..." her voice trailed off.

He couldn't remember the last time he cried, or if he ever had. But he recognized the feeling of it, the threat of tears; his throat tightened, and his jaw clenched; heat pooled in his cheeks and nose and mouth while his eyes watered.

He leaned his forehead against hers, his fingers dug into her hips, pulling her against him. "Do no ever say you're sorry to me. No ever again."

He kissed her savagely then, so much fury inside him, so much he needed her to know, to understand. She apologized to him! He was the sorry one! He was to blame. How could she even stand to look at him? *Jesu*, how could she kiss him? His mouth covered hers hungrily, devouring her softness, her willingness.

Ah, but damn her soul, it was wrong. Jamie halted, his lips hovering just near hers. "Why do you let me kiss you? Strike me," he growled, "or curse me. Smite me, even. But I dinna deserve your kiss."

Softly, she breathed against his mouth, "I did strike you, and oh, how I cursed you." And then, the part of her that was beyond brave, that both terrified and awed him, said, "And now that's done. I far prefer the kissing."

Ada confirmed this by touching her lips to his, boldly tracing the seam of his lips with her tongue. It was ridiculously easy, selfishly satisfying, to give in to her untutored attempt to coax his mouth open. But he waited, curious as to the extent of her daring—or was it only her desire to assuage his guilt? Whatever it was, she did not disappoint. Her wet tongue speared into his mouth, seeking his, curling around it with enough unpracticed fervor that Jamie's cock's sprang further to life.

Understanding—and gladly so—that he wasn't doing anything she didn't want him to do, Jamie took control once again. With great reverence, he lowered his head and touched his lips to her breasts while Ada drew a sharp and startled breath, her hands clasping his head, her fingers curling into his hair. He showered first one, then the other nipple with attention, until both were hard, and she was all but sagging against him. He grabbed her close against him, chest to chest, watching her eyes pop open at the feel of this, as he rubbed his own naked chest tortuously against her breasts. As frantically as an untried youth, he fumbled with the ties to his breeches, dropping them to the ground.

Jamie straightened and stood before her, both of them naked, separated now by several feet. She swallowed and her shy gaze left his to look upon him, her lips rolling in as she confronted his erection, which only lengthened with her innocent but curious perusal.

Jamie was not at all immune to the sight of her. Her legs were long and lean, and he pictured them wrapped around him while he pressed into that triangle between. Her belly was flat, untouched by the violence John Craig had visited upon her. Her arms, it came as no surprise, were thin and toned, and those magnificent breasts sat perfectly upon her, being neither too large nor too small, but perfectly shaped.

Jamie took one step forward and lifted her hand to place it on his chest. Briefly, she'd met his eyes again, aroused as well as curious now, he fathomed, before she shifted her gaze again to his chest. Jamie held her hand even as she splayed her fingers wide and discovered him. Her breathing increased. She moved the tip of one finger over his nipple, the touch so sensational he flexed, bringing her eyes back to his. He allowed the slightest hint of a grin to encourage her, though imagined it must appear pained, with the restraint it required to not pull her violently against him. She traced a long thick cut line where it began near his nipple and followed its path up past his shoulder. Ada stepped closer and pressed her lips to one part of that old scar.

Jamie sighed, and with a hand at each of her hips, he lowered himself to his knees, pulling Ada along with him. He guided her onto her back, onto her fallen cloak. coming over her, his mouth low, touching first her navel. His tongue tasted her skin, warm and soft. Moving upward, leaving a trail of kisses along the way, he captured one nipple, holding himself up with a hand on either side of her, while he pinched her nipple between his teeth. Ada cried out, the sound wispy and needful, and Jamie fought valiantly against the urge to couple with her as hard and urgently as his need demanded.

He stretched out his legs beside hers and lifted his face to hers. Her eyes were liquid with passion, her lips swollen and parted. Jamie touched his mouth to hers, back and forth, inserting his tongue, playing against hers. He trailed kisses down her throat, back to her breast, running his fingers along her thigh, first outside then inside. She went still, her fingernails digging into his shoulder. He joined their lips again and reached between her thighs, into the dark curls, teasing her hot flesh.

"Oh," she moaned, and instinctively tried to close her legs. Jamie followed, persistent, knowing more than she what she desired. But he needed to be gentle, to go slow, and that was becoming more and more unrealistic. Lifting his head, he watched her; her back was arched, her eyes were closed, hair haloed about her head, her body bared to him. Pale and soft, with a lean but voluptuous figure he'd not entirely been prepared for, Jamie wondered if he was indeed capable of reining himself in, keeping the pace unhurried, unthreatening for her.

He sought her lips, closing his eyes, tasting her, his fingers still about their play, wandering inward, filling her. Ada cried out, a bit shocked at this foray. Her sigh then, as she settled against him, was a bit dreamy as she became accustomed to the motion of his fingers. After a moment, as her need increased, she began to move herself against him. Her hands left his hair, thin fingers inflaming his own rampant need with a southern trail, down his back, onto his hips.

"I want to touch you," she murmured. And because her hands already had sampled so much of him, he knew specifically what she meant. He reached for the hand in his hair and guided it between them, showing her how to wrap her fingers around him. An unintelligible sound escaped him; he held his breath, but dared to demonstrate, with his hand covering hers, how she should move. She did so, with aching slowness, that Jamie deemed it wise to leave off teaching her more in this regard. He could only stand so much and did so only until he sensed she was comfortable, though he most certainly was not.

"No more lass," he instructed, pulling her hand away. "A man can only take so much."

He applied himself to making sure she was wet for him, sliding his hand again between her legs, teasing her nub, and entering her again.

Their lips met again, hungrier, more urgent, the rhythm increasing. And when her breaths became steadily audible, little gasps of wonder while his fingers moved inside her, Jamie pulled back, eliciting a startled, unhappy cry. But this was replaced by a husky moan as he shifted and came on top of her. Her legs naturally fell open and Jamie settled between them. With his forearms on either side of her head, his fingers in her hair, he met her eyes, telling her how truly thankful he was for this. And then she enflamed him by saying, "I like the way your body feels against mine, skin to skin."

An answering sound emerged, and he kissed her lingeringly, touching his penis to where she throbbed for him. "I canna lie, lass. I've been thinking about this every day upon that blessed horse, and each night when you lie next to me." He pushed forward fractionally, opening her.

Ada moaned. "This is desire, then," she surmised.

"Aye, and mountains of it."

"I like it," she said, ever honest. "I shouldn't, I think. But I do."

Relief and excitement flooded him at once. Slowly, he entered her, controlling the urge to thrust himself inside her and take her hard. She was tight, closing around him, giving great torment. He put his palms onto the ground and rose above her, every muscle strained with the effort to proceed slowly. He reached the barrier of her innocence. And froze. Not for one damn second had he imagined he would encounter this. Honest to God, he'd just expected the loss of this was one more gruesome offense she's surely suffered. Relief, and then guilt, battled within.

But he could no more stop now that he could bring his own heartbeat to a halt. He'd no plans to warn her of the pain, she was too immersed in her own want and needn't know the price for bliss. Expertly, he kissed her until she was more at ease with the invasion thus far and then pushed himself through, swallowing her cry of distress, stopping completely.

"Do no move," he cautioned, forehead to forehead.

"Something went wrong," she said, her brow furrowed, her eyes shiny.

A chuckle escaped at this. "No, lass. A perfect fit."

He ached to move and did so in small, leisurely increments. He grabbed her hips to show her the motion and she matched his pace but soon her quickening demanded that he move faster. In and out. Blood rushed to every corner of his body. He knew when she neared orgasm for her body lifted, her eyes lighting on him with some beautiful question.

Jamie pulled out, ignoring her cry. He sat on his knees and brought her up with him to sit upon him, catching her amazed expression. Now face to face, he lifted her hips and brought her down again, settling his cock once again inside her. Their eyes locked as they moved and panted. Ada gripped his shoulders, finding the rhythm again while Jamie took both her breasts in his hands, his thumbs stirring her nipples.

He watched her bite her bottom lip and arch her neck, her movements more frenzied. "Ah, lass, come with me."

"I...I need..."

"I ken what you need, Ada. Let it come."

And she did. Before his eyes, just as his own ecstasy was about to burst upon him, she climaxed, shivering with delight, her nails digging into his skin. She brought her eyes back to his, bright with excitement, her face then telling him this was quite unexpected. She pressed her mouth to his, capturing his outcry as he exploded inside her.

Filled with the feel of Ada, the taste of her, the scent of sex, he closed his eyes, shuddering with pleasure. Against her lips, "Jesus bloody Christ." It ravaged him, spiraling throughout his body, firing his blood. Jamie fought to steady himself, his breathing. Spent now, with Ada coming down around him, he held her tight, enjoying still the feel of her breasts crushed against him.

Eventually, when he could move again, he lowered her onto her back again, lying himself atop her. Her hands were in his hair again, pulling the long hair away from his face. Finally, Jamie opened his eyes.

She was watching him, her face now utterly unsure. Of how to act. How to proceed. How to express herself.

Jamie kissed her. Tenderly. "You are beautiful, Ada." Shifting just a bit, he slipped to the side, but remained half lying atop her, kept his face buried at her neck.

“If I’d known what it was,” she said into his hair, her voice seeming to float, “if I’d had any idea...I’d have been thinking about this for the last few days as well.”

Jamie chuckled against her before lifting his head. “And now, lass, when we bed down tonight, or when we ride again tomorrow...?” She was already nodding her head against the ground beneath her that he needn’t finish the question. “Aye, me too. More so, like as no.”

ADA CLOSED HER EYES, nearly trampled by the sentiments raging through her now. She dug into them but could find no remorse. It should be there, she felt. Quite easily, though they were new, she recognized the physical reactions, the now waning passion, the tingling in all of her limbs, the heat coursing still through her, that particular fullness and throbbing at her woman's place. But while her emotions just now were a jumble, she could barely decipher any negative. Surely that must follow what they had just done, shouldn't it?

"I dinna want to move," Jamie said against her shoulder, "but we must."

He removed his body from hers and Ada waited for the embarrassment to come, as he stretched his hand down to her and brought her to her feet. It didn't, though. Instead, only a need to look and touch and know more of him filled her. She reached out her hand, his chest its destination. Her fingertips had barely grazed him, and she'd received only the beginnings of a lifted brow and lazy, satisfied grin from him when Will crashed down onto the beach. This meant Wallace and Roger had returned from hunting, as the hound had accompanied them.

Ada's eyes widened. Jamie bent down and grabbed her cloak, shoving it at her, and steered her back into the brush where her clothes were hidden. He had only his breeches to don and did so hastily, just as Will reached him and pranced around, sniffing the very ground where Ada and Jamie had lain only moments ago.

Ada dressed hurriedly, happy to be wearing clean clothes again, and stepped out to find Jamie waiting for her. She'd have thought he might have returned to the camp, to at least give the impression that they hadn't been bathing together, as their hair was damp yet. But he'd waited, and Ada decided if Jamie weren't concerned with the impropriety, she wouldn't be either.

He yanked his sword from where he'd thrust it into the ground and they walked along the bank, Ada clutching the bundle of soiled clothes to her belly.

"They're going to know," she lamented, "for I fear I won't be able to hide it from my face." Her entire person must look different, she imagined. How could a person just be party to that most miraculous thing as she just had, and not have it clearly written all over their face?

Jamie stopped and considered her, head to toe, his gaze rather raking and suggesting he liked very much what he saw, or was seeing it again minus her garments. "Aye, they're no idiots. We shouldn't pretend they are. But, lass, we'll keep our hands to ourselves while keeping company, aye?"

She smiled at this. She'd done a very bold thing with Jamie MacKenna just now, made even more audacious for her lack of regret, but she didn't suppose she was some hussy to be openly fondling him. Yet, "Best find a tunic then, sir, and remove the temptation."

He chuckled at this and kissed her fleetingly.

WILLIAM WALLACE DID indeed have an idea what had transpired between Jamie and Ada, if Ada read correctly his unusually persistent grin, which he happened to focus more on Jamie than her. But Ada was truly unperturbed. The world could end tomorrow, and well it might, but she had this. She cared not that her future was still uncertain, cared not that she was, for all intents and purposes, a ruined woman. Her history and her scars made the latter so trivial a matter, and Torren's mantra, *your life now can and will be whatever you decide to make of it*, repeated often to herself, reduced the amount of worry she invested in the former.

And when they eventually settled down for the night around the dwindling fire, and Jamie pulled her into his arms, his chest pressed against her back, his breath warm against her hair, Ada knew a sense of hope she'd not entertained in years. Entwining her fingers with his at her waist, she considered that she'd certainly not had an unpleasant life, prior to Dornoch. True, it had been rather hum-drum, Ada ever imbued with a sense of waiting for something to happen, for life to come to her. But she had never, she concluded, entertained as much hope as she did now, certainly not a hint since Dornoch—hope that she was entitled to happiness, hope that something good could be hers. And the beauty of it was that it wasn't specifically or necessarily attached outright to Jamie MacKenna. While she was quite obviously attracted to him, and intrigued by him, she'd only just realized that he'd only shown her that joy was something she could know again.

"Are you thinking what I'm thinking?" Came his whisper at her ear.

Ada grinned into the darkness, and returned in a matching low voice, "I only met that tone in your voice today, but I'm sure I do know what you are thinking. I'm sorry to say, my thoughts were more... cerebral."

There was a smile in his voice, "Have I taught you nothing, lass?"

"There's more?" She teased.

Jamie pressed himself against her bottom and Ada's eyes widened at the hardness she now recognized. Immediately, a heat pooled between her legs. She held herself very still, even as her breathing quickened, not sure if responding or encouraging him was the right thing to do with William Wallace and Roger so closely situated.

And, in her frank manner, she wondered, with her head turned back toward him, "Is it your intent to dangle a temptation before me, one that I cannot enjoy presently?"

His hand slipped away from hers at her middle and rose to slide over her breast, lifting the fullness of it. "What's no to enjoy, lass?"

Thus fascinated, Ada blew out a breath and rather innocently wiggled her bum against him.

"Aye, and now, you trot out your own enticement?"

"'Tis only fair," she said, covering the hand at her breast with her own, willing him to stop. It wasn't fair at all, actually, to tease her so.

Jamie went still. Several minutes passed.

And then he murmured at her ear, "We'll get to MacBriar's tomorrow, lass. I had an idea we might find a cleric to see us wed."

In all her life, Ada could not recall a moment when she'd been more stunned. Not minutes ago, she'd given up her care of the future, had decided to live in the present, had made peace with it. Jamie MacKenna just proposed that they wed. Ada was beyond befuddled.

She'd been speechless in her life, she guessed. Mayhap many times. But she knew of no such occasion that left her gape-jawed and her thoughts so tangled as to render her unable to process them. The most persistent one, however, was silly, thinking that she'd not have supposed Jamie MacKenna the type of man to perceive or attach affection from a lone encounter. He was much too hardened, too cynical for such tedious sentiment.

And then it occurred to her, came as rather a slow dawning of understanding. It was guilt. Because he'd taken the last of her innocence, as inconsequential as it was. She couldn't help it, she recoiled, both emotionally and bodily.

"That will not be necessary," she said rigidly.

All the lightness that had stayed with them throughout the day dissolved in that instant.

"Aye, it's no," he said, his tone hinting at a bit of surprise, a bit of defensiveness.

"Though very considerate of you," she said, believing she'd been successful in keeping the resentment from her voice. "Still, I think a wedding pointless, if you're concerned somehow that I bemoan today's loss." True, it had been the last untainted thing she owned, but she was not sorry to see it gone, did not fret for one moment that it affected her at all, all things considered.

"You mistake me," he said, a new severity reflected in his tone.

"You are asking me to believe that today's encounter has suddenly made you realize you are in love with me?"

"I dinna say that, lass," he clipped. "You want to assume more? Or do you care to hear my thoughts on the subject?"

Her harrumph was possibly undetected. Mentally crossing her arms over her chest, she waited, prepared to have no liking for any coming words.

Behind her, Jamie heaved his own sigh and said, "Lass, I dinna think you can argue that somehow, and for whatever purpose, our fates are entwined—and have been since that night at Dornoch," he began. "Mayhap that's why what we did today seemed so...natural, or only inevitable. But you ken, there will be many a terrible battle waged before this war is done. I'd like to ken you're safe and, should I no survive, it would sit well with me to have you looked after. As the wife of the MacKenna, you would be taken care of always."

Ada relaxed ever so slightly. This sounded reasonable, indeed, much more realistic, though it still hinted at guilt being the prevailing motive for wanting to marry her.

When she did not reply to this, he added, "Also, this thing we've just done, I'll be wanting to do it again, and often." With these admittedly thrilling words, his arms flexed, bringing Ada more firmly against him. "Aye, but I dinna want you doing this with anyone else. Ever. So, I say all that to say all this: we'll be wed before we reach Aviemore."

Ada digested all of this, and it was a lot. The fact that he'd pronounced, not explicitly asked, bothered her least of all. In her continued jumbled contemplations, she pulled out the idea that she'd initially been quite enamored of John Craig, when first they'd met. She had misjudged him terribly. How well did she really know Jamie MacKenna? Might he prove to be a monster as well? No sooner had these doubts presented themselves to her, did she dismiss them. She was unworldly and naïve, she knew, but by some means had every confidence that she had not misread Jamie MacKenna.

And with that—apparently her only inner argument—settled, Ada could think of no other reason not to say yes.

With as much grace as she could muster, she admitted, "I did like what we did today." She chewed her lip for a moment. "I think you did as well."

"Aye, verra much."

"If we wed, I am able only to do that with you?"

"Aye, I've said as much. I'll insist upon it."

"And you can do this thing we've done with only me then?"

"If you insist," he allowed.

"I would," she said firmly, and then wondered, "I assume Aviemore is much the size of Stonehaven?" At his nod, felt against her head, she confessed, "I do not know anything, or have any experience, overseeing a keep that large."

She felt him plant his chin atop her head, but it was several minutes before he spoke, in which time Ada became fairly anxious that he was reconsidering.

Finally, he said, "You were fair happily ensconced there at Stonehaven, but you came away with me, with a man you weren't entirely sure was honorable. You keep company with the most sought after man in all of Scotland and only yesterday, you near slew a man in battle. Earlier today, with nary a bit of hesitation, you lay down with me. And you're worried that you dinna ken how to take care of a big house?"

She nodded.

Another minute passed. "So your answer is aye, then?'

"Aye."

From across the fire, Roger's voice reached them. "You two ken you've no been whispering for half of that? Aye, but please I am for you."

William Wallace spoke up, his voice groggy but not without a hint of good cheer. "Weddings are a fine beginning to joy and other things."

"Aye," agreed Roger.

Ada giggled silently, covering her mouth with her hand while Jamie kissed the back of her head.

He was right, she knew, their fates had been linked from the moment she'd walked down into the dungeon at Dornoch. She couldn't yet process all that wedding Jamie MacKenna might signify, but she knew a certain relief to put into his hands the matter of her well-being and safety, and indeed her future.

Chapter Thirteen

In the morning, when William Wallace was fully wakeful, he approached Ada while Jamie took himself off into the scrub brush.

"Ada Moncriefe, 'tis pleased I am for the decision you've made."

Ada smiled, thinking just now that Wallace's clever blue eyes nearly danced with delight within his long face. "Thank you, Sir William."

"I daresay Jamie MacKenna will give you plenty instances that you'll wish for a stout club to correct his thinking, lass. But I promise you'll no regret the choice you made."

She considered that William Wallace was surely an intelligent man, his very calling seeming to require that he be a very good judge of the character of many a man.

"Sir William, I think I'd come to the same conclusion, but to have this verified is much appreciated."

They reached the MacBriar's Hawick House in the late afternoon.

"You should ken that our present itinerant circumstance will no allow for an actual wedding feast," Jamie had said to her earlier.

Ada had replied, "Nor, I imagine, will I be afforded a wedding gown or a bouquet of blooms or even an attendant to stand beside me." All this, with a shrug, to indicate she truly was untroubled by the lack.

"Aye, but there will be a consummating," her bridegroom said.

She was surprised by the blush that pinkened her cheeks, but heard herself say, with her newfound knowledge of this, "I'm rather counting on that."

Hawick House was neither so large nor so fine as Stonehaven, unable to boast more than two towers, and possessed of an outer wall and gate that surely had seen better days. William Wallace insisted, however, that it was a safe haven for them presently, as the numbers within were so slight. This explained the four of them riding into the bailey, Wallace in their midst and not secreted somewhere just away from notice.

If it had not been made known to her that the castle was so sparsely populated, Ada might have considered it abandoned. No sentries manned the walls, nor even patrolled at ground level near the open gate; no persons milled around the bailey, nor in the smithy's shed; and not one horse was seen inside the stables.

"MacBriar is a bit of an enigma," Jamie described as they dismounted, greeted by no one. "Almost dares an army to come charging in, but the truth is, he hasn't much to protect. Wallace suggested Hawick only aged out."

"What does that mean?" Ada saw Will trotting inside the yard and straight up to Wallace as the giant dismounted. William Wallace was the only person the hound could stand beside and not seem so overlarge and threatening. Next to Wallace, he appeared only a normal sized pup.

"The numbers dwindled. Maybe they lost too many to war. Mayhap too many women and not enough men, or the other way around, or too many not breeding, so that no new persons are born into MacBriar's fold, and those here get old and die."

"But what benefit can he possibly provide to the cause?" Ada wondered, as they stopped here strictly for that purpose, more recruiting.

Jamie dismounted and lifted Ada down from the saddle. "In this region, MacBriar still has great influence. There are thousands of soldiers all around, in neighboring clans. If MacBriar lends his support, others will follow."

"I would have thought his influence would have been weakened by his apparent diminished circumstance here."

"Aye, it dinna look like much," Jamie agreed and ducked his head toward her and lowered his voice, "but they say he's buried more gold around here than he and Hawick can spend in a lifetime. And he loans more coin than Longshanks borrows, so his influence remains strong."

"Or bought?"

"Aye."

William Wallace, as if a regular visitor to Hawick House, punched open the door to the tall and square stone keep and stepped into the hall. Roger and Jamie and Ada followed, standing still just inside, letting their eyes adjust to the gloom. The hall was an abomination, the rush strewn floor sticky and odorous. Dark and faded tapestries hung on the walls, covering any possible windows or light; a stale and heavy fog of smoke and dust and foulness hovered in the air; only one table occupied the large space, though the base of this was cracked so that it leaned crookedly to one end, unsuitable for any purpose.

"A fine venue for a wedding," Roger teased, throwing a wink back to Ada, just as Wallace called loudly for MacBriar, his deep voice echoing throughout the cavernous hall.

A person—Ada could not tell if it be a man or woman—appeared in an archway at the end of the room, but only briefly before bobbing and scurrying away. Ada was left with only an impression of a long tunic-ed body with scraggly hair and a questionable mien.

And then a noise turned their heads toward the other end of the room, where a set of crumbling stairs hugged the wall and led to a shadowy landing. Ada could not hide her surprise at the figure that appeared and now walked down those steps. A young woman, lovely in a gown of fine red wool, with hair the color of honey, descended and greeted Wallace as if happily familiar.

Wallace turned and beckoned to them and rather as one, Roger and Jamie and she moved closer.

"'Tis Katherine, wife of Duncan MacBriar," Wallace informed them.

The woman, older than the distance had hinted at, but lovely nonetheless, turned pretty gray eyes onto her first, smiling a welcome as Wallace introduced the three of them.

"Jamie and Ada are wishing to have nuptials this day, madam, if you could lend any assistance to their cause," Sir William sketched, his gaze and grin fatherly, settled upon Ada.

The gray eyes lit up. Katherine MacBriar took up Ada's hands, seemingly unaffected by Ada's scars, and said, "Oh, but a wedding would be delightful. Hawick House hasn't seen one since my own, and that was a decade ago."

"Mayhap you ladies will discuss some arrangements while Roger and Jamie and I visit your husband's sickroom?" Wallace suggested.

"Aye, and I'll send up some ale and sweets," Katherine said, still holding one of Ada's hands. "We will convene in my solar, dear Ada. A wedding, indeed!"

Ada sent a glance to Jamie, who lifted a brow at this glorious creature's excitement.

Not long after, Ada waited inside Lady Hawick's solar, while that kind woman spent time in the kitchen and in discussion with Hawick's steward about some immediate tasks to initiate. Ada considered the rather sumptuous room, so absurd when compared with the first impression of the hall. These chambers were clean and fresh and bright, with white-washed walls and fine chairs fitted with plump cushions and carved backs, wonderfully artistic tapestries in a myriad of colors, and a table set under the window with colorful glass jars, which caught and shared the light. Ada had only rarely seen glass pieces, sometimes poorly done inside windows, but never so perfectly presented as these bottles and jars of blue and green, two of them filled now with white and pink spring blooms.

The woman appeared then around the open door, carrying a tray set with two pewter cups and a plate of sweet breads.

"Here we are," she cooed and placed the tray on the table, pushing it backward so that those glass jars moved away, closer to the wall.

Ada stared at her. Her own sisters had been intrigued by fripperies, had spent much time on their own toilette. Ada could never quite understand why. The same question seemed to pose itself now, as she gazed upon all the pristine beauty of this woman. Her hair was pinned back in some elaborate coiffure, curls coiled precisely all around her head, braids falling around her shoulders; her dress was immaculate, and costly, Ada imagined, colored wool being far more expensive than the browns and grays; the fingernails of her lean and soft hands were trimmed and rounded so neatly, Ada was sure it must be intentional; the lips that smiled at her were unnaturally red, as if some tint or stain had been applied, giving them a rosy appearance.

The lady handed Ada one of the cups and offered the plate to her. Gingerly, Ada plucked at one of the sweets, and smiled her thanks.

Katherine MacBriar seated herself on the matching chair across from Ada, her back straight, her posture rather formal, inducing Ada to raise herself neatly.

"You are very gracious, my lady," Ada said, not without a trace of awe.

"We so rarely see visitors," said Katherine, "and even more rarely a woman with whom I can share time. You are quite lovely, Ada Moncriefe. Of course, one cannot mistake the scars, but lovely nonetheless—they give you a certain boldness. Your entire look fair screams tragedy, but I can see in your eyes that you'd be no one's victim."

Ada's bottom lip fell. She did not know if she should be offended by such blunt speaking. Quickly, she decided not; Lady MacBriar was nothing if not genuine, she guessed, meaning no disrespect, Ada had to assume.

"But a wedding—and to that glorious man, the MacKenna," Katherine MacBriar said, near to giddy, thumping her hand over her heart. "You are very lucky, indeed. Was it he who saved you from—" the chatty lady swirled her hand around, to indicate Ada's appearance, "—whatever did that to you."

Still taken aback by her careless chatter, Ada could only shake her head and murmur, "He did not."

Katherine leaned forward and winked, "But I bet he wishes he had."

If only she knew. "I'm sure he does," Ada intoned, warming to the woman, despite—or because—exactly how different she was from anyone Ada had ever known.

"You've been wed to the MacBriar for ten years?" Ada aimed to turn the conversation away from herself.

Katherine sighed with a smiled grimace. "Aye, since I was seventeen. He's not awful, and I haven't had to lie with him in years." And then, with greater enthusiasm, "I have the prettiest wardrobe north of Perth—and isn't this room just darling?"

"But the hall...?" Ada wondered, before she caught herself.

Thin shoulders fell, gray eyes crinkled at Ada. "Horrid, is it not? We've no servants or serfs, not as we once did. The more sickly Duncan gets, the tighter the purse strings become. I used to keep it up, but truth be told, it was ruining my hands and what was the point? No one comes to Hawick, and when they do, they only beg coin of Duncan and then they're off."

She was just absolutely riddled with information to share, almost as if she'd waited for someone to come, that she might entertain them, as if all these words had been building up.

Ada's curiosity overrode her politeness, that she dared to ask, "But your husband, when he...dies, what will become of you?"

Her face lit up, the pink lips spreading wide. "Oh, then I'll find a strapping young man—of good honor and fine manners," she was quick to assure, "someone like your man, mayhap. We'll fill the house and land with bairns and return Hawick to its former glory and I will be a grand lady, indeed."

Ada smiled, and her response was both spontaneous and sincere. "You are already a very grand lady."

Katherine accepted this with a happy face for this praise, and then chirped, clapping her hands together, "But now there's to be a wedding! We can have the hall cleaned in only a day or two. I'll tell Moira in the kitchen to start baking for a feast. We'll invite everyone from the village—and oh! We must find you something to wear. I have the perfect gown!"

Ada hated to disappoint her but felt she should straighten her out before this went too far.

"My lady—"

"You must call me Katherine."

"Katherine, you are very kind to offer so much—and to complete strangers," Ada began, and hurried it along when it seemed the woman would brush it off, "but I think it is not our plan to stay overlong. And I'm not sure Jamie would be comfortable with anything...fancy, as far as our wedding goes. Nor I, truth be told."

The pout offered up by her pretty painted lips nearly caused Ada to laugh out loud. With a thought to allow for some concession, to appease the woman's excitement, Ada said, "But I would be quite thankful for some help with my hair and something to wear."

Suddenly graceless, almost childlike, and while the pout remained, Katherine acquiesced. And then her eyes lit up. "Oh, but you must have a bath. That big strapping man of yours won't want a road-weary bride in his bed on his wedding night."

"A bath would be most welcome," Ada allowed, feeling as if she were much older than this woman.

"You've probably already lain with him?" Katherine shocked her again. Reading Ada's blush with a sly grin, she added, "I knew it. It was the way he was watching you, all heated glares, undressing you with his eyes."

"Oh, my." Ada had no other words for Katherine's assumptions and opinions, but somehow was still not put off, but rather entertained.

"You probably wouldn't share him?"

No longer entertained, Ada's eyes widened. Her jaw dropped for the second time in this woman's company. She managed only a very firm, "I would not." And then wondered at the vehemence in her own voice.

"I would not either, were I you."

Admittedly, Ada was thankful when Jamie showed himself only a few minutes later. She jumped up from the plush chair, but Jamie only asked if she needed anything from her bundled belongings.

Katherine answered. "She will not. I've the perfect wedding gown in mind."

Jamie looked to Ada, who tried to convey with her eyes that she was beginning to think the woman was batty. But he seemed not to understand and only announced that he and Roger were for the village, to find the priest.

"You can be ready by sundown?" He asked.

"Aye," Ada said with a sigh, for his lack of help.

Jamie stepped fully into the room and stood before Ada, having misread her meaningful look. "Almost too late for second thoughts, lass."

Ada shook her head. "No such thing," she assured him. Movement next to her showed that Katherine had come to her feet and now stood very close to Jamie and Ada, watching them. Jamie considered her, with only a fleeting curious frown before he was off, with a promise to see Ada next before the priest.

AS GOOD AS HIS WORD, Jamie stood with the collected cleric—Father Edmund, a man who struck Jamie as being ill-at-ease in the long black robes—and waited while Wallace fetched Ada.

He felt they'd been successful and had swayed the MacBriar to their cause earlier. The oversized and sickly man, who hadn't risen from his bed in months, he'd told them, had not ever declared for England, but neither had he necessarily supported Scotland's want of freedom. But he might do so now, Jamie and Wallace believed, and was kind enough to allow them to stay the night—"but not no more, dear sirs," he'd said after some wracking cough, "lest you put a target on my own head as well"—and had been agreeable to their request to see the wedding performed at Hawick House, with little ceremony.

Jamie looked down upon his person, double-checking the pleats in his fresh plaid, aligning one fold with more care. He swiped at the sleeve of his blue tunic, the best he owned, and then ran his fingers through his newly-shorn hair. Roger had assisted him, as there was no barber to be found in town, chopping away at the length, and then—as Wallace had laughed—saying, "Aye, shite, and now I'll needing to hack off more to even it out."

So it was, that his fingers barely found any hair to run through, which felt unfamiliar to him; however, he couldn't say he did not appreciate the lightness of it, even as he suspected his ears might often be cold going forward.

And then all thoughts of his own person and appearance were forgotten as Wallace stepped out onto the landing, his raised hand bringing Ada into view.

Next to him, Will stood, and his tail wagged.

Jamie nearly gasped, and shifted on his feet, settling his hand onto the hilt of his sword.

"Would you look at her..." Roger sighed next to him, no small admiration in his tone.

The Lady MacBriar had seen to it that the unkempt hall was at least lighted well for the nuptials, which cast the entire room into shades of gold. So here came Ada, dressed in a provocative kirtle of white, with some gold threads shimmering in the glow of a dozen tapers. The gown was nearly indecently low but oh, so alluring, rendering Jamie breathless for the space of a second. He swallowed as Wallace led her down the stairs, embracing the role of proud patriarch. She tipped her head, to watch her footfalls, showing him the circlet of flowers that adorned her otherwise unarranged hair, save that the sides seemed to be held away from her face. But Jamie's eyes were drawn again to the gown, being so close-fitting it might have been made only for her, the sleeves long and hugging her lean arms, the bodice snug and low. While Jamie welcomed wholly the display of cleavage offered to him, and while he knew in loftier circles, this would not at all be construed as daring, he was surprised that Ada had been willing to show so much of her scarring. The swell of her breast above the pinched seam of the gown showed to one and all much of the abuse she'd suffered. But Jamie saw only those breasts, pictured them once again in his hands, naked to his gaze.

He'd never thought much of the simpering fools who showed such weakness as to allow their fondness written so plainly on their faces, but felt a slow smile crease his face just as William guided Ada to his side. He met her gaze and was sure that every bride's hope was found in her eyes, and it was no hardship to answer her unspoken question. "You have taken my breath away."

All at once, she seemed to breathe, and relax. Her gaze lifted to his hair, that Jamie found himself now holding his breath until she smiled, with her own appreciation. "You clean up right nice, sir."

The priest began the ceremony, his monotone words intimating he might rather be home, in front of a warm fire, mayhap with his own hound at his heels, but Jamie did not care. And he allowed only a passing recollection of his first wedding, so very different from this, elaborate and false, promising himself he'd not make the same mistakes he had with his first wife.

He took Ada to wife to protect her, because he was indebted to her. And, as he'd said to her, there was much more he wanted to know and to enjoy of her body. But he would go away again, he would revisit the war, and he was unlikely to return to Aviemore so very many times, if at all. He wouldn't allow himself to become attached to her, no matter that he was utterly intrigued by her person, and enormously fascinated by her body. Their marriage would likely be of a short duration; they needn't wrap themselves up in it, or worse, get lost in it.

FOR THE THIRD TIME that day, Ada tried to coax the immoral bodice of her borrowed gown up over her breasts. She caught Katherine's sly eye across the table and dropped her hands at the woman's impatient shaking of her head. She hadn't actually agreed to wear the gown but had been rather shimmied into it by an eager Katherine after a bath in perfumed and heated water. Of course, she'd been appalled first at the amount of skin it showed and then at the quantity of scars it displayed. But she was a woman, and she could not ever recall a dress this fine, the fabric sumptuous, the bodice embroidered with golden threads. And with Katherine's insistence that it was certainly not in poor taste, Ada had acquiesced. If she'd had any idea how often she would be in jeopardy of spilling out of the thing, she'd have refused it outright.

Just as she fussed with her daring décolletage once again, Jamie leaned over to her and whispered, "It's perfect. Leave it be."

Ada tilted her head up to him and in an equally quiet voice responded, "I thought the dress exquisite, but the display questionable. Katherine insisted you would not be put off by my disfigurement being so openly—" Ada stopped, actually going pale at the darkness that entered his gaze. "

With his face very close to her and his voice given so that only she could hear, he said with a scowl, "My wife is no disfigured. Dinna say that ever again."

Ada did not know what purpose compelled his words. They were fierce, as if the slight had come from another. As he did not move, appeared only to await a response, she nodded briefly and removed her eyes from him. She knew it was silly, she'd chided herself about this very thing many times over the past year; just because she took her gaze away from a person didn't mean they also removed their gaze from her face, from her scars. Not seeing them look at her didn't mean they did *not* look at her. Her cheeks pinkened under his continued heated perusal.

My wife.

Ada sighed. She glanced around the table, that earlier-noted broken one, which William Wallace himself had put to rights. Only she and Jamie and Wallace and Roger, and naturally, their host, Lady Katherine, sat round the linen topped trestle table. Whoever it was in the kitchen who'd had a hand in those perfectly moist sweet breads Ada had sampled upon their arrival, had by some miracle managed to put out a feast after all. The table was laden with three kinds of game and fish, more of those sweet breads, a mouthwatering pottage amazingly loaded with vegetables, and cups of wine that seemed to magically always be full.

William Wallace was jovial, livelier than Ada had ever seen him, actually flirting with Katherine, whom Ada realized was not immune to either the giant's smooth words or his overfriendly hands.

From his seat next to Wallace, Roger met Ada's gaze, now removed from the unlikely pair, giving a humored grin at this happenstance. He then engaged Jamie in some debate over a weapon he called a *falchion*, which Roger explained to Ada combined the weight and power of an ax with the versatility of a sword.

"Has no reach," Jamie scoffed, defending his use of a broadsword.

"But the power!" Roger exclaimed, and added, "And a useful tool outside of battles."

Jamie shrugged. "They're generally cheaply made, and you'll find the power is impractical when the blade snaps off inside your enemy."

Strangely, Roger guffawed at this, and then wondered at Jamie's views on the stiletto knife, whose thin pointed blade, he was sure, might wreak havoc against the English's liking of chain mail.

Ada was happy to sit back and listen, letting the warmth of the bitter wine soothe her nerves, happy to steal glances at her husband.

Her husband.

She was wed now to Jamie MacKenna. And wasn't he so brilliantly handsome today, with his fresh cut hair and clean shaven face? He wore a blue tunic, one she hadn't noticed before, which brightened the magnetic blue of his eyes, even within the dimness of the hall.

She listened to his voice, hypnotized by the deep cadence of his words, and blinked several times, guessing the wine must surely be more potent than the usual ale. After a while, Jamie, who was still in conversation with the very affable Roger, slid his arm behind her, along the back of her chair. Ada smiled sleepily and leaned her head onto his shoulder.

It was a very good day.

She hadn't realized she'd said any words aloud, until her husband ducked his head at the sound and asked her to repeat herself.

But she could only smile, hardly recalling what she might have said, and lifted a hand to his smooth cheek. Her smile widened. "I have a very handsome husband."

Laughter followed this pronouncement and Ada swung her gaze around to the blurry wedding guests. "Oh my."

"Oh my, indeed," said Jamie, standing from his chair. "And I have a very intoxicated bride," he surmised, inspiring more chuckles, and used both his hands to pull Ada to her feet.

She stood, weightless and airy, smiling still, hoping Jamie might kiss her again. He did not, instead scooped her into his arms, as if she weighed no more than a sack of grain, holding her close against his chest, with one arm around her back and another tucked under her knees.

As Jamie called a cheery good night to the others, Ada waved a hand over her head, having some idea now that he took them up those narrow steps and into the chambers they'd been given for the night.

He laid her on the bed, the very spot where hours ago she'd sat to don the delicate silk hose Katherine had gifted her.

"I like wine," she cooed, flopping her hands onto her belly.

"Aye, I can see that." Oh, but she loved the sound of Jamie's chuckle.

"I feel very safe."

"'Tis good." Ada couldn't be sure if she heard laughter still in his voice. He was removing his sword, she knew that sound, was used to it by now. She liked the familiarity of it. When next she was aware of Jamie, he was lifting the hem of her gown up over her knees and untying the thin garters that held up her hose. Tilting her head on the very thick pillow, Ada looked down at Jamie, just as he stripped the smooth silk from one leg, being very leisurely in this endeavor. Ada's gaze was rooted to his hands, his fingers gliding along down her thigh and over her knee. Her gaze adjusted, beyond her own legs, and realized Jamie had removed his own clothing already.

"My husband hasn't any clothes."

"My wife is about to lose hers." He removed the hose from her other leg in much the same manner, slowly and tantalizingly. The sleepiness and slight drunkenness evaporated swiftly, her eyes widening and her body reacting already to his hands so adoringly upon her.

Jamie stood and collected her hands, pulling her to her feet. He cupped her face and kissed her soundly, delving into her wetness with his tongue. His hands slid downward, across her throat and over her breast. Ada shivered. Those hands moved further still, pulling at the ribbons tied about her gown, pushing the kirtle off her shoulders, leaving it suspended at her waist. Pulling back, he glanced down, and Ada suspected she heard something akin to a groan escape him as he lifted both breasts, pushing their fullness together, while only her thin chemise remained to separate their flesh. He lowered his head, his mouth landing atop the mounds, his hands then lifting to slide the chemise straps off her shoulders. Ada watched him, her hands coursing through his short hair as he kissed the bare flesh of the top of her bosom. When his lips touched her nipple through the fabric of her sheer chemise, Ada tipped her head back, her mouth forming a silent *O*. He suckled her nipple, first one and then the other and Ada thought she might die a gorgeous death right then and there.

Inserting his thumbs between her hips and the gowns, he pushed them lower and soon the garments slid off her slim body, his hands easing them down over her hips. They pooled about her feet. Having followed with his body the descent of her gown, Jamie was now on one knee. He lifted her foot and swept the fabrics out from under her while Ada kept one hand on his wide shoulders to steady herself. He pressed moist kisses on her shin and her knee and her thigh and higher, upon her belly and again her breast, taking the nipple between his teeth, and suckling then that Ada was quite sure she couldn't have recalled her name had someone asked.

He steered her backward as he kissed her, until her legs touched the bed frame. But he didn't lay her down, only separated again, as if just now desirous only of looking at her. While his hands remained on her hips, Ada reached out to take his hardness in her grasp. Seemingly absorbed by her inquisitiveness, he allowed her slow moving fingers to touch him, making him even harder.

"Jesus," he rasped, a jagged sound undoing the silence.

She looked up at him, but his eyes were closed. When he opened them, his gaze was bright and heated. She took him more firmly, circling him after a moment of exploration about the head. The corners of his mouth lifted as he did now move her backward, so that she sat down. He tipped his head toward the headboard and Ada released him and slid back on the soft mattress. Jamie came over her, his hands on the bed on either side of her, pushing her onto her back as he joined his lips to hers. He delved deep with his tongue, teasing and tasting, while his body settled fully atop her.

Ada whimpered in delight at the feel of his hot skin touching so many parts of her. She wrapped her arms around him, accustomed now to that whirling sensation inside her that made her want to move against him, move certain parts against him. She flexed her hips experimentally. His approving groan, delivered into her mouth, told her the action was good indeed and so she began to do it with a rhythm her body craved, against that ever growing part of him.

Jamie's lips left her own, trailing kisses about and around her neck, suckling and licking, his teeth nibbling at her ear. He shifted upon her, lowering himself to reach her breasts, flicking the hardened peaks with his tongue before taking one nipple fully into his mouth, drawing it harder, eliciting a moan from her. Moving ever so slightly off her, their bodies still touching from top to bottom, one hand moved along the outline of her, tracing a delicious pattern along her shoulder, over the well-loved breast, across her belly and hip, to rest lightly on her mound. This simple touch alone, barely set upon the curly dark hair, sent Ada nearly off the mattress.

Of their own accord, her legs fell open to him, and those masterful fingers moved further, to the very center of her. Completely bereft now of any faculties, Ada writhed against his hand, her eyes closed to such blissful torment as this, and she began to move her hips and bottom in a relation suited to his motion. She was aware, and then not, of a building force inside her, begging for relief, making her dance in time to him, making her cry out softly, making her arch her back for more.

One finger slid inside her, bringing out a larger cry, opening her eyes to find him watching her face. In his eyes, she sensed a hunger about him, the same longing she grappled with now, and reached for him, cupping his face, drawing him near, kissing him wildly, wanting more.

Jamie covered her again, settling between her legs, rubbing that hardness against her while he kissed her senseless yet more.

She felt his erection touch her where only seconds ago his deft fingers had, but he did not go further. Instinctively, she moved her hips against him, her heightened awareness telling her that she wanted this above all else.

"Inside me," she begged, her voice sounding unfamiliar to her own ears.

He nodded, kissing her again, and said against her lips, "But slowly."

Her head moved back and forth. She didn't want slow, she wanted whatever his touch made her crave more than breath right at this moment.

Her husband chuckled hoarsely. "Slowly, lass, to make it last."

Finally, he began to enter her.

"Oh, bless you," she breathed against his lips, the fullness inside her allowing for only short gasps, her words provoking another chuckle from Jamie.

She moaned aloud as he slid deeper.

Jamie crooned, his mouth against hers, "I like your passion, lass."

"I like you inside me." Deep inside she felt him reach, felt their bodies grinding against one another, felt again that ascending need for something more. "Oh, this feels very good indeed," she told him truthfully then, pressing her lips to kiss his shoulder and his neck, her hands finding leverage against the stone hardness of his arms.

Soon, they moved as one, Ada answering each of Jamie's thrusts with a rising of her hips. She liked how his chest brushed against her hard nipples every time he surged forward into her. He increased his speed, pumping into her, harder and faster while she continued to respond to his rhythm, her small tapered nails digging into his triceps. She gasped as pleasure, pure and explosive, crashed over her. Her senses spun as the shock of it scorched her body, surrendering completely to this only recently discovered ecstasy. Minutes later, Jamie cried out, gruffly, and she thought he might be experiencing this intoxicating rush as well, aware that he throbbed inside her now as he had not before.

After a moment, he stilled, collapsing on top of her. She loved the weight of him covering her. Her arms surrounded him, tightening, while her body rejoiced. There was a tingling about her fingertips and toes, about her lips as well, but Ada was otherwise too numb with pleasure to afford it any great consideration. When Jamie lifted his head, she smiled serenely at him, and closed her eyes briefly while he pressed a small kiss to her cheek.

Several minutes later, just before sleep might have claimed her, her eyes opened wide, and Ada bucked against him. Ignoring his confused expression, she scrambled out from under him and thankfully found the gaily painted chamber pot, barely in time to empty her stomach of the wine she only had for the first time tonight.

She moaned again, this time in despair, naked upon the floor, only vaguely aware that her husband had come to her, had gathered her hair to hold it out of the way as she retched again.

"Ah, *Jesu*," he murmured, sounding not at all sympathetic, but very angry, so that Ada felt tears flow as well.

She had no idea that her husband was seeing for the first time the damage done to her back by the scoundrel, John Craig.

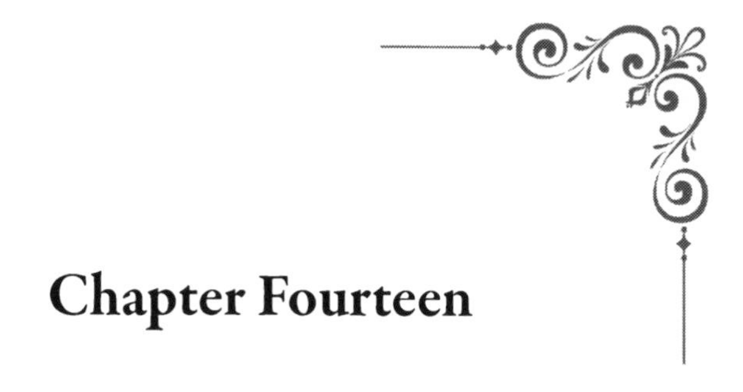

Chapter Fourteen

When Ada woke the next morning, she was naked still, her head ached, and her husband was gone. She sat up slowly, her fingers at her temples. Immediately, she closed her eyes against the onslaught of daylight, pushing the heavy wool coverlet off her legs.

"No, Ada Annabel," she chided herself, "that is probably not the way you intended to start your marriage." Letting out a frustrated growl, she opened her eyes and rose from the bed. It was then she realized that if, indeed, her husband had left, he had since returned. Jamie lounged casually in the doorway, his shoulder propped against the doorjamb, his arms crossed over his chest, and his grin decidedly entertained.

Her first thought was not that she was, again, completely naked before him, while he was fully clothed, apparently ready to leave. Her first thought was that she'd only just humiliated herself more, having now been caught talking to herself.

"Annabel," he said, seeming to test the sound of the name. "Ada Annabel. Is it Ada or Annabel?"

Ada was not at all immune to the playfulness she spied in his gaze, but answered, "My name is Ada Annabel, actually." When he lifted a brow, she explained, "Apparently, my father and mother could not agree on a name," she started, but quickly faltered.

Jamie MacKenna was not attending her explanation at all. He was quite content to rake his gaze over all of her naked body. Slowly. And honestly, quite seductively, that Ada only mumbled the rest. "So I was given both."

She said no more, but he was still doing things to her body with his eyes that might right quick make her forget her embarrassment, and any and all former embarrassments. She knew a blush rose, she knew her nipples had come to peaks for him. She struggled not to cover her breasts, or other parts.

Finally, he met her gaze, giving her the laziest of smiles, telling her unequivocally he was absolutely not thinking about her missteps. After another moment, Jamie pushed himself away from the door and clapped his hands together. "Get dressed, lass. We'll be ready shortly."

And then he was gone.

Ada's shoulders fell. She stared at the open and empty doorway, wondering what had just happened that she felt achy and wanton just now. Could a man—Jamie—do that to her with only his eyes? Good Lord!

Shaking off the effects of what he had wrought within her, Ada dressed quickly in her plain brown wool kirtle and donned her own heavy hose and her gray cloak. With great efficiency, born of many a day in that shack in the woods, she twisted her hair around her hand and used a scrap of linen to hold it away from her face.

She spent some time neatening the gown Katherine had lent to her, lamenting the fact that it was not to be hers, then left the chambers and found her way back down to the hall.

Katherine stood with William Wallace and Roger, near the door. Bracing herself, Ada marched on, hoping there wasn't anything that she could not recall from last night that she didn't even know she should be mortified by.

"Good morning, Lady Katherine, sirs."

Katherine disengaged her hand from Roger's and took up both of Ada's. "I truly wish you did not have to ride away so quickly."

"I, as well. I do not know how to thank you for the kindness you have shown me. You made a very impromptu wedding into a memorable occasion. I am indebted to you."

Katherine kissed each of Ada's cheeks, which suggested she was so much higher born that Ada herself. "Honestly, it was my pleasure. I've already assured Sir William that he will always be welcome at Hawick House, and I extend the same to you, dear Ada."

"Thank you."

And while the gentlemen seemed yet to have more to say to the woman, Ada excused herself and stepped out into the yard.

Jamie was just lifting the saddle onto his mighty steed. Will pranced around, trying to engage the immobile horse into play. Ada walked over to Jamie and began speaking, which turned him around, and showed his mesmerizing blue eyes to her. She was hard pressed to understand how it could have been only minutes ago that his eyes had stirred her to passion. Only his eyes.

"I seem to be often apologizing to you," she said, stone-faced. When he only raised a brow, she explained, "First, for misjudging you, and then, argh—" she covered her face in her hands "—for striking out at you, something for which I will never forgive myself." Heaving a great sigh, she lowered her hands and faced him, squaring her shoulders, determined to get it done. "And now, for imbibing too much on our wedding night. I feel

I've...I hope I did not bring you shame." And because she was nervous, and because he was only staring at her, looking neither angry nor exactly cheery, she babbled, "But I've never had wine before and though it was simple, honestly the entire evening seemed rather magical. And I was thinking that I—"

He kissed her. Ada felt a smile against her lips. Kiss, or smile, didn't matter. It effectively silenced her.

"Lass, if I had a coin—even a wooden one—for every bride who overindulged on her wedding night, I'd be a rich man." He walked around the horse and cinched up the straps to the saddle.

"Truly?"

And now he chuckled. "Truly." Shrugging, he tossed the saddlebags over the back of the horse, tying those straps now. "My father was a great man, Ada," he said over his shoulder. "Once we're at Aviemore, I'll tell you more about him, and you'll hear and learn about him from his people. I wish I could recall every bit of wisdom he ever gave me. Alas, I can no. But one nugget stands out." He faced her again, their belongings secure. He struck his hands onto his hips and grinned at her. "This one nugget had to do with how he dealt with my mother—a great lady, but a strong one, too. My father told me, '*You pick your battles, son. Choose the hill you want to die on—no every hill is to be your grave.*' Having too much wine on our wedding night is no my hill, lass. Dinna let it be yours."

Ada absorbed this. Then, with some thoughtfulness, she told him, "You are so much nicer than you look."

Jamie stared at her, rather nonplussed, before he threw his head back and shouted out a wild laugh. "I ken you're no trying to insult your husband, lass, but for the life of me, I canna be sure."

"No. No, I only meant that you *appear* so... hard and mean, so intimidating—often apurpose, I believe. Yet, you've never been anything but kind to me." And because he seemed still so very amused, Ada shrugged and concluded, "Laugh all you want, I'm sure I've made the better bargain here." She stepped closer to the horse, waiting for Jamie to lift her into the saddle.

He closed in on her, his hands leaving his hips to cup her face, a gesture that Ada was accustomed to, one that she liked very much. She rather sighed as he said, "Was no a bargain, lass. 'Tis a good match for both, aye?" She nodded and then he ruined those very lovely words by adding, "Save for when my bride drinks too much wine."

His grin was downright devilish. Ada chose to allow him his fun; it was worth it, to glimpse that boyish grin of his.

Wallace and Roger exited the keep then and Ada remembered that they would be parting ways. Sir William said farewell to Ada first, taking her hands in his and giving them a squeeze.

"Off to Aviemore you tread, lass."

Ada reached up and kissed his cheek. "It has been my honor, sir, to have met you and have kept company with you."

"The honor is mine, Lady MacKenna. God willing, we will meet again."

Smiling and nodding, Ada wished him Godspeed and then accepted Roger's farewell, hoping that these men met with continued success in their recruiting endeavors, and then the battles to come.

She was not surprised to see Jamie and Wallace exchange a long embrace, with Wallace whispering something into Jamie's ear that had her husband nodding. Knowing still too little about her husband, she did appreciate that he kept company with such fine people as Wallace and Roger and the Kincaid, assuming that it spoke to his own character.

Soon she and Jamie were settled onto his massive destrier, turning left outside the gates of Hawick House, while Wallace and Roger headed east. With one last wave around Jamie's shoulder, Ada faced forward again, and settled in for another long day in the saddle, with Aviemore as their next stop.

But Will's barking caught her attention, as it seemed to grow further away. Ada pivoted and saw that the hound was following Wallace, and that he was pointing at her and Jamie, trying to get Will to chase them instead.

"Will! Come!" Ada called as Jamie spun the horse around.

All three men stopped and turned their mounts to face each other, with a fair amount of space between them. Will sat and stared longingly up at Wallace, who could not help the smile he sent down to the wolfhound.

"Go on, you silly beast," Wallace said, but only half-heartedly.

Even from the distance, Ada could well discern the lightness about the giant, William Wallace, unable to hide his pleasure at being favored by Will. For so long, Will had been her most trusted and steadfast companion. She couldn't imagine having survived the winter without him. Everyone should be so lucky to have a companion such as he, quiet and adoring and strong.

Though she feared it might well break her heart, Ada called across the space, "You'll take good care of him?"

Wallace's eyes met hers. The look he gave her, his great blue eyes warmed and alight with pleasure, told her it was the right decision to make. She smiled back at him. "Godspeed, Sir William."

He bowed his head and sent her a truly thankful glance. "And to you, Lady MacKenna."

The men yanked on the reins then and turned again to their routes. Ada heard Wallace's voice. "Come on then, dear Will."

True, a sadness did blanket her. But Jamie tightened his arm around her and kissed the top of her head. "You are a fine lass, Lady MacKenna."

After a while, when she was sure she would not cry, she mused aloud, "Lady MacKenna." She hadn't considered this when she'd married Jamie.

"Agnes Nairn will show you how to go about it, taking charge of the household," Jamie advised.

"Will Agnes Nairn resent my coming, essentially taking her position?" Ada asked, happy to have her thoughts diverted from losing Will.

"She's no like that. Very practical, she is. Like as no, she felt rather wheedled into the job, as there was no one else at the time."

"I'll try to make you proud," she said, determined to learn quickly.

"Were Wallace still with us, lass, he'd cut right in now and tell you to make your own self proud. That's all you ever need worry about."

Ada considered this. Was she proud of herself? Others, she supposed, would tell her she should be. But they would attach this to her time at Dornoch, for having survived it. Ada wasn't sure pride was the feeling she would consign to having survived John Craig's treachery. And what else had she done, to have pride in herself? Her life, as a whole, struck her as completely unremarkable up to this point. She would give this some thought, to find something that would give her value, if only for herself.

Jamie's voice broke into her reverie.

"Lass, why did you come with me?"

She knew immediately that he referred to her agreeing, so spontaneously, to leaving Stonehaven with him. She believed she'd figured out the answer to this, just took a moment now to put it into words. "I'm not sure you'll appreciate this response, but it's all I have to give. I think I did it because of Will—not the hound. I knew him only for hours, but he is never far from me, from my thoughts. I guess it must have something to do with going through something so...traumatic, maybe some bond is formed."

She let that settle, gathered more words then. "When Anice told me you were leaving, I was so upset. First—naturally—because of how I had treated you. But underneath that, I was so afraid to lose the only connection I had to Will. Even when I hated you, I was...drawn to you, because of him." He remained silent for so long, she felt compelled to ask, "Did—did you expect a different answer?"

"Nae. I dinna ken what to expect."

"You knew Will, obviously better than I. Do you think he'd be happy...with this? Us?"

"I dinna ken about that, lass, but it makes me wonder now, did you wed with me to please Will?"

Did she? "You married me because you felt you owed me the protection of your name. And, of course, for the...." She searched her vocabulary, only knowing ill-mannered words for what she wanted to say.

"It's called lovemaking."

"For that as well. Is it so awful if I wed you, hoping to somehow keep Will's memory with me?"

"Comes off as a wee bit macabre."

Ada sighed. "I didn't think you would understand." Maybe she did not exactly comprehend it, either. While she did not care very much for his opinion, she could not quite read his tone to say there was definite disapproval. "You make it sound wrong."

"Nae, lass. It's no that. My memories of Will are pierced with guilt and shame, for having failed him. What was done to you at Dornoch is perhaps made bearable by you keeping him close. Aye, and he was a great man, and a great friend, so 'tis fitting. He would be well pleased to serve as your anchor."

Ada was rather startled by her immediate reaction to this. She hadn't known Jamie MacKenna very long at all, despite the fact that he was now her husband. Indeed, the majority of her thoughts about him over the past year had been negative, in fact leaned toward violent at times. Yet, just as he'd said he believed Will would be pleased to be her anchor, the initial response, inside her head, had been, *You are my anchor.*

This disarmed her, so much so that she was thankful she had not spoken this aloud.

Huddling deeper into the folds of her cloak, Ada nestled further into Jamie's warm arms and turned over this new revelation in her mind.

They traveled at a slightly faster pace than they had over the last several days, only stopping once to see to personal needs and give the horse a rest, so that Aviemore came into view well before the sun set that evening. It was, actually, the first keep or building of any kind they had seen today, owing to the remoteness of the MacKenna lands.

Jamie reined in just as they crested the tail of a steep crag. He pointed out over the amazing view, swinging Ada's gaze beyond the gray rock directly beneath them and over the fawn colored rolling landscape, across a sun-silvered loch and to a mountain in the distance, whose peak touched the fast-moving clouds. At the base of the mountain, upon a scrap of earth which jutted out into the loch, stood Aviemore. A massive curtain wall of red sandstone flanked two sides of the castle, the north and the west where it faced the mountain, the ends of these fringed with square towers four stories high.

"The northwest tower," Jamie said, into her ear, referring to the tower in the corner of the L shaped wall, "is the Dougal Tower, named for my grandfather, who built the wall. That tower is seven stories high. The entire wall is twelve feet thick. You see the gate house, in the middle of the north part? The barracks in that wall can house one hundred men. The parapet walk, above the crenels, connects all three towers."

"It's so remarkable," said Ada, in awe of the splash of color the red stone presented against the background of the gray and brown mountain. "But why is there no wall on these two sides?"

"It's no necessary with the loch, just wide enough that no trebuchet could send anything, rocks or fire, so far across."

The keep itself was not connected to, but stood close inside that curtain wall, its north and west walls being parallel to the outer wall. Ada imagined the courtyard within to be about the size of Stonehaven's. She noted that to the east and west of the loch and the castle were scattered dozens of cottages, only a few here and there grouped together. 'Twas not then, precisely, a village, but rather a smattering of people who made their homes in the shadow of Aviemore.

Excitedly, she pointed to a herd of deer, coming out of the trees to their immediate right, at the base of the crag on which they perched.

"They come 'round sunset often, will drink at the loch, chew the grasses and shrubs and heather near it. Every one of them has antlers," he noted and explained, "a bachelor herd."

Jamie clicked his tongue and sent his steed carefully down this side of the crag. They skirted around the loch to the left, Ada noting the brown packed earth of this worn trail. From the tail of that crag where she was first shown Aviemore, until they'd ridden around half the loch to find the gate took almost twenty minutes. Ada was weary and suddenly nervous. The people of Aviemore might rejoice at the return of their chief, but would they accept his mutilated and unknown wife? Without thinking, she clasped both hands to Jamie's forearm at her midsection when they approached the gate.

Ada tipped her head back, into Jamie's chest, to take in the height and breadth of the fifty foot high wall. This showed her a thick-helmed soldier glancing down at them.

"Chief?" The man called, and without waiting a response, disappeared from view and soon a call followed, "Raise the portcullis! Open the gate!"

The portcullis, a latticed grill of metal, began to rise, revealing it's pointed ends as they were lifted from the earth. Even before this had been completely lifted, the wooden doors, half the height of the wall, were pulled open and Jamie dug his heels into the horse's flanks to urge him forward.

Ada scanned the bailey as they entered, boasting a well in the center, and several persons come to greet their laird. Ada recognized the smithy's barn and the stables, on the ground floor of the outer wall. She supposed the free standing round building, with its pointed roof, sitting just at the end of the northeast wall, might be the dovecote.

Jamie dismounted and grinned up at her, "Are you ready for this, lass?"

Ada tried to smile, about to lift the hood of her cloak up onto her head, to put her cheeks into shadow.

Jamie swept her out of the saddle, hands at her waist, before she could cover herself. He stood her on the ground, with her back against the horse, and lowered his head to her, meeting her gaze. "Remember lass, my bride is no disfigured. She is beautiful."

Weeks later, when she looked back upon this moment, Ada would come to believe that this was when she fell in love with Jamie MacKenna. But just now, she could only manage a tepid smile, digging deep for that bravery he'd previously claimed to have seen in her.

Jamie turned then and met those who came, soldiers all. He took Ada's hand and drew her toward the keep, even as he bid greetings but put off so many of their questions with a promise to tell of his travels of the past year come supper time.

The keep itself was a wide and tall building, rectangular in shape, accessible by a set of stairs that raised a person off the ground floor and onto the first, setting them directly into the hall. And this, Ada discovered, was unlike anything she had ever seen. Possessed of the usual high vaulted ceiling, it also boasted a gallery, which circled the entire hall, two floors above it seemed, and was protected by a carved and crenellated waist high railing.

Ada spun in a circle to take in all of it.

Jamie explained, "That's the third floor gallery—my grandfather was a wee bit fanciful. There are four corridors up there, which lead away from the gallery in four directions, toward the family quarters."

"How astonishing."

With no small amount of pride, Jamie admitted, "There's really nothing like it."

As they had entered the south end of this long hall, the hearth stood at the opposite outer wall, with the laird's table directly in front of it, this being a thickly carved wooden masterpiece. The chairs of the table, with their backs to the fire, were all high backed and carved as well, the center one, the laird's chair, being easily twice the size of any other.

When Ada had looked her fill, she wondered at the lack of greeting, as no person as of yet approached them inside the keep. Jamie, seemingly untroubled by this, turned as a soldier entered, one who had not been part of the group in the yard that had welcomed their chief.

"Callum!" He called heartily and strode forward, clasping forearms with the man.

Despite Jamie's words, Ada kept her head lowered while she considered the man who Jamie was apparently pleased to see. He was as tall as her husband, but broader, and could easily claim twice as many years, she guessed. His hair was dark and long, as Jamie's had been, brushing the MacKenna plaid angled across his shoulder. Weathered skin creased around his eyes and mouth as he greeted Jamie, and he showed a row of crooked but very white teeth when he smiled at something her husband said.

Jamie turned then and led the man to her.

Just as Ada was sure there was something familiar about him, just as his aged face seemed to show a similar reaction, Jamie said, "Callum, you remember the lass from Dornoch?"

The man's bottom lip fell open, but Jamie's words also proved to Ada that she did indeed know him. He was one of the persons she'd released from the dungeon.

Jamie said, "This is Ada Moncriefe—MacKenna," he corrected quickly. "We were wed only yesterday. Ada, meet Callum Penry, captain of the MacKenna army."

She smiled shyly, extending her hand. "How do you do?"

To his credit, his initial reaction to her scars, before Jamie had mentioned Dornoch, had been polite, almost sympathetic as he'd grazed the entirety of her face right quickly. Once Dornoch had been revealed, he studied her keenly, making a careful examination of each mark on her face and neck. His expression never changed, save for a cord bulging in his neck, hinting at clenched teeth.

Callum Penry amazed her by taking her hand and dropping to one knee. Much as a faithful subject might pay homage to their king, Callum bent his head over her slim hand and closed his eyes. He did not kiss her hand, seemed only to embrace it, almost reverently, holding it firmly with both of his and pressing it against his face.

Thoroughly ill at ease by this display, Ada jerked her gaze to Jamie, who only nodded, seeming to say it was her due.

Callum stood then, and still holding her hands, stared directly and intentionally into her eyes. His were kindly and green, as green as the north sea when the sky was gray.

"I—I dinna ken even where to begin," he said, stammering a bit, as staggered by her presence as she was by his response. His voice was thick, rumbling low, and so heavy with a northern dialect, Ada struggled at first to comprehend. "But married now to the lad? 'Tis perfect."

She smiled at this, certainly at Jamie being referred to as the lad.

Vaguely, as explanation for this, Jamie informed her, "Callum was also my sire's captain."

Ada nodded and said to Callum, "Jamie tells me his father was a great man. Seems you might be the perfect person from whom to beg tales, as I mean to learn all I can about my husband's family."

The captain nodded, and was still holding Ada's hand, one large paw underneath, the other patting the top of hers. "Aye, and we'll get to that, lass. But I'll be saying now—that the shock has waned—that I owe you my life and I will lay down my own for yours. I vow to protect you, Ada MacKenna, first and foremost, all my days."

In no way did she want to diminish the significance of his pledge, or the very seriousness in which it was issued, but she undeniably wanted him to understand he owed her nothing, in regard to Dornoch. Tilting her head, she wondered, with only a whisper of a grin, "Would you not have that obligation, sir, merely by means of my status as the MacKenna's wife?"

He stared at her. Thick dark brows, sprinkled a bit with gray as was his mane, furrowed over the green eyes, until he comprehended. Then he threw back his head and howled with laughter, and shouted out, quite merrily, "Aye, lass, but now I'll do it smiling, you ken?" And he turned his head to Jamie, "Aye, now, lad—I like this one!"

"As do I," said Jamie, with his own grin. "But you can release her hand now, aye? That's enough of that." The words were meant to be lighthearted, Ada thought, but in fact Jamie stepped closer and actually removed Ada's hand from his captain's, holding it in his own.

"Jamie MacKenna!" Called another voice.

The three turned toward the hearth wall, where a doorway suggested a corridor began. A woman stood there, hands on her ample hips, an apron covering most of her brown kirtle and her head covered in a cream colored wimple.

"Agnes," Jamie greeted, and the woman moved, almost running across the hall and enveloping Jamie in a great hug. She then took his face in her hands and spent some moments looking him over. "Oh, your uncle will be pleased to see you, lad." And then, to Ada's delight she turned her head back toward the corridor from which she'd come and startled a bird from the rafters with her strident call of, "Malcolm! Show yourself, you daft man! Jamie's home!"

The woman talked quietly then to Jamie, which showed him tipping his head down at her and nodding at whatever she said.

A man came then from the same doorway from whence had come the woman, Agnes. He might have been Jamie's own sire, the resemblance being so striking. Tall and broad shouldered, with hair that likely was once a burnished blond, and eyes as blue as the evening sky, gave any onlooker an idea how Jamie himself might age. One significant difference was his very pronounced limp, the cause of which was the wooden leg he thumped into the timber floor as he strode toward his nephew with a pleased and welcoming grin.

"Aye, and aren't you a sight for these ancient eyes!" He grabbed at Jamie's tunic when he'd reached him, drawing him into a big bear hug. Jamie returned it with equal fervor, patting his uncle on his wide back. Over Jamie's shoulder, Malcolm's gaze fell and stayed on Ada. A frown lowered his brows onto his eyes. "What's this you've brought us?"

Jamie turned, showing the barest hint of a suggestion that he might have, momentarily, forgotten about his wife.

"Ach, but what have I done?" He returned to her, where she stood still with Callum, and collected her to present to his uncle and the woman, Agnes.

"Uncle Malcolm, Aunt Agnes, this is Ada—formerly Moncriefe, now a MacKenna."

Two sets of crinkled, confused eyes stared at her. His aunt recovered first.

"What you've done? Taken a bride?" Agnes gave no effort to hide her thoughts on this, beaming a smile back and forth between Jamie and Ada.

"I did," Jamie said. Ada could not tell if his own answering smile accompanied his response or was only a reaction to his aunt's delight.

Agnes settled her merry gaze on Ada. "Well, come on, then, give us a hug. You're family now."

There was no way Ada would, or could, refuse this. She accepted the older woman's welcome, and her very warm embrace.

"It'll be a feast, then, aye?" Suggested Malcolm. "Now, dinna be stingy, lass. A hug for Uncle Malcolm, too." Ada had barely found release from Agnes when she was taken up in Malcolm's sturdy arms.

"No feast, Uncle," said Jamie. "We had our bride meal, and in fine company, aye, lass?"

No one waited for Ada's response, but reacted forcefully to Jamie's words.

"Ach, you gonna have a feast, lad," argued Malcolm. "Brings good tidings."

Agnes piped in. "And maybe we'll be asking your pretty bride what her choice would be?"

"Oh, but I don't really think—" Ada started.

"Nonsense," Agnes overruled these words as well, in such a jolly manner, Ada could not be upset. "Every bride needs a feast," she said and enunciated the next words with a dip of her head with each syllable, "with her own family."

Ada looked to Jamie. It was his decision to make. She, herself, needed no other banquet by which to celebrate. Holding her gaze, he shook his head, suddenly without his recent good humor.

Because he said nothing aloud, Ada assumed it was left to her to deny this very dear and very excited couple.

"Truly, it is not necessary. We are road weary, Jamie more so than I, I'm sure. Mayhap an announcement at supper this evening would suffice?"

She immediately felt awful, and as if she were solely the cause of their crestfallen expressions.

Callum, bless him, spoke up as Jamie seemed disinclined to do so.

"Agnes, there'll be plenty of time for feasting and plenty to celebrate in the future. The lass is right. She's probably now even dreaming of a good hot bath with that sweet heather soap you ladies are so fond of."

Ada turned a thankful glance to the captain. He winked at her just as Agnes took up with this cause. "Ach, but where are me manners! Aye, aye, come along then, lass. We'll get you settled."

She tugged at Ada's hand and called over her shoulder as she led her away. "Malcolm, set the pots to boiling for her bath."

Chapter Fifteen

Thirty minutes Later, Ada was seated inside a huge wooden barrel tub, not complaining at all that the water was a tad too hot. It felt luxurious, she decided, sliding down so that she rested her head against the lip of the tub, and the as-promised perfumed water settled over her breasts.

Idly, she let her eyes wander around the room that was to be hers. Hers and Jamie's. It was sparsely furnished, offering only the very wide bed; one aged and weathered trunk, the carvings long worn by now; and a cupboard against the wall behind the door, in which Agnes now hung Ada's very meager belongings. Ada would consider this bed the first they would share, having no exact recollection of the bed, or sharing it, on their wedding night. Happily, she did recall the 'lovemaking'.

Agnes, Ada was not surprised, who'd seemed completely immune to the scars she surely must have seen on her face while down in the hall, fussed over Ada's naked body.

"Who made sport on you like that, lass? Why, they're everywhere!"

Ada pulled a face, not sure how much to reveal. Best to begin as you mean to proceed, she thought a wise choice. "Actually, 'twas a man I was betrothed to." She sighed then, awaiting the expected questions that surely must follow.

But Agnes only tsk-ed and said, "Aye, and likely our Jamie got to you just in time."

Ada hadn't the heart to correct her.

"He's always been like that, but you probably ken that by now. Running half-cocked, rescuing this one, and saving that one. Seems the lad canna sleep unless he's done some good that day."

Hoping to steer the subject away from herself and Jamie, Ada asked, "How long have you been at Aviemore, Agnes?"

"Aye, let me see." She'd laid one kirtle on the bed, flattening the folds of the skirt, picking away grass and whatever else had attached itself in their travels. "More than twenty years, to be sure. Maybe closer to twenty-five?" This last, with a shrug, before she lifted her friendly gaze to Ada. "You ken I'm no really his aunt, aye, lass?"

Ada nodded, and grinned to show her she was bothered by this not at all. Who was she to judge?

"I didn't always look like this, lass. Used to be a pretty young thing, like yourself."

"But do you mind me asking, why did you never marry Malcolm?"

"Aye, it's a sin, and dinna I ken it, but he was already married, lass. But she'd gone back to London, from whence all devils come," she said, and crossed herself. "Couldn't stand the cold and rain, said Scotland was 'fit for neither man nor beast'. But aye, how we celebrated when she'd gone." And she giggled—cackled, really—and used her apron to cover her cheeks at such impertinence. "Aye, and wasn't it the same twenty years later when Jamie took his first wife? She come from the south. Just the same as England, you ask me. Too drafty, she thought, and too wild, she said, always looking down her nose at us. Ran the poor lad in circles, she did, and all the complaining, still had no problem spreading her legs for whatever walked by, pardon and all, my lady."

Ada could only stare, now at Agnes's back as she attended again shaking out the wrinkles in the two spare kirtles, shocked as she was by this carelessly given news. Jamie had been married once before? She supposed first, that it made sense—he was laird of a large number of people and a great house in the highlands, and he was almost thirty, she had assumed. But...he should have told her, shouldn't he have?

Agnes turned, caught the look of astonishment that had drained all the color from her face.

"Ach, you dinna ken, did you?" And she grimaced, her usually cheery mouth widening as it was pulled. "Now, dinna fash, lass. She's gone and away for good and ain't nobody missing her."

Not even Jamie? Ada wondered.

"Gone where?"

"Dead, and with her babe," came the answer, which made Ada gasp and brought her hand over her mouth, with this distress, that Jamie had lost a child. She was quickly corrected, "Wasn't the lad's bairn—he hadn't been home in more than a year at the time. Likely, she could no even name the sire. Never did, at any rate, expecting us all to believe we're waiting on a wee MacKenna to come."

"She was not a nice person," Ada concluded.

Agnes harrumphed loudly, and with raised brows and puckered lips. "Aye, she was no. Never met a more unsuitable bride. Not like you, lass. You're just what Jamie needs, aye, and dinna I ken it?"

Ada tried to smile with this validation, but really could not, not having just learned what she had. She could not help but wonder if this was sometimes, or part of, what often stained his gaze with sorrow.

AVIEMORE, THOUGH GRANDER by far than Stonehaven, didn't house even half as many people, but mayhap just as many soldiers. But Ada was still surprised when she entered the hall for dinner, to find it moderately crowded.

Thankfully, Jamie might have been waiting for her. As she waited, upon the last step at the end of the hall, nervous as ever about meeting new people who would not all be able to stifle their shock or dismay or upset at the sight of her face, Jamie came to collect her. This put her only somewhat at ease. They whispered still. Perhaps word had traveled that they were married. This had Ada imagining they only wondered why this so remarkably handsome man would have taken a bride so horribly disfigured as she.

Ada suddenly wished they were still on the road, with Sir William and Roger, just the four of them. Jamie squeezed her hand and settled a reassuring grin onto her which might also have hinted at an appreciation for her freshened appearance. He led her to the long table before the fireplace. People stood, gathered around the other half dozen tables in the room, and sat all at once only after Jamie had seated Ada and assumed the chief's chair next to her.

"Aunt Agnes take good care of you, lass?" he wondered, rather whispered at her ear.

Ada pivoted toward him, trying to smile. She nodded, but tightly, feeling so much as if she were on display for these people.

Malcolm and Callum came, Malcom taking the chair next to Jamie while Callum sat next to Ada. She was disheartened to see Agnes take a seat upon the bench at one of the common tables.

The tables had already been set with jugs of ale and either pewter or wooden cups. Jamie filled Ada's cup and then his own, and then stood and waited while all around the hall, people likewise poured out the ale.

After a moment, Jamie raised his cup. "I ken you've heard it by now, as word travels fast within the curtain wall, but this here is Ada—Lady Ada, my wife."

Admittedly, the cheer that rose was tepid, while more furtive and frowning peeks were cast her way. Shamed now, Ada settled her eyes on Agnes at the closest table, hoping to maintain only a serene expression. Agnes's face contorted with a fair amount of shock and a bit of dismay at the unenthusiastic reception, her distressed look assisting Ada not at all.

And no one drank, even as Jamie lifted his cup to his lips.

The tips of her husband's fingers of his free hand just grazed the table as he stood next to her and were visible themselves in Ada's periphery. With the silence that followed their lackluster cheer, his fingers began to drum, not softly, upon the table.

Ada bit her lip and she cursed, *damn them all*. And with that, she lifted her chin and began to meet their eyes. *Say it to my face*, she almost dared them.

And then Jamie spoke again. What seeming joy had accompanied his first pronouncement was gone. His tone was unflinching now. Ada could swear she heard his teeth clenching. Even Callum, next to her, turned to look at Jamie.

"Do you ken where I met my bride, your lady?" No one answered. "Aye, I met her at Dornoch Castle in the south of Scotland."

Ada froze, her own teeth clamped now. *Oh, please don't, Jamie*. Her nostrils flared.

"Callum was with me," Jamie said, turning, throwing a hand out vaguely in his captain's direction. He pointed forward then, to a lad. "You were there, Henry." The boy's mouth gaped, his youthful gaze swung to Ada. "You ken the tale, all of you. Callum surely laid out the entire gruesome story. But here it is, the rest of it. Ada Moncriefe did not ken me or mine from the Lord's Adam, but she'd no let the fiend John Craig take another life. She walked down into the dungeon, with no care for her own safety or any consequences, and she set us free." He let this be absorbed. Ada remained tight-lipped at his side. "She asked one boon in return, that we take her with us when we go." He hesitated. Then, "Like as no, you've the next part from Callum as well. He and Henry and I get out. But Ned did not. And Malys did not. And Will did not. And neither did the lass. They killed Ned and Malys quick. When I returned—" he stopped, and turned to Ada, "On my honor, I tried...."

She nodded, keeping her eyes on Agnes, even as she dared not register that woman's expression. She just wanted it done now.

"I could not—did not—return for five days. Will was dead. They'd cut him up as well, but he was fortunate and died sometime that first night. This was done to the lass over the next four days and four nights."

Complete silence gripped the entire hall. Not even candle flames dared to flicker.

"She talked to Will throughout the night."

Ada began to shake her head. *Please stop*. Her hands shook in her lap.

"Hers was the last face he saw, the last kind voice he heard," Jamie said, his hardened tone having softened, as if moved by his own words. "Callum and I and Henry stand here today, because of her."

After a long pause, he lifted his cup again. "To my bride, *your* lady, Ada MacKenna."

The noise then was deafening. It literally shook the rafters, moving the candelabras hung from metal rods. People cheered and screamed and cried, men pounded on tables and lifted their cups and called her name. Next to her, Callum rose to his feet, and the entire hall followed suit, the clamor rising with their bodies from the benches.

Ada never moved, her chin stayed elevated, her eyes remained fixed on Agnes. She could manage no response to their persuaded fervor. Tears fell from Agnes's eyes as she pressed her chafed fingers to her lips and stared back at Ada.

She wasn't quite sure how she succeeded in getting through the meal. The food had no taste, the noise became just a din, the entire room and the faces blurred. As soon as was tolerably polite, she excused herself, claiming a lingering fatigue and found their chambers. She knew when Jamie came to their room that night, felt him slide into the big bed next to her, felt his hand settle on her hip, but kept her back to him and held any further tears, and pretended she slept.

TRUE, SHE WAS ANGRY at Jamie, but she chose to begin the next day fresh, with her husband, and with the people of Aviemore. This was to be her life now, she meant to make it right. She did not want to be known or befriended or have her company sought out solely because of Dornoch. She was more than that. She would show them.

When she considered how Jamie had—however well-intentioned—made her once again feel as if she were a specimen, to be ogled and pitied, his words to her the morning after their wedding came to mind. *No every hill is to be your grave.* She owed him at least this courtesy, this once, to repay his generosity to her.

Aiming for a cheerfulness she had not yet grasped, but determined nonetheless, Ada bounced down the steps and into the hall.

Breakfast was obviously done, so that only a handful of soldiers remained, sitting around one of the trestle tables. To a man, they stood, so quickly in fact the bench on one side was bumped out from the table.

"Good morrow, sirs," she greeted them, though several of them were surely younger than Ada, still lads.

They remained standing, some feet shuffling, some eyes averted, and greeted Ada in return. One man elbowed another, frowning up at his head. He looked up, and quickly doffed his felt hat, scrunching it between his hands at his waist.

She rather hoped they might ask her to join them, as sitting at the family's table, so far removed and by herself, seemed rather silly.

They appeared more tongue-tied than rude, but no one offered her a space at the table. Not quite the auspicious start she'd hoped for, she was about to *ask* if she might join them when she heard Agnes, bustling in from the kitchen. "And here you are, lass. Come on to the kitchen, then, and we'll get you fed. You canna be spending time with these humdrums."

Ada shrugged and smiled at the men and gave a small wave as Agnes led her away. One man, perhaps about Jamie's age, lifted his hand and wiggled his fingers in his own returning wave.

"The lad says you're wanting to learn how to manage Aviemore," said Agnes as they walked through the corridor at the rear of the keep.

"I do. Will that be all right, Agnes? I don't want to step on your toes."

The dim passage opened up into a high, stone-ceilinged room easily half the length of the hall. The kitchen was neither dreary nor bright, but showed daylight streaming into the room from an open rear door. But this fresh air and brightness were quickly attacked by the smoke and steam and grease hovering just overhead.

Agnes tittered, her rosy cheeks rising with her smile. "You'll no be able to step on my toes, lass. I'll be putting my feet up, is what I'll be doing." She pointed to a stool near a long and narrow counter. "Sit there, lass. I'll fetch you bannocks and honey."

Ada sat upon the smooth and glossy seat of the stool and looked around. A slim and young girl stood at the end of this counter, chopping leeks and onions, casting shy glances at Ada from under hooded eyes. When Ada smiled at her, she looked at Ada no more. A lad, too young to be training with the army, scooped ash from the cool and presently unused sections of the hearth. He, too, sent cautious and curious glances her way, but soon he'd filled his tin bucket and scampered out of the kitchen.

Above this table, suspended from the ceiling with thick curved hooks, hung dozens of different sized pots and kettles. The hearths and ovens encompassed one entire wall of this room, and another wall housed shelves of crocks and cups and woven baskets. On the third wall, a man stood, his back to the room, while he worked over a table piled high with dead pheasants. His knife hacked and skinned and chopped, with seeming quiet efficiency. Next to that, two troughs were nestled side by side, at least one filled with water, as attested by the rising steam.

Agnes returned, setting before Ada a wooden plate showing a thick slice of a heavy bannock, which the dear woman had generously covered in honey.

Ada thanked her just before Agnes called to the man readying the pheasants, "Baldwin, come meet your new lady." And then she whispered to Ada, "He's Flemish, lass. Canna understand a word he says."

The man turned and Ada saw a short and robust man of middling years, with piercing brown eyes and ruddy cheeks. He wiped his hands on the linen wrapped 'round his waist and approached, showing a mild frustration at being taken from his work. His eyebrows were only slices over his eyes, and Ada supposed the hair under his unusual head covering might be the same reddish-brown. His headwear was similar to a wimple, enveloping his head in many turns and folds, but his sported three different colors, one a band of shiny blue, which covered his forehead and was tied at his nape, and seemed to hold all the other folds in place.

"'Tis Lady Ada now, Baldwin."

He closed his eyes and bowed his head. And when he opened his eyes and looked at Ada, he seemed only to be waiting for something.

"I am very pleased to know you, Baldwin. You are the cook?"

He nodded. It was curt, abbreviated, yet somehow very formal. Ada felt his mannerisms might be more at home in a royal kitchen, or indeed, the court itself.

"And how long have you been here at Aviemore?"

He tipped his head to Agnes, so that she answered, "Years and years, I think." And with a grimaced smile, she excused him with a wave of her hand.

"Does he not speak?" Ada wondered, after that odd encounter.

"Aye, he does, lass. But I've asked him not to. No purpose to all his noise when I canna understand him."

Ada gasped, but this went unnoticed by Agnes as she had bent and was fetching something from under the counter.

Having rather began her day with the mantra, *I am Lady MacKenna*, to hearten herself, Ada determined to set her own course.

"Agnes, I am very happy to assume the role of managing the keep, but I will ask that you allow me a few days to find my own way around Aviemore. I'd like to meet some of its people."

Agnes stood straight again, holding a plain brown crock. This was plunked down onto the counter as a pained look passed over her face. "Oh, lass, is that a good idea?"

Surely, Agnes was thinking of the initial cool reception at dinner last night.

And now, so was Ada. Bravely, she nodded. "I don't want to hide away in the kitchen all my days."

"Aye, then, lass. You traipse around for a wee bit. Let them see how sweet you are; the kitchen and the stewardship will keep."

Half an hour later, Ada returned to the hall to find it empty now, the soldiers all gone.

She imagined that, like Stonehaven, much of the day's business took place outside the walls of the keep. Reflexively brushing away any crumbs that might have attached to her plain brown kirtle, she set her shoulders back and stepped outside and went down the steps into the yard of Aviemore.

She spotted Callum straightaway, with some thankfulness, and strode toward him as he had his head bent to a lad, their backs to Ada.

"Good day to you, Callum," she called out, which turned around the man, and the boy to whom he was speaking. Ada was pleased to see it was Henry, whom she'd been hoping to meet.

"Lady MacKenna," Callum said, looking truly happy to see her.

Ada stopped just before the pair, noticing that Callum held a strange small hook in his hand, while Henry held a length of thin rope in his.

"Henry, say good day to your lady." Callum instructed the youth, who stared open-mouthed at Ada. He recovered, or gathered himself, and made a gratuitous bow, which raised Ada's brow.

She laughed, to put him at ease, though her own awkwardness was heightened by his show of misplaced worship. "Aye, we haven't any need of that, Henry," she said lightly. "How do you do?"

"Yes," was all he said, which had Callum smiling sympathetically at the lad.

"Will you be fishing?" Ada asked, pointing to the line in his hands. "Is that what this is?"

Henry nodded.

Callum expounded. "Yesterday, my lady, we gathered the nettles and stripped them of their leaves. Aye, Henry? And the lad learned how to soak and pulp the nettle, and earlier we wove the strands into this line. And here I was, just fetched these barbed hooks from the smithy, about to show the lad how to string his line and stone." Callum held both hands, palms up, for Ada's inspection. In one hand sat two iron hooks, one end with an eye closure; in the other hand were several stones, no bigger than Callum's thumb, with holes bored straight through their middles.

"And you catch the fish—or hope to—in the loch?"

"Aye," said Callum, "Called angling, my lady."

Henry hadn't said another word but continued to stare at Ada. Purposefully, she kept up conversation with Callum, allowing the boy to become accustomed to her scars, to look his fill as needed. "What might I do to have you stop calling me *my lady*?" Ada wondered.

"No much you can do...my lady." But Callum smirked with this delivery.

"Will you be fishing—angling," she corrected, "just now?"

"Aye," answered Callum. "Out the back gate to the loch. There's a nice spot on the east bank."

Ada addressed Henry then, "Would you mind if I joined you?"

Still silent, the lad shook his head left to right.

Chapter Sixteen

On the loch side of the castle, which was actually the rear of the keep, there was a fortification of a much shorter wall, being only twice as tall as Callum. Henry dashed ahead of the captain and Ada, showing the way to the man-sized door built into that stone wall. Outside this door, Callum pointed east, to where Henry was already running. They followed a trail of matted grass, and traversed a wide but short wooden bridge, which spanned a gap of a small stream that angled away from the loch. Once across the bridge, it was only a short distance to a neat little area, as Callum had promised, in a wide open spot upon a shallow part of the bank.

From a thick-trunked but squat tree, Callum retrieved two smooth brown poles made from the branches of a nearby yew. He and Henry hovered over these, Callum showing the lad how to tie the line onto the pole, and how to affix the hook, and the stone, which he called a sinker.

Ada happily sat at the shore, presuming this was indeed a well-loved spot, as there were several chopped thick trunk pieces, upon which a person might sit. But the sun was shining, and the grass was dry, so Ada opted to feel the earth beneath her and plopped herself down onto the ground.

When Callum had demonstrated to Henry how to toss the hemp line into the water, the captain took a seat on one of those furnished stumps while Henry stood nearby.

By way of conversation, Ada admitted, "I rather cajoled Agnes Nairn into allowing me to shirk my duties, or the learning of them, for a few days while I familiarized myself with Aviemore."

"A sound plan, my lady," Callum said. "The kitchens and the keep can wait."

"I will not abuse it," Ada vowed. "Although, I don't think even I supposed I'd be lazing about the banks of the lake so soon into my reprieve."

Callum assured her, "You can do no wrong here, I assure you."

Ada pulled her hands from the ground behind her and sat forward, tipping her face to the captain. "Do you say that because of the tale that Jamie told last night?"

Callum frowned lightly. "Lass, 'twas no tale, but truth. What you did at Dornoch—"

Ada interrupted him, slightly frustrated. "Is done, Callum." And then, softer, "It's done. I do not want to be treated differently just because of...that. You'd have done the same. Or Jamie would have." When he scowled still, unwilling, it seemed, to give up the veneration, she decided to set him straight. "Did Jamie tell you how I attacked him? Nae, I thought not. The truth is, I believed he—and you—had abandoned us at Dornoch. 'Tis truth. I berated him fiercely and accosted him physically, called him the worst sort of names, and blamed him for Will's death and... for this," she finished, waving her hand in front of her face, while Callum's eyes widened in his. "Callum, I'm not special and

I do not deserve to be treated so. Won't you please just consider me a friend? One who errs and cries and rages at times, mayhap one who is just like anyone else?"

Callum stared at her, broodingly, and for several long seconds. Finally, he shook his head, his gaze in some way saddened. "You're no like anyone else, Ada MacKenna. No at all. But I owe you my life, and if you beg no singular care, I'll do my best to appease you. Aye, my lady, it would truly be the greatest honor to have you as my own true friend."

Ada smiled at him. "Thank you."

Henry made some exclamation then, drawing their attention. Callum jumped to his feet and attended the lad, who appeared to have snagged some prey on the end of his line. The fishing instruction continued then, with Callum showing Henry how to incrementally draw in the line. In only a few short minutes, Henry had slapped a fair sized fish upon the bank, his smile bright with his success.

Ada clapped her hands for his accomplishment, while Callum announced he actually did have other duties that needed his attention.

"But you stay right here, my lady, with the lad, and straight back to the keep when the angling wears thin."

When Callum had trotted off, Henry cast his line again, as he'd been shown, and then surprised Ada by taking a seat on the ground quite close to her.

She commended him once again on his first catch, but he seemed to have some agenda for their discussion and asked, in a rather frank manner, "Is it true, what the laird said?"

Ada had an idea of what he asked but wasn't sure specifically which part he wanted confirmed. "I shouldn't think your laird would lie, Henry," she said, gently, not with any chastisement. "But what would you like to know?"

"I remember we waited for you," Henry said, haltingly. "The laird and the captain and me. We waited for a while, and the laird was right angry, stomping his feet, and using bad words."

Ada frowned. "What was he angry about?"

"He wanted to go back. But he ken we could no. Captain said everyone would die if we did. Said our only hope was to find our own soldiers, or maybe the MacGregors."

After a moment, Ada wondered, "Were you very frightened, Henry?"

He shook his head, his shaggy hair shaking. "Not then. I was tired. I was real scared earlier. I wanted to be with the others. But is it true, that you and Will were...?"

Ada nodded, plucking at the tall grass around her. "Aye. Will was a champion that night, lad. So very brave." Giving herself a mental shake, needing to lose the maudlin thoughts around the boy, Ada said, "It's all done, Henry. And in the past now, where we should leave it. Here we are, safe and well protected." A good lesson for herself, as well.

They were quiet for a while, watching the part of the line above the water sway somewhat with the slow breeze.

"Do you live inside the keep, Henry?"

"Aye."

"With your mother and father?"

"Nae. I dinna remember my mum, she died when I was a bairn." He hesitated before adding, "My da died last year, after Dornoch."

"I'm sorry, Henry."

"Do you have a mum and da?"

"I do. And several sisters and one brother. How old are you, Henry?"

He shrugged. "Captain said I might be twelve, said I had to wait few more years to start training with the army."

"Will you like that?"

"Aye, then I can save myself."

"Aye."

Voices sounded behind them, coming closer through the brush. Two soldiers, one who had been at the table in the hall this morning, erupted onto the quiet scene.

They stopped suddenly. Whatever had brought them here, they hadn't expected to find the lady of the manor keeping company with a lad while he fished. The man she had not seen before dropped to his knee, bowing his head before Ada. The other, not to be outdone, quickly followed suit.

Ada stared at their bent forms and lowered heads. She glanced at Henry, who's matching confusion was evidenced in his scrunched up face.

Ada stood, feeling fairly put out by their display, and then quite disadvantaged by her seated position. "Kind sirs, there is no need..."

They rose and faced her, but their stances remained formal, feet braced wide, each with one arm tucked at his back, the other resting on the hilt of his sword.

Ada sighed. "Please, there is no need...for this. Can I not just know your names? Know you?"

They exchanged glances. The young man she'd noticed in the hall earlier spoke first. "I am Simon, my lady, and I am at your service." He made to bow again, his cheeks and ears pinkened.

Ada nearly lunged at him, arms extended. "Please, no more," she said with a laugh. She faced the other man, as tall as Jamie, and nearly as handsome, with smiling gray eyes and close cropped black hair.

"Peter, my lady."

Ada smiled beautifully. "There, perfect. I'm pleased to meet you. What brings you to the lock today?"

Again, they looked at each other, before Simon answered. "For truth, my lady, we were about to have a quick dunk, now that our training is done for the day."

"Pray, do not let me—oh, you'll want to..." *be naked*, she thought, biting her lip. "Um, I can leave you—"

They wouldn't hear of it, both chirping at once. They would join her and Henry, they said. Their baths could wait.

Ada was overjoyed with this, and then even more so when they sat and the four of them chatted amiably and easily. Simon insisted Henry was angling all wrong, but his own attempts bore no more fruit than the lad's. True, more than once she'd caught either one of them staring overlong at the marks upon her—Simon seemed particularly curious about the legacy of the rope upon her neck—but politely, they asked no questions, so that Ada enjoyed her time with them.

An hour later, their baths apparently forgotten or forfeited, Simon and Peter walked back to the keep with Henry and Ada. Henry proudly swung his day's catch, three small fish, which Peter said were tasty brown trout, expanding Henry's smile.

Gallantly, Peter offered his hand to Ada over that small wooden bridge. Once crossed, Ada was surprised to find Jamie waiting for them near the postern gate. Her first instinct, to smile at him, was tempered by the glare he currently leveled upon the foursome.

"I've been looking for you," he said specifically to Ada, his tone bearing no pleasantness.

"Callum knew where I'd gone," she said with some hesitation. "Is aught amiss?"

With pursed lips, all but glaring at Simon and Peter, so that they rather scurried by him and into the yard, Jamie shook his head.

Only Henry, proudly lifting the strung-up fish to Jamie, lessened his scowl. He ruffled Henry's hair and told him, "Well done, lad. Get 'em on up to Baldwin. He'll be happy to make use of them."

Henry nodded and scampered off and Jamie's glower returned.

"Jamie, what has happened?"

"I dinna want you outside the walls, lass."

No, that wasn't what he was upset about. She didn't know what had wrought such a foul mood in him, but she knew somehow that if her being outside the wall were truly the issue, Callum would not have allowed it. She spared him only a slight frown and walked past him. She had her own moods to contend with, she couldn't try to manage or interpret his as well.

HE WATCHED HER WALK away.

I'm ten kinds of an idiot, he chided himself with a heavy sigh. She is not Diana. Not at all.

He knew that.

Truth was, he hadn't cared what Diana had done, hadn't been around much to notice. He recalled returning to Aviemore, only weeks after Diana and her babe had died. The only thing he'd felt, or recognized, at the time, was guilt. Guilt that he felt absolutely nothing else.

The marriage had not begun as such. In hindsight, Jamie had determined that neither was to blame explicitly, yet both were at fault. He'd quickly learned that the bride his father and the guardians of Scotland had chosen was a spoiled and needy girl, not a woman at all. When Jamie had remained unmoved by her tantrums, she'd only acted out more. But in her defense, he hadn't cared enough to make the marriage work, or even to stay around to try and figure out his bride. He only found more reasons and more missions to take him away from Aviemore. That pattern had stuck with him, repeated often, despite the fact that Diana was gone now more than five years.

He had to wonder now, what seeing Ada so cheerfully engaged in company with obviously smitten soldiers, would do to him, to their marriage. While only disgust had plagued him when it had been Diana so blatantly peddling her wares, he knew this time around his reaction was entirely different. And Ada and her intent were entirely different—she had not, he was somehow sure, enticed any man to her side. It just wasn't her nature. He would do well to remember that.

He would do well to be unaffected by it.

But to do that, he would need to have much less feeling for her.

Unfortunately, it appeared that it was already too late for that.

Jamie spent the rest of the day upon the training field with Callum, being shown the drills which Callum ran them through daily. Presently, the army housed at Aviemore numbered exactly sixty-eight. Yesterday, Malcolm and Callum and Jamie had poured over the records kept of the entire army, having determined that Aviemore could call up one hundred more. Malcolm had also hinted that there was coin aplenty to hire additional, if he desired. Jamie did, and the necessary letters had been sent this morning.

When he'd returned from the field, Jamie reacquainted himself with the stablemaster, Donnan, and then the smithy, Finlay, and only returned to the keep in time for the late meal. People were just coming in, finding seats at the trestle tables. He wondered where Ada might be and knew a twinge of guilt when he realized he had, more or less, left the lass to her own devices today. He supposed he'd just assumed Aunt Agnes would have taken her under her wing. But mayhap that had not been the case, as he'd found her at the loch earlier, seemingly uninterested in getting on with the running of the keep.

He found his wife only seconds before the meal was delivered to the hall, as Ada came in from the yard, and not the kitchen. At her side was Henry, and the pair laughed, rather in a burst, as if one of them had said something only moments before they'd crossed the threshold.

The pair parted ways near the table closest to the family's table, where Henry took a seat upon the long bench. Ada's gaze found Jamie's, and she smiled at him, though he was keenly aware of her hesitation, likely a remnant of their brief encounter earlier.

He might have smiled back at her—he'd planned to do so—but that was before he caught sight of all the eyes on his wife. These were not the stealthy gazes of persons curious about her scars, nor even the hooded, frowning stares she'd been subjected to at the beginning of yesterday's meal. These glances were cast from men, soldiers, some furtive, some overt, but to a man, every one of them was appreciative.

Jesu, but the last thing he wanted was to be thrust into a role of jealous husband.

She is not Diana, he reminded himself darkly.

Curling his lips into a smile, leaving off the snarl he wanted to give, Jamie elected to make a point. To Ada, and all her admiring onlookers. He closed the distance between them, even as she was walking toward him, and without preamble, wrapped one hand around her neck and kissed her soundly. She did not exactly balk, but she was clearly taken aback by his very public kiss. When he lifted his head, the hazel eyes regarded him warily before the arched brows dropped into a suspicious frown.

THREE DAYS LATER, ADA was confused and frustrated and not entirely happy.

She laid the blame for her confusion directly at her husband's feet. Her experience with marriage was only days old, and her limited knowledge was based solely on observation of others—Gregor and Anice, most recently—but she was fairly certain that what she and Jamie were living since coming to Aviemore was neither what she'd envisioned as wedded life, nor what she imagined might be normal. She saw Jamie only rarely during the day, about the castle or keep. When she'd happened upon him yesterday and today, he'd kissed her openly, possessively, just as he had in the hall three nights ago. He'd come upon Ada and Henry exiting the dovecote yesterday, where the lad had told her more than she'd ever thought she'd need to know about the pigeons and doves of a castle. Jamie didn't seem to have any purpose to approach her, and truth be told, the smile he'd given her hadn't quite reached his eyes, so that when he'd kiss her then, with a seeming hunger, Ada was left with only an impression of falseness. The kiss was empty, lacking both passion and promise, which should have served more as a portend, as she and her husband had yet to share their bed as a wedded couple. True, the first night was her choice to avoid him. But every night since then, Jamie hadn't even come to their chambers until the wee hours of the morning.

Were the daytime kissing and petting then, every time he saw her, only given essentially as an apology for being unavailable—uninterested?—at night?

Honestly, she had no idea what was happening. And with Jamie, and his inscrutability, could anyone possibly hope to make sense of the first days of their marriage?

The frustration, however, was an entirely different circumstance, and this could only partly be attributed to Jamie. The issue really was the people of Aviemore, and their perception of Ada. While she had become friendly with Agnes and Callum and Henry, to the extent that they treated her as Lady MacKenna, or in better moments, as simply Ada, most other persons regarded her with something akin to silent adulation and nervous reverence, better reserved for men such as William Wallace, and even their own laird. It made Ada terribly uncomfortable, and truth be told, hampered her efforts to get to know people.

Just this morning, Henry had taken her by the hand and dragged her over to the alehouse. The castle brewer, Mona, a woman whom Henry had assured her was 'right nice', had gawked at Ada, unable to make or form any words. When Ada had tried to engage her in conversation, asking about the process of ale-making, the middle-aged woman had only smiled and bobbed her head repeatedly, so that Ada wondered if she had somehow spoken in tongues.

They'd left the alehouse and twice, while crossing the yard, people had stopped and had dropped to their knees as Ada passed. One woman, whom Henry named Mary and had said was from outside the gates, yanked at the hem of Ada's gown, pressing kisses onto the fabric.

And therein lie her unhappiness. Aside from the fact that she was extremely discomfited by their adoration, believing it both overwrought and misplaced, she lamented the fact that it would be near impossible to have real and true friendships within these walls while the people of Aviemore continued to regard her as some sort of consecrated being.

As it was, she was just now returning to the keep, intent on finding the kitchen and mayhap less adoration and more industry. But there was Jamie, inside the hall, holding court with his officers and Callum and Malcolm, likely about some castle business. She had no plan to interrupt and only sent a pleasant smile in the direction of the men as she passed, seeing only a short-lived frown crease her husband's brow, presumably at her lack of attention. The smile was tainted then as the men surrounding her husband—all of them—made smart bows in her direction that Ada had all she could do not to roll her eyes.

"Bloody Lady of Aviemore," she mumbled with some vehemence as she reached the corridor and was out of sight.

She found the cook, Baldwin, in the kitchen, but there was no sign of Aunt Agnes. Several youths, lads and lasses, scurried around the room, about some chore as the supper hour drew near. Ada approached Baldwin while he bent over a kettle in the hearth.

When he stood and turned, he seemed neither surprised nor pleased to see her. Ada pasted on another cheery smile and wondered, "Might I have a chore as well? It would suit me to be helpful."

Baldwin nodded and walked around her, busying himself with mixing some dried herbs into a wooden bowl, in what she guessed must be butter, on a table near the wall.

"Sir?" Ada pressed. Perhaps he had not understood her.

He turned again, heaved out a sigh, and gave her that formal stance and what looked to be an impatient glower.

Nonplused, Ada stammered. "Pardon me, I thought I might be of some assistance."

He stared at her, making her feel as if she intruded, quite unwanted, into his domain. "You may not be of assistance, dear lady. I have no need of interference, and I would prefer that you remained away from this room."

Somehow, Ada was now shocked that he actually spoke. His voice, or rather his accent, was thick and clipped, and any *d* at the end of a word sounded like a *t*. Ada was mesmerized by the sounds, though definitely not his intonation, nor the message.

She sputtered the beginning of some rebuttal, "I—that is, I—"

The oily cook lifted a brow at her, almost daring her to continue. *Hmph*, and to think that she had felt sorry for him yesterday, when Aunt Agnes had said she'd asked him not to speak.

Now, with a very verbal harrumph, Ada gave him a good glare of her own and stomped out of the kitchen, marching along the corridor and then through the hall, to the far side and the stairway.

With little grace, she hiked up the skirts of her gown and trudged up the stairs. In another minute, she was inside her own chamber and slammed the door, not without a belated grimace for that childish action. And then she didn't care and flounced across the bed, burying her face in the coverlet. What was the point of being Lady MacKenna? It afforded her no privilege so far that she could see, she concluded. The people were either afraid of her, or ridiculously worshipful, or outright rude—one reaction was worse than another.

"Not allowed in my own kitchen?" She groused into the bed. "And all that scraping and bowing! Bloody bollocks, I am no saint!"

"I hear words," said a voice above her, "but I canna interpret those blown into the mattress."

A weight upon the bed shifted it and her, just as she recognized her husband's voice. Ada rolled over to find Jamie poised above her, a hand on either side of her, pressed into the firm feathered mattress.

Her gripes, which had brought her into this room, and her thoughts about these, fled as Jamie's eyes showed so much more attention than they had over the last few days. Even as he said,

"I'd come to see what had you stomping around the keep, lass," he was staring at her lips and lowering himself onto her. He pressed a kiss against her mouth and then her cheek and then further, along her neck. The heated trail took him up to her ear, "But I'm forgetting just now to care about anything but the sight of my pretty bride in our bed."

Suddenly, Ada could recall nothing prior to this moment, as his body covered hers completely and his lips returned to her mouth, favoring her with a scorching kiss. She closed her eyes and lost herself in the moment, hoping it lasted for hours as she slid her arms up around his broad shoulders and into his hair. And all the worry she'd experienced over the last few days, when he had not sought her out thusly, dissolved to wisps of smoke in her head. One of his strong hands found her breast, his nimble fingers brought the nipple to peak. Ada moaned as the hand left her breast, but it reappeared, rucking up her skirts, delving between her legs, and her moan became a cry of increasing delight.

Their kissing was needful and urgent, their clothing bothersome and hastily pushed aside. And then happily, wondrously, Jamie was pressing himself into her, instructing with some urgency, "Wrap your legs around me." She did so, and he drove deep. Ada arched her back and curled her toes as she crossed her ankles at his back. She lifted her hips and met each thrust, pushing back, sliding her hands under his tunic and all over his chest. All at once, she wanted this to never end even as she begged him, "Oh, please," to give her what she needed.

They came quickly and nearly at the same time, Jamie's hand pinning her hip to the bed as it washed over them, while he closed his eyes and even his cheekbones bunched and moved with all that coursed through him.

"*Jesu*, lass," he breathed raggedly, "how do you make it feel so damn good?"

Ada could not stifle in time the very unladylike snort of laughter. "I'm not sure, being relatively new at this." Her husband's chuckle rumbled against her shoulder, where he'd collapsed. But his question begot her own. "Are you telling me this is a game of chance? Does it not always feel like this?"

Jamie slumped onto his back beside her. He inhaled deeply and exhaled slowly. "Nae, lass. This is..." he broke off, searching.

Love? She almost supplied but bit her lip quickly to forestall so daring a suggestion, having no idea where that had come from.

"I dinna ken," he said. "But I'm no complaining, wife."

Ada had gone completely still, flummoxed by her presently churning thoughts. Love?

When his breathing had returned to normal, Jamie pulled her away from these fanciful notions with, "What sent you off from the kitchens in such a lather, lass?"

Pushing out a tortured sigh, Ada's brain was too twisted to explain Baldwin's rudeness, yet she bothered to ask, "Am I allowed, as your wife, to manage the household as I see fit?"

He turned toward her, though did not answer, mayhap even threw out some questioning frown, so that Ada softened the inquiry. "Am I allowed to make any necessary changes for the betterment of Aviemore?"

"Aye, so long as it's no too drastic a change." There hung still a question in his voice, but he qualified his response with, "You're a clever lass, I ken. You need only to rule fairly but firmly."

Ada smiled, pleased with this reply. Nevertheless, she remained fairly overwhelmed with the idea that she might be in love with her husband.

Chapter Sixteen

Ada entered the kitchen the next morning, less sure of her plan than she was of her objective. She bid a cheery good morning to Agnes and announced her presence to Baldwin. While Agnes was delighted to see her, the cook showed not nearly so warm a welcome. The natty man in the colorful turban shot her what Ada could only surmise was a warning look. This, she chose to ignore. She introduced herself to the kitchen staff, most of whom were present now.

She met the young lasses, Fiona and Moira, who were tasked with much of the serving and the washing. The lads, John and Boyd, were merrily called the 'foragers and gatherers' by Agnes, as they were charged with lifting and lugging and, according to Boyd, "the grimy work". Ada met Joanna, a young woman perhaps only a few years older than herself, who seemed only a browbeaten slave to Baldwin, if Ada's short time in the kitchen were any indication.

Twice, while Ada had been in conversation with the woman, Baldwin had barked out some order, his face turning red at finding Joanna talking with Ada.

Ada ignored him, smiling serenely at Joanna, sorry for her flustered uncertainty. She was a mousy thing, whose entire body seemed to jerk with each sound from the cook's mouth.

Ada suggested softly, "Mayhap, Joanna, you would do well in a different part of the keep?"

Joanna was surprised by the offer of escape, glancing nervously around to see if Baldwin had heard. Truly, Ada was more shocked by the woman's refusal. Her liquid brown eyes focused on Ada with some regret. She lifted a plump hand and squeezed the fingers into her palm.

"Aye, and you're verra kind, my lady," said Joanna, "But betwixt you and me, I love the cooking and the creating. I'd no like to be anywhere else."

Baldwin stepped between Ada and Joanna, where they stood near the prep counter, his face angry with a blotchy redness.

"I had spoken only yesterday to you, my lady. Your presence is not required—"

Ada reddened his face yet more when she held up a hand, very close to his face, to silence him. He had, after all, interrupted.

Joanna's eyes widened, sending her brows up into the scarf upon her head.

"How long have you labored in the kitchens, Joanna?" Ada continued.

"M—many years now, my lady." The poor thing. She remained perfectly still, only her eyes moving, darting back and forth between Ada, her hand, and Baldwin.

Ada gave her an encouraging smile. "Oh, you probably have so many favorite recipes?"

Joanna returned with a slow nod.

Baldwin tired of waiting, and with a not so quiet growl, took himself away.

"My husband tells me," Ada went on, lowering her hand, "that down at a house called Inesfree, they bake apples into the bread, and use something called cinnamon to flavor it."

Joanna's eyes lit up. She lost her trepidation and with Baldwin further away, warmed to the topic. With a fair amount of excitement, she said, "Aviemore has its own orchard, my lady. Though we willna see apples until the end of summer."

"And cinnamon?"

"I've never heard tell of that."

"Perhaps I can beg my husband to collect some when next he is at Inesfree. He says it's his favorite food."

The shy woman grinned at this, at the laird's lady wanting to please him.

Baldwin was barking again, this time at young Fiona, whom he was chasing out of the larder and back into the kitchen. In his anger, he was certainly more difficult to understand. Fiona wrested her arm out of his grasp and tried to apologize. The meaty fisted cook cracked her across the face, yelling louder.

Ada rushed to the girl, who held her cheek and flinched with each harsh syllable.

"Stop this at once!" Ada called. Stepping between Fiona and Baldwin, Ada hissed into his face, "You will not ever strike this girl—not any person—in this kitchen! Ever!"

She couldn't have been more stunned by his response than if he'd slapped her, too. He switched to his native tongue, stabbing his finger in Ada's face with whatever angry words he spat at her.

"Get out," Ada said, her own ire risen, her words fierce. "Get out of this kitchen and get out of this keep."

The red-faced cook only snarled at her and turned his back, taking up whatever work he'd been about, as if Ada had not just spoken to him, had not indeed just kicked him out.

Stymied, Ada glanced around. Agnes stood, eyes as wide as trenchers, her chubby little fingers covering her mouth. Joanna was mute as well, her jaw gaping. Fiona stared up at her with a similar expression of shock and awe.

"Baldwin," Ada called to the man's back, "your services are no longer required at Aviemore."

He turned, only his head, and said, with a curled lip, "You do not make those decisions."

Oh, the arrogance of the man!

Ada ushered Fiona away from the man and put her into Agnes's care and then left the kitchen. The hall was empty, but fortuitously, Callum was walking in from the bailey just as Ada wondered how far she might have to go to find help.

"Perfect timing, Callum," she called. "I need your assistance."

This seemed to please him, and he stepped lively to reach her. The soldier Peter was with him and followed.

"I need you to remove Baldwin from the keep," she said.

God bless him, while he appeared truly befuddled, Callum only nodded.

She applauded his immediate trust in her decision, and while he'd asked no question, she explained curtly, even as she began walking back to the kitchen, "He struck the kitchen lass, Fiona," she said over her shoulder as Callum and Peter followed her. "We will, of course, not tolerate any abuse of our lasses."

"Aye, my lady, we will no."

Ada was quite sure she detected both pride and purpose in the captain's voice. At the end of the corridor, he instructed, "Step aside, my lady," while touching her elbow.

She did, and Callum and Peter entered the kitchen first.

All eyes turned at their coming. Apparently, in the very short time Ada had been gone, Baldwin had already bullied the staff back to their work.

"You come on with us, Cook," Callum ordered. "You're done here now."

"She," Baldwin hissed, pointing sharply at Ada, "cannot dismiss me."

"Aye, she can, and she did," Callum assured him.

Baldwin raged, "I am descended from nobility. I am named for a king!"

"I am descended from a merchant," Ada said and shrugged, showing him lineage meant nothing. "But I am the wife of your laird. And you are a rotten person."

Peter stepped forward, placing a hand on the hilt of his sword.

"I'm going to be right pissed if I have to come fetch you," said Callum, lifting his brow, giving the cook the opportunity to leave without incident.

Baldwin's face, at this moment, mottled with several different shades of red. To Ada's surprise, after a very tense moment, in which he flexed his hand that held a knife, he displayed again that courtly grace, gently lying the knife upon the counter and leaving the kitchen under escort.

Callum shot a wink at Ada as he followed Peter and Baldwin out of the room.

Ada pivoted, as the three men disappeared, to find four females regarding her with speechless wonder. Then Fiona rushed over to her and hugged her tightly around the waist. Ada returned the embrace then put her hands on the young girl's face, bringing her gaze up. "No man is ever allowed to mistreat us." She looked around at Agnes and Moira and Joanna. "Not any of us."

"You are so brave," Joanna said, her tone imbued with admiration.

"I'm not sure about that," Ada said with a nervous laugh. "However, I'm not a ninny. I fight the battles I can. I seek help for those I cannot."

Agnes clapped her hands at this and chortled, "Aye, a fine thing you've done, lass, and good riddance to the pig." Her chuckle only grew larger as she wondered, "But are you to be cooking our meals yourself?"

Even Joanna slapped her hand over her mouth at this unforeseen consequence.

Ada considered this, recalling Agnes's words about being excited about having lesser duties. And here, she'd just created more work. She looked to Joanna. "Might you be interested in the position?"

A very tongue-tied Joanna could only gape at Ada. "But my lady—"

"But nothing. You said only moments ago, you love the work. You have the experience. You'll likely have a more efficient staff—people work better when they work without fear."

Joanna's smile was slow. She pressed a hand over her heart. "I would be honored."

Everyone smiled now, and Agnes wondered to Ada, "What you going to get at tomorrow, lass?"

ADA FOUND CALLUM AGAIN a short while later, near the smithy shed, holding three short, handle-less daggers in his hand, in discussion with Aviemore's blacksmith, Finlay, about the possibility of fashioning a handle that was made specifically for his hand. She'd not have interrupted, save the smithy saw her coming, and offered a respectful, if awkward, bow when she reached Callum's side. The smithy was stocky, his skin pocked and freckled and aged, but his eyes were kind, Ada decided.

"Good day, sir. Please do not trouble yourself to bow every time I come near. It makes me feel as if I haven't dressed properly for the occasion." She glanced down at her plain brown kirtle, then back up at Finlay, giving him a winning smile. To Callum, she said, "I won't keep you from your business. I wanted only to thank you for what you did. You agreed to champion my cause before you'd heard what it was. I appreciate that very much, sir."

Callum accepted the gratitude with a tip of his head. "I'd no been thinking you were unlevel in the head, lass. And you dinna strike me as the irrational sort—I've ken plenty of them over the years."

"Thank you."

Callum lifted a brow, bending his head toward her. "I'll no take up every cause, my lady. No if I believe it untoward or undeserved. But Baldwin's had it coming, and we're none the worse, aye?"

Ada nodded and turned at the sound of a rider coming through the gates.

"I wondered how long it would be until he found out."

Jamie came, and brought with him an unreadable expression, though well his gaze was trained on her.

Any nervousness she might have felt at having to explain herself to her husband was quickly replaced by what the sight of him did to her. Truly, he was magnificent upon the black destrier. The warm summer sun glinted off what little was left of the blond in his hair. Ada liked his shorn locks so much better, save that the blond was gone with the length, showing mostly just a very light brown, several shades lighter than the stubble that adorned his cheeks and jaw.

Under the metal and leather breastplate, he wore only a sleeveless tunic, which put on great display his thick and muscled arms. He reined in, bringing the huge beast to a stop close to Ada, those muscles in his arms shifting and moving with every motion, putting Ada in mind of being wrapped up in his embrace.

He dismounted and strode purposefully toward her, forcing Ada to leave off admiring his body and instead, consider his mood. The dark blue eyes held hers intently.

"The keep is large, lass, but no so big I don't hear tales. And just a few minutes ago, I heard some fantastic story about the lady of the keep sending her own cook packing."

She bit her lip. He didn't necessarily seem displeased. But he didn't necessarily not seem displeased. "I did." Only a light hesitation weakened her words. With greater firmness—very difficult to achieve when he now stood so close, and his lips were so tempting—she added, "And I will not allow it to be undone."

"Fair, but firm, aye?"

"You gave me leave to—"

"I did no give you leave to sack the cook!"

He was definitely angry.

Ada remained stalwart, defending her decision. "You did, actually. I specifically asked if I might make changes that were for the betterment of Aviemore."

Callum, standing close, made to speak up, likely in Ada's defense.

"No, Callum. My husband needs to trust my judgment." Jamie lifted a brow at her. "Otherwise, he insinuates that at best, I am not fit to manage the keep, and at worst, that I am no more than an idiot."

Jamie stared hard at her, trying to read her, she guessed.

"And you believe it was better for Aviemore to have no cook?"

She sensed his lessening fury. And she liked the way his mouth moved when he spoke, liked to see his lips shaping and forming around his words.

"We...do have a cook. Her name is Joanna."

To his credit, he challenged her no more. In fact, while he looked rather longingly upon her lips, he invoked a previously used defense when he said, with that beautiful grin of his, "Aye, like as no, I agreed to whatever you asked, only pretended I understood, or even heard. But it's possible I didn't hear a thing you said."

Ada allowed a small answering grin, but thought to ask, "Perchance, were you too close when you pretended to understand?" She had, after all, begged this boon, only yesterday after they'd made love. "Was it the proximity?"

"Aye, lass. It was at that."

ADA DID NOT SEE JAMIE again that day. Whatever took him off usually in the dark of night had called him earlier. Ada watched him and Callum and several others ride away before the dinner hour. Part of her considered this a blessing, as she hadn't any idea that Joanna actually could put out a decent meal. But she needn't have worried, the changeover was seamless, and if any person in the keep hadn't yet heard the news that Baldwin was no more, they'd not have noticed any difference.

Ada poked her head into the kitchen after supper to congratulate Joanna, who accepted the praise with a nervous smile and pinkened cheeks. She was kind enough to include all her staff in the accolades.

While he had departed Aviemore much earlier than normal for whatever took him away, Jamie still did not return until the wee hours of the morning. But Ada woke this time, turned over on the bed at the sound of him relinquishing his sword to its place near the headboard. She stretched with some grogginess, and then found herself more wakeful as Jamie only stood at the side of the bed, looking down at her.

"Are you angry yet with me, because of Baldwin?"

He shook his head, his eyes raking over her. "Nae, lass. I'm no angry with you. Dinna ken that I ever was."

"Then the brooding stare is...?"

A short chuckle escaped. "Is me wrestling with the same thing, night after night, wondering how selfish it would be to wake my bride and have my way with her."

And now she was fully awake. Every nerve in her body lifted its ear.

But first she asked, not holding out any hope that he might actually answer, "Where do you go off to for such long periods of time?"

"About the same business we were on our way to Aviemore," he said. "Recruiting."

"Successfully?"

He shrugged, and said, "Sometimes," but his expression told her whatever success he had found was less than what he'd hoped for.

Sliding away from him, from the center of the bed, Ada flipped back the furs and the coverlet.

Jamie smiled and lifted his tunic up over his head, tossing it onto the trunk near the foot of the bed. His breeches followed, and Ada wished for more light than only that of the dying fire.

When he climbed in beside her, she whispered, just before his lips met hers, "Thankfully, your bride is awake just now."

"It's verra cold, lass, but I can no be sorry that I'm about to make you naked," he returned against her mouth.

"I trust you'll have me warmed in no time," she said on a sigh.

Ada was sure she would never tire of the hunger he showed her, the hunger he'd created in her. She closed her eyes and blissfully gave herself up to her husband's lovemaking.

Sadly, these would be the last moments of peace between them for some time.

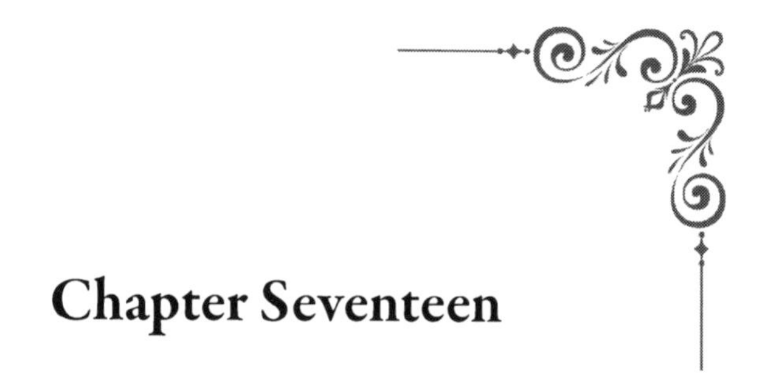

Chapter Seventeen

Ada was at the well, in the center of Aviemore's yard, fetching a third bucket-full of water for the laundering being done within, when Simon approached her. Chivalrously, he shooed Ada aside and easily carried this load for her. She followed him in and then back out of the keep, needing one more filled bucket of water.

She'd given up insisting to him that she was perfectly capable of moving water from one point to another. He was sharing with her some tale of his and Peter's drunken escapades one night in Perth years ago—truly a story more befitting the soldiers' barracks, Ada thought. She'd not said as much, and smiled and laughed appropriately during the telling, happy that at least he was speaking to her and not bowing before her.

Jamie found her that way, leaned against the well while Simon reeled in the next bucket, grinning at the young soldier. Jamie walked his horse into the yard, seeming to spy Ada immediately. She couldn't say that he'd not been frowning before finding her, as she realized his presence belatedly, but he was definitely frowning now. With casual grace, he slid from the saddle and while at least a dozen people watched, Simon included, as he'd just hefted the bucket away from the hook, Jamie strode right up to Ada and kissed her. It was not exactly a chaste kiss, but neither was it warm, nor meant to stir her.

Awkwardly, Simon excused himself and took the water to the keep.

"Why do you do that?" Ada asked of Jamie, crossing her arms over her chest. She hadn't meant to sound so put out by it, had intended for a more casual tone. As it was, she supposed it was her tone that lifted Jamie's brow.

"What's that?"

"Why do you kiss me like that, in front of everyone?"

He grinned, though this did not extend to his eyes. "Am I no allowed to kiss my wife?"

"If it's kissing you want, then aye. But it....it comes not with any of the things that should come with kisses."

His brows creased and he harrumphed. He did not meet her eye, instead busied himself with untying the leather pouches from the horse.

The reason Ada knew that something was false about these kisses was because she'd spent several weeks in the Kincaid household at Stonehaven. She'd learned there that husbands might regularly show such affection to their wives. Anytime Gregor Kincaid walked into a room in which Anice was, he did exactly what Jamie did, walked directly to her and kissed her. Truth be told, Ada had been made quite uncomfortable by this daily, sometimes hourly, demonstration, until she saw the entire picture and not just her own discomfort. There was warmth and love and peace in there gazes. It then became so obvious to Ada, watching the Kincaid enter a room, watching as his eyes scanned until they found her. And honestly, any witness could discern the change in his expression the moment he spotted his wife. His gaze—indeed, his entire person—softened at the sight of her, as if simply having her near turned out any and all negative, turned away everything but her. It had been truly something very special to see.

In no way did she compare herself and Jamie to Gregor and Anice. The Kincaids clearly adored each other, their love was a palpable thing to feel and see and know. Ada and Jamie had not that. They had a marriage rather of necessity and a passion that might well be enough for a time. Mayhap that's what bothered her so much about his kissing her in front of so many people all the time. It wasn't done with the same intent as Gregor Kincaid kissed Anice, so that it only seemed so dishonest, or at the very least, a matter of pretense. Hence her question: what was the point of it?

It came with no warmth, no promise, seemed only a perfunctory action, and one which she was beginning to resent very much. Mayhap that was the issue, she considered. Maybe she was in love with him and was only bothered by awareness that her husband, while enamored of her body and their lovemaking, was certainly not in love with her.

Perhaps her prolonged silence wrought some turmoil in him. He lifted his head and asked, "What should come with the kissing, lass? I canna be accosting you in the middle of the yard."

Ada shook her head, dismissing the whole subject. She knew she was right but didn't know how to explain it to him.

And then a lad, younger than Henry, one Ada had never seen before, came up to Jamie and Ada. With only a passing glance at his laird, he dropped to his knees before Ada, and literally bowed his head to the ground in front of her.

She stifled the frustrated cry that so wanted to burst forth and managed a tight smile, inclining her head benevolently at the boy when finally he rose.

Jamie stared, dumbfounded. "What the hell was that?" He asked, when the lad had darted away.

"*That* is your doing," she accused.

"How am I to blame for—what *was* that?"

"That, husband, is the result of your fancy and needless discourse our first night here."

It took him a moment to understand of what she spoke. "That was necessary, so they understood what you had sacrificed."

"It was not necessary, and it stands now as the basis for all the fawning madness."

"It has nothing to—"

"Aye, it does! And you had no right to tell that tale, by the way. In that moment, you were no better than George Goody."

His frown darkened. "Goody used you for the cause—'twas not right. I did that for you. They needed to know!"

Since his voice had risen with his vexation, so then did Ada start shouting as well.

"That is not your story to tell! It belongs to me! I decide who knows it!" She thumped her chest. "I say who gets to hear it!" This rendered him speechless, though well she could see his mind working. Before he gathered his defense, she plodded forward, lowering her voice again, "They stare as if I'm some holy relic, they're afraid to touch me or talk to me. One man begged a blessing for his sick bairn."

"I canna take back the words, lass, nor bend the truth," he said. "They'll come 'round, is my guess, once they ken you."

"Jamie, I do not think it's that easy. I suspect I could light fire to the entire keep and they might only see it as a sign to repent and follow my ways."

This elicited a chuckle, but Ada could sense no humor in the sound. She cared not one whit for his dismissive attitude for her grievance.

THAT EVENING AT SUPPER, Agnes informed Ada that Malcolm was abed with a touch of the ague, which Agnes announced with such lightness Ada imagined indeed it must be a mild case. So when neither Jamie nor any of his officers showed themselves, Ada partook of the meal seated next to Agnes at a lower table. Agnes sat on one side of her and Peter on the other, with Simon and two other men, Duncan and Fergus, across from her. True, the meal began quietly, the soldiers a bit unnerved, no doubt, to have their lady sitting with them. Ada engaged in conversation with Agnes at first, while they grew accustomed to her presence, until Peter asked her if she had any plans for more angling down at the loch.

She had no plans, she told him, but wouldn't be sorry if she found herself in that circumstance once again. A banal reply, but it allowed for the conversation to open up to all the table.

"Did you catch anything, my lady?" Asked Fergus, who appeared a serious sort, with a constant pensive frown over his dark eyes.

"I did not. Truth be known, it was Henry who had charge of the pole. I was no more than a happy bystander."

"Good eel to be had in the loch," Peter commented.

"You'll no catch them with Callum's hooks and sinkers, aye?"

"How do you catch an eel?" Ada asked. "And what do you do with it when you catch it?"

Many eyes shifted to her face, their surprise evident.

"What do you do? Aye, my lady, you ken you eat it," said Simon.

Agnes said, "It's sweet and soft, tastier than salmon, you ask me."

"But eels are so...squiggly," Ada said, making a face, which produced several chuckles.

"Squiggly?" Fergus repeated, as if he'd never heard the word.

"Aye, Fergus," teased Simon, "as any lass you'd be wanting to—"

He stopped abruptly, jerking upon the bench. Ada suspected he'd been kicked under the table before any bawdy words had come. She bit her lip to keep from laughing.

Peter bent toward her and whispered, not nearly soft enough that it went unheard, "My lady, you may not believe this, but ol' Fergus toils nearly in vain with the lasses."

Gamely, Ada asked, "Because of the squiggling?" She winked at Fergus, to lessen her teasing, but it did not diminish the loud chuckles and guffaws that followed.

And then Jamie appeared, standing at the end of the table, looking pleased about nothing at all. The advent of the laird effectively silenced the entire table, completely and abruptly, that one might think he'd tossed a gauntlet onto the wooden tabletop.

His gaze swept all those seated, seeming to linger on Peter, when came a curl to his lip.

And suddenly Ada understood.

She wasn't sure how. She had no experience with jealousy, however misplaced. As quickly as that idea had come to her, she amended her theory. It wasn't jealousy at all. Just as Jamie settled a decidedly dark look onto her, she realized it was, in fact, distrust.

Agnes's tale of his first wife's faithlessness rang in her head.

It had nothing to do with love, of course. Likely, it was more entrenched in concepts such as masculinity and pride and power—not insecurity, she quickly considered and abandoned. Jamie MacKenna might well suffer the quirks and foibles of many a man, but insecurity was not one of them.

Ada stood, having to climb over the back of the bench, as she'd sat in the middle, and asked of her husband, "Will you take your supper now? And your officers as well? I'll get to the kitchen and inform Joanna."

He nodded and walked with her, in the same direction, tossing his leather gloves with some annoyance onto the head table, while Ada continued to the kitchen.

AND THAT EVENING, AS Jamie found their chambers at nearly the same time as Ada, as he rarely did, she hoped to address with him his misplaced cynicism.

But Jamie spoke first, standing just inside the door, his hand still on the handle.

"I dinna like you keeping company with the lads," he said, with nary a prelude.

Of course, the complaint came as no shock to Ada; his tone, on the other hand, most certainly did, being given in that low, controlled voice that bespoke of a seething, simmering anger.

"Yes, I gathered as much," was all she allowed. It was his claim to state, and she would allow him to make his case fully before she let him know how ridiculous he was being. She was perched on one side of the bed, brushing out her hair, having already changed into her night rail.

She waited, watched Jamie close the door and begin to remove his belt and sword. The brush stopped, mid-motion, when it seemed he would say no more.

Ada swallowed and asked, "Might I know why?"

"No, you dinna need to ken why." He leaned his sword against the spot where the headboard met the wall, then lifted his gaze to her, showing a challenge as he said, "'Tis similar, in fact, to me no questioning decisions you make, lass, like sacking the cook."

"God's blood," Ada groused. The brush dropped to her lap, and she laughed sharply. "That is the most childish thing I've heard—"

"I've said I dinna want you keeping company with my soldiers," he barked out at her, "and that is that."

Ada stood and faced him, only the bed between them, planting her hands on her hips. "Well, that is not enough. You cannot just—"

"I just did!" he shouted. "I dinna want them eyeballing you the way they do!"

"I think you are overreacting," she suggested softly, as this had escalated with greater speed and far more derision than she had expected.

Through gritted teeth, he said, "I am no overreacting when I come into my own hall to find a man leaning so close to my wife as to be offensive and my own bride tittering back at him like some taproom jade, while the rest of them are gawking at you, only waiting their turn."

She was so stunned by this unbelievable and unprovoked attack, she could only stammer. No words came, so that he must have considered the discussion ended, that he sat on the side of the bed, facing the door, and began to remove his boots.

Ada finally recovered. She laughed, sounded almost hysterical. "You've got to be kidding me! Nobody—no one!—is looking at this face and thinking about—"

He shouted again. "You're the only one who sees the fucking scars, Ada."

When she gasped at his vulgar language, and at his tone, he sighed brutally and softened it. "They dinna see them, lass. They see what I see: a beautiful woman looking to be loved."

This rocked Ada, dropping her shoulders. He still sat on the side of the bed, with his back to her. A boot dropped to the floor.

Barely above a whisper, she said, "Only by my husband."

Dully, with near rudeness, he squelched any hope in that regard. "That is no why we wed."

Ada blanched. "But surely—"

"I canna let you be everything to me," he insisted, with a fair amount of fervor. "That will no happen."

"What does that even mean?" She strode around the bed, to face him, as he seemed disinclined to do so. Her hands found her hips again. "Why did you bring me here, then? Why marry me?" Shaking her head, she swished a hand through the air, telling him not to bother with an answer. She knew what words would come—to give her the protection of his name, to bed her more at his leisure. "Yes, I recall the reasons," she said curtly, disbelief warring with a surprisingly painful knot in her chest, that had come with his declaration that he would not allow himself to love her. "Are you saying that was an absolute? Our marriage can never evolve or...become something more satisfying?"

"I see no need," he said, without meeting her fiery gaze.

"How is it that I can forgive you, the man who left me behind, but you can hold against me crimes committed by another?" It was a stretch, she knew, accusing him now of something she'd offered vindication for before, but thus was her state right now, flustered and frustrated, and very, very wounded.

"What are you talking about?"

"I'm not your first wife. I did not betray you." She could also make an argument out of the fact that he hadn't told her he'd been married previously. But that annoyance seemed to pale when measured against what befuddled her now. "Yet you treat me as if I have. Or will."

"I dinna ken that you will no."

She stared at him, aghast by this foolish reasoning. With a strong sense of how important this conversation was, she worked to bring herself under control, considering her words carefully. Ada went to her knees before him, put her hands onto his thighs. "Jamie, I know you wed me out of pity, or guilt. It wasn't ideal, but I truly imagined that more—respect, trust, companionship—would come. I was so very heartened by our beginning, before we reached Aviemore." He was very still, unmoved. Ada dropped her hands from his legs, sat back on her heels. "You're telling me you will not allow it. You will choose to hold me at a distance, even as I tell you I want to be closer." He said nothing.

Ada stood, felt the heat of tears gathering. "I don't want that. I can return to the house in the wood and have that."

Ada returned to her side of the bed and picked up the brush from where she'd left it and set it on the table. She slipped her feet into her slippers and managed still to keep the tears at bay.

"You, of course, understand how newly come I am to the lovemaking." She couldn't help it—nonetheless, did nothing to correct it—that the word *lovemaking* emerged with a snarl of mockery. "But I swear to God, I assumed all that tenderness implied some affection between us."

Jamie had stood, faced the bed now, and regarded her. Yet he said nothing.

Ada walked to the door.

"Where are you going?"

"I'm going away from you," she said evenly over her shoulder. She stopped near the door and pivoted to face him. "You don't deserve me, or even this very insignificant 'us'. If you change your mind, if you...want anything other than...this, I will behave as your wife. But not until then."

His frown was heavy but still, he said nothing.

The part of her that was so very undone with sadness over his rejection, for that's exactly what it was, made her lash out at him, with some final thoughts. "If you plan to throw the point of my argument back in my face, kindly recall all the parts of it." Yesterday, defending her decisive action against Baldwin, she'd told him that if he could not trust her judgment, then she must suppose he deemed her an idiot. And just so there was no question as to the difference between what they'd discussed yesterday and just now, she clarified, "You are an idiot, Jamie MacKenna."

Finally, he spoke, just as she stepped through the doorway. "You canna leave Aviemore."

She turned one last time, met his fierce glare with her own. "I'll not leave. Not unless you actually do not come to your senses."

"My wife will not—" He began, thrusting out a pointed finger.

Ada had had enough. "Your *wife* will behave as such when my *husband* does so as well."

JAMIE STARED AT THE vacant doorway, from which Ada had just disappeared.

Stubborn lass.

Quickly deciding that she was irrational, and certainly too hopeful for her own damn good, he returned to undressing, removing his tunic and breeches and hose. Eventually, he slid into the empty bed, stretching out on his back, one forearm bent under his head. His hands were still fisted.

Let her stew, he decided. She'd be back come the morrow. He would nobly listen to her possibly stilted apology—he couldn't quite imagine Ada cajoling—and perhaps he would offer some conciliatory gesture of his own. Or like as not, he'd end up making love to her, and the entire ridiculous circumstance would be forgotten.

Save that he would remain resolute on those two points: he would not suffer her being friendly with his soldiers, no matter how innocent she believed it to be; and he would not at all disillusion her with hopes of having love between them.

He was bound to die, he often believed. Loving Ada would only bring heartache, to both her and him. And, too, he'd witnessed what loving your wife—any woman—did to a man. Bloody hell, Gregor Kincaid was kicking down doors to get to Anice, when the key was only minutes away. Never mind that he had, more than once, wondered if what he felt when Ada smiled at him was anything at all like what Gregor must surely feel when Anice smiled at him—he'd dismissed the very possibility outright.

He had neither the interest nor the time to suffer such a distraction as that, being in love with his own wife.

Jamie chewed the inside of his cheek, replaying the entire conversation in his head once more. All would be well tomorrow, he was confident.

You are an idiot, Jamie MacKenna.

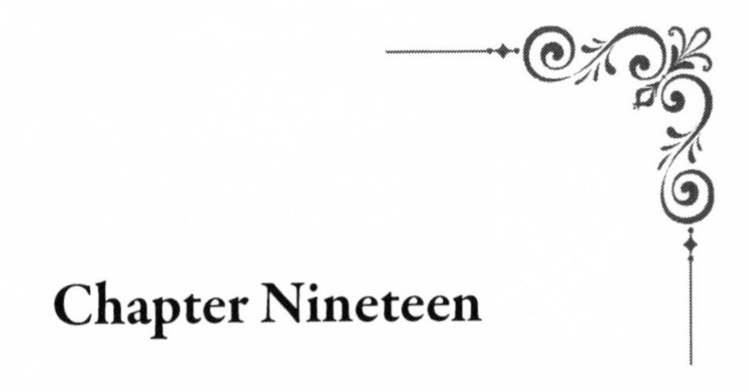

Chapter Nineteen

All was not well the next day, nor even the next several days. Jamie had discovered, with a bit of nosing around, that Ada had taken up in some unused chambers in the south wing. But that was all he knew of his wife in the days that followed their confrontation. To her credit, he did not see her at all keeping company with any of his soldiers. Twice he'd spied her heading into the kitchens, seeming wholly unaffected by their fractured state, laughing with Agnes as they'd left the hall. She'd sat next to him at dinner, smiling at this one and that, but never said a word to him, having some earnest conversation with Callum on her other side throughout most of the meal.

He'd been atop the battlements one day, only surveying a crumbling section of the wall that needed attention when he'd noticed her down at the loch. His teeth clenched immediately, about to march down there and reprimand her for going outside the gate by herself. But then Henry showed himself, moving away from the trees that had blocked him from view. And then, to Jamie's surprise, his aunt also appeared, chirping about something that had her clapping her hands together excitedly while Ada tossed her head back and laughed with Henry.

From within the shadows of the stables one day, he watched her cross the bailey, from dovecote to keep, with Aviemore's new cook, Joanna. He witnessed again the scraping and groveling of persons not yet friendly with her, as a serf from a nearby cottage came barreling through the gate, babe in arms, and all but fell at Ada's feet. The woman held the infant up toward Ada even as she kept her own head bent. Ada gasped and covered her heart with her hand, looking anxiously from the woman to the babe to Joanna. Finally, her shoulders slumped, and she took the babe in her arms, pulling back the swaddling to coo and fuss over the child. While the woman watched with keen adoration, Ada pressed a kiss onto the child's forehead. Jamie almost found himself laughing then, at the face she made when the babe began to bawl. With a near comically guilty expression, Ada pushed the infant out to arm's length and beseeched his mother to claim him. But yes, he could clearly see how that occurrence, repeated again and again, would make Ada extremely uncomfortable.

Three nights after their unfortunate clash, Jamie had exhausted all his patience, waiting for Ada to come to him, begging his forgiveness. He'd just come from the garder robe and a lengthy bath, to his empty chambers and bed, and decided enough was enough. She'd certainly made her point that she could pretend better than he that she wasn't bothered at all by their present situation. Wearing only the breeches he'd donned to see him from the bath to his bed, he left their room and strode with purpose toward her temporary quarters.

He found himself standing outside the door, debating which might serve him better: knocking first, and waiting admittance, or barging in as laird of the keep, asserting his dominance to set the tone for what would come next.

"Did you need something?" Came Ada's voice.

From behind him.

Jamie rolled his eyes at his own dumb luck, and for tarrying too long with indecision. He turned to find Ada anticipating a response, her slim brow lifted, while her arms were filled with a stack of freshly folded linens.

Jamie cleared his throat. "Aye, we should talk, lass."

With no hesitation at all, and with an exasperatingly unreadable tone, she suggested, "It's late. Maybe tomorrow?"

"Aye," he heard himself agreeing, his eyes on her lips. With a mental shake, he caught himself. "Nae." He moved to block the door completely, just as she'd moved to be through it. Away from him. "Nae," he said again. "We'll talk now."

He half turned and opened the door, and then took her arm and pulled her into the room. He'd already closed the door behind him when it occurred to him that he should have marched her back where she belonged, to their chambers.

She faced him, her expression inscrutable, which only allowed Jamie to be thankful he'd not read anger. She did that thing that he'd noticed previously, when she was on edge, where she rolled her lips inward, while she watched him warily.

"Ada," he began, not truly knowing where he was going with this, except to say, "that's enough of this now. Come back with me."

She did not move. Her expression did not change. She did not even blink.

For the love of all that was holy, he would like to know how, between Stonehaven and here and now, she'd learned to hide her emotions. There was a time, he happily recalled, that every sentiment she felt played across her face like ripples waving across the surface of the loch.

"Your teeth are clenched," she noted in an even tone, "much as they were during our last conversation. This has me thinking that you cling still to your ideas of how and what our marriage should be, with no care at all for my preferences. That being the case, my position has not changed."

His jaw only tightened. "Just like that? With no discussion?"

She laughed and stepped around him, toward the bed in this room. "You didn't come here for discussion. You came and barked out an order." She dropped the stack of linens onto a chair beside the bed and pulled one from the top, shaking out the folds.

There was not any part of him—not even the very large part of him that quite often found so much pride in her bravery—that appreciated her very aloof, seemingly unbothered manner. As he would never believe that she'd managed to hide her true self from him for so long, he had to imagine that her coolness now was all for show, a façade she'd created to...what? Befuddle him? Vex him?

It didn't matter, the why. It mattered only that he break through the wall she'd erected.

He knew of only one way to do that.

Jamie strode to where she stood. And just as he reached for her arm, to turn her toward him, he saw that she swallowed hard when he entered her peripheral. A near predatorial grin crested; she was not unaffected. If she had stiffened when he touched her arm, he might have thought twice about his next move. But she only closed her eyes and held herself very still, either willing further courage from within or praying he didn't seduce her into acquiescence, because she knew he could.

She turned and he kissed her, but only partly to deconstruct her wall, and mostly because he'd missed her. That notion rather slammed into him just as his lips touched hers. He should never be too long gone from her kiss. His own stubbornness over the last few days did not extend to rejecting his desire for her kiss. He wasn't that strong, and frankly, he did not particularly mind being tortured by thoughts of kissing Ada.

He let his lips and tongue demonstrate his desire. Her resistance was small, half-hearted even. While she didn't seek more, she did respond to his kiss. She didn't wrap her arms around his shoulders and stretch her fingers into his hair the way he liked, but she did have her hands on his chest between them. When he slanted his head, she adjusted accordingly, and her tongue met his with equal enthusiasm. Nae, she was not so stoic as she'd have him believe.

Many days without her in his arms had created a powerful need and he pressed this against her belly. He kissed her lips and her neck and her cheek...and tasted a saltiness.

Ah, but why did she have to cry?

He wanted to ignore the tears, pretend he hadn't tasted them. "God damn it," he cursed against her lips. "I know you want this." This, breathed raggedly.

"I don't *want* to want this," she said in an incredibly small voice.

Jamie chuckled without humor. "'Tis a curse, and don't I know it, lass."

"What's the point of desire, if there's nothing more?"

He did not let her go but lifted his head to better see her face. "Desire is the point." *Desire is the by-product*, something whispered inside him. He ignored it.

"You won't force me." There was only hope, not any surety, in her voice.

"I will no have to."

Jamie watched her face fall at this pronouncement, so very thankful that she had abandoned the pretense of indifference, and he was able to read her again. She knew it to be true. Had known it well before he put it to words.

He wouldn't, of course, damn his own honor. Releasing her now was not an easy thing to do, not when what he wanted was within his grasp. Heaving a tortured sigh, he dropped his hands from her arms and stepped away. He did not give up the room, only took the chair near the hearth, watching her.

With stiff, almost trancelike movements, she regained the discarded bed sheet and began to lay it out over the linen covered mattress. He revisited their conversation of the other night, reassessed his own inner debate about their marriage and his part in it.

And he considered her and his desire for her. He couldn't say he'd ever felt this degree of desire for another. His first wife had been naught but a thorn to Ada's rose.

He watched her stretch across the bed, smoothing out the soft linen, her arms lean within the sleeves of her kirtle, slim fingers brushing against the fabric. She moved around the bed, obviously intent on ignoring his presence, even as she must feel the very heat of his gaze. She flattened and fitted the linen on the far side, leaning across to offer him a fine view of her collarbone and the swell of her breast as it pressed against the bodice of her gown.

Ada was...so very desirable. Every damn inch.

And he was no fool.

The desire was comprised not only of the need to feel her, to have his hands on her, his lips touching hers, but much, much more. He leaned forward, putting his elbows onto his knees and threading his fingers together. No fool, indeed. He knew well the effect she had on him, almost from the start. Seeking her out in the middle of the day when he'd have been better served by distance between them. Awaiting her entrance in the dining hall with near teeth-gritting anticipation. Rising from his bed and having thoughts of Ada be his first of the day. Salting his dreams with images best saved for people who believed that happily-ever-afters really existed.

Jamie was intimately acquainted with what havoc she wreaked upon him, upon his entire life. But he was ever practical, and there remained the fact that he would leave soon, and for the life of him, he could not dispel the notion that he would return no more to Aviemore. He was pleased that she had so quickly acclimated to Aviemore, and to those that mattered. If he'd managed to get her with child already, a boy would one day be laird of Aviemore. If there was no bairn—he guessed this more likely, certainly considering their present circumstance—Uncle Malcolm, and then his son by Agnes, would rule the MacKennas. He'd already spoken to Malcolm, had made known that his sole objective in marrying Ada had been to see her cared for all her days. Unquestionably, he rested easier having this settled.

That was all he'd wanted, right? That had been his only objective.

It had been, at one time.

He sat back again. She had just finished with the coverlet and could no more ignore him. She faced him, managing to look all at once unnerved and resolved. The hazel eyes blinked and regarded him warily, even as she straightened her shoulders, surely about to request his departure.

"What is it you want, Ada?" He asked before she might have spoken.

One brow arched. "We've already discussed—"

"Tell me again," he insisted.

She sat on the side of the bed, rather fell back upon it as if the motion were only an exasperated sigh. "Jamie, it doesn't matter. And truth be told, it's an uncomfortable conversation to have again. When last we spoke, I—I misunderstood what you were trying to say. I see that now. And—well, never mind. Please, just give me a few more days and I'll return to our chambers. We can...carry on."

She was not looking at his eyes. Her gaze had settled on his chest. He couldn't say for sure that it did so with desire, as it had previously, or if now it was only an evasion, to avoid his eyes.

"What did you misunderstand?"

Still, the hazel eyes stayed on his naked chest. She did not answer his question. Instead, she offered, "You have done a very honorable thing, to have married me, given me this life, and Aviemore. Everything will be fine." She tried to smile.

"Ada, you are the bravest person I ken. Why can you no answer the question?"

Now her eyes met his. He raised a brow. The look that crossed her face was all at once weary and cross and completely disenchanted.

"Because it does not matter." Pointedly, she added, "Hills to die on, and all that."

They were talking about the state of their marriage, what was expected and needed and hoped for, and she'd just told him that it wasn't important enough to engage her. While his hackles rose at this, he acknowledged that his stoniness of the other night might have something to do with such a bare statement.

"Just give me a few more days," she pleaded again.

He nodded and stood. A fantastic inner debate waged just then, to go to her, to kiss her senseless, to kiss her into admitting she lied, that indeed, it did matter. But to do so would require him also to examine why he was so bothered by her suddenly dismissive attitude. He wouldn't love her, would rather she didn't love him, why was he so angry now that she'd given him what he said he wanted just three nights ago?

The other side of the debate won out, and Jamie left, closing the door behind him, his mind whirring with how unrealistic his expectations had been, about everything. Her. Marriage. Tonight. His need of her. Hills worth dying on.

Jesus bloody Christ.

ADA WAITED UNTIL THE door had closed before releasing her breath. It burst forth with a cry. She slapped both hands over her mouth, stifling any further noise, whimpering silently while a shudder racked her whole body.

Dear Lord, but that man had just tried and challenged every fiber of her being!

She understood why he'd come tonight. In truth, she'd expected him sooner. But why did he feel the need to dredge it all up again? How had he imagined his coming here tonight, using the same cool attitude of the other night, might have seen her returned to his bed? He'd said his part three nights ago; she'd figured out, a day later, what he'd meant. There was no reason to put her through it again.

When he'd reminded her the other night that they had not married for love, and then had said, basically, he would not allow himself to love, she had mistakenly thought he'd meant that he wasn't interested in becoming a victim of love again, didn't want to be hurt by it—perhaps as he had in his first marriage. She'd believed that he truly was being stubborn, choosing not to even entertain the possibility of love between them.

What a fool I was!

She understood very little about love, but she knew this: you did not choose who you loved, or who you did not.

You just...loved. Or you didn't.

Upon reflection, it was clear the drivel he'd offered had been given in an attempt to soften the rejection, when in fact the truth was, he had no feeling for her, outside of the desire for her body. He couldn't force it any more than she could *make* him love her, nor any more than she could *not* love him.

How unsettling. And embarrassing. And so incredibly heartbreaking.

She'd had now several days to come to terms with it. She hadn't been in love with him when she married him, she didn't think, so she couldn't even claim that she wouldn't have married him if she'd known this aforehand. All it had done, truly, was dash any hope of true happiness. Resolutely, she'd determined that with hope out of the way, and with her having a firm grip of her own reality, life would actually be easier. She would define and embrace her role as Lady MacKenna and never give him cause to regret affording her a life she'd likely never have known if not for him. And damn it, in another day or two, she was sure she could smile while doing it.

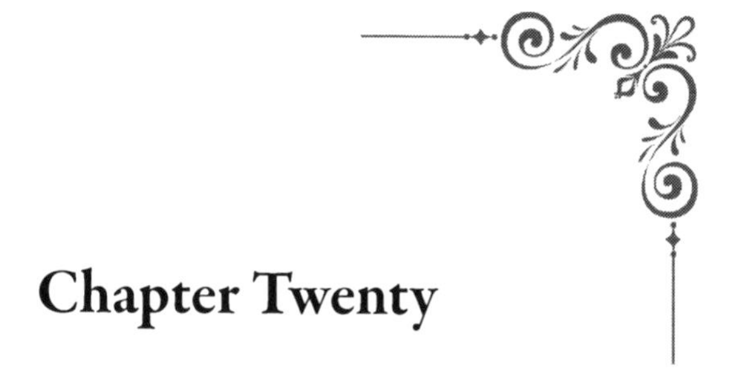

Chapter Twenty

Two mornings later, in which Ada had seen little of her husband but knew she hadn't much more time before she must oblige him and returned to their chambers at night, she stood in the kitchen, discussing the day's menu with Joanna and Agnes. The daily task of feeding so many people was more involved than she'd ever supposed, and Agnes had harrumphed while explaining the process, telling her with a fair amount of gloom, "Just wait, lass, until the winter comes, and your choices are so few."

"Lots of pottage and bannocks," Joanna agreed, with a similarly discouraging face.

"But we'll plan ahead and be prepared?" Ada assumed.

Agnes and Joanna exchanged a funny look and simultaneously burst out laughing.

"Be prepared, she says!" Agnes chortled.

A long trill sound disrupted their merriness. Agnes grabbed Ada's hand. "The alarm," she breathed, her mouth forming a long and narrow *O*.

Ada rushed from the kitchen, knowing the two women weren't far behind. She ran along the corridor and through the hall and out into the yard. The gate was pushed closed and secured, the portcullis slowly rattling down. The attack on Stonehaven was made disturbingly fresh in her mind as she noted the scrambling and scurrying in the bailey. She bounded for the gate house, and used the stairs to the battlements, hiking up her skirts to reach the roof. She ran around the perimeter, following the sentries as they all raced for the south side of the keep to see what came.

At the far side of the loch, well beyond the reach of even the most skilled archer, a huge army came, with wagons and banners and more soldiers than Ada had ever seen all in one place. They were too far to see yet who dared to cross onto MacKenna land without so much as a by-your-leave, and moving at only a fast crawl, but Ada still cried out with fright. Whoever they were, their numbers were easily ten times those of Aviemore.

Jamie! She panicked and raced around to the west side of the battlements, but not one MacKenna soldier was out on the training field.

She heard her husband before she saw him. Running again along the rooftop wall, she found the stairs once more to get back to the keep just as Jamie's voice rose above the din and clamor of an army and keep readying for battle.

"Where is my wife?" And only seconds later, while she descended the stairs within the enclosed walls, she heard a more frantic, "God damn it! Where is your lady?"

Ada stepped into the yard again and saw Jamie at the other end, dismounting swiftly. "Ada!" he roared, which rose her brows. She stopped, her hand on the wooden jamb of the doorway. Mesmerized, she watched him sprint toward the keep, calling her name, his tone sounding almost frantic.

"Jamie!" She called across the bailey to him, bringing him up just short of the door to the hall. He turned and scanned the yard, his anxious gaze finding her near the gatehouse.

Confusion battled within. Why was he so panicked?

Jamie raced over to her, pulling her into his arms. The look on his face was eerily reminiscent of the exact look he'd worn as he'd raced to her rescue when the enemy had come to Stonehaven. "Jesus, lass. I was worried you weren't within the walls." He hugged her tight, pressed a kiss onto her forehead.

Ada was dumbstruck. And when Jamie loosened his hold and looked down at her, he mistook her stunned expression as fear. "Ada, I will no ever let harm come to you. Do you understand me?"

At this moment, with an invading army only minutes away, the proper response might have been a quick nod, maybe an "aye". But Ada could not lose that image or the sound of her husband, the one who'd claim there would be no love, nearly fraught with terror when he feared for her.

Jamie gripped her arms, giving her a shake. "Ada, I *will* keep you safe. Do you understand me?"

Ada tilted her head back, saw all the worry reflected in the depths of his gorgeous blue eyes and said to him, with a serene smile, "I do understand...despite the proximity."

His frown deepened, and then disappeared completely. He breathed a ragged breath into her face with a short and surprising chuckle. "Aye, proximity," he said. All that was harsh and hardened melted into some new awareness, softening the whole of his handsome face, erasing the darkness in his eyes. And he kissed her, fiercely and hungrily, with his own new understanding of what such unbridled worry for her might mean. But there was precious little time to explore this. "I need to get on that wall, and I need to ken you are safe inside. I'd lock you in the chapel if I had time," he said, pushing her away and kissing her again at the same time.

I'd lock you in the chapel if I had time, were possibly the most glorious words Ada had ever heard. Lock her in the chapel, as the extremely loved and valued Anice Kincaid had once been locked in Stonehaven's chapel when danger had come.

Her husband, bless his soul, was in love with her. He must be!

Just as his fingers finally released her, a loud cheer came from the top of the wall.

Jamie and Ada exchanged glances. Cheering?

"MacGregors and Kincaids comin'!" Callum leaned over the wall toward the bailey and shouted down.

Ada had begun to smile, with this happy news, until Jamie said, "That is no a good sign, lass. No reason for them to come, save to bear sorry news."

Now that the coming horde had been identified there was no reason to take to the wall to mark their progress. Jamie gave the call to open the gate and he and Ada waited just inside. Within five minutes, Gregor Kincaid and another man, whom Ada did not know but presumed was the MacGregor walked their massive steeds inside the walls of Aviemore. Ada spied Torren coming alongside one of the wagons, a covered conveyance drawn by a team of four. A similar wagon followed this one, this one strewn with the same colors as the plaid of the MacGregor laird.

Gregor dismounted and marched straight up to Jamie. The men clasped forearms. Jamie seemed to hold his breath, while Gregor shook his head, prepared to deliver bad news indeed, Ada guessed by his tortured expression.

"Wallace has been arrested."

Ada gasped and covered her mouth with trembling hands. She looked at Jamie, saw his face go pale with acute shock. Indeed, his entire body seemed to go limp, shoulders dropping and hands falling. Ada's heart broke for him.

The MacGregor reached the pair, stretching out his hand to Jamie, who recovered as necessary.

"Let's get the lasses settled," Gregor said, "and we'll fill you in."

These words made Ada consider those wagons again. Torren was at the back of the first one, just lifting a very pregnant Anice onto the ground. Unprecedented circumstances, indeed, if Anice had been allowed or made to travel at this time. Torren reached back in and brought forth another woman, Ada saw, this one about Anice's height with long shiny hair in a most unusual shade, who lifted magnificent green eyes to the three lairds as she took Anice's hand and came forward.

Ada ran to Anice, who cried out when she noticed her.

They embraced without words. What might they say now, with the fate of the magnificent William Wallace in such grave peril?

Oh, but she was so happy to see her friend!

Anice cried into her shoulder. "This was the only good thing, that coming here would allow me to see you."

"I've missed you," Ada said, wanting to squeeze her tighter, but for the belly between them.

When they parted, Anice took up her hand and turned her toward the other woman. "This is Tess MacGregor. Tess, meet my friend, Ada Moncriefe."

"How do you do?" Ada said.

Tess stepped forward and embraced Ada. "I do just fine, and I'm so happy to meet you. Anice told me about you as we traveled."

Tess MacGregor's immediate warmth was a wonderful thing, that Ada minded not at all that Anice had shared her story, however much. With a small and wry smile aimed at Anice, Ada announced, "Actually, I am Ada MacKenna now." She assumed this news would come as quite a shock.

But Anice only showed the loveliest smile, dimpled and all. "Welcome news, indeed."

Behind Ada, a cracked and ancient voice said, "Aye, but it feels good to put me stilts to the ground."

Ada turned, and saw a charming blonde lass leading a tall and gangly old man toward them. The young girl, maybe seven or eight years old, held the man's gnarled hand and giggled at him, "Mine feel like Eagan's custard."

Ada noted immediately that the man was blind, though his slow and plodding step seemed more an affliction of age and not his sightlessness.

Tess introduced the child as her daughter, Bethany, and the man as her friend, Angus.

Remembering her role as Lady of Aviemore, Ada invited them into the hall. "I'll have Agnes prepare some barley tea."

Ada met Jamie's gaze as she led the group toward the keep, which prompted him to usher the growing circle of men in as well. His face was stricken still with disbelief and fear for the grim news they'd brought with them.

The gray and cool day compelled Ada to sit Anice and Tess near the hearth, while she begged of Henry, who hovered nearby, to stoke the fire.

Agnes, too, was nearby and after introductions to the party near the hearth, Agnes beckoned two serving girls to the kitchens with her, that they might begin preparations to feed so many weary travelers.

JAMIE STOOD AROUND the family's table, with Kincaid and Conall MacGregor. Torren and Callum had exchanged greetings as old friends and Callum gave a hearty bear hug to the MacGregor captain, John Cardmore, a huge mountain of a man, with more years and experience than any man present. Malcolm had joined them, his frown heavy, his face pale.

The grim news of Wallace's arrest had nearly floored Jamie, but only partly explained the presence of Conall and Gregor, and less so Tess and Anice and the rest of the retinue they'd traveled with.

Gregor provided some answers. "We thought to combine our armies—as we would have in another month to join Wallace—but now to London instead."

Conall added, "We left half our forces down near Haddington. They'll await us, or word from us, as we head south."

Jamie did not question this. He'd be riding right now for London if not for the fact that they obviously had decisions to make regarding what they planned to do for Wallace and how they hoped to accomplish it.

"We considered Stonehaven for the lasses, with the sea as means of escape, but figured Aviemore was further, and so much less accessible," Gregor was saying, and added grimly, "should things not go our way, and there come repercussions."

Malcolm nodded, taking it all in. "You're sure Wallace is in London now?"

"Aye, they moved him straightaway," Torren provided.

John Cardmore added, "Trial to start forthwith."

"Aye," agreed Conall, "Will be no more than a farce, meant to appease Longshanks and give only the appearance of impartiality."

"The whole God damn effort will fall apart, without Wallace," growled Gregor.

"We ride into London, we're riding straight to our own imprisonment," cautioned John Cardmore. "Be no help to Wallace then."

"I'll no leave him—do you ken what they'll do to him?" Jamie said with a great fierceness. "He'll no receive a fair trial."

Conall nodded and suggested, "We'd planned to leave skeleton crews at Stonehaven and Inesfree, and a quarter of the entire force here with the lasses."

Gregor finished, "And march into London a thousand strong, bring him back."

"Might be all we have," Conall said pensively, mulling over the plan. "Bruce might've accepted Wallace's invite to meet, but he's no in a position to do much else just yet."

But Jamie allowed, "They'll suppose some plan to retrieve him. How many do you think Longshanks will have in London proper?"

"More than we'll ever amass," Gregor said. "We canna save him by numbers and brawn alone. There has to be a plan, and it likely will require more stealth than brute force."

"We've no time to sit and strategize," said Jamie.

Torren chimed in, "You can ride and plot."

"Aye," said Conall, "we need to go now."

Jamie looked at Gregor. "I understand if you bow out. Anice needs you with her."

Gregor was shaking his head even before Jamie had finished. "Anice and our child need to live free." He looked to Torren, "She won't stand for both of us to go."

"I'll no leave her," Gregor's captain vowed. Torren looked to John Cardmore. "That puts you in charge of these three," he said with a humorless smirk, and then tossed his thumb over his shoulder at the lasses. "You answer to those three if you dinna bring 'em all home."

John harrumphed, but nodded, knowing it was true.

Conall ironed out a few more particulars. "Callum, you're on logistics for the movement. You've got one hour to mobilize the MacKenna army. We'll leave forty each, Kincaids and MacGregors. Figure out the rest to assure Aviemore can hold its own. Malcolm, if needs be, you send for the food stores at Stonehaven and Inesfree, if we're gone too long, as you'll have a full army to feed."

Gregor asked Jamie about spare horses. "We've got a few lame just from the day's journey to Aviemore. We'll leave them to your stable master and swap out for fresh."

"Aye," Jamie allowed. And he motioned to Simon, who stood close with several other officers of the three armies, who then pivoted and left the hall to see to this matter. "How are we on food for travel?"

Conall shrugged. "We brought what we could. We'll eat when Wallace is safe."

"Aye," came a chorus of agreement.

ADA AND TESS AND ANICE sat completely silent near the warm fire, listening intently to every word from the strategizing men. Angus, sitting with one long leg crossed over the other, chewed the inside of his cheek while he listened as well. The child, Bethany, seemed to sense the very air of solemnness within the hall and stayed still and mum at Angus's side.

Ada excused herself quietly and went to the kitchens to find Agnes. Luckily, Moira and Mary were there as well.

"Quickly," Ada instructed, "we need to prepare rooms, one for the Kincaid, and one for the MacGregor. The ladies will need space and rest, and they'll want privacy for their farewells."

Agnes nodded, her face pinched with her worry. "Moira and Mary will attend that now, aye, lasses? And I'm just bringing out the tea and cakes."

"Thank you," said Ada, and she returned quickly to her guests. The number of soldiers within the hall was diminishing one by one as men dashed off to see to any assigned tasks set by their lairds.

They've done this before, Ada thought, as she watched Anice and Tess. They sat, side by side, holding hands, their faces showing none of the anxiety or fear that Ada grappled with, looking all at once serene and stoic. Putting on brave faces, Ada decided, when she noticed how white were the knuckles of their clenched hands.

As the men still were gathered and plotting, Ada spoke softly still. "They are preparing rooms now. You'll want a quiet place to bid your husbands Godspeed."

Fifteen minutes later, and with Tess and Anice shown to their borrowed quarters, Ada stood inside the room she'd not shared with Jamie for almost a week. Jamie lifted the lid on the trunk at the end of the wide bed. She waited just inside the door, fearful and silent, watching him prepare to depart. Rifling through the contents of the trunk, he extracted an extra plaid and several tunics and breeches and several pairs of hose. Aviemore's armorer would have at the ready Jamie's chain mail and weaponry. Ada supposed she herself, as Jamie's wife, was responsible for what he was about now.

Oh, but how she wished they had more time! Groaning inwardly, she chastised herself for being so selfish. His time and his attention were properly and proudly obligated in service to William Wallace now. Yet, she would not allow him to leave with so much unsettled between them. She would flaunt that bravery with which she was so often attributed, she would put her heart out there again on the slim bow of her sleeve, and she would make sure he understood that it belonged to him, if he wished it.

She stepped forward, then stopped, unsure how any attempt now to smooth their recent aloofness might be received. Her understanding of what had transpired in the bailey was rightly a precarious and delicate thing; while his fear for her had led her to believe there must be love, she had since considered a late-coming argument that it could, just as well, lead her to believe that the keen excitements of a looming calamity had predicated such intense concern for only the lady of the manor.

Jamie turned toward her while she continued to gather her courage. One look at his remarkable blue eyes, so heavy with undeniably tormented thoughts and suddenly, Ada did not care about anything else, not even any possible rejection. She moved again, this time walking up to him and wrapping her arms around his middle, while his hands were filled with his rolled belongings. For just a moment, before he left her, she wanted to know the warmth and security of being pressed against him. Tunics and hose and the plaid were pressed against her back as his arms closed around her. Ada closed her eyes, committing this to memory, hoping she did not need it for long.

She would say her peace; what he did with it was his business. But she'd not have regrets hanging over her while he was gone. With a fierceness she truly believed she'd only discovered *after* she met Jamie MacKenna, she lifted her head and took his face in her hands, waiting for him to meet her eyes. His jaw was clenched, she noticed, but could not know if this was because of Wallace's predicament, or because she touched him.

"I do not want to send you off with so much unsettled between us," she said.

"It'll keep, lass, until I return."

And that was what she feared. She remembered him once saying he wasn't afraid to die, as he hadn't much to live for.

"But please come back to me," she begged, tears pooling. "I am in love with you and I want you to love me and you cannot do that if you do not return. I don't want to be foolish or afraid or...without you. I want to be your wife."

All the harshness evaporated instantly. His brow lost its crease and his eyes softened; he almost smiled, save that leave-takings were always sorrowful. He lifted his hand and smoothed his palm over her face, tracing his thumb along the scarring. "You are my wife, Ada MacKenna, with the silly other name."

Ada grinned and cried at the same time.

The kiss that followed was greedy and devouring, and Ada returned it with reckless abandon, savoring every second of this moment. She didn't know what became of the garments he'd bundled, but both his hands slid around her waist and onto her bottom, which he pulled enticingly against himself.

"Aye, I'll come back to you, lass," he breathed against her lips. "And there'll be a reckoning for what you've kept from me this past week—for which I now will have to wait so much longer."

Ada wiggled her hips against him, so needful of him just now. She needed to know they had a chance. "Take a bit now, to think on, to remind you that you need to come home. To me." To her own ears, her voice sounded husky, provocatively so.

He needed no other urging or insistence but ducked his head and covered her mouth almost feverishly. "A bit will no be enough," he growled.

"Then take more," Ada breathed into his mouth. Boldly, she lowered her hand, rubbing it between his legs.

Very slowly, he shook his head, but his refusal came not with any dedication and he pushed himself against her hand even as he lifted her skirts to find the center of her. A heat gathered in her loins while her breasts prickled with sensation as his fingers met flesh inside her drawers and slid between the folds to dip inside her. Ada moaned and sighed against his mouth, fumbling with the ties of his breeches, yanking and pulling at them to free his erection to her hand. She circled him but was allowed only seconds to touch him before he groaned and lifted her off the ground and against him.

Instinctively, she folded her legs around his back, and Jamie pivoted smoothly, taking several strides, and pushing her up against the wall.

"Move your skirts," he demanded hoarsely, his lips at her throat while she arched her back and leaned her head against the wall. She obeyed and hoisted the bulk of the heavy fabrics up to her belly. She felt the hardness of him searching against her, between her legs, and knew she was wet for him when he slipped so smoothly and wonderfully inside her, filling her. Under her fingers, she felt every muscle of his arms and shoulders flexing as he suspended her and pumped into her. She found purchase against the wall and struck one leg out as leverage against the tall cupboard next to her, lifting and lowering herself on him while heat roared and crashed within her.

Ada saw only a brief flash of his expression, clenched jaw and flared nostrils, his gaze riveted on her, before he captured her lips again. They kissed noisily and sloppily while he pumped faster and faster into her. Her foot slipped away from the cupboard just as she came so that she rather sank against him, crying out as wave after wave of pleasure exploded inside her. Jamie found his own release only moments later, with some guttural sounds escaping before he breathed, "You are mine," against her neck.

THE LEAVETAKING WAS dreadful, almost as if so many expected it to be permanent. The yard of Aviemore was filled with so many people, lairds and ladies and soldiers and serfs,

Malcolm and Agnes stood at the top of the steps to the keep, wearing matching sorrowful faces, Malcolm's thick arm around Agnes's drooping shoulder. Three youths held the reins of a trio of huge destriers, awaiting their lairds, who each stood just beside their own mount, bidding farewell to their ladies. Conall MacGregor was stoic, insisting to Tess that all would be well, and that he would absolutely return to her. Gregor Kincaid's face was imbued with both determination and guilt, for having to leave Anice at this time. She angled her head up at him, a brave smile upon her face, meaning to send him off with his mind set to the daunting task ahead, and not left here with her. Torren waited and watched, at the bottom of the steps, below Malcolm and Agnes, his thumbs looped into his sword belt, his countenance grim.

Jamie held Ada's hand, pulling her along to his mount, where he crushed her to him in one last embrace. Ada closed her eyes and her mind to everything else but the feel of him, so warm and strong and real.

"You'll come back to me," she reminded him and assured herself.

"Aye, I will, lass," he ground out against her ear. Eventually, as the others gained their mounts, Jamie pulled back and gave her an impassioned blue-eyed stare. "I'm very proud to call you my wife, Ada. I'll come back to you, as we've some unfinished matters between us, aye?"

Ada nodded and tried to smile. A tear rolled away from her eye. "I love you, Jamie."

And then he kissed her and was gone.

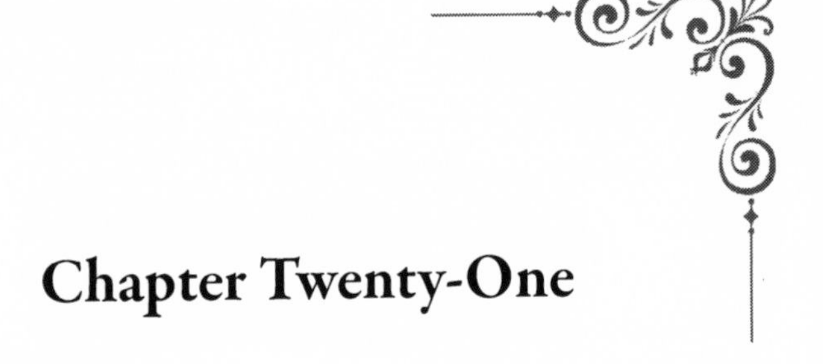

Chapter Twenty-One

"Ada, I think now would be a grand time to tell me exactly how you came to be *married* to Jamie MacKenna," Anice said.

Ada smiled at her friend, admitting, "Honestly, Anice, I'd thought to hear this question hours ago."

Anice grinned. "I was *trying* not to be nosey."

Truth be told, if they'd come yesterday, Ada was sure she'd not be smiling as she related the events of their journey to Aviemore to Anice and Tess, as the ladies sat in the nearly empty hall later that evening. Yesterday, she'd been so miserably unsure, so fearful that Jamie might never love her, that had Anice come then, she'd surely be crying on her shoulder now. But with Jamie's behavior earlier in the yard, and his swoon-worthy good bye shortly thereafter, Ada was hard pressed to contain her grin through the telling.

This did not go unnoticed by Anice, who declared, with dimpled pleasure, "You are in love with him."

Ada rolled her lips inward and nodded, though she needn't have bothered with the latter. It was written quite plainly on her face, in her shy smile and happy eyes.

Anice crossed her hands over her chest, exclaiming, "And I bet he's madly in love with you as well. How could he not be?"

Ada rather blurted out a funny laugh. "Mostly, I'm afraid he's just mad. At me." As both Tess and Anice favored her with brows raised in question, she expounded, "So often he seems so angry, always so harsh whenever he stares at me."

Tess and Anice now shared an odd look and simultaneously let out their own giggles.

"Oh, then he's definitely in love with you," Tess advised her.

"How does that say love?" She wanted to know.

"Well, that's him fighting it, my dear," Anice provided sagely.

Tess nodded, and offered, "When Conall began to fall in love with me, he was so moody, all simmering madness and furious glares. In hindsight, it's actually quite sweet, to have witnessed him understanding and finally accepting—embracing—what it was."

"Gregor kept sending me away," Anice said with a shrug, and then another laugh, "as if that would have made it disappear."

"Why is it that men are so afraid to love?" Tess wondered idly. "Do they consider it a weakness?"

"Aye, but it is," said Angus, who'd been quietly taking it all in, unmoving as to be unthreatening, so they'd continued to speak.

"Why is that, Angus?" Tess wondered.

The old man shrugged, his slim shoulders riding up and down under the soft wool of his tunic. "Their entire lives, from the time those three trained at the knee of Sir Hugh Rose and formed this closeness, they were taught and trained to be fearless. Forced, by the very world we live in, to have no weakness. You three represent the most vulnerable part of them, the one thing they cannot live without, the one thing that could be used against them." Angus lifted a hand, turned it over with his thoughts. "At the same time, you are also the very thing that makes them exactly the men they are, you ken. Remind them what all the fighting is about—love and honor, someone worth living for."

"That's some deep shite there, Angus."

All heads turned toward the doorway, where lounged Torren, his arms crossed over his chest, his grin wry.

Angus chuckled, an aged and craggy sound that Ada liked very much. "Aye, lad, but the lasses seem to like it," he teased as Torren joined them.

Anice touched his hand as he stepped past her to take a seat next to Angus. "And here's my poor Torren, tasked with the ignoble job of safeguarding me."

Angus sobered and stated with profound seriousness, "If you think his duty is no important, you're no as clever as I'd believed, lass."

"Aye," Torren agreed. "Those three need clear heads for what they're about."

"'Tis a great honor," Angus added, and defined, "the lairds chose him, above all others. They can ride away and ken you are safe, and in good hands, and concentrate on the task at hand. Torren's role is invaluable to them right now, aye?"

THE NEXT MORNING, TESS found Ada in the kitchens shortly after breakfast.

"Anice will be lying abed a little longer today," she said and quickly waved off Ada's concern. "She is only fatigued and promises that is all."

Agnes turned from the counter where she plucked feathers from pigeons, and pronounced with good cheer, "Aye, and she'd better find her rest now before the bairn comes and takes it all away." This was followed by a delighted cackle, given by a woman whose very age suggested vast experience in the matter, and whose voice insisted it was so.

Tess and Ada shared a smile before Tess asked, "Might I have a chore to prove useful?"

Ada resisted. "Tess, you are a guest, and not expected to labor while you're here at Aviemore."

"I did not think I was, but I will be extremely annoying to you," she said with a beautiful smile, "if I'm left to my own devices."

Ada grinned at this, understanding the need to not be idle. And then a thought struck her. "Tess, maybe you can help Joanna and I. Jamie once told me that some bread baked down at Inesfree, with apples and something called cinnamon, is his favorite. Might you be able to help us with the recipe?"

"And the cinnamon?" Joanna added, standing beside Ada, as they'd been discussing the plans for the days meals.

Tess's gorgeous green eyes widened. "I remember when Jamie tasted it for the first time. His eyes lit up, and he kept looking down upon the trencher, as if he couldn't believe such a thing existed. It was so funny to watch. But yes, I'd love to help."

Ada and Joanna looked at each other and smiled with excitement.

Tess stole of bit of this. "Of course, we'll have to wait on the cinnamon. Angus's son, Fynn, provides that from his trading, but I can send some up when I return. Aviemore has an orchard, I presume?" At Ada's nod, she said, "Then let's see if any apples are ready this early, and we can make it with honey in the interim, and at least you'll have the recipe."

Twenty minutes later, Ada and Tess had wrapped themselves up in their cloaks, as the wind was fierce today, and headed outside the gates and toward the orchard. Henry and Bethany ran ahead, Bethany following the flight of a butterfly while Henry scampered alongside, maddeningly trying to send the butterfly further out of her reach. Two soldiers dogged their heels, after the usual bowing and scraping toward Ada, and several appreciative but furtive glances at Tess's uncommon beauty.

Tess threaded her arm through Ada's and whispered, having checked that the two men-at-arms were far enough away, "I can rarely get a soldier to form sentences in front of me, but you've outdone yourself, Ada. The genuflecting is well done, indeed."

There was much mischief in Tess's tone, but Ada insisted on clarifying, "That is not to my liking. I'm about to enlist Torren to start knocking heads together."

"It's charming, but quite curious."

"I assume Anice explained exactly how Jamie and I met?"

"She did," Tess acknowledged. "Which makes you my hero, as well."

Ada rolled her eyes, sensing that Tess was only partly serious. "When we arrived here, and it was told that the great laird of Aviemore had taken a wife, these people were none too happy with his choice—likely having hoped for someone who matched him leastwise in beauty."

Tess, bless her, did not instantly refute this, insisting with any hollowness that of course Ada was beautiful, despite the scarring. She said only, "But of course, you know that you are more beautiful because of your scars."

Ada smiled at her and continued. "So Jamie shared the rather inglorious details and now they all think I'm the second coming of our Lord."

Tess giggled at this. "A weighty mantle to bear."

"Annoyingly so. Please tell me that you and Conall had a more conventional beginning."

Tess chuckled. "Alas, I cannot. He kidnapped me, to spite my father, who'd wronged him years ago. I spent the first five days at Inesfree locked away in a tower and believing I was bound to die."

"Not so ordinary at all!" Ada realized. "But how remarkable, that you turned hate to love."

"As did you," Tess reminded her. "But where is your hound, Will? Anice mentioned he was at Stonehaven with you."

"When we left Stonehaven, it was in the company of William Wallace. Will took to him straight away, and Wallace to him." She shrugged, more dismissively than what she felt, being not at all unaffected by how much she missed her hound. "When we parted ways, Will followed him instead, almost as if he sensed that Wallace needed him, a companion.

"How lovely. Animals are very intuitive, I've always felt."

Kindly, Tess did not put into words the fear that Ada had been wrestling with for days, that if Wallace had been captured, Will might likely be dead.

They reached the orchard, with Henry and Bethany racing ahead, running between the scrub brush and trees.

And by mid-afternoon, with both Tess and Ada aproned and dusted with flour, as was Joanna's round face, they'd created what Agnes referred to as a masterpiece, and which Ada resolved must absolutely become a regular staple at Aviemore.

"And the cinnamon makes it even tastier?" Joanna asked, with a skeptical lift of her brow.

"I cannot imagine," Ada chimed in, savoring the last bit of her piece of the apple bread.

"But it's true," Tess assured them. "Just you wait."

Anice finally showed herself, looking rested and calm. Of course, Torren wasn't far behind.

"She sniffed out the food," Torren teased.

Anice ignored him but gave away the truth of Torren's statement. "But what is it? It smells heavenly."

Happily, Joanna cut two more slices of their new favorite food, the apple bread. One piece was significantly larger than the other, which she proudly handed to Torren, having first given Anice the smaller of the two.

Anice considered the size of her share, against that of Torren's, her gaze envious.

With a roll of his eyes, and while all the watching women giggled, Torren switched their wooden plates and grinned at Anice's now satisfied smile.

THREE WEEKS AFTER THE lairds and their armies had departed Aviemore for London, a rider came to the castle, bearing a sanded missive written in Gregor's hand. It was brought into the hall by Henry and handed to Torren. He'd been hovering over Anice, seated near the hearth and feeling poorly this day. Ada, Tess, and Angus were present also, as it was nearing the supper hour.

With a steady hand, Torren snapped the wax seal, and perused the words before sharing the report with everyone. The change in his expression, from fairly still with breath held, to darkened scowl with a long breath blown out, told one and all there came no good news.

"Wallace is dead," he told them, seeming to lose a bit of his fierceness, looking all at once so much smaller and suddenly unsure. "They did not reach London in time." He paused and looked at the words scratched upon the vellum once more. "*All are well,*" he read aloud. "*Expected to Aviemore in three to four weeks.*"

Ada sat, fell really, into a chair next to Angus, her tears instant. She covered her face with her hands and wept, thinking of William Wallace's constancy and perseverance, and of his warm blue eyes. Tess moved behind her and rubbed her back and shoulders.

Angus's voice was scratchy and sorrowful, as he said, "That'll be the end of it, then. Freedom will no be ours."

A long span of silence, interrupted only by soft sniffling, stretched out upon the hall, until Ada was revived and pulled from her abject sorrow by Torren's words.

"It's time, lass?"

Lifting her head, Ada saw Anice biting her lip while pain gripped her, one hand sitting on the top of her belly. "Aye, I think it is." She said when the pain had passed.

Ada's heart broke for her, for how truly terrified she looked, her beseeching eyes fixed on Torren. The big man quickly tamped down his own apprehension and went to her side. "We'll be fine, lass." He scooped her up in his arms and Ada led the way up the stairs and around the gallery to find the Kincaid chambers.

Tess had called after them that she would alert Agnes and had dashed off toward the kitchens.

Inside Gregor and Anice's chambers, Torren carefully laid Anice out on the bed. He knelt at her side, while she held his large hand, their thumbs interlocked. Ada adjusted pillows behind Anice and then could only stare and wait, feeling supremely inadequate and unqualified. Tess came into the room and stood by Ada, the pair joining hands as well.

Torren's voice soothed them all. "Just do as Agnes says, lass. And you scream when you want, and you call me when you need me. The lasses are here to comfort you and you'll be just fine." And then, because he sensed her anxiety, he teased, "I'll be drinking myself senseless below stairs, aye, lass?"

Anice managed to grin at this but was soon overtaken by another contraction just as Agnes appeared at the doorway, smiling as if the unease and fear within the room wasn't something you could actually see and taste and touch. "Aye now, it's a birthing, folks. No call for the long faces," she said with a merry chuckle. "Get on with you, Torren Beyn. 'Tis women's work from here on out."

Torren did not leave immediately, not until the contraction had waned and Anice released his hand. For his sake, Anice nodded and smiled at him, as best she could, but no one in the room believed that she was unafraid or perfectly at ease.

Anice labored for nineteen hours, in which time she'd been changed and bathed twice, while always Ada and Tess were at her side. Not once did Anice release a strip of Kincaid tartan, which she held so dear, squeezing it mercilessly as the pain came and sometimes holding it to her face, with thoughts of Gregor, Ada had to assume. Agnes came and went, as needed, having pronounced early on that the work load was all on Anice. "We can only make you comfortable, lass. And in that, there'll be no comfort until the bairn comes and gives us a good wailing."

For some time, Tess sat behind Anice, rubbing her back while Anice moaned quietly. Agnes brought rose oil into the room, which Ada rubbed all along Anice's thighs and hips. She was fed sugared water and vinegar, but accepted this only sparingly, choosing sometimes only to suck on a linen square dipped into water.

Torren tried twice to enter the room, but Agnes would have none of it. On the second occasion, Anice was in between contractions and managed, in a clear and seemingly strong voice, to call out to him that she was well.

So it was, just after midnight then, on the third day of the ninth month, in the year of our Lord, 1305, that Ian Kincaid, son of Gregor, finally greeted the world. He came wailing, just as Agnes had hoped, and howled yet more when he was taken immediately to be bathed and swaddled. "Aye, but he's a loud one, your mighty Kincaid bairn," chortled Agnes, charged with the babe's care as she was the only one in the room with any experience.

Anice slumped against the pillows, her brow damp with the sweat of her labors, her face ashen, and her smile wondrous. Ada stayed with Anice, still holding her hand, exactly where she'd been when the babe had come, while Tess assisted Agnes. When finally the infant was presented to his mother, Agnes beamed a bright and red-faced smile, proudly placing the swaddled bairn into Anice's tired arms. This enlivened her, and tears fell as she met her son, her joy overwhelming her. Tess and Ada shared a glance across the bed, their own eyes misty as well.

An hour later, Tess and Ada had changed and bathed Anice once again. The new mother sat up against the pillows on the headboard, covered in a fresh night rail of fine linen. Her serene and pleased smile had barely left her child, even as he was now held in Torren's arms while he sat in a chair near the bed. The babe was a "right nice size," Agnes had said, but still looked so astonishingly tiny enveloped in the big man's huge arms. Torren showed no embarrassment at all for his own watery gaze, as he beheld the little cherub, whilst the babe fisted one entire hand of fingers around only half of Torren's thumb.

THEY TEASED OFTEN OVER the next several days that if not for the fact that Anice was regularly needed to breastfeed her own child, she would be able to hold him barely at all. The bairn came into the world as so many did, with a plethora of people just waiting to love him, that Anice's chambers rarely contained less than two or three visitors.

After one week, Anice was thrilled to be allowed out of the bed and her rooms—Agnes and Torren had agreed—so that she rejoined the daily activities in the hall. The babe's coming was indeed timely, and for certain had lessened the pall that had shrouded Aviemore since the news of Wallace's execution, but the truth was, there hung still an air of dread, while Scotland's future and the very fate of their husbands was yet unknown.

The routine of Aviemore settled and then continued for the next few weeks. The ladies met every morning to break their fasts, always in the company of Torren and Angus and Bethany. Of late, Henry had joined them, at first in awe of Torren's massive size, and then, slowly, beginning to warm to conversation with the big man. Ada was pleased with this occurrence, thinking Torren Beyn a fine model for whom Henry to emulate while both Callum and Jamie were absent, being both fearless and gentle and wise. Ada and Tess had traded happy smirks over the way Bethany constantly had her pretty blue eyes on the lad, stealing glances while she hovered always near Angus.

Ada's mornings were kept busy within the kitchen and with household duties, and she was thankful for Agnes's continued help in this regard. While she might well manage the keep by herself, learning as she went, the advent of their welcome guests did make for more chores and labor, and Agnes's assistance was both valued and necessary.

Ada often came across Torren keeping company with Malcolm, who'd since recovered from his brief illness. The two men oversaw the constant training and upkeep of the mixed armies housed now at Aviemore, with Henry always underfoot. And there was hunting to be done, which often took so many units far outside the walls, with mostly successful efforts to keep the large numbers well fed.

The afternoons usually found the three ladies in Ada's solar, a private chamber next to her and Jamie's, which Agnes had told her Jamie's mother had used to entertain favored lodgers. Here, they busied themselves with needlework, making and mending, Tess having supplied so many bolts of fabric that Anice had teased they might have new kirtles, each of them, for every day of the week, if they were to employ all the yards of material. Malcolm had kindly tasked Aviemore's carpenter with the very important job of fashioning a cradle for the babe, one he suggested, with a wink toward Ada, might see use even when Anice and her bairn were gone from Aviemore. Thus, when Torren was not present, and the beautiful babe was sleeping, he was settled quite nicely in the cradle, upon a soft coverlet of fine linen, which had been the first item Tess had made and then gifted to Anice. When Torren was present, it was a rare occasion that the babe was not found in his arms.

Suppers at Aviemore, while the three lairds and their armies were still far afield, and because of the additional details that had reached this far north, specifying exactly how unspeakably Wallace had been put to death, were unsurprisingly subdued. At this time, the meal had not the usual societal agency, being neither cheery nor animated, but only a venue at which to receive sustenance.

And at night, while Ada lie in their big bed, which sorrowfully had now seen too many nights without Jamie beside her, she thought of him, and dreamed of him, and talked to him. Somehow, despite knowing firsthand that life might not always or exactly choose the course to which you'd set all your hopes, Ada still succeeded in never once doubting that he would return to her.

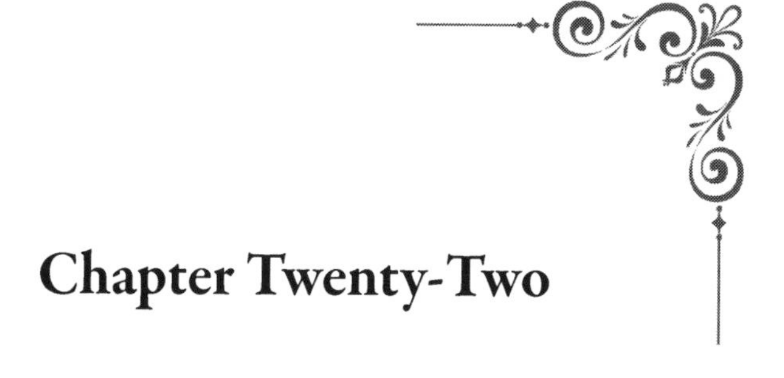

Chapter Twenty-Two

Ada stepped into the hall, surprised to find only Angus in the room, seated near the hearth. While the old man certainly needed no regular tending, he was rarely alone, being ever in the company of either Tess or Bethany, and of late, sometimes Malcolm and Torren.

"Where has everyone gone, Angus?" She asked.

He cocked his head only slightly at the sound of her voice. Surely, he'd known someone came and who that person was, well before she'd spied him. His senses were a matter of wonder to Ada.

"Gone to the loch, lass," he said. "These bright and warm days will no be upon us for much longer."

"Anice and the babe, too?" Ada asked with some surprise, taking the chair next to Angus, before the low afternoon fire. She glanced up at the thick pillar candles in the hanging lanterns overhead, making a note that these all needed changing, likely before the week was out.

"Aye, after a fair amount of wheedling and cajoling with the big man," Angus said, a grin teasing his features. "Torren finally agreed, but only if the babe went by way of the basket, and only in his hands."

"That sounds fair," Ada allowed, her own grin coming for Torren's protective bent. "And here, Anice thought she'd have some freedom from his worry, once the babe came."

Angus chuckled. "Only doubled his workload, you ask me."

"Your hands are idle today, Angus," Ada noted, as no leather pieces sat near, which Angus deftly worked into bridles and bits and other goods. He held only his pipe, the scent of whatever he smoked mossy and thick. "Will I send for more hides from the tanner?"

"No today, lass."

"You are happy to sit here with your own thoughts?"

"Sit with my thoughts, aye, but no so happily," he acknowledged.

"What brings you grief this day, Angus?"

"Truth be known, lass, I'm thinking on the death of William Wallace, and now the broken spirit of our own people."

Weighty reflections, indeed. "Jamie said the spirit of Scotland was never the same after Falkirk, that it died on the field that day, with all those thousands of men."

"Aye, like as no. But what might Wallace's death mean now?"

Ada concurred, plagued by the same questions. "It seems we might only limp along, scarred and defeated, until something comes along to stir our passions again."

Angus turned, and Ada was sure he looked directly into her eyes. "Like you, lass?"

She gasped at this, but upon consideration, supposed she was truly not so surprised. She'd kept company with Angus now for many weeks and was continually amazed how much he actually saw. Ada abandoned the chair and knelt at Angus's feet. She placed a hand on his knee and lifted his one hand while he moved the other, which held his pipe, out of the way. With her palm at the back of her hand, she pressed his palm to her cheek.

With this permission, Angus leaned left and set the pipe on the ground at his side. He put this hand, too, on her face. While his fingers were spread out over her ears, he used his thumbs to find and trace over every mark on her face. His thumbs moved slowly and then back and forth several times over the larger, deeper scars.

"Aye, I suspected as much, lass. Or something like this."

"But how...?"

"It's in your voice, lass. No your words, but in the sound."

Ada grimaced and took one of Angus's hands and moved those fingers down over her neck. He nodded while he felt his way along the thick abrasion from the rope. "Aye, I ken it. But that's no what makes the sound, lass. Sorrow is what creates the sound I hear."

"But I..." she stopped as Angus shook his head.

"It'll be fine once your chief comes home. Aye, but you remember, lass, your husband can make you *feel* safe, can bring you joy—but only *after* you find these things inside yourself. Aye?"

Slowly Ada nodded, while the old man's hands slipped away from her face and neck. Ada stood and found again the chair beside Angus. He was a wonderful man, was Angus, so she didn't feel the need to tell him that, proudly, she knew these things already.

Bethany bounded into the hall, flushed and smiling, holding what Ada was quite sure was Henry's peaked felt hat. The lass sidled up to Angus, casually laying her arm across the old man's thin shoulders. Angus extended his arm around her waist.

"You're causing trouble, lass, I can smell it." His tone now was light and happy.

Bethany, standing just about the same height as Angus's seated form, leaned close and whispered something in his ear. Chuckling, Angus patted her back and said, "Aye, I ken you do. But you leave off bothering that poor lad. He's got his work, and his training, and he'll no want this distraction." And then, with another chortle, "No for another ten years, at least."

Henry himself bounded into the hall, his hand on the door frame as he came to a quick stop and scanned the room. Spying Bethany, he made straight for her, only showing slight frustration. Truly, he seemed enlivened by the play. Bethany squeaked, and with a quick peck to Angus's cheek, she was off, around the table as Henry gave chase, and back out the door.

Ada and Angus laughed at this. Not two seconds later, Tess showed herself in the same doorway, just as breathless and as flushed as the children.

"They've come!" She called, her excitement a living thing, breathing around her. "Ada, they're returned!"

Ada jumped from the bench, darting toward Tess, before thinking of Angus. She turned and offered to bring him outside to await the armies. "Come, Angus."

"Go on, Ada dear, see your man. I'll sit right here in the quiet and listen to the happy reunions."

Tess was waving her on from the doorway.

"Where's Anice?" Ada wondered as she met Tess and they left the hall, stepping out into the quiet, mournful air of the bailey. The sentries on the wall, under different circumstances, might have whooped and hollered, raising swords and MacKenna banners in salute. This homecoming, while thankful, was somber. To celebrate their return with glad hearts, with any exhilaration, seemed false. They could not rejoice, not when William Wallace had been so tragically, so mercilessly, and so traitorously, cut down.

The gates were swung wide and the portcullis creaked and groaned as it was lifted.

Tess pointed to Anice, holding her bairn, her smile the most gorgeous thing as she glanced teary-eyed up at Torren next to her. Torren carefully took the beautiful babe from Anice, cradling him snugly in his big arms and hands. "You'll want to throw yourself at him, I'm guessing," he said to Anice.

The ladies stepped forward, poised still just inside the yard, holding hands.

They came as one, Conall and Gregor and Jamie, riding side by side through the gates of Aviemore. Their faces were grim, even as their eyes lightened upon seeing the lasses waiting for them.

Ada kept her gaze on Jamie, his tight and grief-stricken countenance drawing forth a whimpered cry from her lips. Her eyes scanned every inch of him as he dismounted, finding him whole in body, if not in mind. As Gregor and Conall had also dismounted, the three women released each other's hands and rushed to the men.

Ada ran to Jamie, throwing herself at him. There were no words, none that needed to be said now. She was in his arms, he was holding her tight, his face buried in her neck.

Jamie was home.

True, she would have liked immediately to have taken him to their chambers, to have stripped him of his clothes and his sorrow, and to have been loved by him as she'd dreamed for so long. But they had guests yet, friends all, and they would grieve together now.

Jamie lifted his head and stared over Ada's shoulder, turning her around. They watched as Gregor loosened his hold on Anice while Torren walked closer, with Gregor's son in his arms. Gregor moved as well, closer to Torren, tugging Anice along by her hand. He met the proud and happy gaze of his old friend. Before Gregor glanced down at his son, he wrapped a hand around Torren's neck and drew their foreheads together, the babe between them. "Thank you, my friend." No one who heard had any doubt about what he so much appreciated, keeping his Anice safe.

Torren inclined his head, and Gregor released him to look down upon his child. His very handsome face softened with awe while his son stared back at him with the amazing blue eyes of his mother. Gregor took the child from Torren, showing none of a new father's uneasiness at holding something so small and fragile. Anice stood at his side and moved a bit of the swaddling out of the way, to show all of his angelic face and some of the spiky blond hair.

Ada teared up, seeing Gregor's silent joy at beholding his son, noticing his watery gaze.

"He's just a miniature Anice, swathed in a blanket," Gregor breathed, mesmerized, while those around laughed at this silly though perfectly apt statement.

MUCH LATER, WHEN THE supper was done, when the sad tale of how they'd arrived too late in London had been given in low and weary voices, when a haunting and mournful song in the delicate, innocent voice of Fiona had been sung to Wallace's memory, when the new babe had been fussed over by all those gone for so many weeks, they finally retired, finding quiet and peace in their chambers.

Jamie sat on the edge of the bed, having removed his sword and belt, about to remove his boots. Ada pushed the door closed and leaned against it.

He was home.

Setting his boots aside, Jamie lifted his gaze and his hand to her. "Come."

Ada put her hand into his and Jamie pulled her onto his lap, lifting her skirts for her so that she straddled him.

He did not kiss her, just brought her close against him, pressing his chin against her shoulder while his arms slid around her back. They sat like this for many long minutes, quiet and still, while Ada ran her fingers through his hair, against his scalp.

Finally, Jamie whispered into the hair at her nape, "I've missed you."

"And I you." She closed her eyes and held him still. Another few minutes passed before Ada asked, "Is there more we need to talk about? Do you need to unburden yourself?"

He shook his head against her, and finally straightened and faced her. He swiped a hand downward, from her temple to her jaw, moving strands of her hair off her face.

"Lass, I canna talk about it anymore. Conall and Gregor and I—that's all we've spoken of for weeks. I've railed and raged, and I've cried, and we've struck out. And I'm done with all that. I need to look toward the future, this one here with you for right now."

"But Scotland's freedom?" He couldn't give up on that.

"Aye, it'll keep, lass. We've met with Robert Bruce, that's what kept us away for so long. He requests that we three, Conall and Gregor and I, fight with him, as we had with Wallace. But it'll wait for the right time. Aye, the war survives, lass, even as so many do not. But for now, can I no have you in my arms? Can you no tell me you love me again? For weeks, I've naught but heard the words in my dreams, or in my head. I need them from your lips."

Ada pressed her lips to his, breathed against him, "I love you, husband. I am yours."

"Aye, that's all I need. But I owe you more and beg forgiveness from you. I left here with Wallace on my mind, fearing for his life, and I did no do justice to what you gave me before we departed. You gave me your heart and I promised nothing in return."

Ada disagreed, "Oh, but you did, Jamie—"

"I did, with my body, but I never want you to no ken that I love you. This time was no too dangerous what we were about, but it could've been. If something had happened, you would no have ken that I love you, lass."

Ada sighed and tucked her head against his chest. "But you *will* still show me with your body, aye?"

The smallest of chuckles escaped. "Aye, I'm thinking about that verra thing just now."

This raised her head, brought her lips to his. Ada melted against him, her joy at having him in her arms once again nearly undoing her. Over the next hour, he showed her love, and said, "I love you," with more than simply words.

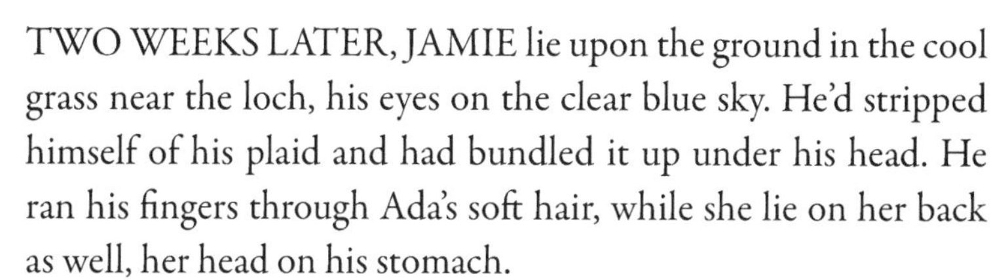

TWO WEEKS LATER, JAMIE lie upon the ground in the cool grass near the loch, his eyes on the clear blue sky. He'd stripped himself of his plaid and had bundled it up under his head. He ran his fingers through Ada's soft hair, while she lie on her back as well, her head on his stomach.

Truth be told, he'd thought to re-introduce his wife to some outdoor loving, but they'd been quickly joined by Henry who was eager to show his laird his prowess with the trident Torren had commissioned from the smithy while he'd been here. The lad stood now, ankle deep in the water, the trident poised and ready while his eyes scanned the water. His efforts might well prove fruitful if the eels would be so kind as to show themselves.

The Kincaids and the MacGregors were gone almost a week now, and sorry though he was to see them off, Jamie was happy to have his wife to himself again.

"Favorite sibling?" He asked his wife, knowing she had three sisters and one brother.

"Muriel," she answered without hesitation. "She's bossy and autocratic, but the most level-headed and friendly."

"Favorite...season," he suggested next.

"Summer, of course," she answered quickly enough. "Do persons exist who like rainy springs or harsh winters?"

"Autumn is—" he began to defend, appreciative of the different colors presented in great bounty all around them even now.

"Colorful but cold," Ada finished. "Ask me who my favorite person is."

Jamie could well detect the smile in her voice. "Nae, lass. My intent is to learn more about my wife. I'm no looking for confirmation for things I already ken."

She giggled aloud at this but challenged. "That's some pretty huge self-importance, sir."

"Did I misspeak, Ada Annabel?"

"You did not." She turned onto her side so that she faced him. "My turn."

"I've only just started," he grumbled.

"I have better questions."

"Mayhap your sister is no the only bossy one in the family."

"Mayhap," she allowed and wasted no time before asking, "Favorite city?"

"Glasgow, I suppose, though one of my favorite places is the Isle of Skye."

"Favorite boy's name?"

He shrugged. "I'm no sure about names. They're just sounds, really."

"You likely cannot see it," she said, with a hint of playful exasperation, "but I am rolling my eyes at you. Do you have a favorite girl's name?"

"I once ken a lass named Fawn," Jamie told her evasively. "What does that mean? Her mam thought her a deer? I dinna ken it."

Ada laughed again. "Very well, so you wouldn't name your own daughter Fawn."

"I would no. Unless I was planning to name her brother Buck, which I ken I would no."

Jamie lifted his head, gauging Henry's progress. The boy had barely moved. Jamie decided he would take him hunting, where his seeming ability to stand perfectly unmoving for long periods of time would serve him well.

"So what would you like to name this child, then?" Ada asked, being very still against him.

Taken aback, Jamie shifted his gaze to his wife. She smiled beautifully at him, but not without some nervousness. While he remained still, stricken actually, she sat up and faced him.

Jamie's gaze widened and moved back and forth from her belly to her now smiling hazel eyes. "A babe?" He sat up.

Ada nodded, waiting for joy to spread across his face. It did not. Every inch of his face melted with wonder. Cautiously, he reached out a hand and touched her still flat belly.

"This is mine," he said, so much reverence infused in his words, his tone. He splayed his hand out on her middle and bent to place a kiss just above her navel.

"'Tis ours, sir."

Jamie stood and pulled her to her feet. He kissed her again, knowing he would never grow tired of this, his lips on hers. He tilted her head back and let his gaze linger over all the parts of her beloved face. He'd been right, he knew, thinking of all the times while he'd been gone he'd brought to mind the picture of her. Memory did no justice to the warm hazel of her eyes.

And no memory, no dream, nor any imaginings could ever compete with the reality of having her in his arms. "Have I ever told you, Ada Annabel MacKenna, how fine you are? How beloved you are?"

"You have," she said, her smile a glorious thing. "But you should do so again, I think."

"Aye, and it's true, lass. You are everything to me."

Ada closed her eyes. She pressed her head against him, and his arms slid around her.

This was all he needed.

Everything that was good and right and beautiful in his world, in this world, was right here in his arms. There was hope, then, that men like William Wallace did not die for nothing.

Something never before known to him before he'd met Ada surrounded him, something warm and welcomed, settling over him in the form of peace and joy and hope.

Epilogue

Summer 1307
Stonehaven, Scotland

ADA MACKENNA FOLLOWED Anice Kincaid and Tess MacGregor through the tunnel of Stonehaven, and down the slope of the majestic seaside keep. At the bottom of the hill, they angled toward the right, over a well-worn path that flanked the north side of the keep and onto the magnificent beach of the North Sea.

Henry came bounding around the turn in the path as well, waving a pink ribbon in his hand, and darting around and about the three ladies. A giggling squeal, half-annoyed, followed, as Bethany gave chase, nearly bumping into Anice.

"That's my ribbon, Henry!" Bethany cried out. "Mother, tell him!" But neither she nor Henry gave Tess time to react to the dictate.

When the path opened and the beach was presented to them, Ada saw that everyone was here. She smiled, with something so much greater than fondness. They hadn't all been together like this for more than a year. And, oh how she'd missed her friends.

Anice had put so much planning and time into this gathering, Ada was amazed at all she'd accomplished in the few short weeks since the letters had gone out, with the invite. The beach had been transformed into a great dining hall, trestle tables and benches and chairs lugged all the way down from Stonehaven's hall. Fluted metal rods had been struck into the sand, spaced all around the gathering, filled with thin beeswax tapers, should these friends linger longer than the daylight. Summer's bounty of flowers were gathered and dotted the sandy landscape, in various baskets and urns and crocks. Four huge metal barrels had been rolled down onto the beach, and were arranged as four corners, filled now with low burning fires.

Ada stopped, short of the entire group, letting Anice and Tess continue toward the party. She felt misty-eyed. She would blame it on this pregnancy; Anice had teased her only this morning that it must be a girl this time, if she were so emotional. But here was everyone she held dear, and wasn't she just the most blessed person? Idly, she placed a hand over her rounded belly and looked around at all those assembled.

Tess hovered over her baby, Archie, snuggled in John Cardmore's arms while dear Angus sat very close, playing with the baby's feet. John Cardmore glanced up at the sun, giving it a mean glare, before rearranging the bairn's bonnet to shield his so very new eyes.

Anice had collected her daughter from Torren, walking back and forth, bouncing little Katie gently and rhythmically to soothe the fussing babe. Torren rejoined Muriel at the table, pressing a kiss onto her cheek, while she smiled so lovingly up at him. Ada still could not believe her sister was here and married to Torren.

To the left of the table, near the cairn rocks, stood Jamie and Conall and Gregor, entrenched in earnest discussion. Gregor was holding his toddler son, Ian, who watched Henry and Bethany running around with a curious, interested frown. Jamie had his eye on his own son, his smile fond, watching as Callum happily allowed young William to use his thumbs as anchors as he trudged unsteadily through the sand.

Jamie lifted his gaze to spy Ada taking it all in. His smile faded, replaced by concern, as he quickly strode to where Ada was.

"Is it the babe, lass? You look pained. I ken we should no have traveled now."

Ada placed her hand lightly on his chest, which quieted him immediately. She settled her gaze onto his perfect blue eyes. "Tell me you love me."

Without hesitation, he did. "Aye, I do. More than life," he said. And then with that so dearly beloved boyish grin of his, he added, "And I believe that was me demonstrating said affection just this morning when we woke."

Aye, it certainly was. "There, the day is now perfect. And complete."

Jamie smiled and kissed her lips, far too hungrily for the company they kept now.

"You might return the favor, lass. Make my day perfect as well."

She smiled against his lips, just as his words had been spoken against hers.

"I love you, husband, never less than yesterday, never more than tomorrow."

"I am a lucky man."

Jamie led Ada to the tables, sat her down on one of the benches, and stood close, his hands on her shoulders, kneading them ever so softly.

Ada listened to all the conversations around her, understanding it was peace and joy that curved her lips.

"Torren," her sister was saying with a very tolerant grin, "Anice can tend her own child."

"Aye, but Katie's wanting her nap now I'm thinking. It's about that time. I should take her back up to the keep." He was facing away from the table, watching Anice walking along the beach with her babe.

"Gregor," Muriel called, "he's fussing again. Please let him hold Ian to calm him down."

Torren turned and favored Muriel with a long-suffering grin while several chuckles followed. But Gregor brought the boy over and placed him in Torren's arms and the gentle giant's brows smoothed instantly. Ian was equally delighted to be held by Torren, smiling infectiously at the big man, knowing some manner of fun was in his immediate future.

Angus said, to no one in particular, "Aye, but aren't they magical, the bairns?"

"It's no magical, what this one just dumped into his nappy, I ken," John Cardmore said, lifting baby Archie away from his chest while Angus chuckled and waved a hand in front of his nose.

Tess stood and collected her son, whisking the bairn away to the huge woven mat Anice had made, which served as a fine barrier between the sand and a person. Conall watched her, his own contentment evident in his adoring gaze.

At the far corner of the mat, well away from the gathered friends, six massive swords formed almost a perfect standing circle, their tips struck into the sand, their blades glinting in the sun.

She heard Will barking before she saw him, but turned and found Kinnon chasing him, laughing as the hound ran straight for the water. The hound had returned to Stonehaven, likely the only place he could call home, about six months ago. Anice had written to Ada, had said he was just there one morning, standing outside the gates, and that he was well and loved and would wait for her.

Henry and Bethany had ceased their play, the pink ribbon returned to the lass's shiny blonde hair. They sat near Tess and the woven mat, attempting to make a replica of Stonehaven out of the sand. Ada considered the pair, and their awkward circumstance; half a decade possibly divided the pair, but as they were neither adults nor babies, they had only each other when these families gathered. Bethany screamed and then giggled when Will, the hound, crashed right through their creation. Henry huffed and threw sand at him, but immediately began to fix the sand walls of the castle.

Gregor stepped away from the group, went to Anice and took the babe from her arms. He rocked and hummed quite naturally, as if he'd done so a thousand times before. He and Anice continued to walk, her hand threaded through his arm. Her face was tipped up to him; she said something and he ducked his head down to her, smiling affectionately. Behind them, Kinnon and the hound followed, Kinnon scooping up seashells and tossing them back out to sea.

William, still walking with Callum, had spotted his mother. His eyes lit up while a cherubic smile broke across his face. Callum steered him in her direction. Ada turned on the bench and showed a mother's happy smile as he neared. She scooped him up and hugged him tight, her darling Will, as Callum took a seat next to John and Torren and Angus, happily accepting a cup of ale from John.

Not long after, soldiers and servants of Stonehaven filed down from the keep, bearing a feast to set upon the tables, and more wine and ale to refill the jugs and cups. Before they partook of the grand buffet, Conall, sitting at the end of one table with his sleeping son in his arms, raised his glass in a toast.

"To freedom. May we no rest until we ken it completely."

"Aye, aye," came the agreeable chorus as cups were lifted.

Gregor added, raising his cup, "May we see peace in our lifetime," and with a nod to present company, "outside the circle of our friends and family as well."

Cups were tapped against the tabletops, accompanied by calls of harmony.

Anice chimed in, "To the brave and noble companions of the hero warrior William Wallace, may they continue to serve his memory well."

"Aye, aye."

"And to the lasses who love us," offered Jamie, his eye on Ada. "God bless them all."

"Aye, aye." John Cardmore's voice rose above the rest.

Angus tipped his cup, his smile soft in his wizened and weathered face. "Aye, you're better men for the love of a fine lass. And there ain't no finer than who's gathered here."

The End

Thank you for reading ***The Shadow of Her Smile***. Gaining exposure as an independent author relies mostly on word-of-mouth, so if you have the time and inclination, please consider leaving a short review wherever you can. Thanks!

You can read Conall and Tess's story in Book One,
The Touch of Her Hand[1]

You'll find Gregor and Anice's tale in Book Two,
The Memory of Her Kiss[2]

Watch for Torren and Muriel's love to be written in
Mountains To Move
A Highlander Novella
Coming 2020

And Henry and Bethany's tale will be available as
Stay With Me
A Highlander Novella
Coming 2020

Sign-Up for My Newsletter
Stay Up To Date![3]

1. https://www.amazon.com/dp/B07X7D1SCV
2. https://www.amazon.com/dp/B07XPDQ4ZX

And hear about all the upcoming books.

3. https://www.subscribepage.com/o1o9t1

About the Author

Rebecca Ruger has been a lover of romance books since the seventh grade, when her mother introduced her to Victoria Holt, and her sister shared her Barbara Cartland collection. She is the founder and former editor of *Glassing Magazine*, the first ever print periodical all about sea glass and beach glass (which she sold in 2018, and is now called *BeachCombing Magazine*).

She is the mother of four (her greatest loves) and lives in Western New York with her perfectly supportive husband, Larry, and their just-ok dog, Brody.

The Touch of Her Hand is the first in the Highlander Heroes Series, to be followed by *The Shadow of Her Smile*, available October 2019, and *The Memory of Her Kiss*, available November 2019.

www.rebeccaruger.com

Thank you!

Read more at www.rebeccaruger.com.

Made in the USA
Coppell, TX
22 March 2022